THE BLESSED CURSE

Sarmad Sehbai

T0244019

We acknowledge the support of the Canada Council for the Arts for our publishing program. We also acknowledge support from the Government of Ontario through the Ontario Arts Council, and the support of the Government of Canada through the Canada Book Fund.

The publication of this book has been supported by Arshad Mahmood, Munir Pervaiz Saami, the Canadian Community Arts Initiative, and the Progressive Writers' Association Canada.

Cover by Sabrina Pignataro

Library and Archives Canada Cataloguing in Publication

Title: The blessed curse : a novel / Sarmad Sehbai.

Names: Ṣahbā̉ī, Sarmad, author.

Identifiers: Canadiana (print) 20230588352 | Canadiana (ebook) 20230588379 | ISBN 9781774151495 (softcover) | ISBN 9781774151501 (EPUB) | ISBN 9781774151518 (PDF)

Subjects: LCGFT: Satirical literature. | LCGFT: Novels.

Classification: LCC PR9540.9.S44 B53 2024 | DDC 823/.92—dc23

Printed and bound in Canada by Coach House Printing

Mawenzi House Publishers Ltd.

39 Woburn Avenue (B)

Toronto, Ontario M5M 1K5

Canada

www.mawenzihouse.com

Dedicated to Taufiq Rafat who exorcised our colonial ghosts
by giving the English language a native hue and local habitation

"Even obscenities uttered by a saint, are words of God."

A Sufi saying.

Chapter 1

Corpse in a Luxurious Coffin

Fifteen years of marriage and he never saw his wife naked.

Nawabzada Noor Mohammad Ganju's mind swelled a porcupine with erotic probes.

"Hello? Are you there?" The chief of intelligence panicked on the other end.

Ganju tried speaking but he was snared by his intruders.

"Hello, hello!" shouted the chief.

"It's just the weak signal," Ganju sighed, recovering, "I am very much here," he said.

"Ah, these mobiles, never mind," chuckled the chief.

Ganju intoned a faultless "Sir!"

His wife rustled into the room with dim anklets and fidgeting gold bangles. Layers of silk dutifully concealed her body.

"I'll see you at the dinner tomorrow. Don't miss it, the General is expected to be there. And yes, congratulations," said the chief cheerfully.

"I am flattered, sir," Ganju filched a look at his photograph in the newspaper smiling at him from the side table. "It's all because of friends like you," he said.

"And by the way my warm regards to our respectable Bhabhi," tingled the chief, referring to the Nawabzada's wife.

Something twisted in Ganju's thigh; the porcupine had left, shedding behind its quills.

Two canoodling pigeons, her hands, perched on the table

as the wife neatly placed a hot cup of tea on the table. Ganju glimpsed through his gold-rimmed glasses a face folded in a chadder and a neck impatiently disappearing into a silken blouse. She collected the newspapers from the table, not sparing a look at his photo. The day before, Ganju had been awarded the Presidential Medal for his efforts at rehabilitating the victims of a recent bomb blast, and the papers had duly given him the top headline on the front page. Everyone had called him to congratulate, except the General.

Ganju dared a steady look at his wife. What he could snatch from the forbidding folds was a slice of hand and a partial face. He slouched back on the armchair and took a sip from his cup. He could remember seeing her during their childhood, but as a young woman she had withdrawn into the woodwork of draped balconies and curtained rooms. He had seen her again as he sat beside her in his bridegroom attire. They were not allowed to see each other directly; eye into eye, but a mirror was placed between them to steal glimpses. On their wedding night all his passionate attempts had failed against a bundle of coyness huddled on the bed. It was an exhaustive night of perspiring futility. She wouldn't let him into the bed without putting off all the lights. In that dark, even a faint movement of her body would drive him into mad desire that was only deflated by her virginal stubbornness. He would struggle like a child not tall enough to reach the fruit on the tree but at the same time never losing hope. Fighting a crusade against heavy jewelry and heaps of bridal linen, it had taken him more than a month to reach the knot of her undergarments.

"Your shoes." She bent, layers of her dress rising into fulsome curves.

His eyes fumbled. "Could we go to bed? I mean, early tonight?" For a moment, he was thrilled by his boldness.

"Yes, you have to catch the morning flight."

"Oh no, I've decided to go by road, sometime in the afternoon," he revealed excitedly.

"I'll order your lunch for tomorrow." She stood up to leave, unruffled, without a smile.

Long-drawn silences hung over the brooding corridors, the distant pillars, the piles of trunks, and the cupboards. The haveli was a hushed world of secrecy, where sweets were offered in gaudy dressing and a glass of water came covered with beaded gauze. Members of the family were addressed by their positions and not by their given names. There were rules and signals. A nod, a glance, a cough guided daily life. There were codes for fetching water, closing doors, drawing the curtains, bringing slippers. But there was no code to transmit the craving Ganju was experiencing that night.

All those years he had made love to his wife like playing blind man's bluff. He would rush into a pool of rustling darkness, a turtle scuttling towards an invisible shore. Negotiating with multiple folds of crumpled sheets he would wander through the fluffy confusion, etching a figure in his mind, reading zips and buttons. He could never reach her mouth, as she would keep it sideways to avoid kisses, the spiteful sins. All night, flippering in wet nothingness like rowing without oars, he would hang in the void, pushing upward only to recoil in despair. At last she would let him pull her shalwar half down and he would perform a missionary in her midwife position; a pantomime of awkward limbs and dull weight.

"You want me to make another cup of tea for you?" she said, speaking under her chadder as she entered with her bag of embroidery. Ganju's eyes leapt at the floating flame, her full lips. He thirsted in silence. Finding no answer, she took out her embroidery kit and sat quietly working on the picture of a swan she had traced out from a wildlife book.

His daughter entered the room. Head down, she greeted him. Ganju's hand patted her.

"Papa, I saw your picture in the papers."

"Oh, really!" Ganju held her in his arms.

Barely fourteen, she was already a woman. The image of their maid turned in his mind, panicking at her birth, "Sir, it's a daughter!"

"Daughters are Allah's unique blessings," Ganju had corrected her.

That was a quiet day without guns and fireworks.

Since then the unique blessing was guarded by the sacred order of the Haveli. She had grown up like a phantom, moving in closed cars and living in the protective isolation of the women's quarter, the zenankhana. Unnoticed.

"Why didn't you bring bhai with you?" she asked.

"Oh, he had to take his exams. Why? Are you missing your brother?"

She shied away nodding her head.

"Well, he'll be here for his summer vacations," he said.

"Papa, my friends also saw your picture," she giggled.

"Oh, did they?"

The cat had appeared from nowhere.

"They said you looked like the General in our history book."

"Oh really?" The cat had started rubbing herself against his leg. He didn't like the cat, but that day it felt pleasant.

"But they said the General had a bigger moustache," said the daughter naughtily.

"Ha-ha, a bigger moustache?" Ganju laughed.

The mother threw a glance at the daughter, who left, head down, trailed by the cat. The mobile rang. Ganju took the call. It was his uncle Zahoor, a Member of the National Assembly and father of his wife. Why was there no call from the General?

As his wife needled into and out of the stretched framed cloth in her hands, the desire to see her naked kept mounting in him. He was possessed by his fantasies, banished for so long by the force of good breeding. He had walked through his life blind-folded, but tonight there had appeared a chink; a frantic eye to unveil. Was it the shot of power that had roused him to such impossible dreams? "Y'Allah, what's happening to me?" Ganju quivered a prayer, but inside he was stampeded by hooves of lust.

Something had tingled under his skin ever since he left the city. The inspector of the police had stopped all traffic on the roads for his vehicle to pass. The doorman at the airport's VIP Lounge had fixed him a salute, stiff with obedience. Inside, waiters had served him with impeccable keenness and rows of necks had lifted up to see him as he was ushered inside the plane. That day he was on the satellite strutting his success on News at Nine. The air hostess bore a never-ending lipstick smile on her face and the pilot had greeted him with a navy blue salaam.

During the flight, Ganju kept looking out the window. Floating clouds offered him whatever he desired; camels, dogs, elephants, and at times, to his bewilderment, huge reclining women. When he landed, he was garlanded by his devotees. Flanked by armed bodyguards then, he was driven to his village in his Pajero. It was early March. The earth showed off its new growth in the unpredictable wild flowers. It was the mating season. The air was giddy with animal heat and the smell of ripening sugarcanes. Everything had looked bigger and abundant with life.

At the Haveli, Gul Khan the chowkidar, opened the gate with his larger hands, his teeth glaring behind his youthful beard. The mossy red bricks looked redder. Terraces had spread out, walls had retreated for him and the vines had jettisoned bigger bouganinvilleas.

Ganju stood up from his chair and took off his coat. "It's hot in here," he said.

The wife put her embroidery down and moved to the air-conditioner.

The quills bristled. "The bitch is a bucket of ice, a corpse lying in a luxurious coffin. Crush those conspiring anklets, the bangles ravaging in hollow sleeves, hooks scheming in silk robes. Strip off her trappings!"

"Your clothes are ready," the wife said, stifling Ganju's erotic spree as layers of clothing hovered before his gold-rimmed eyes. How could he have dared such a thought? A woman, especially a wife should never expose her modesty. It was a matter of honor and decency. There were matrimonial principles, charted in moral books. How unbecoming of a man who had received a medal from the President himself? What would she think of him? A vulgar commoner. Ganju sweated in shame. Wasn't there a difference between a wife and a whore, between a mosque and a pub? He looked at his cup.

The cup stared back.

Finishing the tea, he headed for the bathroom.

White lights washed the floor, baring the brilliant tiles. Outside the window, voices shouted, "Zindabad! Ganju, zindabad." People had made their pilgrimage to the Haveli from their far-flung homes to catch a glimpse of their Master.

Ganju listened and then hushed the voices by closing the window.

The old ancestral toilet had been replaced by a European two-seater. A chromatic Muslim hand-shower dangled by a side hook like a luminous snake. Large mirrors watched him. A thousand reflections cloned him into a crowd of selves. He shuffled to the bathtub.

Under the water, he felt almost perfect. The distant sound of people chanting slogans in his name was music to his ears. In cool serenity the ripples of the water kept refreshing the images of his award-winning ceremony at the National Day parade: soldiers marching along the bagpipers with tilted turbans and swirling Scottish kilts, strutting around like puffed peacocks. Lying snug in the tub, Ganju lifted a languid foot. His eyes stood on the humps of his parted knees. Tonight, in the thick of muscled thighs snoozed a bigger penis. "Ladies and gentlemen, the head of state." He heard the booming voice on the loudspeakers. Naked swords offering a salute. He saw himself standing up for the national anthem. Amused at his performance at the national parade, Ganju stepped out of the tub, rubbed himself with a pink towel, and removed the Japanese hand-mirror from the sideboard. It was one of his bath rituals. He flashed the mirror down to his navel. Other mirrors watched it swelling a wrist out of a thumb. "Ladies and Gentlemen, Here, I call upon Nawabzada Noor Mohammad Ganju. We award him the Tamgha-e-Khidmat in recognition of his unparalleled services for our nation." The ripples in the tub tossed up reflections of Ganju somnolently walking to the President. The President extending a royal hand. Ganju kissing that hand and lowering his head. The sheen of erect swords sent a lasting sensation along the water and the wonder mirror, blowing him up to a size and girth more than a man could ever desire. Ganju melted in a narcissistic swoon.

Drowned inside the shimmering mirrors, he was shaken by a nasty twitch, the familiar pain shooting from his rectum. He lost his balance. Stumbling towards the medicine chest, he picked up a tube with a plastic nozzle. Collapsing on his haunches, he paused for breath. The nozzle looked at him. Angling it to his palpitating anus, he lightly pressed and eased it in. The plastic finger filled him with minted calm. Etherized, he slipped into his well-pressed achkan, the national dress, and giving himself a last look in the mirror walked out of his bedroom.

On his way along the corridor, Ganju slinked into a passage receding to the unlit stairs which led him down to a basement, where he unlocked a cupboard and hurriedly pulled out a shiny briefcase. Clicking a combination, he opened the briefcase and went for the bottle.

A shadow in the dark. He turned around. A pair of narrow searchlights stared at him. Ganju moved a step. The cat disappeared, leaving behind a furred sensation. Turning back, Ganju downed the contents of the bottle in gulps, firing up his chest. Shoving the bottle back, he reached for the cardamom in his pocket. Brisk bites. The taste lit up his mouth. Tipsy, with an incensed mouth, and a bottom breezing with cool ointment, Nawabzada Noor Mohammad Ganju advanced towards the waiting crowds.

As he entered the hall, waves of scruffy turbans stirred. His guards pushed away eager hands wanting to touch him and cleared the way for him to sit on the ancestral chair that stood enormously on a platform. Ganju's trusted servant Juma Khan respectfully touched his knees and stood behind the chair. Allama, the local religious scholar, promptly stood up and recited verses from the Quran. They all listened in silence. Allama finished the recitation and offered special prayers for the family of Ganju, his forefathers, and the people of Noorpur village. They all responded with devotion, "Amen! Amen!"

Ganju's family tree had roots in Islam's sacred lands. The family were regarded as the direct descendants of the early religious leaders. The sick sought cure and women hoped to get children with their blessings. The Haveli, their ancestral home, was known as Bab-e-Musarrat, the Abode of Happiness.

The hall breathed with reverence. He felt moved.

"Ya Allah, give me the strength to lift them from their fated sloth. They need me," Ganju spoke in his mind. With tears in his eyes, he waved a hand that knew how to send shivers of awe and grandeur across an audience.

From the fog of murmurs, an old mother surfaced. Her arms outstretched, face a bowl of wrinkles. Spreading her chadder on the ground in front of Ganju, she screamed her plea to him to avenge her raped daughter. A father of a son in prison begged with wet eyes. Ganju nodded, smiled, raised his hands. Hands surged in response, clambering to touch his compassion.

Somewhere in the crowd, a heap of rags opened like a cave. There he saw a head with matted hair flung back.

"Pir, the Invisible Saint sends you the blessed curse!" the head spoke.

A stunned hall watched. Ganju felt a weird elation come over him in a wave.

"Pir the Invisible Saint sends you the blessed curse!" The whirling head danced.

Guards jumped at the man.

Who was he? Some *musst* possessed by a spirit? Ganju tried leaving but he was nailed down by the man's stare. Ganju held his composure. Juma Khan waved to the guards.

The guards took the man away.

Ganju was led to the zenankhana by his attendants. Once they left, he knocked at the bedroom door and coughed, identifying himself.

"Please wait a minute, I am changing," whispered the wife from inside. In her voice, Ganju smelt her armpits. His obsession returned, he wanted to ram the door and grab her without clothes. The eyes of the madman he had seen earlier flashed in his mind. To his surprise a sudden flush of energy welled up in his limbs, and he coughed again. The cough this time signaled something not known before: the grunt of a horny bull, rending the air. No answer, but frightened silence.

Ganju would have never dared to do this ever in his life, but all astir, on rubber feet he moved a small table from the veranda and climbed up to the ventilator window. There she was, tall under the light, unaware of the voyeuristic gaze. His eyes zoomed into the hands that wandered around her neck to unbutton the blouse, a bosom about to be revealed. Ganju stared without a blink.

She turned off the lights.

His grunt was muffled by the timeless quiet of the Haveli.

Entering the bedroom Ganju dumped himself on the sofa.

"Here, your vitamins." She handed him the capsules.

In his mind the omen buzzed with "Pir the Invisible sends you the blessed curse." What the hell did he mean by that? The blessed curse? Some spiritual gibberish! Bastard, son of a bitch, a worm from the slime, how dare he? Guards must have tied him up by this time, or beaten him to death, he reassured himself.

"I've warmed the milk for you." She brought him the glass, covered on top by a beaded doily.

Ignoring this white signal, he threw the power pills in the bin and took off his achkan.

The beads snickered in the sly drone of the air-conditioner.

His wife turned off the lights, expecting him to retire.

"What brews inside the veil?" Ganju wondered, slipping into his nightclothes. Women can conceal what they concoct in their minds, pretending innocence, smirking behind a poker face. History is full of their wiles. Who was Eve but an agent of Satan; what fatal tricks a woman can play.

Was it unnatural for him to think such a thought? Ganju pondered uneasily. Doubtless, it's the man who is the Lord and the Master. It's he who gives the moral frame, women merely design the embroidery on the cloth. Their minds are as intricate as the knots of their needlework. Ganju had a sudden urge to switch on all the lights in the room, tear off her clothes and hammer her to the hilt. But then she coughed.

Ganju stood up and smelling his way to the bait fell into the bed.

He heard the landline ringing.

"Who could that be at this hour?" He got out of bed.

"Congratulations." It was the General.

"I am greatly honored, Sir," Ganju's voice shrunk into a squeak.

"We are very proud of you," the General's voice rose.

"I know it, Sir. After all, you are behind me," Ganju mumbled.

"I hope it's not too late for you," the Metallic Tone amplified and before Ganju could say a word, he saw a spooky string streaming out from the phone's mouthpiece. Ganju did not believe his eyes but in the dark, he could clearly see the tiny holes emitting strings of meat like a mincing machine. Ganju went dizzy. The string spinning on the floor formed a plasmatic quiz that solved itself into a moustache, thick and waxy. Then appeared lips, eyes, the full face, and finally it settled into heavy limbs. Within seconds he saw the General rising, decked out in medals, flicks, and brass buttons.

"Sirrr!" screamed Ganju.

The General switching on the lights, began taking off his pants.

Ganju blushed.

Out came two pillars of curly ants, the General's hairy legs. Ganju began to shrink, his arms and legs crammed in, shaping into a meat puppet. He eagered himself between the large thighs of the General. His torso dangled out and hung on the hook of the General's pelvic bone, the General's mock penis.

The General flaunted the venal whip.

The wife giggled under the sheets.

"Frigid bitch, who's she saving it up for? Worms? She needs a poke, a real one." Ganju stood alert at the command, his face red with anticipation.

"Charge!" bellowed the General. "Blow off that cold mine."

Ganju jostled inside the sheets, fuming and frothing, fighting pillows and blankets, climbing hazards, pushing boundaries.

Head up, he nuzzled inside the dark pit of miasmic smell, sniffed the whiff of flesh that was sucked into a tiny nipple of pure delight.

The bed jolted with militant thrusts.

Ganju heard his wife moaning with pleasure. "Bitch, is that what you wanted?" Sinuously winding, steering, lolling, squinting, he met his end. Spent and shrunk, he sank into his own futility.

Ganju saw the General disappearing through the tiny holes of the mouthpiece. His hairy absence hung in the stillness of the Haveli. In that blurry emptiness, Ganju sensed the cat. She was lapping up the spilt milk on the floor. The cat looked at him, sharp and quick.

Ganju tried to hit her but fell from the bed like a cut-off limb.

The cat bared her fangs.

Terrified, Ganju rolled over.

Her taut whiskers stirred the air and a pink tongue lunged at Ganju.

Ganju fought for his life. Mercifully, his arms and legs popped out. He was shuffled back into himself before the cat could chew off the tender treat.

An upright Ganju walked to the table and discovered the General's massive moustache stuck to the mouthpiece of the phone. Calm and collected, his wife slept in the bed, all covered under the sheets.

He touched the moustache. Lightning flashed, a thunder reverberated.

Without thinking he tried it on and checked himself in the wall mirror. The mirror gave a royal smile.

A repeat from the history books.

Chapter 2

Nazrana — the Holy Kickback

"And indeed Allah is watching you."

Against the posters on walls flashing doomsday warnings sat Juma Khan in his office.

A mug head perched on his longish neck that housed a lump of Adam's apple. He wheezed and it inflated under his skin like a lazy toad. Below a bulging forehead wriggled two worms, his eyes. A thin mustache sickled his upper lip that helplessly gripped a set of abrupt teeth. His mouth bled of betel leaf.

Juma was the front man of the Ganjus in the city. He handled key appointments and profitable contracts on commissions that would eventually stuff the pockets of the Ganjus. For a decent charge, his office published pamphlets carrying scientific proofs of Heaven and Hell. Each month, with the help of local astrologers, the exact date and time of Armageddon was determined along with the whereabouts of the ultimate savior of the world. Apart from unraveling the mysteries of the universe, Juma planned fundraising projects for the victims of floods, earthquakes and other unforeseen calamities. Lately he had managed to collect an impressive amount for the Ganjus to support the bomb blast victims.

Juma pressed the buzzer on his phone and asked his personal assistant to send in the police inspector who had been waiting since morning. The inspector stepped in, dressed in plain clothes.

"Do sit, Sher Mohammad!" said Juma without lifting his

eyes from the pamphlets on his desk.

The inspector, who had lowered the pointed ends of his mustache before entering the room, nervously took the seat and coyly lifted a packet hidden in his lap. "Sir, you are the mother and father of us, our Mai Baap! Some mithai to sweeten your palate," he said.

Juma, without looking at the packet, kept his eyes on the pamphlets.

"It's nazrana, Mai Baap, a humble offering. No matter how small it seems, it acknowledges the indisputable power and authority to whom it is offered."

The inspector put the packet on the table.

"Come to the point, inspector," Juma said and calmly took the packet.

Sher Mohammad, the top cop in Heera Mandi, the red-light area, was losing business; prostitutes were shifting from the old walled city to join beauty parlors run by elite Madams in the newly developed areas. The inspector was desperate for his transfer to a place where he could line his pockets. But to talk Juma into this was like expecting an egg from a rooster.

"Mai Baap, you know this poor slave of yours regularly pays bhatta, the commission, never a penny less and . . . " the inspector gave a sly pause.

"And?"

"And still not promoted, Mai Baap!"

"Look, Sher Mohammad, I got you appointed in Heera Mandi where even a smile carries a price tag." Juma neatly put a paan into his mouth and picked up the pamphlet from the table.

"Oh, Mai Baap, I don't know how to tell you but . . . " The inspector mopped his face with his arm sleeve and blurted, "I am in love, Mai Baap!"

"What?" Juma raised his head from the pamphlet, "Who's she?" He chewed briskly at the paan.

"Mai Baap, she lives in Heera Mandi."

"Ha! Ha! Don't you have a minting machine then?" Juma's mouth ripped into a wide grin. "Playing the big Daddy? Sher

Mohammad, a whore is a whore. There's something in their blood," Juma aspirated, sawing the air with his buck teeth.

"Mai Baap, it's not that my Mano, God forbid, is a child of loose morals. She only does it out of poverty, my poor dove . . . " The inspector burst into tears. "Mai Baap, I swear by Allah, I don't care if I am not promoted, but even if transferred I'll be at peace. Why, Mai Baap? Because I'll be too far to see her disgracing herself with every other man. Mai Baap, a customer is a customer." The inspector raised a sleeve to his tears.

"Look, I'm not here to warm your pocket and loins at the same time. Now go away." Juma returned to the End of the World pamphlet, cool as a cucumber.

The inspector fumbled at his pockets and pulled out a photograph. "Mai Baap, I bet you would have never seen an artist like my Mano, the kitty with blue eyes. Oh! How she shakes her young body . . . Mai Baap, when she arches her back with her hips thrusting and her mounts pointing to the sky, men go wet in their pants." He discreetly placed the photograph on the table.

Juma's eyes shifted from the End of the World and halted at the uplifted breasts of Mano. His mouth wet with lust, he felt the cardamom under his molar. He chewed it hard.

"Mai Baap, Mano was born after offering constant prayers— and . . . " The inspector became lipless.

Juma had pressed the buzzer.

"Don't let anyone in, and no calls," huffed Juma into the intercom.

The inspector beamed with joy. He had succeeded in arresting Juma Khan's attention. With renewed vigor, he went on, "Mai Baap, when the mother became pregnant her husband died. An old Wadera, the landlord, bought her belly on the condition that if a girl was born, he would get her in marriage. And Mai Baap, the Wadera was so happy at the birth of Mano that he sent two tons of mithai to her mother to be distributed among neighbors and the poor. And Mai Baap, when the midwife placed her out in the sun for a bath, she was thunderstruck to find that the baby had a lovely mass of flesh around her thighs and a chest which normally females develop when they are well in their teens. Discovering a miraculously well-formed child, the midwife touched her ears in praise of Allah and told the mother that she had given birth to a fairy with blue eyes. And then, Mai Baap, to ward off the evil eye, nature had blessed her with a nazar butto, the black mole on one of her smooth buttocks."

Juma squirmed in his chair.

"Mai Baap, the Wadera was sixty-eight when Mano started menstruating. But poor man expired soon after he deflowered her. Everyone thinks the mother killed him by mixing small doses of poison in his aphrodisiacs."

"Yes yes," Juma chanted.

"Mai Baap, her mother disappeared and never came back. Poor Mano didn't have anyone to protect her from the sharks. But one has to give credit to her; she has an amazing power to defend her chastity, Mai Baap."

"What?"

"Yes, Mai Baap! May Allah forgive me, but this girl knows thousand and one ways of remaining a virgin; just a pelvic twist and the man sheds like a puffball, without ever entering her. And Mai Baap, she also sings ghazals. And I tell you . . . "

A buzz.

Juma was kicked out of his lustful reverie.

"Idiot, I told you to hold all calls," he shouted.

"What?" Juma's face turned pale. Ganju had sent for him. He quickly put the phone down and glared at the inspector. "Idiot, get lost, you have wasted too much of my time."

"Oh, Mai Baap, do forgive me, but I pray of you, don't forget this slave of yours," said the inspector walking backwards. Near the door he clicked his heels, saluted, and left.

"Take me to Zahid Sahib's house," said Ganju to Juma, who took a sharp turn to the Blue area of the Capital. Ganju lit his cigar and looked out from the car window. Carefree youngsters chatted by the wayside cafes, fashionably dressed men and women ate in restaurants, and shopping plazas sparkled in their neon glory. Ganju loved urban life. The heady smell of power and glamour released him from his dull village life. The pace of life lifted his senses and gave his soul a joyful sprint. Floating in the river of rushing lights, he thought of Zeenat, his wife. Maybe he should bring her to the city. They could go to the cinema and dine together in some romantically lit corner of a restaurant. She could play tennis at the club and go swimming . . . Zeenat in a swimsuit? The thought took a voluptuous turn. Oh God what was he thinking about? How would she ever wear a swimsuit? And if she comes to the city with him, could he ever touch a drink in front of her? What'll she think? Was he pimping her to the city's delights? And his followers in the village? They'd hate him for unveiling his wife to others without shame. And his father-in-law? He'd lose his face in public. Damn the uncle! It had taken him more than a year sucking up to him to get this award. How long should he suffer in the dark ages of that Haveli? What was he to his uncle? A palfrey trotting behind the steed of power! In that blanked-out moment his mind rattled with the madman's curse, "Pir the Invisible sends you the blessed curse."

"Tell me, Juma," he asked abruptly. "Who's Pir the Invisible?"

"Sarkar," said Juma, slowing down the car, "like our five senses, there are five Pirs in the world and the Invisible Pir is like our sixth sense, it's some kind of intuition, Sarkar, which we cannot see." He peeked at Ganju in his mirror. "Is something wrong, Sarkar?"

"No, not really, move on, we are getting late," Ganju said, cutting him off.

When Ganju arrived, Zahid was standing at the door with a beer mug in his hand.

"Pleased to meet you," Ganju extended his hand, formally.

"Congratulations! I saw you on TV with the President at the National Parade. Very impressive! General Sahib is on his way, he'll be here any minute." Neat and showered, Zahid in his shorts had a sunny look even at this time of the night. "I just came from my swimming. Please don't mind my casual dress." Zahid, trotting like a young boy, led Ganju to the basement.

Elegant stairs with enameled banisters spiraled down to the hideout, with its blend of avant-garde and ethnic furniture. Artistic nudes stood on top of the fireplace, figurines of dancing dervishes whirled atop the white stillness of the marble. Near the fireplace, a sculpture of Shiva and Parvati curved in a tantric asana. In a corner, a round table displayed alphabets in gothic style with hoary images from some voodoo book. A tiny glass rested on it. With soft Persian carpets and a cool sprawl of creepers, the basement was a sensuous uproar.

"Shall I get you some whisky?" Zahid in his Hawaiian shirt was being effortlessly pleasant.

"Yes please," said Ganju sitting next to the table with the tiny glass. He looked at the glass.

"Oh don't be intrigued, every Thursday we invite spirits," said Zahid, pouring the drink.

"Do you really believe in spirits?" Ganju asked, casually picking up the glass.

"Oh it's great fun. We are in conference with the dead."

Something stirred in the glass. Ganju, with a start, put it back on the table. "Oh, by the way that's a nice shirt," he said, trying polite conversation to normalize himself.

"Cool, isn't it? Picked it from a shop in Bali. I know you are too sophisticated for such casual rags," said Zahid, moving to the bar. Ganju gave a guarded smile and discreetly loosened his necktie.

Zahid had arrived a day before from one of his business trips to Bangkok. He loved duty-free shops. Often he would show off to his guests his fancy clothes, aftershaves, deodorants, cigarette lighters, flashy goggles, and at times pens displaying floating topless women.

"*Banti nahin hey bada o sagher kahey beghair.* Sir, Ghalib the great poet has truly said, nothing works without wine," Zahid said, placing a bottle on the black felt counter of the bar. "Even the liquor breathes," he sighed as the slow sparkle of liquid resounded in the half-lit bar. Zahid handed the whisky glass to Ganju, saying, "What fun, all our poetry is full of wine and women."

"Well yes, but I guess they are more or less used as metaphors," Ganju said and took a careful sip.

"Oh that's a smart one," said Zahid, his face glowing with a mischievous smile. "My dear sir, it's the forbidden that haunts the poets. Cheers to the forbidden!" He clunked his beer mug against Ganju's glass. "Let me play something for you." He slid a disk into the hi-fi music system.

"*Madh key bharay toray nain.* Oh, those eyes are goblets of wine," a clear female voice sailed through the ornate ambience of the room.

"This is the chaste style of singing thumri, purely a creation of Muslim courtesans," he said, humming a line. "Can you see how she touches the ghostly note? Just like Eve shaking the forbidden tree. Oh God, she's not singing from her throat but from her genitals." Gyrating his head Zahid sat on the settee, all absorbed.

Zahid, a divorcee, lived by himself. Apart from purchasing defense equipment for the army, he was involved in a couple of other major deals and had made money by judiciously sharing kickbacks with his benefactors in the government. He enjoyed familiarity with politicians, sportsmen, fashion models, air hostesses, madams, beauticians, film stars, and other celebrities, real or fake, with a halo of glamour around him.

There were many who appeared as pious Muslims in public and visited Zahid's abode of forbidden pleasures. He was their host angel at the door of Heaven. He arranged mujras, where dancing girls jolted the abating passions of senile men. Thrilled by a single female firing their slow blood, they would drink all night and repent at dawn on their prayer mats. Zahid offered them hijab, the Solomon's cap that made them invisible to the rest of the world.

Ganju's self-restraint and sense of propriety had always held him back from such gatherings. His share of earthly delights was his wife and children, and for him that was enough to be a complete man. But lately he had felt a strange desire to soar above his ordinariness still dreading the temptation to touch the forbidden.

Madh kay bharay toray nain.

Oh those eyes are goblets of wine. Zahid looked lost to the nostalgic music of the Mughal Empire, a lament of defeated grandeur, scratchy wails of a broken sitar. The receding hairline had left a fuzz on his balding head and the Hawaiian stretch shirt had accentuated his beer belly.

A teenager gone old in a t-shirt.

"Here, a Honolulu cigar," Zahid opened a cigar box. "It's thigh-rolled."

"Thigh-rolled?" Ganju took the cigar.

"Yes, rolled on the thighs of Hawaiian women." Zahid sniffed around the rolled length, breathing in the thigh rub. Ganju wanted to do the same but refrained.

No armchair Casanova, Zahid was an expert on the erotic arts, a Sinbad navigating the oceans of female smells. A compulsive bed-hopper, familiar with escort services, health clubs, and massage parlors all over the world. He practiced yoga to enhance his virility and was proud of his dawn-to-dusk erections.

"Can you believe this woman in Thailand was down on me for forty-five minutes," Zahid announced as he fixed another beer for himself.

"What?" Ganju gulped his whisky. He thought of leaving but something held him back. Zahid had tickled a nerve in him, which he had never discovered before. "How interesting." He took a quick puff of the cigar.

Ganju had a self-image too large to be reduced to the common sport of womanizing, but somehow he seemed to go along, amused by the tales of Zahid's sexual escapades. "What exactly happened?" he cautiously asked.

"Oh, her mouth was a cave of honey, and her tongue? A real cock-jacker! Mind you, it's not just the baser instinct, it's a higher calling. A dick for them is not dirty. They adore it as an article of faith. And what do we have here? Dead pelvises, cock-shy, coffined females. Have you ever thought our wives don't even take off their clothes when we want them real bad? Lights are switched off, and you jump in the slushy mess like a blind frog."

Ganju nodded nervously, keeping mum about his own blind matings, his secret rendezvous with the Japanese mirror and his nagging hemorrhoids.

"Now my wife was a cunt with an attitude. I would get horny and she would pretend a migraine. Sometimes, when the bitch did condescend to have sex, she acted like a queen. Oh, but these women? They turn you into gods, yes my dear, but you got to have lead in your pencil." He laughed naughtily.

Ganju tried hiding his embarrassment under a smile. "Now she was a supermodel, rather expensive," Zahid winked and moved closer to Ganju.

"Aren't they all the same?" Ganju sounded naive.

"No, my dear sir, it's not the woman's body, it's the very fable of female legend, a mega fantasy. Title-fucking is no joke. Next time you come with me. I bet you'll have a swell time." Zahid slapped Ganju's thigh, with familiarity.

The butler showed up at the door.

"I think they are here, the General's ball players," said Zahid and waved to the butler.

Two army officers stepped in with bomb detection equipment. They saluted and carried the quick operation all over the house, starting from the whirling dervishes.

"I've got Russian vodka, all ready for him, that's his favorite," whispered Zahid to Ganju and leapt to the door.

The General marched in wearing a loud necktie and a printed maroon jacket. He filled the room with his wide presence.

"Sir!" Ganju stood up to greet him.

"Oh please! Now don't you sir me. I'm not in my uniform and I've known your family much too long. Zahoor Din, your uncle plays golf with me every Sunday. Call me Sana, that'll give me pleasure," said the General, giving him a warm handshake.

"You look great, sir," Ganju responded in confusion.

"Oh, you are quite perceptive, it's the new style of my moustache," said the General, twisting the pointed ends upwards. Ganju, averting the hairy flares, took a quick sip of whisky. How come the General still had his moustache? Did he dream the whole thing? No, no! Sometimes dream and reality can overlap. Perhaps his intense admiration for the General's moustache had got him one. It's like sympathetic magic, he reasoned out.

"Sir, your drink." Zahid brought over the vodka as the General settled himself on the sofa. "Ah that's good," said the General and took the glass. "Cheers!" He lifted his glass and guzzled the vodka full belt.

"Now tell me, what were you talking about?" The General signaled for a refill.

"Well, sir," Zahid placed the glass in front of the General, "I was just telling Ganju about birds and bees."

"Oh, your trip to Bangkok. I know you go there to warm yourself up."

The General cocked his head and took over. "Do you know the first comfort house for exclusive military use came into existence after the Rape of Nanking? I've read somewhere that among other services, sexual service was equally important. It relieved the soldiers of their blue balls. Well, frankly speaking, whores are extremely helpful in putting soldiers back to normal life. Biting off a nipple or gouging out a breast kept those footsloggers calm and committed," pronounced the General with authority.

Another round of vodka and he was in charge, "Guess what we did in our Captain days," he said. "Well, Ganju, you must listen to this."

Ganju managed a smile.

"You see, every Saturday at midnight, we would march to the banquet hall and light candles around the portrait of our General that was hung on the wall. Once the portrait glowed in the halo of flickering candles, two smart cadets would slowly reverse the frame revealing a bombastic pair of boobs and glossy thighs. You see, we had this nude bunny from Playboy thumbed right behind our General's portrait. She would wink and the dark hall would reverberate with rhythms of heavy breathing, our fingers going frantic. It was a candle-lit orgy, a massive uprising in the military camps. We would masturbate solemnly till our wrists ached. Ah, what timing. All of us, just in one go, would explode into a marathon orgasm. O God, what magnificent teamwork it used to be. Even our regular drill was not as impressive."

The General laughed, full belly, Zahid followed, and Ganju attempted a polite smile.

The Sri Lankan maid tiptoed up to the stairs. Zahid stood up, "Sir, you'll excuse me," he said. "I've to check the food, the cooks can't be trusted. Sir, you understand there's a heating time. One has to flicker softly around the surface. It's like warming up your woman and if your attention is diverted you are in for a soggy disaster. I certainly don't wish to make a burnt offering. Do allow me to perform the last minute rites of a palate-blowing gourmand while you enjoy another vodka, a stiff one sir?"

"Sure. Go ahead," said the General. Zahid made a quick drink for him and left after the maid.

"Sir," Ganju tried to make some conversation, "I must say those jawans at the parade were just perfect. And those jets in the air were awesome."

"Yes, yes," the General's eyes shone with pride, "You see, manhood has to be earned, tested, and proven. Men who can't defend their motherland have in fact lost their manhood." He gave a sidelong glance at Ganju.

"You see, war is essential for us. It gives us national heroes. In history, warriors and conquerors are remembered, not eunuchs," he said with a smirk. "But once war is over continuity is screwed up, no more call-ups and they are back on the city street, dragging heels. Sissiness takes over. Those thumb-suckers posture masculinity by buying chocolates for their wives. Once denied an enemy, you are in deep shit. The question is, what should one do during this crisis of uselessness?" The General lowered his head to face Ganju. "Well," he said, resuming his posture, "I play poker with my wife to keep the action going. You won't believe it, but I turn into a cushion."

"A cushion, sir?"

"Yes, yes, a big spongy cushion." The General, for a moment excitedly packed himself together, acting out a cushion. "You see, she sits on me without being aware of me. Not a sound, I just hold my breath and savor the face-sitting. Well, she's built for comfort and I love the pressure, especially when she jiggles on the cushion, which as you know, is me."

Ganju nodded in affirmation.

"Now she gets up and lazily spreads her legs to set the target for me. O God," the General stared into blank space, "what a view from that cozy trench. Charge! I shout and she runs to the closet, completely ambushed. I crawl on my belly, very slowly until I reach the enemy post. Surrender! I command and there she stumps out of those silky shades of lingerie and nightgowns with her hands up, totally defenseless." The General winked at Ganju, "You know what I mean by defenseless? Ha! Ha!"

"She also keeps those air force chaps busy by sending them her favorite meat kebabs from the South. The saber jets airlift them for her in exactly twenty minutes. I tell you there is something to that meat. I've no idea how it works on me but she turns into a real hot filly," said the General with an orgasmic shiver in his voice. "Hey boy," The General shook Ganju by the arm and said, "Why don't you talk about your matrimonial adventures?"

Ganju felt a lump in his throat.

Zahid, the star chef, entered with a series of servants who carried a huge thaal of giant-sized mushrooms and a large steaming fish. He placed the thaal in front of the General. Servants laid the table and the butler opened the wine bottles.

"Sir, this mermaid is a special one from the Bay of Bengal, a gift of nature to man and I truly mean it. I've devoutly marinated it with my own hands. Sir, pamper your palate with this nipping wine. Ganju, take a sip, wet your whistle." Zahid conducted the dinner like an orchestra.

"Ah what a feast." The General attacked the food. Zahid and Ganju joined him, taking cautious bites.

"Come on, Ganju, try a piece of this princess from the Bay of Bengal," the General halted mid-bite, his fingers clutching a succulent piece. "Bhabi will be too happy with you," he said gleefully with a jerk of his moustache.

Ganju blushed.

"He's still wet behind the ears," Zahid said pouring wine for the General.

"Well, he can't sit still, can he? He is in the spotlight now. Receiving a medal from the President is no joke, it's a buzzer to power, a mighty turn-on, and mind you, they don't want to see a daisy there. Young man! Wake up to the call, show your mettle," commanded the General.

"Excuse me, could I use your washroom?" Ganju stood up abruptly.

"Sure, right there." Zahid pointed to a side room.

Inside the bathroom, Ganju washed his hands and his sweating face. Walking out into the room, he was transfixed by a huge waterbed lying on the floor like a heaving cloud. The room was designed exclusively for Zahid's erotic theatrics. Surrounding the bed were large mirrors to repeat the performance of the valiant knight. Next to the bed on an ivory table stood a menagerie of crystal bottles. Walls displayed paintings of copulation in all conceivable positions. Overpowered by the vision of a venal paradise, Ganju was tempted to touch the fetish colognes, miracle oils and magic creams. They could swell male virility, sustain power over a female partner. Condoms in all kinds of variety, colored rough riders, silky black magics, minted ones that could turn your penis into a stun gun, dotted ticklers with hurting spikes and an S&M kit, ready with whips and chains. Haunted by the mesmeric glare of erotic totems and ghosts of perfumes, Ganju stood still, until he heard a voice. It swirled around his neck like hot breath. The giggle of a woman blurred into a song. Bewildered, he saw in the waterbed a flutter of colors that slowly ferned into a lilt of haze. A voluptuous turn of curious hues tossed the layers of feathers, overlapping with cascading rainbows. Spangled among shells, on a hammock of ladling waves, the mermaid beckoned him. Enchanted, he jumped. Water dimpled into the whirlpool of her arms. She touched his crotch and he turned into the nervous skeleton of a shrimp.

The ocean rocked with a sudden flood. Caught in seaweeds,

Ganju struggled. The bed burst open and water splashed all over the room sweeping the menagerie of occult potions. Ganju was hurled to the doorstep. He hit the door, which flung open.

"Are you okay, young man?" Zahid went up to him. "Yes, oh yes, I am fine," said Ganju in a daze. He walked back down to the basement.

The General had munched the fish to the last fin.

Late at night, when Juma brought Ganju back to the house, both were in a pleasant mood. "Did they look after you well?" asked a tipsy Ganju.

"Very well, Sarkar," said Juma, without looking up.

"Go, have some sleep," said Ganju and ambled off to the bedroom.

Steaming with booze and fleshy tales, Ganju's mind was wrought by a graffiti of horny images. He tried sleeping but something kept him awake. He was used to sleep alone in the city, but tonight the bed felt bigger, vacant and cold. He turned inside the sheets. Why couldn't he ever talk about his sex life like others? He sat up in the bed. Was he not equal to those powerful men? He got out of the bed and went to the living room.

"Sarkar, have a drink." Juma tiptoed behind him, his eyes peeking at the mopish face of his master. "I am sorry, Sarkar. I saw the light on," he said.

Ganju took the glass.

"Sarkar, I'll be awake till you retire. Just ring the bell if Sarkar needs me." Juma turned to leave.

"No Juma, sit here with me," said Ganju in a tired voice.

"Sarkar, as you command." Juma sat down on the floor.

"Tell me, Juma Khan, Allah has blessed me with every good thing in life and yet I feel so empty. Why? Is there something missing?"

"Sarkar, if I, the dust of your feet, may say so, Sarkar needs a companion in the city who could keep Sarkar in good spirits." Juma had started pressing Ganju's legs.

"What do you mean?"

"Sarkar, have you ever thought about why in old times, the kings, nawabs, and maharajas had their harems?" Juma had moved up to Ganju's calves.

"Why?"

"Because, Sarkar, a single woman is never enough for a man in power." Ganju gave in to the lull of the gentle rub. Juma continued, "Sarkar, Bade Hakim sahib says, 'Once the wife becomes a mother, the house turns into a sacred place, and one can't sully the place of maternity.'" He thumbed Ganju's ankles.

What was he talking about? Did he want him to betray his wife, abuse his body with another woman? Ganju tried pulling away his legs but they had turned into jelly in the hands of Juma Khan.

"Sarkar, from the ribs of this city I'll carve a woman for you."

"A woman?"

"Yes, Sarkar, a girl with youthful urges and a raging passion." Juma's eyes flickered like golden cockroaches.

"Really?" The image of a young girl had fired his loins. "Who's she?" he mumbled.

"Sarkar, I know a pious widow who wants to offer her daughter to Pir Ganjus as nazrana. And who knows better than Sarkar himself that declining a nazrana is an act of arrogance, almost a sin. She's fatherless and our Allah commands that His people should act justly towards orphans and bring them to their fold."

"Yes, yes, I know. But isn't she too young for me?"

"Sarkar, virgins and apples ripen early in our kind of climate. And then as Bade Hakim sahib says, a horse and a man never get old."

"Is that so?"

"Of course, Sarkar! And she's no ordinary girl. She is an evergreen virgin." Juma shook the tree of his soul.

"What?"

"I know it's a bit strange, but Sarkar, her mother who was married to a nawab, couldn't have a child. So she prayed to the Pir the Invisible and slept one night at the shrine. Next day she was in the family way. Sarkar, since the daughter was born of prayers, she was free of the original sin. No matter how often she's deflowered, she remains a virgin. The local Mulvi thinks she is a divine child sent from heaven for only hoories have such virtues."

"Unbelievable!"

"Sarkar, its hundred percent true. And Sarkar, she can also sing and dance. Her great grandmother was a singer in the Mughal court."

"*Madh kay bharray tooray nain.*" Ganju heard an echo; he was whizzed to the exotic harems of the Mughal Empire.

"Sarkar, you are already blessed by Pir the Invisible. You must give your manhood a taste of blood," Juma said, showing his beetle-red teeth.

"Blessed curse? How can a curse by the Pir be a blessing? Are you out of your mind?"

Ganju pulled away his legs.

"Forgive me for saying, but Sarkar knows more than myself that a man's sex organs are his bestial self. In moral books they are considered a curse, but when Pir the Invisible blesses them they become sacred. The curse in fact is a gift to your masculinity."

Ganju felt a stir in his pants. He shook his head, half sunk in a wet dream.

He could no longer hear Juma Khan.

Chapter 3

Nazrana 2

Inside the walled city, Mano had made a special effort to wake up early that afternoon. A day before, some film wallas had come in a car looking for her. They were told by the tea boy that Mano, an all-nighter, moved with her body clock and since she needed her beauty sleep she wouldn't show a leg until late in the afternoon. They had left a message with the boy, who had promptly relayed it to the entire neighborhood. Overnight, the news had spread like a delicious virus among whores, who often dropped names of the rich and the famous in front of Mano.

Buckets of warm water were fetched from the local hammam, on credit. Mano took a long bath, washed her hair and scrubbed herself with a foreign soap. She used an expensive hair remover to scrounge off the kinky curls from her body.

She wanted to feel brand new.

On top, she sported a diving neck with a trendy push-up bra. It gave a shocking height to her breasts. A see-through orange shirt, doubly starched, nipped her pert hips and a white cotton chooridar, the accordion pajamas with heaving folds, hugged her nifty legs. She smudged her lips with a pink lipstick and kajaled her blue eyes. Garnished with a silver scrunch, a ballast of makeup tarted up her baby face. She was ready on time.

Expecting a paan-chewing, pot-bellied, burly producer from Lollywood, Mano was surprised to see a tall lady with padded shoulders and very short hair. A crinkled dopatta frilled her front, and like an ampersand between her breasts was stuck a yin-yang emblem. Trailing behind her was a small chubby girl holding a bag.

"I am Nazo Jan, the woman activist." The tall one extended a stiff hand. "And this is Riffat. She is assisting me on this project," she said.

Riffat smiled an assistant's smile.

Nazo had a throaty voice, thick and metallic. She had had an unhappy married life. Every night her husband would hit the bottle, spank her, and call her a cock-freezing Antarctica, a kick-start. Then it all happened so fast, just in a day. A historic moment, when she returned early from shopping to find her husband and their maid all bundled on the master bed. Nazo jumped at her husband. All nails. The maid, tucked in green feather bikini, playing a fantasy duck, ran out of the window, screaming in horror. Nazo grabbed her husband by the balls and butchered his penis with the kitchen knife. The husband was rushed to the hospital by the neighbors As facts came to light, the lady doctors took sick leave and nurses went on strike.

Tabloids beefed up the news and bannered the headlines:

"A traditional housewife tears her veil to hoist a flag."

"Exposes male hypocrisy. Cracks the hard nuts."

Now known as "hunter wali" the woman with the whip, Nazo had become the heroine of the feminists.

A day after her divorce, she joined the Liberation Club, an NGO where among her male sympathizers she had met the dashing playwright and actor, Afzal. An underground communist, Afzal was a wannabe Lenin, lovingly called Ley-lunn by the poor workers, which meant, "take the prick." Both he and Nazo had clicked like titch buttons. She directed his street pieces for social change and practiced her feminism on him as well on the peasants and workers of the nation.

"Please sit here."

Mano had borrowed two elegant chairs from the shop that rented furniture for weddings. The owner was a regular customer.

Nazo and Riffat both sat plum on the cushy chairs. Mano had a pert nose, teased by a silver ring. She was in the habit of curling it up under a raised eyebrow that would nearly hook her upper lip. It was Mano's nakhra, the theatre of her face. "So, you are the producer?" Mano curled her nose.

"Oh yes, we are making a film," replied Nazo.

The tea boy brought in the tea in chipped cups with broken handles. "You son of a pig," Mano glared at the boy, "I told you to use my crockery. Look at those cups, like the siblings of a whore, none matches the other. Sorry sister Ji," she smiled to Nazo, "this kid is careless."

"Oh, you don't have to bother." Nazo smiled demurely.

"No Baji Ji, I mean sister Ji, you are my special guests. It's my honor to entertain you." Mano swung her hips as she strutted around setting the table with an array of fashionable china cups.

Other prostitutes, pimps, and street bums appeared in the windows. Agog.

"Wao, Mano is going to burst the big screen with her horns," someone in the crowd whispered.

"Go, go, get to your work." Mano waved to the spectators politely.

Some ducked, others hid behind the walls. No one left.

"What is the story of your filum, Baji Ji?" Mano breathed out her breasts to a strategic heft.

"Ha ha. I think the poor girl has misunderstood us," Nazo archly giggled to Riffat in English.

"Look Mano behen, my sister, it doesn't have any make-believe story."

"But Baji Ji, tell me how many dances, how much disco, how many wet scenes, and how many rape scenes you have in this filum?" Mano inquired like a pro.

"Oh no, no, you got it all wrong," said Nazo like chiding a child.

"Please don't tell me it's a meatless filum. No, Baji Ji, no. I tell you all box office hits have wet scenes. Even the censor people run and rerun these scenes till they get piles. Why, Baji Ji? Because in the rain, when your clothes are dripping, it's natural, isn't? And rape? Well, you should know what happens after the rape? The villain is always punished, if not by the law then by Allah, who sends a hurricane or an earthquake to show His wrath. Now Baji Ji, how can the villain be punished if there was no rape. Do you see my point?" Mano aired her cool judgment on the art of filmmaking.

"What a tragedy, she's crazy about those cheap flicks," said Nazo to Riffat, who grinned.

"Oh, they are from Amrika." Windows buzzed with whispers.

"Yes, from Hollywood."

"They talk angrazi."

"Gitmit, gitmit."

"But they are dark like us."

"They are kali mames. Black mame sahibs," spectators hooted from the balcony.

"Look, Mano behen, we are not producing any song-and-dance film. We are doing a documentary."

"Dako muntry?" Mano was confused.

"Yes! Yes! It's about real life, about truth."

"What truth?"

"Truth about us women. The naked truth," Nazo raised her tone.

"Angraz makes naked films."

"Films with three crosses," snickered someone in the window.

"Goras don't eat spicy things."

"They carry cold sausages between their legs."

"Fluffy rolls of dough. Tihlla atta."

"They can't hold for long."

"Our Mano can flatten a gora any time."

"Go fuck yourselves in your own places." Mano took off her shoe and brandished it at them.

All faces about-turned, backs of their heads in the window.

The mobile phone in Nazo's bag rang, yelling like an infant. She pulled out the slim instrument and pressed a button, "Oh yes I am in the Heera Mandi, right in the heart of the flesh market," she said in English. "I know you don't believe me, but I'm very much here, among real people. It's exciting. Oh no, no,

I am fine, safe and sound. I'll get back to you the moment I'm through." She switched it off. "It was Afzal on the phone," she said to Riffat.

Mano was overawed by Baji's English accent.

"Well, Mano behen, you must understand that we are here to help you," said Nazo putting the phone in her bag. "We'll shoot on actual locations, expose the conditions you live in, your fears and dreams and yes, your health . . . your brothers and sisters . . . "

Nazo looked at Riffat.

"Well, she means if there are any unwanted children or if you had any abortions etc." Riffat looked at Nazo, who joined in, "And yes, we wish to show the world how our sisters are harassed and humiliated in a male-dominated society."

Mano felt cheated.

"Why don't you make some stills?" Nazo whispered to Riffat who promptly took out a camera from her bag and fixed her eyes on Mano. "Let us wait for the right expression," she said, adjusting the flash. Her hand went for the tea cup.

"Don't touch it, you'll catch herpes," warned Nazo. Riffat blenched and let go of the cup.

"Will you remove that ugly confectionery?" Nazo pointed at Mano's makeup.

"Mano behen, we want to take your photographs without makeup," Riffat smiled to Mano.

"What?"

"You see, we don't wish the camera to lie," said Nazo.

"Lie?" Mano went dim in the face.

"Yes, we want to show the real you," said Riffat and took out some tissue paper from her purse to rub off Mano's makeup.

"Yes, that's it. This is the real thing. I want pathos," said Nazo hovering over Mano. "Chin up, tilt your head, a little to the left, go for it, that's the look."

Riffat zoomed in, the tele lens lunged. Click click.

The sudden glare of the camera flashes hit Mano's face. She felt stripped of her props. The camera chased her face, her push-up bra, her chipped cups, frayed cushions, silted walls, stained curtains, borrowed chairs, tattered carpets, and her brand-new skin. Among a volley of flashes, the tea went cold. A film of brown coat crusted under an umbrella of flies. The heads in the windows grew larger. Mano was watched in her shame. She tried to avert the gaze but Click! Click! Click! The mocking eye of the camera kept hounding her until she pulled herself away and rushed to her bedroom.

Inside, she dashed to the bottle of rum that belonged to the inspector. Guzzling in anger, Mano looked in the mirror, watched her face in a close-up without the festive shine of cosmetics; the face of a stranger. "Bitches!" The liquor sparked the silent wires of her imagination. "Hit of a swine, vomit of a pig, soor dhi satt. Here they come sistering their cunts with us. Behen chod, go and grow your tits first, those eggs you nest in your blouse." The mirror magnified her face. "Fuck the truth." Mano spat at the blowup, cleaned it with her dopatta and started rouging herself up. Frantically.

"Baji Ji, would you like to drink with me?" Mano stumbled out of the bedroom hugging the bottle. Her face a coloured nightmare.

"Oh no, thank you, we don't drink," Nazo said politely. "Poor girl is alcoholic," she whispered to Riffat. "Look at her, this is what they do to wash away their guilt."

"Baji Ji, you wanted the truth, didn't you?" Mano sat on the floor, thighs apart.

"Oh yes, we want a kind of social realism. Good, you understand." Nazo nudged Riffat. "This is the moment to drive home our message."

"Yes! Yes!" said Riffat shifting her bottom to the edge of the chair.

"Trust us, Mano behen, don't feel embarrassed to tell us about men. We know how they visit you as meat shops, weigh you, feel you up and harass you. Sexually," Nazo patted Mano with her phallic tone.

Mano curled her nose, took a deep swig and looked her in the eye, "Baji Ji, you call me behen, your sister, right?"

"Right," Nazo replied with relish.

Mano scratched her thighs and said, "Baji, can you scratch your thighs like this?"

"What?" Nazo looked at Riffat. Aghast.

Mano laughed, like the vamp in movies.

"She's pissed drunk. Doesn't know what she's talking about," Nazo panicked in English.

Mano curled her nose in slow motion. "Baji Ji, what is a man?" Mano pointed in between her parted thighs. "This is his grave," she said.

The crowd hanging on the windows clapped. The Bajis got scared. They tried smiling but Mano was in some mystical trance.

"Here, on this front, the Generals disarm without resistance. Their armors are shed like dead skin. The rich part with their riches, and the pious pawn their piety. Their senses blur and minds cease to think. They all fall on the mighty mount of Mano."

"Bravo! Balley balley!" The crowd rejoiced.

"Mano Ji, tell them about Goga. Tell them all, yes! Yes!" prompted the crowd.

"Oh Goga the wrestler," Mano smiled to the crowd. "What a powerful man," she said, "lifting rocks with his moustache. Baji Ji, no one could ever defeat him. He was always the winner. Well, this beef bum used to pass by my house every day. All muscles. I would call out for him, Hey, I want you. He would never stop, just walk away twisting his moustache and show-ing off his well-oiled body. But Baji Ji, I was not to give up. I kept calling him, hey is it only good for a leak? Where are your balls? Don't you have extra meat for this little pussy? Did you lose it in a wrestling match? Don't tell me you are a khassi."

"Yes! Yes! Don't tell me you are impotent, a khassi." The crowd repeated.

"But then Baji, a day came when he could no longer resist," continued Mano. Both Nazo and Riffat cringed in their seats. "As he walked in, I threw my legs up for him," said Mano rais-ing her legs, a replay for the Bajis. "Allah knows, he jerked inside me for three seconds and then fell on me like a corpse.

I kept shouting, 'Goga Ji, fuck! Fuck me on the double! Where has all your strength gone? I don't want to die a virgin!' I pulled his moustache, slapped his thighs but no, Goga was khalass. Baji Ji this was his grave." Mano once again gave the sign.

"Balley! Balley! Bravo! Mano Ji bravo!"

"Sadi Mano aavay e aavay," sang the crowd.

Nazo and Riffat looked at each other, appalled.

"Baji Ji, will you join me to celebrate our cunt rites?" Mano said in a drunken voice.

"What rubbish are you talking? Don't you have any shame?"

"Baji Ji, shame un-shame is a fad with the shariefs, the decent folks. We don't have such hangups." Mano smiled. Childlike.

"How dare she talk back at me?" Nazo grumbled to Riffat.

"Tell me Baji Ji, can you raise your legs without knowing who is on you? No, you can't. Because there is a white collar on your snooty twat and you sit on the sagging prick of respectability."

"Oh my God, how vulgar, toba toba." Nazo stood up, shaking with anger.

"Baji Ji, we are artists. We can only give you song and dance, warm your body and soul. This is the truth. The naked truth." Mano had finished the bottle.

Outside in the street, shops were opening. There was barbeque, the taka tin of gurdah kapooras, an aphrodisiac scramble of goat's kidneys and testes. The spicy mix of chicken kharai and the yeasty smell of tandoori roti. Boys with garlands of jasmine flowers appeared in the doors. Whores stood in balconies throwing their charms. The crowd in the windows had dispersed. Time for business.

A drunkard, all decked in jasmine garlands, entered the room. He held in his hands a few bundles of currency notes.

"Mano Ji," he announced. "Here we come to your astana, the threshold of your immortal beauty. Throw the alms of your youthful charms in our bowl of desire." He softly flicked the deck of notes. "Mano Ji, here is our humble nazrana. We sacrifice Money, the worldly god to your heavenly Beauty," he said releasing the pile of stapled notes. A handful of hundreds swirled up like a fan and sailed down like feathers, covering Mano with an invisible veil.

"O, the lamp of Beauty
Burn us with your flame
We are moths ready to die,"
the man recited the verse from a famous ghazal.

"Oh my God this is what men do to please them," said Nazo to Riffat. Both started to leave.

"Ah Mano Ji, is she a navaan dana? A fresh sapling?" the man grinned lewdly, pinching Musarrat's padded behind, fumbling for some flesh. Nazo shuddered in disgust.

"Oh she's a bundle of twisted matchsticks. No meat. Mano Ji, she won't fetch even a bad penny, khotta paisa," he said with a wide grin. Nazo kicked the man in his balls. He fell, befuddled. The mobile rang, like a fire alarm. Nazo shoved her hand inside her bag. The hand came out with a fancy vibrator.

"Madame! Madame!" Riffat whispered to Nazo, who for a moment went pale in the face. Sliding back the object, Nazo pretended as if no one had seen anything. The phone rang off.

"They are visitors from the city," Mano said to the man, with a knowing smile.

"Oh, Allah may forgive me," the man groaned, lifting himself from the ground holding his balls in the cup of his hands. "Toba toba!" Keeping one hand on his balls, he touched his ears, one by one with his other hand.

"Sorry Madame, will you have some cold drink or hot tea?" The man had become extremely courteous.

"Shut up." Nazo took her bag and brusquely walked out with Riffat, who kept looking back at the man.

"They need to be educated," said Nazo on the way. "I will tell Afzal to write his next play on these ignorant victims."

"Very good idea." Riffat nodded in compliance.

"Mano Ji, who were these women," asked the man as the two women disappeared.

"My sisters."

"Sisters?" The man looked shocked.

"Yes, my stepsisters from the shariefs, the decent folks."

Mano smiled reaching for her ghungroos, the anklet bells.

"No wonder they had a fashionable hand phone." The man laughed his head off, forgetting the pain.

The tea boy stealthily walked in and whispered in Mano's ear. She winked at the man. The man immediately fled away. Mano waved to the musicians. A trail of attar, a strong perfume followed them as they entered the room with tabla, sarangi, and harmonium. The tea boy closed the doors and pulled down the curtains on the windows.

It was a muggy night and the air was heavy with fog. Juma slunk out of his car. His stork neck was shrunk inside his shoulders. He entered from the back door while the inspector stayed outside on duty. Mano raised her right hand to her forehead and hooking her upper lip with a twist of her eyebrow flourished a salaami. Juma's neck craned up, his eyes puffed, and his Adam's apple bobbed under its skin. Mano offered him a paan. He took it with a toothsome smile. The sarangi struck the melody of a ghazal, the harmonium followed and the tabla thumped. Shaking her ghungroos, Mano gyrated to the thrusting beat.

The night had begun.

Outside, under the dim pole lights, people moved like tarred shadows.

Chapter 4

Nightfall

Like a child who pulls a toy cart by the string, Ganju's uncle Nawabzada Zahoor-ud-Din had led his clan from its humble origins of blacksmiths to the status of nobility. He had changed not only the fate of his kin but also their blood.

Zahoor, the rightful owner of the jagir, was younger than Ganju's father, Allah-yar. Their father Haji Noor who, in colonial India, fixed horseshoes at the stable of the British commissioner, had gained access to his masters by spying on freedom fighters and persuading village folks to enlist their sons in the Imperial army. Allah-yar was killed in action. The British had rewarded the martyrdom by allotting Haji large chunks of land and by raising him from a horseshoer to their recruiting agent.

For the blacksmiths, the horseshoe did bring luck but without honor. Land was not enough to command respect in a world that also demanded superiority of race and caste. Soon after Haji's death, Zahoor took an oath at the hand of Pir Ganju Shah, a local saint whose ancestry could be traced back to sacred Pirs. On Shab-e-Baraat, the holy night of fireworks and the revelation of the Quran, Zahoor heard the laughter of the Pir's eldest daughter and was shown the way. He prayed all the time, performed chillas, the rigorous meditation, and generously spent money on lungars, the free food for the poor. Pir Ganju Shah found in him a true believer and eventually decided to give him his daughter.

The marriage gave birth to a new genealogy that reincarnated the low-caste horseshoe-fixers into respectable Pirs and Nawabzadas.

Zahoor rebuilt the shrine at the site of Pir Ganju Shah. Elegant minarets with green tops were erected. Golden arches appeared with tiled floors, and a large dome dominated the skyline. The catafalque was raised to an impressive height over the marble. A sparkling chadder with the hundred names of Allah covered the sacred mound. Zahoor held the Urs, a huge festival, with drums and dhamal, ecstatic dancing, and hundreds of oil lamps. The schoolmaster traced the family tree, successfully proving the legitimacy of Zahoor's claim on the holy blood.

After the death of Pir Ganju Shah, who was without a son or a relative, Zahoor in a grand ceremony became sajjadda-nasheen, the custodian of the shrine and was now known as Pir Zahoor-ud-Din Ganju the Bade Sarkar, which meant the big ruler.

As he gained influence, Zahoor fought elections and clinched a seat in the National Assembly. When his nephew Noor Mohammad Ganju came of age to take over his father's jagir, Zahoor married off his daughter to him, making sure that his property remained within the control of the family.

"*Wato izzo min tesha wato zillo min tesha.* Allah alone bestows either wealth or poverty upon humans," Zahoor quoted a verse from the Quran as he rinsed his hands in a finger bowl after the lunch he had hosted at the Capital Club for ministers, bureaucrats, and other distinguished citizens. He was to leave for his village, where he needed to spend time before the upcoming elections.

While he picked his teeth with a toothpick, Zahoor lashed out at the rampant corruption and lack of justice in the country. "They have forgotten their graves," he said. Slipping some toothpicks into his pocket, he addressed the guests, "We have to think about our akhrat, the afterlife where every sinner will be punished."

Heads at the table nodded in approval.

Noor Mohammad Ganju, sitting at the edge of his chair, had shrunk to a nobody in the overpowering presence of his uncle. He wanted him to leave as early as possible so that he could talk to Juma about the nazrana girl, but after his lunch Zahoor decided to sit with Ganju to go through some routine matters.

Inside Zahoor's suite at the club, Ganju placed some files in front of him. He had to get his uncle's stamp on the papers Juma had given him. They included an application by the inspector, requesting promotion and transfer to a city with the highest crime rate in the country. Zahoor signed the papers without looking at them. Ganju waited for him to say goodbye, but Zahoor went on with his long instructions about the fundraising schemes for the upcoming elections. Ganju sat still, listening, but his mind buzzed with images of the Mughal princess, the nazrana girl.

It was a clear day in the late summer afternoon when Zahoor entered his Pajero flanked by his guards to leave for his village. Waving to the uncle, Ganju turned back to Juma, who stood behind him.

"Juma?"

"Ji, Sarkar."

"How long does it take to get out of the city?" He handed the signed papers to Juma.

"Well, Sarkar, Bade Sarkar likes to go fast, it shouldn't take him more than two hours."

Perhaps it was safer to think of the nazrana girl once his uncle was out of the city, thought Ganju.

Juma coughed discreetly and said, "Sarkar, do you have any engagement this evening?"

"No, Juma, there is nothing. Nothing at all." Ganju wanted Juma to say what he wanted to hear, but Juma, who could normally read his thoughts before they were born, was quiet as a mouse.

"Why do you ask?" Ganju asked.

"Sarkar, I need your permission to be excused for the evening."

Son of a bitch. Was he suggesting that what he had said a day before was a joke?

"Juma were you there with me at Zahid Sahib's house?" Ganju asked firmly.

"Yes, Sarkar."

"Did you say something about a nazrana?"

"But Sarkar, that's what the work is, what else?" He gave a weird smile. "She's only waiting for your orders," he whispered in confidence.

"Who?" Ganju got confused.

"The nazrana girl, Sarkar!"

"No, no," Ganju felt a flush of embarrassment. "I think you should wait. Look, I've got to go to a dinner tonight."

"Very well, Sarkar. May I leave now?"

"Well yes, I guess you can." Ganju's voice came like the reluctant stroke of a wet matchstick.

Inside his bedroom, Ganju fell on the bed and anxiously hugged the pillows. Was he committing adultery? Betraying his wife? For a moment he regretted having listened to Juma, but then from nowhere in his mind swelled the porcupine with its thorny questions. Wasn't he the one who was rebuffed by his legally wed wife? Didn't he have to hide to steal a glimpse of her? How long could he mate with a shadow?

He rang for Juma.

"Sarkar?" Juma appeared in the door like an apparition.

"Juma, do you think Bade Sarkar would be out of the city by now?"

"Long before, my Sarkar," Juma said matter-of-factly.

Ganju felt stupid.

"Well, Juma, I called to tell you that I've cancelled the dinner appointment. Maybe you can go right now and do what you have to do." Ganju threw a meaningful glance at Juma.

"I understand, Sarkar."

As Juma left the room, Ganju went weak in the knees. He needed a drink. Somehow he still felt the unsettling presence of his uncle. He poured a large quantity and gulped nervously. Who knows, the uncle might change his mind and return from half way? Maybe he should wait, but Juma said Bade Sarkar must be out of the city by now, and once she is here, he would have certainly reached home. What about her? Was she really a virgin?

Young and untouched? Would he be able to perform? He was
not used to her body and hadn't got much experience in bed. But
did she really want him? Of course, she did. She's the nazrana
girl, a sacred offering. What has sex to do with it? Turning down
a nazrana is an act of arrogance, an unpardonable sin.

"Congratulations!" Juma, sitting against the infernal posters in
his office handed over the transfer orders to the inspector. The
inspector kissed Juma's hands and unloaded a bowl of goat's
trotters in front of him. Juma joyfully released his teeth out
of his puny jaw and grabbed the first bite. "I don't want you
to spend much time in moaning and groaning with her. You'd
better say your goodbyes quickly and leave the city as a respon-
sible officer. She's no longer the girl you knew from the walled
city, now she is not Mano but Nasreen Bano, understand?"

"I understand, Mai Baap." The inspector watched Juma
eating; he was not allowed to share food with him.

Mano, alias Nasreen Bano, was away at an expensive beauty
parlor for a waxing and facial. With a new name and flattering credentials, Juma had shifted her to the kothi, a house in
a lesser populated area of the Capital. A trained maid and a
trusted guard were now in her service. Her hair was done in
the traditional style. Long swaying tresses tied with gold rib-
bons reached up to her ample hips. On her lithe form flowed
the embroidered pishwaz that held her bosom in a delicate
grip, restraining the provocative contours to a seductive charm.
Holding her trim waist, the fall of the pishwaz swirled around
her legs, and aab-e-rawaan, a transparent dopatta known as
"running waters" circled her entire body. The bra was a silky
one with subtle wiring. Her hands carried the exquisite patterns
of henna in vivacious reds, and floral jewelry adorned her like
a blooming tree in the spring. Overnight, a new parenthood
and a virtuous family background had transmuted Mano into
Nasreen Bano, the damsel from courtly harems.

All preened and made-up, Mano hailed her newly found

image. In the beauty parlor when she looked at herself in the mirror she was taken aback by her rebirth as the Mughal princess.

She heard the horn.

Juma had arrived to pick her up. The inspector had followed him on his motorbike. He stuck his face into the car window and gawked at the "lady."

"Is that you my dove?" he whispered.

"Why, of course, it's no one but your own Mano." She curled her nose.

"Oh my God! That's hundred percent my Mano." The inspector touched a corner of her dopatta.

"Look with your eyes, not your hands," warned Juma from the front seat.

"Oh, inspector sahib, we have to go our separate ways." Mano blew a kiss, pulling away her dopatta.

"I know! I know!" The inspector slipped the air kiss under his new uniform and hummed a verse, "*Muj say pahli si mohabat meray mehboob na mang.* Oh my love, do not ask me to love you like before. My country is far above our venal love!" Tears rolled down his unshaven face.

"Don't you act like a eunuch now. Wipe those pissing eyes and go back to your duty," growled Juma.

"O, no! I'll not let my Mano leave me." The inspector, in his desperation, tore at his new uniform.

"Don't fuck up your uniform, they'll charge you for it. Come, take a deep breath." Juma calmed him down.

"I am ruined Mai Baap," cried out the half-naked inspector and lunged to grab Mano's hand.

"Get out of my way or I'll squash you under the wheels," yelled Juma, starting the car.

Mano pulled up the window and waved to the inspector, who on his motorbike disappeared from her life at the corner of the main road.

Nightfall.

Juma entered the house with Mano sitting at the backseat like a virginal bride. Ganju heard the door open. Gulping down the liquor, he went to the bathroom and stood before the mirror. He was not that old, only the receding hairline on the forehead had outsized his face a bit, but a bulging forehead could be exciting, it showed his masculinity, he assured himself.

Juma quietly left Mano inside the bedroom on a sofa and left. Curled up in her dopatta, she sneaked a glance at the luxurious bed, rich carpets, and laced curtains. With a purr she rubbed the opulent dream into her closing eyes.

Rising footfalls.

Ganju entered, clad in his traditional dress, a casual bang of hair dangling on his forehead. Mano lifted her head. Ganju was struck by her blue eyes and fair skin. She gently knelt down and waved her hand from her forehead down, flourishing a ceremonial salaami. "Aadab," she almost sang. Petals of roses sailed down at his feet.

Ganju felt like a king.

Bowing her head, she touched his feet, making sure her plunging neckline was at the centre of his vision. Ganju's eyes engulfed the heaving cleavage. He held her up. She trembled like a bamboo shoot, limping down on the floor; her body taut with the pressure of puberty. In all readiness, there she was bundled up at his feet, a sacred gift of unravished youth, a humble nazrana.

Oh God, do I dare? He panicked. Was it the raw youth, or the submission of a defenseless victim? Was it the fear of his uncle, or the fear of willful sin, hell and damnation? He felt his royal robe stiffening. But then, as if in a dream he walked to the secret safe inside his dressing room. There it was, the sacred sign of malehood. He looked at it. It puffed into a grimace. He brushed it lightly against his upper lip. It stuck there happily. He took out the Japanese mirror and tilted it down on him. Suddenly something fattened inside him. He grew taller, rising to the pictures of Generals in the history books. His body buzzed and hair started sprouting from the pores of his skin. With a frothing mouth his teeth hung out and a rapidly growing fur covered his body. Something howled inside him.

On his prowl, he saw Nasreen, all wrapped up on the floor. Driven by the demon of lust, Ganju sprang at the plunging cleavage, his hands scavenging the wired bra. Vivid nipples surged, proud and defiant. He lifted her up and threw her on the bed rummaging at the youthful flesh under a heap of silk. Pulling herself, she folded her arms and tried hiding her modesty. Ganju savaged the drapery until she was stark naked. He was obsessed by her nubile skin lying amidst crushed flowers and shredded silver embroidery. She rolled, covering herself with the bed sheet. Ganju tore it off, baring her luscious thighs. He lunged, she turned over. Mano alias Nasreen Bano was not a woman of easy virtue. She struggled against the brute force with telling patience. He tried slamming into her, she clinched her legs. Mano's resistance made him mad with rage. He hit her hard and tearing her legs apart, rammed into her with splitting speed. Pinioned, she fluttered like a trapped bird until her screams got muffled by the growing fur and her flesh was absorbed by his shadow.

As he lay exhausted in the heat of sweat, the sight of virginal blood on the white sheet made him feel bigger than what he had ever seen in the magic mirror. He had penetrated the impenetrable.

In that gripping silence, he thought he heard a knock on the door.

"Who could that be?"

Another desperate knock.

Mano shifted under his weight.

"Who's there?" he called out.

"Sarkar! It's Bade Sarkar," quavered Juma from outside.

"What? Is he here?" Ganju jumped out of the bed.

"No, Sarkar, he can never come back again."

"What?" Ganju shouted in fright.

"He's dead, Sarkar," came Juma's voice from another world.

"Dead?" Ganju covered his body with the torn bed sheet.

"He met an accident, Sarkar."

Ganju stood still. It made his flesh crawl. His body shed the ever-growing fur. Like dead skin.

Chapter 5

Burialfest

It was one of those days when the sun is radiant and a gentle breeze wanders in the open fields. Everything is calm, but then a tiny fuzz of cloud goes berserk, turning itself into a haze that unnerves the raging sun and wraps the world in a foggy gloom.

Zahoor, sitting on the back seat of his car, had finished a chicken sandwich. After drinking from the bottle of mineral water, as he picked the hollows of his teeth, the wind outside howled itself into a dust storm. Amused at the sudden change in the weather, Zahoor picked merrily until the toothpick got stuck in his teeth. The wind died down like a panting animal and a slow drizzle followed, soundless and invisible.

When they passed the mountainous terrain, the air quickened and like animals prick their ears before an earthquake, the trees shook their leaves. The driver held up the prayer plate for Allah's help. But then from nowhere a huge trailer hit the Pajero. It went flying off the road, tumbling down thousands of feet into a ravine. Zahoor's body crashed against the windshield. His head was crushed and his guts spilled out, his gold buttons sank deep into his chest like bullets. The seat belts hung, like swings of death.

"Shit, what a way to kick the bucket," Zahoor grunted as his cellular phone blinked, and his soul loomed over the debris of his bones.

Sometime past midnight, collected in a plastic sack, Zahoor's body was brought to the hospital. Under the blazing lights on a table lay the litter of his mortal remains. Only a bit of a toothpick remained in place between a pair of jammed teeth. Surgeons in white masks and synthetic gloves kept busy till late, reassembling the organic mess. By forenoon they had tarted up the human junk for public viewing.

The grand show of massive wailing started the moment his body arrived in Noorpur village. Shamyanas went up and carpets rolled on the open space surrounding the Ganju House. The body lay in the basement among thick slabs of ice that stood like walls.

"What a mess," Zahoor grumbled. Though the surgeons had done a good job, the severed tongue was too swollen to be stuffed back in place. Forcing it down, they had stitched his mouth.

Zahoor had to stay in the freezing cold to appear fresh for visiting friends and relatives.

Followers of Ganju's clan, relatives, government officials, women and children, swarmed at the Ganju House. Separate arrangements were made for men and women along a special VIP enclosure with velvet sofas, furred carpets, and colorful cushy chairs. Outside, beyond shamyanas, pushed to the ends of the ground, beggars with hungry eyes and stray dogs with hanging tongues circled the degs, the cauldrons of food. Inside the courtyard, women squatted on mattings and wailed.

Zeenat sat huddled on her bedroom floor, attendants serving her water every time a new arrival entered to weep with her. She had been there from the crack of dawn, waiting for the body.

Taimur, Zeenat's son, walked in. She couldn't help bursting into tears as she hugged him.

"Have you seen your father?" she sobbed. The boy shook his head. "Your sister?"

"No," he said.

She waved to Cheemo, her personal maid, and asked her to bring Razia from the house. Someone came and whispered to Zeenat.

Zeenat kissed her son and said, "Your father wants to see you." The boy left to find his way among the mourning women.

Ganju in his starched white dress sauntered around the VIP enclosure like a bridegroom. Earlier he had sat on his ancestral chair under the common shamyana where followers had kissed his hand, their grief terminating at the edge of his knees. He was their new lord and master, the custodian of the shrine, their savior, the Bade Sarkar.

Taimur entered, head down.

"Here, my son, sit with me," said Ganju fondly embracing him. Taimur sat, his eyes fixed on the ground. Ganju wanted his son to face the facts of life, have his first experience of a proper funeral. Taimur, hardly thirteen, was pulled out of his bed early that morning from his hostel and was brought to the village by the family driver. He had no idea of what was happening around him. Ganju explained to him the reality of death and of reward and punishment in the Hereafter. Taimur's eyes kept straying beyond the enclosure to the scruffy beggars and mangy dogs. Somewhere on the way his father's voice got lost. He felt a chill.

"Open display of grief disturbs the decorum of death," out in the courtyard everyone consoled everyone. "Don't cry too much, it'll hurt the dead." No one listened; all were desperate to display their sorrow. Babies yelled in their mothers' laps who quickly nippled them under their chadders. Children fought and pissed everywhere. No one cared, everyone too busy lamenting the dead. The business of mourning went from huffed sobbing to wheezing, muffled hiccups to hysterical theatrics, beating the chest or just freezing in a sakta, the ultimate stupor with lidless eyes.

Outside the main shamyana, Allama's boys swayed vigorously, chanting verses from the Quran in shrill voices. They looked happy in crumpled caps and unwashed clothes. It was hope that made them sway, the greed for money and the rich food that only came with death. For them it was Eid in black clothes.

Now the courtyard shook with sudden outbursts. Marasans of Noorpur village had entered the scene. These women sang and danced at weddings and childbirths and also mourned, for money. Relatives of the dead watched them with hawkish eyes, selecting the one who cried the loudest in a style that could move them to tears. The Marasans made an impressive spectacle by doing epileptic aerobics, gnashing teeth, rolling on the ground, foaming at the mouth, tearing their hair and grinding their chests to reveal miraculous stigmata. The occasion provided them the license to bare their breasts and thrust their bodies about lewdly. Allama's boys had tough competition with those witches of the doom.

For Razia, the news had awakened the hope of being able to get out of the house, see things, walk on the streets and meet people. She had been overjoyed that her brother had arrived unexpectedly. She had always missed him from the time he had left home to study in the city. He used to play with her and Cheemo, their maid, who was almost of her age. He would tell them all the interesting stories circulating outside the Haveli. At times they would dress him up like themselves and dance for hours in their room. They would put him on the bed like a baby patient and act as nurses, fondling him all over with hugs and kisses. Sometimes when he was called out to play cricket, they badly resented his freedom. Left by themselves among lifeless dolls, they would play boys to fill his absence.

The appearance of Cheemo put Razia into a festive mood. It brought all those hidden desires back. She trembled with the shiver of muffled rebellion as she changed her clothes. She had not been aware of her growing body. The ripening thighs and bursting hips jostled for space in her tightening clothes.

"These are gifts of Satan, they must be gagged," she had been told by the old maid who taught her to read the Quran. At midnight, in her dreams, a tiger with a human face would attack her, sometimes a wild horse or a hairy demon. Among strange breathing rhythms a scream would freeze in her throat. Confronted by grilled windows and sly slants of arches she would recite a prayer and try to go back to sleep. In the sultry silence of summer afternoons, as the breeze entered through the windows, she would lie on her bed and stare at the ceiling. The smells of wild roses and the cooing of doves would make her swoon. She would sit up startled, as though somebody had caught her naked.

Wrapping herself carefully in a large chadder that obscured her bold contours, she sat in the car beside Cheemo. On the way, Razia pushed aside the curtain of the car window and nuzzled at the glass to look at the shops in the bazaar. Cheemo stared at her. Razia slipped a small leather purse to Cheemo. Cheemo hesitated. Razia nudged and pushed it to her, "Take it, it's for you. There's some money too." Cheemo smiled mischievously, the purse disappeared instantly somewhere under her clothes.

Reaching the Ganju House, Razia met her mother and asked for her brother. Her mother told her that he was in the men's quarters with her father. Disappointed, she went out into the courtyard. It was afternoon now and the wailing rage of grief had settled to a drone of sighing and sobbing. Allama's boys were tired and hungry. Their faces were weary and their voices fatigued. Food was to be served after the burial.

Razia met some of her friends. They embraced without saying much. The male cousins and uncles hugged the girls. The occasion provided the freedom of unsuspected touch and discreet caresses. Vibes traveled through shuffling clothes, ritualistic pats, hugs, and kisses. Bodies quickened under the mournful Haveli. For the girls the funeral had turned into a thrilling event.

Outside under the shamyanas village women recited Quran while slipping dry dates through their fingers. A purda, the curtain, hung across the shamyanas that partitioned male from female enclosures. Huge matkas, the earthen pitchers filled with water, sat on a wooden sill with clay bowls. The mourners after spilling pails of tears had to water their dried up bodies. Young girls and children ran enthusiastically to the matkas. To be the first at serving water on this occasion was to ensure Allah's blessings.

Razia watched them for a while, and then finding no one around, got up to fetch the water herself. She moved to the pitchers, but seeing a pigeon sailing down from the sky, she stopped. The pigeon preened and dipped its beak in the clay bowl. Razia went a step forward, it flew up, unfurling a cloud compressed within its wings. Her eyes followed the pigeon till it dissolved in the distant skies. A subtle wind ruffled the curtain. She forgot to pour the water. Two eyes were looking at her from behind the partition. Someone called, she didn't answer. There, he stood tall under the tree, his face covered but his eyes everywhere. The curtain fell back, the breeze gone. Someone pulled her. "Why don't you get the water?" Razia ran madly, back and forth, serving water to the mourners. The capricious wind kept playing with the curtain and her heart jumped with the seesaw vision. Every time she passed by the curtain, she sent her eyes to him.

Preceded by the bomb squad the General arrived at the scene. The squad, after having inspected the grave and the degs, outside the shamyanas, were now busy checking the sofas and the chairs. He was attired in shalwar kameez and a white skullcap that looked rather tight on his plump head. He warmly embraced Ganju. A stiff moustache lashed across Ganju's face as he kissed him on the cheek. The General wiped his moistened eyes with a white handkerchief and eased himself on the velvet sofa. His hands raised in prayer, his eyes closed. After the ritual, he boomed, "What a man! I can never forget his honesty. Unlike our politicians, the late Zahoor was incorruptible, an upright man, always committed to his principles."

Allama walked in, belly first, and embraced Ganju, flicking an oblique glance at the General. "Asalaam-o-alaikum," he said bowing to the General. The General stood up, Allama promptly hugged him, crying out, "*Inna lillahay wa inna illahay raj-a-oon*. Everyone has to return to Allah." His eyes running water. "How's your Excellency?" Allama sleeved his tears and returned to his normal self.

"I am alright Allama sahib, do pray for all of us," the General said with respect.

"Your Excellency, Allah says anyone who fights for Him is a jannati, a paradisee, who shall go straight to paradise. You, mashallah, are a mard-e-mujahid, a ghazi, the soldier of Allah. It's in the Quran that on the day of judgment when the grave of a ghazi or shaheed, the martyr, will be opened, his body will be as fresh as new, as if he had died right at that moment. Aha, what grandeur a mujahid carries even to his grave." Allama had made room for himself in the VIP enclosure. "Aha, Chhotay Sarkar, our little master." He hugged Taimur and kissed him on the forehead. Mumbling something with his eyes shut, he sprayed Taimur's face with his breath. The stench of bad breath and attar sunk into the boy's pores. "God bless you, may you live for a thousand years." Allama once again stamped Taimur's forehead with a kiss and rolled back towards the General. "Now what a man we have lost in Sarkar Zahoor Sahib," he said. "As long as Sarkar lived, our boys never felt like orphans. Allah may reward him; he used to spend at least fifty thousand per month on the orphanage. Full fifty thousand," Allama almost shouted the amount throwing a glance at Ganju.

Ganju heard it, fifty thousand, it was meant for him. He called for Juma. Juma discreetly moved to Allama and once he paused for a breath, Juma whispered something in his ear. Allama fell silent at once. Without a word he left in obvious haste. There was food in the backyard, which he could eat on the quiet before the burial.

Zahid had come straight from the airport. Earlier he had called from Dubai where he had gone on one of his business trips. Dressed in a safari suit he quietly hugged Ganju, shook hands with the General, and sat down beside him. Soon after, Kashif Ali the Intelligence chief was ushered in with his private secretary, who sat far away from the main group in a corner. Kashif was tall and thin with sunken eyes that hardly moved. He had a basilisk-like stare. In his long achkan buttoned to the neck, he looked like an ancient gravedigger. Lifting his large hands, he prayed aloud and the air filled with his gravel voice.

In the room next door, Zahoor's belongings were laid out for public display. His turban, shoes, his framed honors and certificates, his clothes, his large portraits freshly garlanded guns and swords, his photographs with the prime minister and other leading politicians, his prayer mat and his walking stick that lay side by side with the toothpick retrieved during his surgery. Just in a day the living house had become a shrine.

Everyone had a tour.

The passage leading to the basement had become crowded.

One by one people visited the body to have a good look at a face they were never going to see again.

"Why do they wish to see a dead man's face?" Zahoor groaned soundlessly against the ice walls. Perhaps they wouldn't believe him dead unless they saw his face. "They touch it and become certain, absolutely certain that you are gone." His eyes bolted and arms crossed, Zahoor was a useless slab, a carrion to be disposed off to foraging worms.

"Death subverts hierarchy," he mused in the cold void. "She's the ultimate democrat. Under the rule of dust, no one is privileged. All skulls are called by the same name. Skull."

"Look how his face glows."

"He's not dead, he is just sleeping."

"What a divine smile."

"We the sinners are left behind, he's the lucky one." Voices clamoured around him.

"Why don't they die with me if they are so envious of me?" Zahoor tried rising up in vain.

"Who's he?"

A hooded figure entered the room. It was a man, his turban crumpled and a chadder covering his face. He stared at the body with bloodshot eyes. Finding no one around, he pulled the corner of his chadder and spat right on Zahoor's face. "Bastard!" He mumbled and left. After him entered an old landlord's wife, her eyes still like glass. Holding a lengthy rosary she cast her gaze at his face, all sprayed by the hateful spit. "Ah look at the dead man, he's crying," she sighed. "It's all Allah's own miracle. Oh I see tears around his eyes." She left in a state of shock.

Now came some women. As they neared his face, they unveiled themselves. Zahoor saw their powdered faces, plucked eyebrows, red lipsticks, and blue eyeshadows.

"Aren't they whores? How did they get a chance to paint their lustful dreams and come here for a voyeuristic feast," groused Zahoor, mourning the loss of female modesty.

Later when the rush subsided, Ganju came in with Taimur. At the door, he saw a woman clad in an expensively embroidered burqa. She was walking out of the basement. A little boy, munching a cob, followed her. The woman kept looking at Ganju from a distance as if she wanted to say something to him. Taking her to be some needy woman, Ganju ignored her but her eyes behind the veil kept chasing him. The boy showing his crooked teeth threw away the half-eaten cob and left with the woman. Ganju hurriedly took Taimur inside.

"Son, take a look. Say khuda hafiz to your grandfather, Nana Jan," he said to Taimur with paternal warmth. Taimur closed his eyes as he caught a glimpse of the twisted jaw and stitched neck.

"What's wrong, son?" Ganju asked, caressing his face. "Oh my God, you are burning with fever." Ganju quickly took him out and sent him home.

"Poor kid, he can't be corpse-friendly at his age," sneered Zahoor, liplessly.

"*Ash-hado un la illaha illalah*!" Men recited aloud, lifting the charpoy with the body on it. Women hung in balconies to watch the funeral procession. Men walked beside the charpoy to get a chance to shoulder the dead and draw reward in the Hereafter.

"What a magnificent procession! If Bade Sarkar were alive today, he would have been really proud of his funeral," Allama moaned under the weight of the charpoy, flooding his beard with tears.

Gul Khan the chowkidar had been crying like a child, "I was getting married next week, but now I can't. My sarkar has left me alone in the world. How could I be happy without him?" he told the man next to him as he took the chance to rest the body on his shoulder. Now Juma replaced Gul Khan and came closer to Ganju who was on the other side.

"*Ash-hado un la illaha illalah*," he recited aloud and whispered to Ganju, "Sarkar, you have been chosen by fate. Don't wait. Elections are coming and Allah is on your side. *Ash-hado un la ilaha illalah*," Juma shouted the kalima and shifted out for another man.

"I am not buried yet and they are dancing on my dead body. I would have skinned them alive if I were not dead. Good, I am leaving this world to these vultures." Zahoor happily turned on the charpoy without motion.

Towering over the freshly made grave of his uncle, Ganju threw roses. With each petal he released his burden of vengeance.

After the burial they returned to the Ganju house, where food was ready. A mob of people gathered around the degs with hankering hands and hungry mouths. Inside the VIP enclosure, special dishes were catered for the dignitaries. After the meal the conversation turned to the departed soul whom they remembered through poetry, philosophy, and famous quotes.

"*Haq maghfirat karay ujab azad mard tha.* What a liberated man he was. God bless him," Zahid recited.

"Well, it was a bad accident. But if you think of it, it was the best way to go, you see no hassles. I must say he died a decent death."

"I know, if you have a lingering disease you need prolonged and tedious care, and we all know how emotional support is. Tiring isn't it?"

"The accident eased his last gasp, here he went without making any demands or testing anyone's patience. He didn't even ask for a glass of water from anyone. And imagine, no medical bills."

"It was a godsent invitation for him and as the poet says," Zahid quoted from Ghalib, "*Maut ka aik din moyun hai, neend kyon raat bhar nahin atee.* When the time of death is fixed, why have sleepless nights."

"Wah, wah!" said Kashif, shaking his head in appreciation, "Now look at the Pharaohs, who packed everything from shoes to their toothbrushes in their coffins. How considerably neat. Death for them was like going on a journey, therefore all the luggage, how sensible."

Nibbles and the afters.

"Human disposal is tough, it causes lots of anxiety and tension," said the General. "Do you know just one Nazi official presided over the deaths of at least 900,000 Jews in a single extermination camp in Poland."

"What about illegal abortions? How many die within the womb, there are no statistics available."

"Have you read about Dr Death? The mercy killer?"

"Death has become a joke, just a handshake."

"Well, we all have to die, sooner or later so why such a hullabaloo."

"My dear, it's for the Hereafter."

"Well, it all depends on what you believe in."

"I think both Hell and Heaven are on earth. *Yahin say uthay ga yoom-e-mehasher, isi zameen per hisab ho ga.* It's on earth that doomsday will rise and it's here where the judgment will take place," with this verse Zahid concluded the discussion.

It was getting late. Most of the people had left. The trio was animated enough to stay back. They trooped to the living room for a nightcap.

"I believe there's a peasant uprising," Zahid said, turning to politics.

"Oh yes, we have reports of an underground communist movement active in the country," said the chief of Intelligence.

"Do you think they'll come out in the open?" Zahid lit his cigar.

"We have to keep the facade of democracy in this country. There are issues of human rights, freedom of speech, political torture and all that fancy jargon of the political blackmailers. So in case they choose to fight elections, we cannot possibly stop them but can do what we can."

"Like bungle the ballot boxes, harass them, and sabotage their campaign. Release snakes or water in their rallies and murder if necessary?" said Zahid.

"No, we simply put everything in the hands of the army," Kashif said, twisting his nubby fingers.

"That's exactly what I expect from those politicians, cleaning their shit," said the General, swigging his vodka from the hip flask Zahid had slipped over to him.

Time to leave, they all prayed for the departed soul to rest in the eternal peace of paradise. "Amen," they said in unison.

Before leaving, Zahid sat next to Ganju and held his hand. "Ganju Bhai, now you are the head of this grand dynasty," he said. "You'll have to take on all the responsibilities. I know

Bhabhi will be in grief, she only had her father and he too is gone. This is the time to make her busy with something. And I brought a few cans of halva from Dubai, it's with the servants."

The General patted Ganju on the shoulder, saying, "My dear, you have to look forward to the future. We are behind you, and as they say in the army, war always starts in the mind, so keep charging your brains. Now you are our man, after your uncle, elections are coming, this is your chance."

Ganju saw them off to their cars and waved until they disappeared in the dark. Walking back to the abandoned house, he missed the nazrana girl. Why was he thinking of her on such an occasion, he wondered. Perhaps with his uncle's sudden death his zest for life had bloomed. He looked up to the heavens and saw the first moon appearing in the sky like a milk tooth. Oblivious of his daughter still standing against the shamyana, his hands went up in prayer.

Chapter 6

A Briefcase War

Elections are a season of intrigues. The wounds of old rivalries are scratched open and crime rates go up. Bets are laid, voters are bribed, booze flows, predictions are floated by astrologers, and journalists clamor for payoffs. Time to make serious money.

"Zindabad Ganju, Zindabad!" Thousands shouted outside in the courtyard as Ganju in his bathroom minted himself to soothe his piles. After performing his bath rituals, he hastened to the basement, knocked back his usual dose, and chewing cardamom stepped out nervously. Power gravitated towards him as he paced along the corridors approaching the people.

"Zindabad Ganju, zindabad!"

Slogans warmed his soul as he sat down on his ancestral chair. Sudden silence.

Allama had started Tilawat, the recitation of Quran. Above the belly, his mouth shot off through a barbed-wire beard, sending cannon balls of divine wrath. After he barreled down from the stage, an aged poet was helped to the rostrum where, fixing his thick glasses, he quavered a qaseeda in praise of Ganju to a popular folk tune. Showering praise on him and his ancestors, the poet reeled on until his toothless mouth could squeeze out no more.

Now, as if to invoke some sacred deity, the slogans came faster, "Zindabad! Zindabad! Ganju! Zindabad!."

Ganju lifted himself from the chair and shuffled over to the rostrum. A twitch in his rectum disoriented him. He tried speaking but a lump stuck in his throat. He was no orator, only his uncle could sway the millions. He struggled in vain, against a tongue numb with the dead odor of his uncle's memory.

"Gaanjuu! Gaanjuuu!"

His name chanted by the crowd became a never-ending wave, pumping energy into him. A sudden jerk and the knotted tongue opened free. Standing erect, he spoke, and each word evoked passionate applause. Charged with eloquence, Ganju drove them to a frenzy.

"Gaanju! Gaanju!" The voices made him euphoric.

"God must have felt the same when he created angels," absorbing the adulation, Ganju murmured to himself.

The trouble with his piles had vanished miraculously.

On that day, Ganju's spirits kept humming the prophecies brewed by his followers until Juma, pressing his legs at night, broke the spell.

"Sarkar, I am born out of the filth of your feet but . . . " he unleashed his tongue.

"What's it, Juma?" Ganju chirped, still giddy.

"Sarkar, nothing is more intoxicating than listening to one's own praise, but slogans can't fill bellies. Voters no longer look for speeches but for their next meal," Juma slurred.

"What rubbish are you talking?" Ganju pulled away his leg.

"Sarkar, in Bade Sarkar's times things were different," Juma had grabbed the other leg, "but now with Gulf money, sons of kammies return from Dubai with showy transistors and VCRs. The bastards have discovered their golden calf, their God on earth. Sarkar, our Allah is invisible, but money is foolproof. You put your hand in shit and polish up even a penny buried in it, toba toba," said Juma touching his ears in disgust. Ganju tried to withdraw his leg but Juma's pressing argument was too strong. "Sarkar, Allah may punish me," he continued, "but the Maliks are bribing the voters."

"And?" Ganju nudged Juma with his leg.

"Sarkar, they are planning to file an FIR against you and the late Bade Sarkar for a murder case." Juma flashed his red teeth.

"Murder case?" Ganju sat up on the bed. "Do you think this inspector would dare to register an FIR against us? Idiot, are you out of your mind?"

"Sarkar, they have opened a briefcase on him."

"What briefcase?"

"A briefcase full of currency notes, Sarkar," Juma said, his eyes widening.

Ganju folded back his legs. A signal for Juma to leave.

"Sarkar, forgive me, but Bade Sarkar used to say, in their own arena even dogs are lions." Juma left, stepping backwards.

Ganju didn't believe Juma, but he certainly lost sleep on whatever he had said. He must talk to Kashif and get the inspector transferred. But what about his opponents throwing money on voters? He couldn't imagine himself to be elected by purchasing votes. He had an impeccable record, no corruption charges, no assets, no kickbacks, how could he be that low and undignified. Maybe he should get his lawyer and transfer everything in his own name, but did he have enough? Only the lands and a factory and some money in the bank but what about the debts undertaken by his uncle? Where would he go in case he needed money? His mental roulette wheel swung and stopped at one name.

"Oh boy, what are you doing in a godforsaken village at this hour? The action is here," Zahid blared on the phone in his drunken voice. Ganju could hear live music in the background. A mujra was on.

"My dear, we can never be a democracy. Each new ruler promises this whore of a nation a sharif life and then pimps her more than ever to fatten his pockets, ha, ha." Zahid laughed, vulgarly. "But do come, we all are your supporters, I'll drink to you." Ganju heard the ice clinking at the other end. "Waah, this broad has some tits, shakes them well, our friend Anwara has promised a strip show at the end, ha ha . . . "

The line got cut. Disconnection. The tone beeped like an ambulance hooter.

Next day Ganju was at Zahid's door.

Inside, he found a man sitting with Zahid. Both were leaning over the spooky chart on the table with the tiny upturned glass on it. "Shish, Mata Hari is on the line! Meet Anwara, our friend," Zahid said in a husky voice as the glass moved under their fingers. Ganju nodded to Anwara, who smiled slyly back at him. Anwara had a bald head skirted by a white fringe of thinning hair. A red handkerchief bled from the front pocket of his pink suite. It was Thursday, the day of the seance. Observing holy silence, Ganju watched the tiny glass scurrying about, joining letters on the chart.

"Come, talk to Mata, I'll fix a drink for you," said Zahid vacating his seat for him. Ganju put a reluctant finger on the glass, and his body felt an eerie sensation. The glass scuttled along like a crystal insect under his fingertip.

Zahid poured in silence and while passing the whisky to Ganju, whispered into his ear, "Do ask her a question." Ganju shook his head in the negative. Zahid sat down and touched the upturned bottom of the glass with a finger and murmured like a seasoned shaman, "Oh, the sweet spirit of great Mata, you have visited us mortals in your kindness. Please tell us, were you really a spy?"

"I was not a spy," the glass tapped out the letters one by one, completing the sentence, "they killed me for my sexual secularism."

Zahid smiled at Ganju and looked to Anwara, who swiveled his nude head down towards Mata, crizzling her glassy bottom with a sharp one, "What exactly were your political views," he asked.

"I never believed in isms, both capitalists and communists carried the same genitals under their ideological pants," the glass giggled. The two watched with revered amazement while Ganju felt uneasy. He coughed to clear his throat, "Well," he mumbled to Zahid, "I am here to discuss something important with you." Zahid looked to Anwara who, sensing the pressure of urgency in Ganju's voice, made the parting announcement with a flying kiss, "Good night Mata Hari, thanks for being with us tonight."

"Good night," the glass hurried around the chart. Ganju felt as if his finger was being pulled by some magnet. His eyes followed it as it zigzagged and spelled out, "And one of you is blessed with a curse."

"Did you move the glass?" Ganju asked with a start.

"Why? Of course not." Anwara looked at Ganju as if he had uttered something blasphemous.

The glass wobbled, shrugging off the astonished fingers.

Ganju glared at the glass, as if to crush it with his gaze.

Anwara excused himself; he had a live appearance on television that night. As he left, waving his red kerchief, Zahid announced, "Anwara hosts a popular TV show in drag."

Ganju didn't seem to hear anything; he was there for something urgent. Ignoring what Zahid had said, in awkward haste he threw away the lines he had rehearsed the other night.

"My dear, don't rush, relax," Zahid comforted him and made him sit on the sofa. "There's plenty of time," he said and strolled over to the bar.

"Chacha Ghalib, the poet, has said, '*Bazeecha e atfal hey dunya meray aagay*. The world is a kid's game for me.' Come, drink to that." Zahid offered the drink to Ganju. Ganju hesitated but then took the glass.

"How about some music?"

"No, thank you, sorry, I am in a kind of hurry, you know how things are in my constituency. We must talk." Ganju was desperate to have the assurance of money.

"Look, you are like a brother, and your late uncle was like a father to me, but investment," he paused, "especially heavy investment in any business is not something one can take casually," he said.

Ganju didn't like the word business.

"Politicians have their interests and so do the investors. Your family has been successful in politics but now things have changed."

"What do you mean, changed?" Ganju asked.

"Well, our public this time will not be polling on rhetoric but on a solid economic agenda. Conventional tactics won't pay off. We have to come up with some new strategy for the investors to cough up money." Zahid gave a meaningful smile.

"And what could that be?"

"Well, in my opinion, if you wish to win, you have to cross over."

"Cross over?"

"I know it's tough but—"

"Look," Ganju interrupted him, "my party has been in power for the past twenty years. Everyone knows how strong we are. People are loyal to us, they trust us."

"But I've it from the horse's mouth."

"Horse's mouth?"

"Intelligence report. Kashif gave it to me. I asked for it the night you gave me a call." Zahid dropped his head and brought the rim of his glass under his eyes.

"What's it now?" Ganju couldn't bear the silence.

"I see an undeclared war being fought not with weapons but with money." Zahid's voice took the oracular turn of a soothsayer. "Money has taken over the world. We are monetized. Love, faith, honor, they all are listed as *other* items in this new charter." Zahid raised his head from the glass. "Join the other party."

Ganju gulped his drink and hastily poured himself another one.

"Look, my dear, once you change your mind, we can get secret funds and loans that could be waived off once you are in power. We'll win this war not in the battlefield but by sitting in partnership with each other," Zahid said, finishing his drink.

"I could never disgrace myself by getting into the bandwagon of political opportunism. I've my principles."

"Think about it," Zahid looked hard into his face.

"Forget it!" Ganju stood up and left abruptly, bumping into the tiny glass, which rolled over the table and fell on the floor, breaking into pieces.

When Ganju returned to his village, it was in the grip of election fever. The Maliks were going door to door actively bribing the voters, and Afzal and his underground communist group held demonstrations, calling the Ganjus fake Pirs.

Keeping in mind the information he had received from Juma and the offer he had refused from Zahid, Ganju decided to sell some of his lands and invest in his election campaign. On his usual kachehri, the open court, where anyone could approach him, a woman covered in burqa approached him with a boy. Ganju recognized the boy; he had seen him at the funeral. Ganju immediately attended to the woman. She handed over a letter to him, and before he could say anything, she left, pulling the boy along with her. Ganju opened the letter, which was written by one Zubaida Begum, who claimed to be a legally wed wife of his late uncle Zahoor. She was demanding her share in the inheritance. The boy then was no stranger but his own cousin. How come his uncle had married a low-class woman? Maybe she was set up by his rivals? True or not, he had to clean his uncle's shit before it made a stink. Ganju abruptly left the kachehri.

At home he went through papers, account books, and legal documents. He found that the lands he was hoping to sell could be transferred to Zubaida Begum if she succeeded in claiming her right. Who was she? On investigation it turned out that a secret nikah was performed by no other than Allama himself.

"Forgive me, my Sarkar, I had promised Bade Sarkar never to reveal his secret. It was not a promise to him but to my Allah, there is no doubt that she is a legitimate wife of Bade Sarkar, and Nadir is their legitimate son," said Allama beading away his rosary. Ganju snatched the rosary away and threw it on his face.

At night in his room, while Juma pressed his legs, Ganju spoke to him in a tired voice. "Juma, you have told me about the briefcase the Maliks are circulating. I think I need to sell some lands."

"Forgive me, Sarkar, but selling land is not in our tradition," Juma replied, head down.

"It's an emergency," Ganju said.

"Sarkar, no amount of paper money could bring the satisfaction of owning the land," Juma said, stubbornly holding onto the leg. "Selling land is showing weakness, it's like selling one's own mother, Sarkar, it will not please your voters."

Ganju was livid at Juma's comment. He kept simmering in silence until he saw the light in his daughter's room. He jumped up from the bed and shouted, "Juma!"

"Ji, Sarkar," replied Juma.

"Call Allama first thing in the morning."

"Ji, Sarkar," said Juma and left, confused.

Ganju's mind had worked a miracle. To hold on to one's inheritance was the custom, and nothing was improper about it. Razia didn't have to see the young bridegroom, as it was not the custom. Daughters must remain within the paternal fold, Ganju told himself. Razia was lucky to have a godsent suitor. Race comes first in the preservation of the family. When it comes to choosing an animal, one checks its pedigree, its teeth and horns, feels it all over, weighing its worth. A bull terrier's bite is different from that of a mongrel's. The mother was a low-class kammi, but it was his uncle's blood running in the veins of young Nadir. Children are not known by their mothers, it's always the male seed that counts.

The next day Allama performed a secret nikah, a legal engagement. Razia happily signed the papers without having the vaguest clue about her marriage to the nine-year-old Nadir. Having his daughter settled, Ganju pledged his lands against a heavy loan from the bank. He held quick meetings with the party members, sanctioned a substantial amount for Allama's orphanage, and planned his first big show of power at the Ganju shrine. Soon after the Friday prayers, Allama blasted Ganju's opponents, the Maliks, "These heretics are pumping haram money. I am not on anyone's side, I am neutral, because I am on the side of my Allah. Every one of you, like a good Muslim, should be on the side of Allah." Elaborating on the Muslim faith, he declared the Maliks were not against the Ganjus but against Allah Himself. Throwing out his arms towards Ganju, who was squatting among worshippers in the mosque, he commended the Islamic spirit of Ayaz and Mehmood, king and slave standing as equals in the presence of Allah.

On the grand jalsa at the Ganju shrine, minarets were decorated with rose garlands, colorful shamyanas were erected, and deg food was arranged for the poor and the beggars. Ganju, his neck buried in rose garlands, waved to the thousands and vowed to change the fate of his people. Some hooligans started shouting slogans, "Jaali Pir, zaat da fakir," the Pir of the beggar caste. They were promptly attacked by Ganju's supporters and, to the joy of the crowd, beaten senseless.

Ganju kept his cool but then he spotted a heejra, eunuch balancing an oversize cutout of a horseshoe on her pelvis with lewd gestures. As Ganju's eyes met hers, she shouted in her twin voices, "Pir the Invisible sends you the blessed curse!" Ganju's guards grabbed the heejra by the waist and pulled at her breasts. Falsies flew in the air like bursting rag balls. The crowd jeered. One of the men shoved his wrist between her thighs and lifted her up, the other pulled the horseshoe, choking her, and punched her painted face. Blood spurted out. The heejra looked at Ganju, the surface of blood caved into her mouth, and a voice came, "Pir the Invisible sends you the blessed curse!"

A few more jalsas and Ganju felt the pinch; he couldn't afford to feed the entire village every second day.

"Sarkar, do you remember that eunuch?" said Juma as he pressed Ganju's legs.

"Why do you ask?" asked a worried Ganju.

"Sarkar, heejras have been at the helm of affairs in history. They controlled and sometimes ruled the state."

Ganju pretended not to be listening.

"They have been king-makers, secret messengers, and confidants of rulers." Juma raised a finger to draw attention, "And Sarkar, they are neither men nor women, they keep shifting from one side to the other."

Ganju's mobile rang. "Hi, there, how's it going?" Zahid said. "General sahib has been asking about your health. By the way if you need any kind of help, do call. We are all here for you."

The morning papers carried a cartoon of Ganju with a big lota, the ablution clay pot signifying that it could give any bottom a holy wash.

Ganju had left his party.

"Who reads these English papers, only a bunch of chattering classes, not your voters, don't worry. You made a timely decision," Zahid said, walking behind the counter. He brought out a black briefcase with golden locks. "Here, take it," he said. "We need media managers, lobbyists, spin doctors, all those hangers-on to protect you and your reputation. They'll serve as a firewall around you." He punched in the code numbers. The briefcase opened its jaw. It exhaled an aroma Ganju couldn't resist. It seeped through his pores. Thousand-rupee bills danced before him.

"This briefcase is connected with a 'whitener' that launders black money, so it'll never cease pouring prosperity. Good luck," said Zahid, shaking a keen hand, and walked Nawabzada Noor Mohammad Ganju out of the room.

Juma opened the car door for him, but Ganju told Juma to sit on the back seat and took the wheel himself. He liked thinking as he drove.

"Sarkar," Juma coughed as the car stopped, "you really drive very well."

Ganju's thoughts had steered him to the kothi, the house of the nazrana girl.

There was no one inside. Ganju heard someone humming. He followed the voice. There she was under the shower, a nymph in the rain. Ganju had not seen so much bare flesh in his life. He coughed discreetly. Startled, she emerged, covered herself with a towel, and fell at his feet.

With all his wealth and a Mughal Princess at his feet, Ganju felt like a winner. But before he could celebrate his conquest his phone blinked.

It was Zahid. "We all have skeletons in our closets, but don't forget, small-time blackmailers are always on the prowl to sniff out a scandal. If one of them gets a whiff, it'll make a big stink!" Leaving the princess half naked, Ganju rushed out of the kothi. Outside he saw a black jeep without any number plate disappearing into the dark.

"What are friends for, get her over to my place, she'll be safe here and then you could always make your private statement in my side room, which as you know is fully loaded and guarantees complete satisfaction."

Nasreen Bano was shifted to Zahid's house the same night.

Things changed as Ganju started carrying the briefcase

around the village. Within no time most of the opposition workers were pushed behind bars, Afzal had gone underground, and
the inspector was more than willing to enter FIRs against the
opposition. Ganju had succeeded in turning things in his favor.
The black box with a whitener inside had opened its jaws on
every conceivable opposition, sucking off the sting and sweeten-
ing it to absolute docility.

"The Maliks are sending their women for canvassing," Juma
said, driving him to one of the influential landlords.

"Hum," Ganju in the back seat ignored him and kept looking
out of the window.

"To win elections, one has to have contact with people and
the Maliks know that their best contacts are through their
women. Bade Sarkar would say, on the outside it's the men but
on the inside it's women who control them."

"Just slow down," said Ganju pulling aside the curtain of the
car window, "very slow."

Juma almost halted the car.

On the corner of main bazaar, high on a pole was firmly
planted a huge cutout of Ganju. Every time he passed here, he
secretly watched himself standing like a god waving to his creatures. The mammoth hoarding invoked dizzying admiration.
It carried hypnotic power in its size and paint. Under his feet
in the painting was a carpet of green, spreading to the horizon
with floating clouds and tiny birds. They were surrounded by a
clump of palm trees, above which was suspended the glory of
Mecca. Absorbed in his image, Ganju felt the blessings of Allah
on his shoulders. He had a closer look and noticed that the mustache was painted black, thick and shiny without a jolt of gray.
An out-of-proportion fist raised towards heavens penetrated the
skies. The shaded outline had added weight and length to his
body. The slogan on top was a couplet, "Tu shaheen hai bas-
eera kar pharoon ki chatanoon par, you are the eagle who lives
on the rocks." The eagle was his election symbol. Each time
he looked at the hoarding, his eyes would stick to his favorite
spot; down to his waist, the painter had given it a vertical swell.
Looking at that bulge Ganju felt elated.

"Reverse the car and take me back to the city," Ganju ordered Juma. Suddenly he had the irresistible urge to see Bano.

"What a surprise, I thought you were in the village," Zahid said, finding Ganju at his place.

"Please don't bother, I'm sorry I couldn't inform you, but I'm here for a short while, I needed some . . . you know, a kind of distraction from the hectic campaign," Ganju stuttered, trying to manage his embarrassment.

"Of course, I understand," Zahid smiled, putting his arms around Ganju, "I am afraid I've to go swimming. Kashif will soon be here to pick me up, but the servants are here, and there she is, waiting for you in the side room. If you need something, just order, the house is yours. And yes, have a good time." Zahid left as the horn honked outside.

Wrapped in a long chadder, Nasreen Bano was on the prayer mat when Ganju entered the room. In her spiritual trance, she closed her eyes and made sure she prostrated more than what was required by religious dictates. Embarrassed, Ganju lowered his head but couldn't help watching her going down on her knees and raising her lavish buttocks. Nasreen Bano repeated the motion a couple of times, spicing his guilt with excitement. Finally she rolled up the prayer mat and fell at his feet. "Sarkar," she sobbed burying her face between his knees.

"Why were you praying at this time?" Ganju asked, half aroused.

"Sarkar, I was saying my nafals, the voluntary prayers. I've pledged one thousand nafals for your success in the elections," purred young Bano with tears in her eyes.

Here, everyone was after his life and there she was praying for him. Her tears warmed his heart.

"You are a good girl." Ganju lifted her up.

Bano smiled, her nose hooking her upper lip. She took off her chadder and revealed a steaming body in the skimpy dress she wore underneath.

The temperature of the room changed.

Nasreen Bano sat on a laden cloud like a centerfold nymph from a pleasure magazine. The strong smell of magic potions, synthetic creams and deodorants, and the copulating scenes made Ganju shudder with mounting lust. His eyes bulged at the sex weapons. Extensions of enticing lengths pampered his fantasies. He selected one with a pink top.

Throughout that evening, amidst the screams of Nasreen Bano, no one could hear the soft bur of the camera Kashif had fitted in the eye of a Hindu god. Ganju floated on the laden cloud, oblivious of the omnipresent eye.

As the election date neared, one day a helicopter went buzzing over Noorpur like a giant moth, hovering over vast fields and rooftops. The villagers ran out to greet the sky visitor. As it danced in the air, thousands of papers swirled down from its wings, scattering all over the streets and the fields, inside courtyards and open latrines where people watched the iron bird while they relieved themselves. The pamphlets had Ganju's photograph with a picture of the eagle on it. One such pamphlet fell inside the mosque where Allama was about to lead the prayers.

"We have got the message from Heaven," he addressed the praying men, "it's in black and white, which means it's a written order. Now who in his senses could ever deny a written order? Indeed Allah is great." He raised both hands in prayer.

Soon after the helicopter episode, busloads of ghost voters were arranged, ID cards were forged, and meetings with the landowners, supporters, and organizers were held and the strategy for the coming elections was put on the anvil.

Ganju, after he performed the ritual of spreading a new chadder on the grave of Pir Ganju Shah, prayed and thanked Allah in anticipation. Later, he distributed money and free food among the poor and sent mithai to his well-wishers. One day when he had retired to his room the phone rang.

"You have to send your women to the voters."

"What?"

"Pressure is mounting, there's tons of money at stake, we'll be ruined. The Maliks are fucking us up, their women cook food for the poor, tend the sick, play nannies to the kids of the kammi class, while your pirzadies lounge in cushy beds getting pressed by the maids, doing nothing but talk about clothes," Zahid's voice sounded like an emergency alarm.

Ganju's jaw began to stiffen, "Are you out of your mind? How could the women of pirs and nawabs go to these kammies, do you have any idea what you are saying? People get murdered for this," he flared.

"There's no time for us to defend your pseudo honor, sorry, we want something personal, something umbilical which could bring the sympathy of the voters. And don't forget, you could be the Chief Minister."

"I don't care about any ministership. I prefer losing elections than letting my women go and beg for votes."

"Look, the intelligence reports are not in favor of all this, once you lose, the new government will not spare you, they'll come up with hundreds of false cases against you."

"Don't you threaten me and don't you order me around."

"It's not you alone who's fighting this election, we who are supporting you can't afford to lose just because you have some hangups about your family honor. If you don't send these pirzadies you'll end up as nobody."

"Never! Over my dead body." Ganju banged the phone down.

Exactly one hour and forty seven minutes later by the clock, the bell at the gate of Ganju House rang frenetically.

"We have something you might like to see," read the note that came with a video tape. Ganju put the tape in his VCR and pressed the button, "Play." The screen lit up with a clip of Ganju and Nasreen Bano engaged in a battle of sex weapons on the waterbed.

The next day, the pirzadies, their heads covered by chadders, were out in the village, visiting the women folk. People fell at their feet as they entered their homes. Following a written order from Heaven, they were being visited by the sacred women of the pirs. Razia, with her body covered from toes to fingertips, walked beside her mother. She was overjoyed to be out of the Haveli but she did not know what she was doing in the poor dwellings. Poverty stared from every corner of those houses, women with children hanging on their breasts, pale and cranky, young girls and coughing fathers sitting in the backyard smoking hookas.

These visits tilted everything in Ganju's favor. The Trio had already started celebrating the upcoming success.

On the last day of the election campaign, when the pirzadies were canvassing for the Ganjus, a woman beckoned to Razia. Finding her mother busy with other women, Razia followed the woman. They came out in a street. "I am Nazo, a friend," the woman said and as they turned into a lane, she disappeared somewhere in the shadows. Razia found herself in a barn. There, in the dim light of an earthen lamp stood the shadow of a man. Who is he? she wondered with a beating heart. He uncovered his face. Razia saw those magic eyes. "I am Afzal," he whispered to her. She fell on his broad chest like a wounded bird. Afzal looked into her eyes and kissed her on the lips.

Chapter 7

Ganj-topia — the Age of Golden Rule

After the guns and fireworks, drums and flowers, after blessing devotees, Ganju had rushed to the Capital to haggle with
power brokers, strike deals with MNAs, hire informers, and
dutifully suck up to the Trio to pressurize the Prime Minister
into choosing him as the Chief Minister. Possessed by the spirit
of intrigues and conspiracies, Ganju frantically walked up and
down the corridors of the parliament building till he saw his
photograph in the papers with the Chief Justice, donned up in
black robe, taking the oath.

"Oh boy, there's always a strong dick behind a big butt,"
shouted the General, stroking the new Chief Minister's behind,
as the Trio popped off champagne bottles after their private
viewing of Ganju on the screen. "We'll lift your bum and you'll
screw the world," they rejoiced. With wild drunken screams and
hysterical lullabies they rocked him in their arms like a baby.

Excellent camera work by the intelligence chief, a memorable
performance by a rising political star, and innovative props and
décor by a businessman had created history.

The next morning Ganju looked at the world from the clouds.
He was in a helicopter, visiting his village. A long line of turbans
greeted him. In the courtyard of the Haveli, landlords, party
workers, and heads of families respected for their race and caste
sat for lunch with Ganju. After food, while they discussed the
new political scene, he excused himself from the guests to visit

the bathroom. Inside, he couldn't resist a peek at his secret hand mirror. He lowered the mirror to his favorite angle and came out feeling like a stud.

He didn't realize that instead of returning to his guests, he had walked into the zenankhana. His wife, Zeenat, sat on the mahogany bed with her back to him. Standing in the door, he traced her undulating figure wrapped in a chadder and for a moment imagined beyond the folds the smoky smell of armpits, calves, and the inside of her thighs. Excited, he coughed; she turned and kept doing what she was doing. The smell of fresh nail polish hit his head. She was not going to say her prayers now. She had the divine exemption and was free to indulge in the worldly pleasure of self-adornment. And yes, they were not to sleep together until she took her first bath after the seven flag days. The red signal put him off balance. He reeled back and left the room.

Back in the city, Ganju, in a twelve-bedroom house with twenty-two guards, found himself a lonely man as he fell on the king-size bed to sleep. He felt deflated about his visit to his wife in the Haveli. Was it one of her ploys to avoid him? But even in her normal days she was cold to him. He fidgeted with the crumpled sheets. In that gloomy moment, the image of Nasreen Bano shifted into his mind. He imagined her lying next to him, a defenseless territory to be conquered. Virginal flesh keenly yielding to his advances, without any resistance.

"I know its kind of late but I, somehow, can't sleep." Ganju said, having pressed Zahid's number on his mobile. "I was just wondering if I could come over." He coughed nervously.

"I don't think it would be wise of you to do that, sir." Zahid added the sir sarcastically. "Try sleeping tonight and we'll work out something in the morning," he said and yawned.

Ganju fell back on his bed, staring at the ceiling. He hadn't seen Nasreen Bano for almost two months.

The next day in his office, Ganju found a sealed envelope on his table. He opened it; there was a ticket to Saudi Arabia, and the return trip gave him a weekend hotel stay in Dubai. Before he could unravel the mystery, Kashif was on the hotline.

"Sir, the very first thing is to thank Allah. We have arranged everything for your Umrah, the holy pilgrimage. Allama will accompany you as your religious advisor, his orders have been issued, but he'll return earlier to hold a press conference on the significance of your visit to Mecca."

"But could I have some information on this weekend stay in Dubai?" Ganju mocked up an officious tone, but rather unsuccessfully.

"Zahid briefed me about your sleepless night, sir. Things are changed and things must change. You are no longer an ordinary citizen. Now you belong to the whole nation. We can neither risk your reputation nor your security." Kashif was impersonal, all duty.

"I don't get it."

"It's for your other Umrah, Sir." Ganju heard Kashif chuckle on the other end. "They say if you can't resist a temptation, you must succumb to it, smoothly. Even Allah is known as Sattar-ul-Ayoob, the One who hides man's sins," he said.

In Mecca, Arab princes received Ganju at the airport. An air-conditioned limousine took him to the House of Allah. After performing the necessary rituals, he swept the floor and gave it a rose-water bath. The Foreign Office and the Ministry of Information took special care to promote him as a devout Muslim and an emissary of Muslim brotherhood. While Ganju dined with the princes, Allama held meetings with religious scholars. The Saudi government presented him with a gift of forty thousand expensively printed copies of the holy Quran for free distribution among Muslim brothers. Allama on his arrival discreetly sold the same to a wholesale dealer at a "fair" price. His visit to the holy land was well rewarded.

While back home people celebrated his Umrah, the lesser Haj, Ganju, pure and absolved, stopped over in Dubai for his weekend stay. Clandestine in a cab, he sped to an island in the late afternoon and sneaked into the hotel apartments that towered over a luscious beach.

"Come in." He heard a female voice as he knocked at the

door on the third floor. The voice sounded familiar but the
words spoken were in English. "Who could that be?" Ganju
stared at the door anxiously. The door opened to show a tall
lady with cropped hair. A western top and a pair of jeans covered her trim figure. Streaks of gold shimmered in the cascading
darkness of her hair. She wore high heels.

"Welcome," she said.

Ganju stared at her, agog.

A curvaceous Nasreen Bano ushered him in. Ganju followed
her coltish hips and a dress that sang of luxury and flattered her
limbs. What on earth had turned the former docile slave girl
into a living woman?

"Is that you, Nasreen?" he mumbled in disbelief.

"Call me Nussu, that's what they all call me now," tinkled
Bano.

"They? Who, they?" Ganju's eyes chased her like a spotlight as
she waltzed to the bar, took out a whisky bottle and said, "Soda
or water?" Syllables of English language tripped over her tongue
as she tried holding them by her native accent. "Water," he said,
"and I thought I asked you a question." Ganju in his new position hated to be ignored, and that too by a nazrana girl.

"I know, I know." She batted her eyelashes and neatly placed
a coaster on the table outside with two chairs that awaited
them. She mixed his drink and put the glass in front of him.
"I got some wine for myself, while waiting for you." She delicately poured from an open bottle, "Cheers," she sang, lifting
the glass, "to your roaring victory."

Ganju raised his glass.

"Now," she paused to take a sip and softly flopped on the
chair. There glowed a blue haze of clear waters behind her.
"I'll answer your question," she said. Not curling her nose but
squinting her eyes, she pouted her lips and shook a naughty
bang of her hair. "I was sent to Mr Anwara by Uncle Zahid."
She gently leaned against the table and told him about the crash
course, "He groomed me for a few days and then sent me to
a Madame who taught me how to dress up, what lipstick to
put on and what shoes to wear. My diet was fixed, there was

a strict schedule for the day, 10 am, swimming lessons, 12:30 pm lunch, 4 pm gym. English lessons in the evening and social etiquette at dinners with the Madame." She spoke in a charming mix of Punjabi, Urdu, and English. Ganju couldn't take his eyes off her. Was he dreaming? A stop in a fairytale, Hollywood in a room.

He looked down at the beach. Some European couples were openly kissing, youngsters surfed on the high waves, and some women luxuriated on the sand without bras, receiving direct sun.

He looked back at her, a rustic figure honed by urban graces. Nussu. Even the name had a titillating ring, the rhyming syllables NU, SSU produced a sensual effect. From lengthy *Nasreen* to short, bouncy *Nussu*; the abbreviation itself was a jumpstart to civilization.

After dinner they strolled on the beach where with her head on his shoulders and arms around his waist, Nussu honeyed his ears with sweet nothings. Ganju was carried along like an enchanted fish.

When they returned, she disappeared into the dressing room. Ganju stood in consternation until she emerged in a negligee. Revealing a purple pinch of puberty, her nipple, she put her arms around him and rasped, "Noor darling, I love you."

Then she took off his shoes and undressed him like a baby, button by button. She went down on him and blew him bigger and bigger. Ganju had never felt such exhilaration before in his life; to be lifted and blown without sex weapons. He could give away his chaste blood, his lands, his position for it. "Noor darling, I love you," she kept calling him by his first name and he, instead of resenting that, liked it.

"I love you too, I can't live without you." To his utter surprise, he too was whispering to her while he was on her.

Finally, he saw the roses of fresh blood on his bedsheet. Oh, wasn't she an eternal virgin? Ganju marveled at the miracle as she kept saying, "Noor darling, Noor darling." The voice kept coming back to him even during his flight. Ganju, the Chief Minister, sitting in first class, realized that he had hopelessly fallen in love.

"Party time is over. We have to think of Good Governance."

As soon as Ganju touched the native ground, the Trio jolted him into the subject of national priorities. They shouted the Golden Rules.

"Good Governance is when people are manipulated, master-minded, ransomed, and tagged. Sentenced, ridiculed, mocked, harassed, and framed.

Subjugated, punished, killed, gagged, and silenced.

Three thousand seventy-five children in prisons await trial.

Many die in police custody, beaten and coerced into criminal acts.

Eight hundred on death row below eighteen.

Children can be indoctrinated easily.

They can find landmines for us by kicking their heels.

Cross-legged on durries they'll rock back and forth.

Recite from the book.

Mashallah Mashallah!

How are you funded, sir?

Allah funds us.

Remember!

Brains, not weapons win the war.

They'll be our ideological missiles.

Martyrdom is our inheritance.

A key to heaven's door.

Have you ever noticed beggars with crippled children on the road?

In the hot summers they press their faces against the closed window of your air-conditioned car.

To show you fear.

And in winter they throw a naked child against your heated car.

Chase you among neon lights.

Like cloven shadows.

Do appreciate.

The theatrics of poverty.
The sight of hungry children is a cash crop.
Export them to the camel-racing countries.
They can bring good money.
Let's celebrate the day of special children.

OK, the one who lost a leg or an arm in the recent bomb blast, yes that boy will be fine. Come, Mohammed Din show them how to play cricket with your one arm.
Come on, hop! Prance! Jump!
Missing limbs are a blessing indeed.
A windfall.

Ban alcohol!
Banned, it will have more value.
And don't be ignorant of the shameful sight of Hindu idols and animal decorations on the sacred soil.
I obey Allah, you obey me.
Utopia!
Ganj-topia, the ideal state.
Ganj, the treasure, Ganj, the baldness.
Two meanings of the same word.
Topia, the ideal state, and Topia, the cap: two sides of the same coin.
Ganj-topia! The ideal cap for your baldness, your shamelessness, your blatant bigotry.

Goats and lions will drink from the same river.
Children will play with snakes.
Leopards will graze with cows, birds and animals will talk.
Stones will speak the human language,"
sang the Trio.

Armed with the Utopian ideology Ganju took a whirlwind tour of the province and appointed his trusted men in sensitive positions. Within a week Allama gave a fatwa against the mother of all evils, alcohol. To manufacture, import, transport, or sell any intoxicants meant for human consumption by a Muslim to a Muslim was declared repugnant to the spirit of the holy Quran and Sunna. The day the Federal Shariat court issued the order, the Ministry of Health issued the license to Zahid Hussain, authorizing him to manufacture tinctured alcohol for medicinal, industrial, and scientific purposes.

In no time, with the help of efficient bureaucrats and far-sighted colleagues, thousands of stolen vehicles were reconditioned and sold to the public to improve and modernize their living standard. Allama boosted export by selling 40,000 burqas to be used as beach tents in USA.

"We must keep the borders alert, there have to be some killings everyday so that soldiers are in good shape. Constant war is a must," announced the General.

Billion-dollar deals for submarines, old Mirages, British ships, helicopters, minesweepers for the Navy, and aircraft spares were amicably concluded by the civilian government with inputs from the General.

Relations with the northern neighboring country were improved and borders were made porous to facilitate the transport of poppy, which was cultivated and harvested at the border and shifted to mobile laboratories.

All said and done, it was in his hometown, Noorpur, where Ganju became a national hero.

Flanked by guards, Ganju, in his flagged Mercedes with tinted glass windows, halted near the temple where once Hindus had worshipped their deities. A huge crowd cheered Ganju as he announced the demolition of the temple of Noorpur, a legacy of Hindu paganism and idolatry. He appealed to the believers for chanda, contributions to help build a mosque on the foundations of this mandir.

Kashif arranged for the removal of the Hindu gods and safely stashed away the antiques.

There was peace all over the country. Allama and Zahid, Juma and Ganju, the General and Kashif all were drinking from the same stream.

On the way back from his village, Ganju was pleased to see a hoarding depicting him on the main boulevard, but then something interrupted his view. Next to his cutout was a film hoarding with the picture of a woman. He ordered for the car to stop. Emergency lights flashed with ear-splitting danger alarms. Lilly Khanum, the woman on the film hoarding was the spitting image of Nasreen Bano. Among security guards and in a massive traffic jam, he dialed his mobile.

"Where's Nussu, where is she?" he shouted on the phone.

"Where do you think she should be, sir?" Zahid asked cheerfully.

"Who's this Lilly Khanum?" he roared.

"That's her filmi name, sir. You'd better prepare yourself for a title fuck on your next trip abroad."

Ganju looked at the board: Lilly Khanum pointed at his groin, furtively, with a pelvic thrust. His eyes shifted to his own cutout. The bulge moved.

They both looked larger than life.

Chapter 8

The Return of Thumbelina

With ten movies signed in a row, Nussu, known as Lilly Khanum was the new star buzz with a personal manager, Mubarik Michael, a fair-complexioned local Christian with a British accent. Goga, the famous wrestler, apart from doing stunt scenes in movies, had become her official bodyguard. In his new position he had changed his hulia or appearance by tattooing his arms up to the shoulders and wearing jockey caps, leather jackets, and chains, just like the American wrestlers on TV. He could shout like a rapper in his own lingo and could toddle a few steps of break-dancing. Worshiped as a sex idol by the ladies of the red-light area, his position next to Lilly turned them green with envy.

He chewed bubble gum.

Special food in hot pots and a silver thermos full of tea would accompany Lilly to outdoor locations. She traveled first class, had a chauffeur, and her photo sessions featured a new mobile phone for effect. Each paan shop displayed her poster dangling among light bulbs and blared out songs play backed for her.

Lilly, however, was reputed for declining fat offers in the name of self-respect and chastity. Already her role of Razia Sultana, the Muslim warrior queen, had made her a hot favorite with Islamic zealots. And during an intense shooting spell, when she left the set at prayer time, her picture printed in the newspapers had a quote from her, "I am a modern Muslim girl who prays on time and acts on time. One is my duty and the other is my profession." The media had lauded her love for Allah. Allama was quick to give a fatwa for every God-fearing Muslim to watch her movies as a religious obligation.

At the premiere of her new film, which was released on Eid, Lilly's popularity shook the nation. To join the queues, people with charpoys arrived the night before at the cinema door. In the morning they attacked the box office, climbing on each other, tearing their clothes in order to get their tickets. When the first ticket was issued, the ticket-holder looked at Lilly on the cine board and dancing his way to the entrance, shouted, "Na Lahore na Dilli, sadi Lilly sadi Lilly." Neither Lahore nor Delhi, only Lilly.

As the inspector battled the hysterical mob, Juma Khan in a back room was busy supervising the clandestine black marketing of the tickets.

"Isn't she from the walled city?" The inspector heard someone say.

"Well, of course, she's the one," the man said looking up at her image, his hand fumbling at his crotch under his dhoti. "Remember? She didn't even know how to blow her nose, ah," he took a deep sigh, "used to spread her thighs for a hundred bucks. Now she charges one million for a movie, she's an English thing, man, you know, Hollywood stuff."

"Allah is great," the other responded touching his ears.

Fresh from the media bath, Lilly went on a short trip to New York. On her return, her tight jeans torn at the knees, bleached hair, green contact lenses, and baby face perked with makeup covered her humble origins. In her interview on TV, she impressed the elite with her Minglish: a mix of American slang and Urdu, spoken in a nasal drawl. Once the Friday editions flashed her pictures, taken by an America-returned photographer, the story of her mixed parentage was already on the title pages of the tabloids. Her mother, an American ballerina, who after losing her husband in the Vietnam War had joined the flower children during the sixties. She was interested in Zen Buddhism and was doing drugs. In this country she found hashish and Sheikh sahib, both in abundance. Tina Sheikh was their only child; a spicy mix of her mother's Occi- and Sheikh Sahib's Orientalia. Her father had died soon after her birth and her mother had become alcoholic. Tina was trained by her mother in ballet. The media host, Anwara, confirmed the story. "What a man, her father was," he said to the camera, on his face a look of nostalgia. "Sheikh sahib would travel with trainloads of singers and musicians. He had mortgaged his property to pay for his passion. He was a modern Maharaja, a connoisseur of art and music and her mother was a leader of an international group of touring dancers. Tina Sheikh alias Lilly Khanum, mashaallah, has inherited the two cultures. She's the unity within the diversity," he waxed.

Critics specializing in the semiotics of cinema saw in her the primordial Mother Goddess. Others saw in her the return of the vampire, a taste of sin that a society with strong religious orientations relished on the sly. Leading intellectuals thought her to be a postmodernist, while spiritualists believed she was blessed by the great saint, Pir the Invisible. Chronic cynics and chilly males nevertheless dismissed her as another product on the shelf. No one listened to them.

9 pm.

After watching the news on TV, Ganju picked up the green phone, his face stiff with anger. "Sir," came the reflex response from the Information Minister on the other side. Ganju in choice words told him to take care of his media projection and ordered him to stop the supply of newsprint to the paper that had carried a cartoon in which he was shown to be on the state-run channel for more than an hour in a half-hour news bulletin. Somewhere in the middle of his instructions he thought he saw Nussu on the screen. He quickly hung up and pressed the volume button on the remote. Lilly Khanum sat in the studio like a princess, commanding great charm while the editor of a coffee-table magazine described his first exposure to the film idol. "She was in convent school when I had the pleasure of watching her in a drama contest," he reminisced with fondness.

"Nussu in school?" Ganju clenched his teeth.

Big close up. "She played Juliet with natural flair. I happened to be one of the judges."

"Bastard!" Ganju cursed aloud.

The BCU smiled, a flurry of wrinkles bursting through his crusty makeup. "I could see in her the making of a mega star," he crooned.

Cut.

A rush of sizzling visuals; computer graphics and daring camera angles flashing her biography. Lilly Khanum in black and white, in sepia, in florescent colors posing on beach, in garden, on sofa, among mountains, and in a colonial house, a baby Lilly in her mother's lap. Watching her on screen, Ganju had forgotten his appointment with the dentist.

Wasn't that stuff fiction? Tina Sheikh, Nasreen Bano, Nussu, and now Lilly? What was going on? Ganju, standing in front of the wall mirror, argued with Ganju. This bitch called "reality" was just a hypothesis, a hang-up in the brain, an endless ritual of peeling off an onion. And she? She looked real on the screen. He looked at himself in the mirror with a nod.

Why couldn't he recognize this princess in the guise of a nazrana girl? Arrogance! Yes, he had been defiled by arrogance, a vain sense of superiority where one builds the minaret of one's self against the fear of unbalance. He was doped by his own truth, cheated by his own ideals. How could he ever bargain his Lilly Khanum, a goddess, with a common mortal like the nazrana girl? Why should he look down upon her as a piece of mere flesh? A sudden sense of loss came over him. He made himself a drink. A power monger, that's what he was, a hostage to the state where heart didn't matter. He had been on trips outside the country but was always accompanied by the prime minister. He could never see Lilly Khanum, who at times was even shooting at the same places. So far they had met each other only in the newspapers.

All night Ganju kept drinking and fantasizing the fable of Lilly Khanum. To go down on her was to line up with the real men of the world. It was to enrich one's biography.

Some time in the middle of the night a shameless urge sat in his groin like a dull ache, and from nowhere in his nervous system, a tiny cell, trampling down all his rationality, became a call from his heart. "I want her," he howled. "I want her," he heard himself saying on the phone to Zahid.

"Not possible, we are in the middle of parlays with the religious parties." Zahid for a change was sober on the phone. "Even if you leave the country, the prime minister will not approve of it. And you already know, the budget is to be announced," said Zahid in a firm tone.

"I don't give a damn; I am going nuts about her. I've got to see my Nussu," Ganju whined.

"Nussu?"

"Yes, Nussu. No, I mean Lilly, Lilly Khanum the queen of Lollywood. My Juliet from the convent school."

"I told you it's not possible," said Zahid.

"Look, I don't want to listen to any reasons. I am telling you, I'll commit suicide if I don't see her." Ganju marveled at himself as he put down the receiver.

It was during this golden age of Ganjtopia and the rise of Lilly that at a barber shop one day in a remote village of southern Punjab sat a young boy for a shave. He was the younger son of the late Wadera's fourth wife, whom he had married before buying the coveted belly of Mano's mother.

The barber, a devout receiver and transmitter of local gossip, while lathering the boy's face discreetly mentioned the presence of a clandestine haunt of debauchery in the center of the village: a white wall in an open field with a rickety projector. Scared of their wives, the menfolk sneaked into the cinema, their faces hidden behind the folds of their turbans, and found a stray brick for a seat to enjoy the daily show which, as the boy was told, quickened to life soon after the night prayers.

Next day the Wadera's son took his elder brother along and they both saw a familiar bust bounce out of the big wall. It belonged to none other than their long lost stepmother, Mano.

"Look at the bitch, how innocent she looks with that makeup on, she has changed, yes, and even has a new name, Lilly," whispered the elder one to the younger one. "Can you imagine this vampire as the cause of our father's death?"

"I don't think so," replied the younger one, his eyes plastered to the wall. "She was much too young at that time."

"Shameless bastard, you have no honor," the elder one said and spat in the direction of the wall.

"Don't talk, I am watching," the younger one said.

The brothers spent the night quarrelling about how to avenge the murder of their father. The Wadera had transferred big chunks of fertile lands to the mother to rejuvenate his aging bones. The brothers agreed to share the handsome inheritance looted by a whore.

In no time, the news of Lilly's discovery as good old Mano buzzed at the barber shop. The buzz flew and perched right on the ears of Ganju's arch rivals, the Maliks.

"If someone calls, say I am not home," said Lilly to her maid as she entered her house after a live show for TV. "And run the water in the bathroom, I want to have a bath." She threw away her shoes in a huff and went to the dressing room to change.

The Jacuzzi overflowed with perfumed water. Lilly slipped into it. She lay there, still, until the liquid warmth soothed her body to the pores. Ah, what a comfort to lie here, she thought, free from the cares of the world. Reclined, her eyes half closed, she hummed a favorite tune. With the hand shower, she playfully toyed with her body. While she was immersed in this narcissistic spell, the mobile rang. Ignoring it, she dipped her head under the water. The phone rang again and again, incessantly. She pulled up her bag from the floor and took the phone out. The tiny screen flashed the number and the hand shower fell from her hand. Why must the bastard call her directly? If he wanted the monthly payment, he should have called Michael. Behan chod, he thinks if he had slept with her he had rights over her. In a fit of anger, she thumbed the phone off and called for the maid and ordered a shot of vodka.

The maid walked in with a silver tray carrying vodka and tomato juice. Lilly drank in quick gulps; the phone call had resurrected a ghost from her past.

Sher Mohammad, the inspector, was the man whom she had met through a local masseur after her mother's death. The masseur used to service overworked whores in the afternoons. He would ease off their daily fatigue to prepare them for their nightly performances. He enjoyed a good reputation among pimps and was a favorite with the inspector who, after thrashing hardened criminals, would get a long massage for himself. It was the masseur who had requested the inspector to fix her in the Heera Mandi.

Why am I thinking of all this, I am not that person anymore, she tried diverting her mind. But then this phone call? Oh God, all those years she had been paying the bastard to guard her secret. Lilly had a refill, desperate to wash down her sordid memories. Suddenly the bubbles formed images, images of humid nights, she on a bare charpoy, sweat pouring out of her armpits in rivulets, she raising her legs turning her face to the side, watching moths circling around a jaundiced light of a low-power bulb freckled by fly shit, watching, watching until it is all over. Smell of antiseptic and the man washing himself under the tap in a corner of the room. Her mind fading into a migraine. But then seeing money, life coming back to her. Without counting, she, putting it in her unwashed bodice, yes, yes, she, thinking, the mother would be happy.

Why should she be remembering all that? Only an hour ago she had invented a blue-blooded mother from the civilized world, it had been all over the media, a white queen had replaced a scavenger of a mother. Oh that witch who would kick her all over, teach her tricks to extract money from the rich. What did she do with that money? She bought jewelry of pure gold which she would flaunt before the customers. And she would cry in the night while the Wadera snored next to her. Oh no, I was not born of that bitch, no. I've buried that child; it has faded in the glare of floodlights.

"Pay double to the inspector and tell him never to call me again," she said to her manager Michael on the phone.

After that she felt clean. Everything was in place, even the black mole on her left buttock. Relieved, she ordered free food for the shrine of Pir the Invisible. Later, popping her sleeping pill, she thanked God and fell asleep. She had a heavy schedule ahead.

The next morning.

"Action!" shouted the director on the megaphone and Lilly in her hot pants jerked to the heavy metal beat of desi disco. The nightclub set showed in its background a bar displaying bottles with foreign labels, lukewarm tea standing in for whisky. The cameraman zoomed in for her bust shot, and as he focused—

Sudden gunshots. The music stopped. Bottles rolled on the floor and a bunch of roughnecks with masked faces entered the set, firing Kalashnikovs. Lilly screamed. They tied her up and fled the scene.

"Cut," shouted a jubilant director. It was an okay shot, performed with riveting realism. The extras were extraordinary. A limousine with dark curtains sped into a blind alley.

Once her blinkers were removed, Lilly found herself in a dark and dingy room, her mouth stuffed with cloth and her hands tied. A bulb on a wire hung across her face. The hired men had neatly replaced the real extras from the shooting for their purpose. They had brought Lilly Khanum to the Maliks' haveli, a few miles away from the city.

Where was she? In that silence, she could only hear her own heartbeat. She looked around. The unplastered walls stared back at her. It looked like the den of villains in the movies.

"How did you find our performance, Ladyio Lully Khaanum?" A voice came from the dark. Lilly looked around, startled.

"Well, now is your chance to swing your hips for us, tha, tha theyee, theyee," another voice from the left introduced the stereo effect. Lilly struggled helplessly against the gagging cloth.

"We were not born yesterday," the elder son of the late wadera came forward, twisting his moustache. "You thought you'd get away, but we dig out people from their graves."

"Remember me?" Stumbled in the younger one with an open bottle of homegrown wine. "I used to watch you from the window while you took your bath." He leered at her. "Had it not been my father, I would have banged you on the very first night." He sucked at the bottle and squeezed out a kiss. Lilly was petrified. It reminded her of the phone call by the inspector. He must have been trying to warn her about this very moment but she had thought he was calling her for money. Tears came to her eyes. She cursed herself for not taking his call.

"Don't waste time, leave her to me," the elder one admonished the younger one and addressed her in a straightforward manner. "Look, lady, you and your mother killed our father and disappeared with all our money. We just want it back, simple!" He took out the cloth from her mouth. Lilly burst out, "Idiots, don't you have sisters and mothers of your own? Get me out of here, right now!"

The elder brother was stunned by her boldness.

"You got the wrong woman. Don't you know I am an artist of your country? Everyone knows my mother was an American and my father a businessman." Lilly had switched to her Minglish, to prove her breeding. "I've got nothing to do with people like you. Now let me go, I've a busy schedule," she said with a slight frown. The elder one stepped back not knowing what to say.

"Whore!" A knife flashed in the dark, as the younger one pushed his brother aside. "Impresses us with her git mit?" he took a swig. "*Desi bund vallayti pudd*, local ass farting in English? Haan?"

For a convent girl it was too much of an insult.

"Let me tell you who really you are." He leapt at her and slit her clothes.

"Bastard, don't you dare to come near me." Lilly raised her leg to kick him but it only made her slashed pants slide down. He laughed and turned her around exposing her behind to the solitary bulb.

"See, it's still there, nazar buttoo, the black eye to watch over all evil." He rudely stroked the black mole on her bare back. "This is our chief witness, guardian of our money, stuck to these sweet cheeks. Oh, I love this little pinch of darkness. All the sponges in the world can't rub it off. It stays loyal, like the dwarf to the white queen. I told you I watched you naked, Miss

Lulli Khaanum. I was only waiting to get you." He roared, slapping her fleshy mounds.

"Take your dirty hands off me. I'll see to it that you all get behind bars," Lilly said in chaste Minglish, keeping up her bravado.

"We know you, bitch, you warm the beds of the hot shots. That pimp of the Chief Minister, Juma Khan, didn't he take you to his master for a fuck? You think other whores are blind, they don't see what's happening in their neighborhood?"

She tried kicking him again.

"Why? Don't I have what others have? Or you only go for a flagged cock," he said tilting up his pelvis.

"Shut up," said Lilly looking away.

He slapped her hard. She screamed violently.

"Stop it now," said the elder brother.

"Get away, you, Mr Gentleman. I found her first, she's mine," said the younger one and gagged her with the cloth. He drank half of the bottle in a giant gulp and put on some loud desi music. "Lilly Khanum meri janum," he sang doing a lewd filmi dance.

"Are you out of your mind, she's your stepmother!" the elder one said.

"Fuck you and your cowardice, you pussy, you know our father couldn't deflower her, he was too old, now it's the duty of his son to do the needful, leave me alone, I am a mother-fucker, haaa." He pushed his brother away and, gathering her bulk in his arms, bit her nipples. Lilly's screams died in silence. Before he could go further, someone from the dark threw a chadder on her naked body. The music switched off. The son staggered back.

"It is not in our custom to touch a woman," a voice spoke and the elderly Malik appeared from the darkness. Lilly looked at him with pleading eyes. To her he was the legendary apparition that in movies saved the damsel in distress.

"Get some Coca-Cola for the lady," he said, coaxing out the cloth from her mouth, gently. The elder brother ran for the bottle.

Lilly gulped in the air. "Please get me out of here, I've done no harm to anyone. I am sure there has been some mistake. Please!"

"Patience! Patience!" spoke the Malik. "We believe you, lady. Just relax. We are not barbarians, we too are respectable people." He took the bottle of Coke from his son. "Have a sip. Feel easy. Okay." Malik lifted the open bottle to her mouth.

"No, I am not thirsty, please let me go," Lilly said in a polite tone.

"We don't expect you to be impatient, lady. Trust me, we'll let you go, but first you must cooperate with us," said the Malik.

"What do you mean, cooperate?" Lilly struggled against the fetters.

"Lady sahiba, you, mashaalla, are an intelligent lady. I am sure you have a fair idea that people survive in this world by helping each other. You know how humanity is served," said the wise Malik.

"I don't know what you are talking about, and I don't care. I am warning you, if you don't let me go I'll report all of you to the police," Lilly raised her voice.

"Shut up you bitch." The younger one slapped her on the face. "Whore, you have no idea to whom you are talking, he is our elder, the head of the Maliks." He touched the Malik's knees and said, "Uncle Ji, leave her to me I know how to make her cooperate." He roughly pulled Lilly's chadder.

"No, my son, no," said the Malik putting back the chadder on her shoulders. "We don't rape out of sexual starvation but out of revenge. If she doesn't cooperate with us, we all will do this honorable job with great pleasure." He smiled to the lad and then turned to Lilly, "Woman!" he said, "You should know what that bad seed of the blacksmiths has done. The mother-fucker has ruined us and now he is ruining this country. He won the elections by fraud and deceit. We are sworn not to forgive him. Justice has to be done and indeed Allah is on the side of the righteous ones."

"But, sir, whom are you talking about?" Lilly pouted her lips like a five-year-old.

"You know who I am talking about, your lover and our rival,

Ganju, the son of blacksmiths. We want to see him dethroned, back to the streets, powerless!" His voice changed to a hoarse gravelly and his eyes bulged with hate.

"What do you want?" Lilly said in a timid voice.

"Just finish this bastard," said the bulging eyes.

"But how?"

"If you ruin his reputation, we'll win. And once we are back in power, we'll load you with gold. Even consider giving you some political power. Don't forget we believe in women's representation, and we have women's seats in the senate. You can see it's all a fair bargain."

"What if I refuse?" Bare and defenseless, Lilly wanted to weigh the consequences.

"Woman!" the Malik calmly put the chadder back on her head and unrolled a crumpled ashtaam paper, the legal document on the table, "We'll expose you in public. This document shows how the lands of the wadera were transferred," he said.

With her hands cuffed, Lilly looked at the pale old paper bearing the indelible print of her fate, the impression of her mother's thumb.

In the glare of light, it hit her, like a bullet.

She forgot her Minglish.

Chapter 9

Gharjawai — the In-House Groom

"Are these new," asked Cheemo the maid, relishing the shine of her mistress's gold bangles.

"Of course. Can't you see, they match my dress," Razia said teasingly. "Now put that necklace on me."

She puffed up her chest before the large mirror. The mirror, with three cut surfaces, cascaded her triple image in shimmering waves. Cheemo carefully lifted the gemmed necklace and put it around Razia's neck. Razia's face glowed.

"You look like a princess. Is it pure gold?" Cheemo asked.

"Yes, pure gold! What else, idiot," responded Razia.

"He brought these for me," said Cheemo shyly, lifting her arm which was covered with plastic bangles.

"Who?"

"My husband, who else?" Cheemo's dimpled cheeks flushed. A year younger than Razia, she had recently got married to her cousin ten years older.

"What does he do to you," Razia asked with a frown and looked out of the window where Nadir was busy pulling the hair of a maid.

"Oh, lots of things." Cheemo started to comb her mistress's hair.

"What things?"

"Sometimes he grabs me in the kitchen, doesn't let me cook, makes me helpless, you know, Baji," she laughed, her hands going limp on the comb. "*Kuch kuch hota hey*, something, something happens," she sang and spreading her arms, moaned. "He kisses me on the lips, bites me, pulls off my clothes, and rolls all over me. I just faint."

"Don't you say anything to him?"

"What can I say, he's my husband," said Cheemo, lazily resuming her combing.

"Does it hurt?"

"Hurt? Oh yes, a little, but I love that hurt, oh I just love it."

"Don't you have any shame," Razia glared at her.

"Kuch kuch, Baji," she said and shook her breasts which Razia noticed had grown bigger after her marriage. "Oh Baji, I fly to the skies when he is inside me. Oh my God." The comb slid and fell from her hand.

Razia scowled into the mirror.

"Bitch!" she yelled, pulling Cheemo's hair.

Right after Ganju's elections, Razia was formally married in a closed ceremony where the two families exchanged presents and food. Ñine-year-old Nadir had toddled into Razia's life. It was within the custom to adopt the groom, especially in landed families that didn't marry outside their blood relations. At the Haveli, Nadir, the son of late Zahoor-ul-Din Ganju was the new in-house groom.

Razia was happy to be married, happy to be getting all the attention in the world. The sudden liberation from her cloistered life had made her euphoric. She could laugh, dress in colourful clothes, wear jewellery, listen to radio, watch local television, spend money, and keep a lipstick in her purse.

During the wedding, wrapped in her bridal dress with young girls singing around her, Razia was lost in awe of the ritual. She had grown up with a fantasy about an Arabian prince riding a white horse and taking her beyond the horizon, near the stars, where they would live happily forever.

Short in height, the groom had amply inherited the square jaw and stout limbs of his father. With a putty nose and thumped eyes, Nadir, dressed in a silken achken with a red turban on his

head, had sat next to Razia, her dream prince in a toad, a giant
in a midget.

On her wedding night, when Razia entered the bridal room,
she saw among the flowing wreathes of roses, a large bed with
silk sheets and feathery pillows. Nadir was already asleep in his
wedding clothes. She waited for him to open his eyes but he was
fast asleep. Her dowry was spread all over in the room; a wardrobe of saries, embroidered blouses, velvet shawls, and ten jewellery sets. The room overflowed with glamour and abundance.

Razia slipped into the bed and putting her arms around the
sleeping prince kissed him on the mouth. He woke up with a
start. She held him tightly in her arms. Nadir gave a loud scream
and digging his teeth into her arms pulled away. She shouted
at him. He started running in the room breaking things. She
slapped him hard. He became silent and fell back into the bed.
Soon he was snoring.

Razia felt trapped in her wedding dress. She got out of the
bed and stood against the mirror. Lipsticks, face creams, shampoos, and deodorants on the dressing table appeared in the
mirror like tiny buildings in a wonderland. She touched them.
They aroused her gently. Layer by layer, she undressed herself.
Breathing in, she upped her young breasts, straightened her
back and stretched on her toes. Thrilled by her own beauty in
manifold reflections, she eagerly rolled her fingers around one
of those bottles. Her body shook with strange sensations. Her
pelvis turned taut, her nipples hardened. She curved on the king
size bed and copulated with an onanist gigolo, her solitude. It
became a routine.

Sitting next to the mirror, her only window to escape, the
newlywed Razia with her large wardrobe and jewellery was
already a living widow.

She spent her days with Cheemo who was given to her as
a part of her dowry. Cheemo would clean the room, wash
and iron Razia's clothes, dress her up, comb her hair and tell
juicy stories about her conjugal life. The radio was on all the
time. Sometimes when it played film songs, she would dance
to the thrusting beat, throwing her body to the mirror in lewd

postures. Cheemo would clap her hands to the music. Nadir mimicked his wife, put on her doppatta and coloring his willy with her lipsticks pissed around. Razia would kick him out of the room and he would piss all over the courtyard showing off his painted willy to the maids, lifting the tails of their long skirts, mounting them like a horse and farting on their faces. His manners sang of ill breeding and cruel humor. As the son-in-law of the Chief Minister and the son of Zahoor the Bade Shah Ji, Nadir was treated like royalty. The maids accepted his rudeness with traditional docility.

Once out of the room, Razia would hardly be aware of his presence, but at night she would want to take him to the bed. She would bribe him with chocolates, bathe him, dress him up, try to excite him, play with him and in the end if she ever got him into the bed, he would pull her hair, scream, spit at her and kick her out of the bed. In his midget size, he had the energy of a monster.

Television showed local programmes about cooking and religious and children's programmes. English movies were vulgar and obscene, dish antenna a forbidden tree and the VCR only played the satanic tricks. She had heard about it from the mourning women at the funeral but when Cheemo told her stories about her husband renting a VCR and playing dirty movies to train her in how to perform in bed, Razia rushed to the guest room where she knew a VCR was locked in a cupboard. She broke the lock and brought it to her room with a cassette that lay next to it.

At night, once the in-house groom had fallen asleep, she played the film and it took her breath away. She didn't understand much English but was excited to see the exotic beaches, women in swimsuits, bedrooms with couples kissing, drinking and making love. Each night she longed to be on those beaches and be held by the strong hands of the hero. Whenever he kissed the half-dressed heroine, Razia would go wet all over. Sweating in guilt she would quickly wash herself and pray.

One day Cheemo stole a movie from her husband's collection and brought it to Razia. Alone at night Razia slid the tape in the VCR and waited. The moment the screen lit with pictures, she shut her eyes. But then reassuring herself that no one was watching, she opened them. Naked bodies with their steaming flesh filled the screen. The unending copulation in all possible ways fired her up. The heat of the stimulated genitals kept blasting her body until she almost fainted.

Sometimes in the morning she woke up and saw the blank screen. She then dashed to the guest room and put back the machine.

The naked film had upset her biology; she felt a constant hollow in her crotch, an itch tingling her body. Now if Cheemo told a new story about her husband making love to her, she would fly into a raging fit. The gold had started to lose its glimmer, the wardrobe, the roses, the bangles the makeup, everything was beginning to wilt, fade and die quietly. She longed for a man, a full man.

"Baji, I've great news for you," Cheemo whispered going red in her face.

"Don't give me the lie, tell me why are you late, don't make up stories."

"No, Baji, I am not telling you stories, it's true."

"What is true?"

"I am pregnant."

"What?"

"Yes! When I reached home last evening I couldn't eat, I just threw up. My husband took me to the dispensary. The health mistress took some test and asked me to come in the morning, and today, Baji, she said, yes, yes!" She shouted, holding Razia in her arms.

"Stop it and help me change my clothes. I've been wearing them for two days now." Razia pulled herself away.

"Listen, Baji, I met a lady there," said Cheemo.

"What lady?"

"Her name is Nazo. She gave me this for you." Cheemo untied the knot of her doppatta and handed over a carefully folded paper to Razia. "She said not to tell anyone, it's a secret," said Cheemo and went to look for Razia's clothes.

Razia opened the letter. Oh God, it was from Afzal. The kiss she had felt on her lips months ago, refreshed itself instantly. She locked herself in the bathroom and with her hands shaking, read the note again and again. Every time she went over the letter, its words entwined in blue ink aroused her. He was the prince riding the white horse, breezing through the wilderness of her youth. She didn't understand words like *underground, antistate,* or *revolution* but was sure that Afzal wanted her to run away with him. "I will come and take you away from this cruel world," he said in the letter. In a start she got up, went to the mirror and saw her face. To her horror, it had started to grow old, very very old.

Razia hurriedly scribbled a reply on the back of the same letter and gave it to Cheemo. "Just hand it over to the woman and no one else," she said in a rushed voice. "Go now!"

"Ji, Baji." Cheemo carefully tied the paper in a corner of her doppatta and left.

That night something far off had come closer than her breath. Razia felt his presence inside her bed, the afterglow of his kiss floating in the fluffy darkness of her quilt.

The next day, midnight.

Razia wrapped herself in a long chadder and slipped out of her room. Everyone was asleep except the guards. She stepped out into the backyard. It was a moonless night, dark and desolate. Dragging the trunk of a fallen tree to the wall, she climbed on it up to the barbed-wire top. Down on the other side of the wall a tall shadow beckoned her. Without thinking of the sharp wires, she jumped. Afzal held her as she came down. She clung to him. They ran to the motorbike standing nearby. But before she could sit on the bike with her lover, gunfire crackled in the air. She fell, unconscious. The guards shot at the man but he sped off.

In the early hours, Razia was dragged into the Haveli by the maids. Ganju looked away from her. He wanted the matter to be hushed up. He didn't want anyone to know that the Chief

Minister's married daughter had tried to run away from the house. He reported the matter to Kashif, who informed him that the man identified as Afzal was on their hit list, but had fled the country.

It was a few days later that while he was on the phone with the General he heard those hysterical screams, windows crashing and things thrown around.

"Your daughter is suffering from a libido disorder, a kind of sexual anxiety," said the psychiatrist. "Bastard," Ganju flew into a rage. He told the doctor he was sick in the mind, a pervert. To say his daughter was sexually disturbed was an insult to his honor and his family. He consulted Allama.

"Do forgive me, but all these symptoms lead to one conclusion, that choti Bibi the young mistress, is possessed by a Jinn," Allama said, his hand on his rosary. When Ganju learned from an old servant that his daughter had been tearing off her clothes and dancing indecently, he was more than convinced. He asked Allama to exorcise her.

Every Friday, Allama would lock himself with her in her room. He would read the Quran, rub her body with sacred water, massage her with special oils, and beat her on her bottom. That would calm her down.

Razia would dress up for Allama, with makeup on her withering face, high heels, and false eyelashes. Allama would happily exorcise this little demon. Razia would swoon and jerk into a fit, her pupils would disappear, leaving the whites of her eyes. Her mouth would spout saliva and she would revel in her convulsions. Razia having nothing left in her life had become a willing slave to the ritual.

When Allama didn't appear the following two Fridays having fallen sick, Razia became restless. Her body started splitting up; something kicked her from inside. She would go into convulsions with screams and howls. The maids tried wet towels and all kinds of special prayers to ward off the devil but nothing worked.

On a dark night Razia shredded her wedding dress with her teeth and stepped out of her room naked. She entered the guest room, opened the cupboard and looked for the VCR. Her hands touched a leather box lying next to the VCR. It was heavy. She unlatched it and saw a pistol inside. She touched the cold steel with her small hands. Taking the weapon out, she aimed at an invisible target. At that moment she heard someone coming. She hurriedly put the revolver back in its place and left, smiling at it like a newly made friend with a promise to meet again.

Chapter 10

White Noise

Zahid had arrived at the lunch that Ganju had squeezed in between his day-long budget meetings. While they scooped the steaming soup, Zahid told him the news. Lilly had disappeared from the studio during a film shooting and was nowhere to be found. An eyewitness had reported some miscreants entering the studio and firing gunshots in the air. The guns were real and the men were no actors. A man had come and asked for her autograph and then she disappeared. There was also some gossip about Lilly having a secret lover. Goga and Michael were equally ignorant. No one had looked for her as they all knew that Lilly was in the habit of disappearing for days.

Listening to the news, Ganju lost his appetite.

After lunch, at the meeting, Ganju's mind was split into the functional mind coordinating with what was going on in the room and the aerial mind which floated as a giant eye hovering over the puny rag ball of human vanities. Lilliputians without outputs, words, speeches, development plans, taxes, opening and closing of files, covert and overt nuclearization, price hikes, and the common man, all rumbled in his brain like endless noise. Sitting on the high chair, he could no longer hear or understand their language but by the time he uttered the concluding remarks, he had made up his mind to move the entire government to search for Lilly Khanum.

At night in his residence, he was greeted by the wilderness of the twelve-bedroom building. Lying in bed he had nothing to dream about but to look at the four walls filled with his own pictures and a blank ceiling weighing over him. He turned on the TV. Every channel aired the news of Lilly missing in mysterious circumstances. Her images on the screen made him desperate to see her. Shouldn't he talk to Kashif to move his men to find her, or approach the General? No, they would never understand his passion for Lilly. They would accuse him of lusting after an actress when half of the nation was on strike to demonstrate against price hikes and lack of food. He turned off the TV, got up and opened a whisky bottle. The more he tried to shake off that face from his mind the larger became her image.

Suddenly the room became suffocating. He unbuttoned his shirt and walked out to have some fresh air. The guard at the main door salaamed him. Ganju responded with his usual nod and walked into the main gallery where he held open courts for the public. He saw a burqa-clad woman sitting on a distant bench. "What's she doing here at this hour?" asked Ganju.

"She has come from a very far off village sir, she has been waiting for you all day. Sir, she needs your help," replied the guard.

"At this hour?"

"Yes, Sarkar!"

"Tell her to go away, I can't see anyone at this time," ordered Ganju.

The guard saluted and left.

After a brief walk, Ganju went into his living room where he glanced over the evening newspapers. They all ran stories about Lilly Khanum. The whole film industry was upset by her disappearance. Ganju threw the papers down and went into his bedroom. His olfactory senses were suddenly lit by the smell of a feminine scent. He looked around and saw the burqa-clad woman sitting on the sofa with a bag. Before he could call out, he heard her say, "It's me! Lilly." She had taken off the veil. Ganju was stunned to see her with high oriental makeup, molded in wistful suffering.

"Nussu, my God!" He nervously shut the door. "How did you get in here?" For a moment Ganju hesitated but then eagerly went and hugged her. "Are you all right?"

Tears rolled down her rouged cheeks.

"Did they harm you? I'll lock them all up in jail. Bastards! Oh my poor love . . . "

"Ah," she lingered in his arms, "all my life I've been dying to hear from your lips the word, *love*," she said.

"I love you, I love you my darling!" Ganju clung to her as if he was never going to let her go.

"I walked barefoot to the shrines, hung prayer flags on trees, only to wish a glance from you." She gave a pale smile. With a pout of her lips, seeking an unseen kiss, she moaned, "I spent days and nights training myself good manners. My feet got swollen on high heels and my jaws ached practicing English speech, but I kept going all the way only to reach my beloved. Remember the walk along the beach when I sang a song to you in English?" She hummed some words. Ganju smiled and swayed his head to the rhythm. "Oh how happy I am to have you right beside me, alone and all to myself," she opened her arms. Ganju hugged her tightly.

"I hope you know that I was a bride of the Lord when you took me. And I am proud to be the chosen one. Aren't you happy that you were the first man in my life?" She pressed his groin with the crook of her arm. "I know! I know! My love," Ganju moaned. She kissed him on his cheek. Ganju shivered with excitement. He had never felt so happy to be a man.

Removing his gold-rimmed glasses, he kissed her lightly on both cheeks and then gently wiped her tears.

"Would you like a drink?" he chirped.

"Maybe some wine," she said batting her eyelashes coyly. Ganju went up and got the drinks. They kissed and toasted each other like lovers in a movie.

"Why did you change your name?" Ganju asked. Lilly's nose curled up like a serpent, but then she nailed it with a smile. Flicking away the stray curl on her forehead she said, "Why? You don't like it?"

Ganju felt a bit uneasy. "Oh no, I love it, I was just wondering." He sipped his drink.

Lilly stood up from the sofa and walked around the room looking at the framed pictures of Ganju. "Nice pictures," she drawled, "you look so grand and powerful, like a god. Here," she pointed to the one where Ganju was hoisting the national flag. "And this," she moved to another one, "you, shaking hands with the foreign secretary of America . . . and here, my darling standing next to the prime minister," she said, mimicking some TV host.

"Oh, I am glad you like them," said Ganju, bursting with pride.

"But tell me, my love," she said coming closer to Ganju, her eyes still on the pictures, "why did you change your party?"

Ganju became uncomfortable; he was not used to being questioned, not by anyone below him in status. He shot down the drink and after a stiff pause said, "Well that's politics."

"Oh really?"

"Why, what's wrong?"

"Nothing. I thought you had asked me, why did I change my name?"

"Well?"

"Well, that's the politics of art," she said calmly, sipping her wine. Ganju got ruffled. He couldn't help expressing his displeasure. "Well, I enjoyed the wonderful show of yours on TV the other day. Interesting, very interesting," he snuffled. "You seem to be the miracle of change. I guess this goddamned media can do anything, turn vice into virtue, a lie into a truth, black into white, dross into gold, and a whore into an artist."

"Well, if the blacksmiths of Noorpur could wheel their fortune to royalty, why can't a poor girl like me do a little for herself? It's called upward mobility! Who can know better than you, Mr Chief Minister, my Sarkar," she spoke with an easy smirk and a charming frown.

Ganju lost his cool, how dare she? He slapped her. She stood unmoved. "Why? Can't you take the truth, is it too painful for you?" she asked.

"You bitch," Ganju exploded, "what were you? An orphan who was presented to me as a nazrana. I pulled you out of poverty, from that filth you were living in. I took pity on you. And you show me your tongue?"

"This, too, is politics, isn't it?" She fluttered her mascara eyes, "Can you give back my original name to me? No, you can't," she said with a wicked smile and lounged on the bed, her burqa still covering her body. "Jahangir, the Mughal prince left his throne for Anarkali, his maidservant. Will you do the same for me?" She freely curled her nose at him.

Ganju didn't answer. He walked away from her, poured another drink for himself and sat on the sofa. His mind rattled with all kinds of suspicions. How come she never addressed him as sarkar or sir? Not once had she shown any respect for his position. Such dare in a woman was risky. And why didn't she speak about her abduction? Why was she hiding in a burqa? How come she had walked into his bedroom with all his guards standing outside? Ganju's left foot, resting on his right knee, had started to shake.

"What exactly happened at the club scene?" he asked abruptly.

"Let's not talk about it, we don't have enough time, honey," she stretched her body and her burqa slipped up to expose her ankles.

Ganju averted his eyes, his foot still shaking. "You'd better tell me."

"All right," she said, settling her burqa on her bare ankles. "I know you think I am some cheap celluloid face who's used to lying all the time. I am a woman and I've a heart. Oh no, I just forgot that you're the Chief Minister, a self-centered ruler, too stonehearted to feel the love of a woman. That's what people in power do, treat women as playthings. I pity you because you only want me down my waist and miss out the part where my heart beats." With her voice drowning in sighs, she continued, "But I love you and I'll tell you everything. I will open my heart and show you the truth."

An embarrassing silence followed, everything became still except the foot on the knee.

Lilly recollected herself and slowly stepped down from the

bed. She knelt down in front of him and lifting her sad swollen eyes said, "The minute I came to know that you wanted me, I was like a fish out of water," her voice changed and with a nervous rift in her mouth, she slurred, "I couldn't eat, sleep, or even act. Producers didn't leave me any time to see you. I was going insane. It was like 'stars searching their shine, flowers their color and trees their shade,'" she quoted, the verse adding resonance to her voice. "Suddenly I felt that money, fame, comfort, and even my own existence were a meaningless bluff. I had become desperate. I couldn't wait any longer to be with you." She turned her face away from him. Ganju heard a sob. "I know, you won't believe me, but I was never abducted," she said.

"What?" The shaking foot stopped.

"Yes, that's the truth."

"Then who were those men?" The foot resumed its shaking.

"They were poor extras, whom I had paid to set up the scene for my abduction," she said and grabbed his shaking foot.

"Is it the truth?" Ganju's foot slipped from her hand and limped down from his knee.

"Yes, they were the ones who left me here at your door," she continued. "I am sorry I came." She settled her burqa and stood up to leave.

Ganju was stabbed by sudden guilt. There, at his feet sat the greatest movie star, the offspring of twin cultures, the dream girl of millions, who had staged her own abduction just to see him and he was shaking his bloody foot? In sheer repentance he cried, "I love you Nussu, my Lilly, I love you." He lifted her from the floor and hugged her. Sunshine in rain, Nussu smiled behind her tears. Ganju wiped them carefully with the palm of his hand. She looked at him with moist eyes and kissed his hand. Ganju blushed. She held his hand and put it under her burqa. Ganju looked at her incredulously. "Yes, yes," she nodded. Ganju had the thrill of his life; she was wearing nothing under her burqa.

"I knew you'd like it," she said teasing the hair on his chest. "Come see, what you have to see!" He saw himself changing into a crawling little boy. "Don't you want to see my birdie?"

She whispered. Ganju blinked and she engulfed him, warm against her bare flesh.

"Let me also give you a surprise," said Ganju peeping out of the burqa.

"I am waiting. I am waiting," she moaned. Ganju came out of the tent and toddled to his secret safe. He toddled back with the tape that had won him the elections.

"We are going to watch the most passionate lovers in the world," he announced in a thin voice and put the tape on with his tiny hands. The room was filled with moans and groans as images of Ganju and Lilly flickered on the TV screen.

"Oh you naughty boy, how could you do that? Wao, aren't you some man?" She giggled and shied away, covering her face with the burqa. Ganju for a moment didn't believe his eyes, but he saw himself gliding out of the screen waving a larger than life penis. Noor Mohammad Ganju, a Romeo with Dracula's teeth was absorbed in the cozy darkness of the burqa.

Among dim lights, sometime near early dawn when Mano heard the soft snoring and the white noise on the blank TV screen, she quietly got off the bed and clicked the eject button on the VCR. The tape stuck out. She slipped the tape in her bag.

The white noise continued.

Chapter 11

Guilty In a Gilt-frame

Morning.

Ganju in his slumber heard a light knock on the door. It slowly mixed with a vague drone. Another knock and he was up. The TV was on. Why? Did something happen last night? he thought with a fuzzy head. Oh, yes, he had met someone, who? A burqa-clad woman. No, she was Lilly, oh yes, she was. He groped for her on the side next to him, a pillow rolled off. No one was there.

Another knock.

He shrugged his mind and switched off the TV.

Before he could discard the whole thing as a wishful dream, he saw the red spots on the sheets. In sudden joy he sat up on the bed; yet another virginal conquest by him of this amazing woman. He dashed out of the bed, squeaked into the cupboards and twittered to the bathroom walls, "Lilly, Lilly, are you there?" No sign of her. She must have gone, but how did she sneak out? Maybe she left before the servants could wake up, or perhaps no one noticed her in the guise of a needy woman. He calmly got back into the bed, and covering the evidence on the sheets, coughed for the servant to enter.

The servant brought in his tea with a stack of newspapers. His sagging neck puffed as he salaamed Ganju with a wide grin. Ganju nodded back cheerfully. Placing a cup of tea on his bedside table and newspapers on his lap, the servant drew the curtains and left with silent feet.

Ganju took the first sip and hunched a sumptuous glance at the red spots. They assured him of his undisputable virility. "God bless the Invisible Pir," he muttered the prayer and turned to the papers. As usual, they carried flattering news about him. Enjoying his tea, Ganju felt almost complete that day. His wife was back from the hospital, waiting for him in the Haveli as an armchair. His son Taimur was studying engineering in USA on the Asian fund scholarship for the Third World, and the daughter was happily settled with young Nadir, his own nephew, and above all, Lilly, the most glamorous woman of the country as his mistress, was the icing on the cake. He marveled at the smart use of the veil by the evergreen virgin. Lilly had lit a passage to his private pleasures through a moving tent that warded off all ghosts of suspicion. The going for Ganju was all milk and honey. Ganju on that note ordered a black goat to be sacrificed at the shrine of Pir the Invisible and spent more time on his bath rituals. The secret mirror was ever ready to give him the final touch.

"Mirror, mirror on the wall, who's biggest of them all?" he hummed.

The mirror, as usual, had blown back to him a fat answer.

The rest of the morning Ganju drifted in a daze. He kept dreaming about the late afternoon session of his open court. He was there on the button. Sitting on his chair, his eyes hovered around, searching for Lilly. He couldn't spot her in that crowd of veils but the tickling curiosity to find her behind one of those intriguing folds thrilled him to bits. He gave special attention to anyone wrapped in a burqa, listened to her to the minutest detail and didn't leave her until he was sure that she was not his Lilly. But Lilly was not there. She was holding a press conference in a five-star hotel.

Day after.

The sun was unusually bright for a winter morning. Ganju was up, waiting for the routine knock, but the door was silent.

On edge, he rang the bell. A knock on the door. Ganju coughed. Entered the servant, head down. He salaamed him awkwardly pushing forward his head. Ganju returned a curt nod. The servant put the tea on the side table and turned to leave.

"No newspapers?" Ganju asked.

"Haven't arrived as yet, sir, I'll bring them when I get them, sir," mumbled the servant and left quickly.

Ganju wondered about the delay in the delivery of the papers. Normally they were there on the dot, except on rainy days, but there was hardly any rain. After a while, the servant appeared with the papers. He nervously put them in Ganju's lap and started to walk back in haste. Ganju coughed, the cough carried the phlegm of his anger. The servant turned back, hurriedly drew the curtains and left.

Ganju was surprised at this rude behavior, but before he could react, the front page greeted him with his own picture with the prime minister. That put him back into a good mood. He read the story twice, once as a run through and then word-for-word, savoring each phrase with critical relish. While sipping his tea, he flipped to the inside page. A huge portrait of Lilly Khanum jumped at him. Struck by that smiling face, he missed the headline.

"Lilly speaks of her disappearance, sex scandal with the Chief Minister." His eyes went blank. The cup toppled and the tea spilt on the big close-up, smudging her face beyond recognition. Noor Mohammad Ganju wanted to become invisible. Instantaneously.

"Get the top lawyer and sue them for defamation, and yes, issue a press advice to kill this rubbish," Ganju fumed on the Hotline.

"Sir, we wouldn't have dared to allow such a thing to go unnoticed, but I am afraid we have different instructions on the subject." The Information Minister on the other end was unexpectedly calm.

"Different instructions?" Ganju was suddenly hit by a wall.

"Yes sir, from Intelligence," fell the sword. "I thought you knew," the Minister's voice carried a smirk.

"What do you mean from Intelligence?"

"Sir, we have been conveyed orders to give it maximum coverage," continued the Smirk.

"Maximum coverage?" Ganju blew his top.

"Yes sir!" came the answer.

Ganju banged the phone.

"What the hell is going on here? You know the bitch is lying." Ganju was shouting at Zahid on the phone, "she came here in the guise of a needy woman, how come you all want it to be splashed over the media?"

"You never know who's on the line, it's not safe, I'll be with you in a minute." Zahid clicked off.

When Ganju and Zahid came out on the lawn to have breakfast, attendants kept their eyes down and spoke in whispers.

"What must they all be thinking about me? No wonder the servant didn't bring the papers directly to me. They must have been circulated among the staff first. I was the clown for their breakfast show," Ganju grumbled as they sat under the canopy.

"They don't matter," Zahid said with a mouthful of fruit cocktail, "think in broader terms."

"What do you mean, broader terms?" Ganju was glaringly upset.

Before Zahid could say something, Ganju's mobile buzzed. Calls from reporters, his well-wishers, and from his supporters. A mortified Ganju repeated the same answer to everyone, "It's all a setup, they want to frame me with this woman to distract people from all the good work I have done for them."

"Put off that damn thing; they all are junk calls, we don't have time for that." Zahid took the phone from Ganju and switched it off. "Now don't panic, just calm down. Here, I'll pour tea for you."

"Look, to me, you are quite a perceptive man and I believe you are capable of understanding the ups and downs of power. Now, in all seriousness, allow me to tell you that whatever has been done is done absolutely in the national interest," said Zahid, pouring himself a cup of tea.

"National interest? What rubbish is this? You think bringing my bedroom out on the streets is in the national interest?" Ganju gulped at his tea, disdainfully.

"Well, you know we have a disaster at hand." Zahid lathered his toast with cream.

"What disaster?"

"The National Budget, it's being announced this week."

"So what?"

"You say, so what?" Zahid choked, mid-bite, his face a big exclamation mark. "Even a blind man can see it's not a welcome budget. What's touted as a poor man's budget will make the poor poorer and within a few days, the topic for the nation will be nothing but money. And," he gave a pregnant pause, "we want to change that topic. That's all." Zahid resumed his luxurious munching.

"So it's all a setup?" Ganju said, gripping Zahid's hand that was knifing the bread.

"Don't get me wrong," Zahid continued, calmly releasing his hand from Ganju's grip, "no one planned it. It all happened because of your shameless lust for this woman, like a child you have put your hand in the fire."

Ganju looked away.

"Anyway," Zahid paused, giving a relief to the knife and fork, "what's done can't be undone. Now what we, as intelligent people, can do is to bend it our way and think how much political leverage we can get out of it," he said, mopping his mouth with his napkin, looking perfectly reasonable.

"But why should I be the sacrificial goat?" Ganju bleated meekly.

"I am afraid the axe is about to fall. We've already plundered foreign aid and fat loans from the IMF and the World Bank. Out there, those hungry millions will soon be dying of price hikes, inflation, and new taxes. Do you think they would take it lying back? Never!" He put some marmalade on the bread. "They'll lynch you and me on the streets." Zahid continued as he cut the bread, "and there is no bigger fool than you if you think the opposition will watch the whole thing go by as spectators." He finished by raising the knife. "Oh, you make me puke." He swallowed that handsome chunk of marmalade.

Uneasy silence.

"Now if you come to think of it, in this situation, we have to stop those hungry hordes, redirect this lethal missile to some other target and," he nibbled at the cherries, "nothing could be more effective than a sex scandal." He laced his speech with smooching sounds. "Every day, we should have something for them to chew on. And who could know more than yourself that our people forget to eat the moment they see a pussy being rammed. Our film stars are insanely adored, especially if they are endorsed by the West. Lilly is our top heroine and don't forget she has a foreign mother. Sir, this is known as white complex. Our lower classes are illiterate, they live on fantasies, you know the shrine culture? Pirs, prayers, superstitions, black magic, etc. Now who doesn't know that this child is blessed by Pir the Invisible?"

He gave a well-fed smile and leaned back on his armchair with a toothpick in his mouth. It reminded Ganju of his late uncle.

"What about my wife, my kids?" Ganju beseeched like a sinking man.

"It's time to shed clichés of personal honor. I know the conscience creaks like a stunned cricket. Flit it, get real. And let me inform you, it's not just our decision, it has been discussed at the highest level."

He burped heartily.

Ganju looked at him, his face like an empty frame.

"And frankly speaking, if you take my opinion, I think it's a wise decision." Zahid lit his cigar. "Call your staff, let your PR man deny all allegations. We'll be in touch," he said looking at his watch. "Oh no, you don't have to see me off," he stood up and gave Ganju a friendly pat. "Enjoy your tea." He left without looking back. Ganju saw him disappear in the corridor.

Underneath that tinsel she remained a low-caste, nazrana girl, thought Ganju, sitting back in his room, leafing through the newspapers again and again. He should have kept her in her place, but he had given her a pillow next to him. Suddenly he felt naked in that closed room. Lilly had stripped him in the middle of a jalsa and the crowd was jeering at him. One single woman had shattered his infallible world into pieces.

"Will he stand for the next Erection race?"

"Lilly gets a Willy."

"Virgin Island ruled by the Chief Molester."

Headlines triggered new sensations each day. The copies burst with saucy statements by Lilly: "He seduced me, sent presents which included a see-through bra, panties, and some toys. He was fond of giving me erotic torture."

"And he called me his Ideal State, his Ganjtopia," ran another copy.

Within days, the sex scandal had aroused public interest. It was freely discussed at the paan shops, film studios, press clubs, diplomatic dinners, funerals, wedding receptions, army messes, and Hera Mandi, the center of prostitution. Overnight, the mix masala of politics and sex had spiced the dull lives of the masses, and Lilly's juicy statements had launched Ganju as an incredible bed player. His colleagues became envious of him. The General had called him a dark stud, an iron cock, the king of virgins. Others had found in him an epicure, a hedonistic barbarian, a rake, and a loveable rogue. Some influential ladies had expressed the desire to seek an introduction. Even his doctor had asked him, discreetly, as to what kind of bread he ate to have such a fine libido. Ganju had become a fantasy figure that stalked the imagination of both poor and the rich alike, a rage with the indoor parties and outdoor ghetto squatters. The media moles took no time in burrowing information about his background, his height and weight, his waistline, his moustache, his clothes, his deodorant and aftershave lotion. Even his shrug and nod were recorded to track down his charisma as the sex god. He noticed that the number of burqa-clad women appearing at his open court had increased significantly. The delicate secret of seduction through the lacy nebula had been finally revealed to these needy women. From nowhere, a new burqa design had emerged with a double cover for the face;

a thick layer overlapping a transparent muslin. Once they got closer to the Chief Minister to air their grievances, they would accidentally flip the top layer and Ganju would watch their mouths going liquid behind the faint shadow of the flowing chintz.

The reputation that it's not the head of the Chief Minister but his genitals that took decisions, gave Ganju an extra mile.

During this time, the public humiliation that Ganju had experienced earlier was turning into an enigmatic, pleasing esteem. The Trio, at whose hands he believed he had suffered, dazzled in the new light like a holy trinity. No matter how much he denied the allegations, Ganju, in that heat of publicity, hungered for the next headline about him. In-between his statements to the press, he would make sure that he dropped something for them to be picked up for the gossip columns. Without him realizing, his grey and black suits were being replaced by bright blue and white jackets and instead of those sober-looking neckties, he was sporting floral or striped ones on pink, green, and yellow shirts. Ganju had hatched another Ganju: a potent symbol of ultimate malehood, the pinnacle of masculinity.

He no longer consulted the Japanese mirror.

At this time Ganju, however, was reluctant to visit his home village. He was avoiding his people and especially his wife and daughter, whom he had caused serious damage. But he must come clear to them, it was his duty, he thought. Before planning his visit, he felt it safe to send Juma ahead, who as a weather-cock could warn him of any brewing storm. Juma took the first bus to the village and was on the line the very next day.

"Sarkar, the mood is great, they all are looking forward to welcome you."

When Ganju alighted from his flag-waving car in his village, the men who had gathered to receive him stood silently. They didn't raise any slogans but inside their hearts, Ganju could hear each one of them applauding. Their faces gave away a mysterious glow radiating vibes of appreciation, and empathy, a man's feeling. As he walked along them, he felt that bonding.

Walking through the courtyard of the Haveli, he felt proud to be a father and a husband. He had thought of winning the favors of his daughter and his wife by bribing them with expensive presents. First, he went to his daughter's room, which had been renovated after her marriage. He carried a packed hobbyhorse and a box of chocolates for his son-in-law and a ladies' watch for the daughter. He knocked at the door and coughed. A giggling dark girl opened the door and almost fainted at his sight. She quickly settled her doppatta on her breasts and disappeared in the corridor. "Who's she," he asked his daughter.

"Cheemo, the maid," said the daughter, head down.

"Oh I didn't recognize her, she has really grown up fast," he said looking towards the outside corridor.

"She's married now," said Razia coyly.

"Oh, I see, well, you should not let her into the room unnecessarily, she should finish her work and leave," said Ganju and patted her on the head.

"Ji, papa," said Razia.

Ganju brought out the watch from his pocket and handed it over to Razia. "This is for you," he said.

She took the watch.

"Ah, my little prince, Nadir Shah." Ganju moved to his son-in-law, who was sitting on the floor, tearing sheets from a cookery book with his teeth. Ganju with much fondness took him up in his arms. The boy let out a deafening scream. Ganju held him tight saying, "Look, baba is here." He waved to his daughter to unpack the chocolate box. She opened the box and brought it to Ganju, who picked up one piece and shoved it into Nadir's yelling mouth. The boy spat it back. "Hey, look what we've got for our prince here," said Ganju unpacking the hobbyhorse. "Look it runs," he swung the wooden beast. Still at the book, Nadir Shah didn't bother. Ganju tried to attract his attention by sitting on the horse himself, but the little prince didn't respond. Ganju pulled him up. Nadir clawed at his necktie.

"Oh, no, don't do that, not the necktie," said Razia firmly. Ganju realized quickly that he was wearing one of his floral purchases. "She knows, then," he told himself.

As soon as Ganju left the room, Razia slapped her husband. That made him quiet for an hour.

In the late afternoon, Ganju met the leading men of his party and sat with them till dinner. No one said a word. They kept looking at him with some weird admiration.

At night when he retired into the men's quarters, Juma was on his legs, all ready to magnetize them.

"I've been watchful about what they have been talking behind your back," Juma started with his report.

"What?"

"Sarkar, the Pir's blessed curse has come true. It's the virility flowing through the blessings of the Pir, who is linked with cosmic forces. Everyone can see that."

"How do you say that?"

Ganju kept quiet, savouring Juma's compliments.

"Now everyone thinks you have ousted all film heroes," continued Juma. "You have hammered a woman of the big screen. Sarkar, what you have done, our party workers would have loved to do themselves. Since you represent them, they share everything through you."

Juma was not sure whether he had succeeded in conveying his feeling to the master. He fell silent. In that silence Ganju's mind sparkled with luminous insights. Pages from the biographies of the hundred great men fluttered around. There were scandals about world leaders from Europe, Middle East to South and East Asia. The public loves to be ruled by a man with balls, yes, with balls, and no doubt he was one of them.

As Juma left, Ganju entered his bedroom in the zenankhana. He coughed, no answer, the door was open. Where was she? He wondered. Maybe she was out with the maids or in the kitchen. He rang the bell, in came the maid. "Where is your mistress?" he asked, looking away from her.

"She's in the adjacent room. She has shifted," replied the maid fidgeting with her doppatta.

"Oh I see, well, it's all right," he said. The maid didn't leave. "You can go now," he said looking at her. She turned to leave, "Wait," he called out. Ganju had noticed that she was not the usual maid and was one step inside the room which was not the custom of the Haveli. They don't walk in, unless they are ordered.

"Sarkar?"

"Where is the old maid?"

"She's busy, their cow has delivered a calf," she said, red in the face.

"All right."

She left with a suggestive gait.

"Every woman wants to get into bed with you, even the house maids. Lucky bastard," said Ganju in the mirror to Ganju who had started to undress. "But why would your wife shift to the adjacent room?"

"Maybe she felt lonely in this room, maybe she missed you; after all, you haven't been to the village in some time."

"Or maybe she doesn't want to sleep with you anymore. Shame on you, Mr Ganju, you might have seduced the world by this cheap scandal but you could never seduce your own wife," bounced back the mirror-Ganju.

A cloud of disappointment sat on his face. In slow, uneasy movements, he undressed himself and opened the cupboard to take out his night suit. "What?" Inside, in a corner, sat his favorite VHS tape which had a few explicit bedroom scenes. How come it's there when he had locked both the VCR and the tapes in the top drawer? He looked up, the lock was broken.

"Oh God, it means that Zeenat has been watching it," he thought with a smile.

"Waah Mr Ganju, now that you know her secret dreams you could jump into her bed without that silly cough for an invitation. Yes, oh yes!"

He already had a hard on.

That night Ganju moved like Kama the god. His wife who lay still in the bed was to be resurrected by his magic touch. Like a blind man his fingers groped to read the secrets of this change. She moaned in agony, and shifted, pushing him away. Still shy? He thought and got aside, sending his apology through his silence but then the bold cough. She didn't move. He pulled her to his side. With an automatic hand, she pulled her shalwar down, enough for him to enter. Exhausted he performed. As usual.

She's not ready yet; things don't happen in a day, it takes time to transcend the traditional holds. But things have started to move. The magic of the media works gradually, it cooks on slow fire, he thought.

The next morning Ganju left his village as a successful man. He had pleased everyone, including himself. When he arrived at his house in the Capital, he didn't realize but he was whistling. Interrupted by his PA, who had rushed to him, he stopped and in sheer irritation asked, "What is it?"

In jitters the PA handed over an envelope to him, saying, "Sir, it's urgent."

"The bitch has gone to court. I just received a notice," Ganju stuttered to Zahid on the phone.

"I know, I know!"

"What do you know? You know nothing!"

"Well, that's even better," said Zahid in a drunken voice.

"Look you are pissed drunk and don't understand what I am trying to tell you. How on earth can the judiciary hear a case against me when all these judges have been appointed by us?"

"Yes, but don't forget, we have an independent jury."

"Fuck you, there's nothing independent in this country."

"Well, we have already proved that there's a free press and now we have a chance to restore the credibility of the judiciary. I think it's brilliant." Zahid's glass of whisky clinked on the other end.

"Are you out of your mind, I'm the Chief Minister, how could I go to court?"

"No one is above the law. In the West even presidents are summoned to the court. Can't you see, by having you on trial we'll be entering the first world?" Clinked the glass.

"But I can never go on trial."

"Sir, you are forgetting that a trial gives people the sense of justice, it's a reminder of Judgment Day itself. Man is always on trial, without ever knowing his crime. Please, I beg of you, know your Kafka and your Perry Mason. A trial is the most absorbing event for the masses, every hit movie has it," he clicked.

Chapter 12

Fall of the Priapus

"Order! Order!" growled the ageing judge inside the crowded court.

Dead silence.

"I cannot proceed unless the plaintiff appears in person, face to face," said the honorable judge after Lilly, wrapped in a toe-length burqa, took the stand.

"Milord," said the prosecutor clearing his throat, "allow me to submit that my client is privileged to appear according to the dress code specified for women in this country." Lilly was represented by the best lawyer; a closet fan, adept at finding legal covers to his private passions.

"Let me remind the counsel that this court has to be convinced that the person who stands in the witness box is the lady called Miss Lilly Khanum." The judge was brusque.

"Milord allow me to refer to the Shariat bill passed by the highest office of this country, the National Assembly. I may humbly submit that in this bill, it is clearly stated that women in our society must observe purda. Do permit me, Your Lordship, to say that my client is acting strictly in concurrence with the given rule. She is covering the contours of her body, her zeen-ats, Milord."

"Now what was that word you used?" The judge took a lavish pause. Taking advantage of his impaired hearing, he wished it to be repeated.

"Zeenats, Milord, are the female beauties," amped the prosecutor.

"Say it again," said the judge squiggling his ear with a cotton pick.

"Zeenats, my lord, the female beauties," came the echo.

"Oh I see . . . ee!" The judge slurred and giving his folded neck a jocular lilt, asserted, "I am afraid justice cannot remain blind in this case. She must identify herself, if not publicly then privately to me. In my chambers."

"Milord, Islamic law prohibits the male to cast even an accidental glance at the member of the opposite sex unless he is the legally wed husband," said the prosecutor, looking the judge in the eye.

"Objection, Milord!" The defense lawyer shot up from his chair, "The worthy prosecutor is deliberately creating obstructions in the way of justice," he said.

"Objection sustained."

"Milord," the prosecutor glanced over Lilly protectively, "I reiterate that my client should be granted the permission to remain veiled, and," he halted in front of the judge, defiantly, "I should be permitted to proceed."

"Objection, Milord," leapt up the defense lawyer, "the plaintiff is a film actress, her picture appears in all our newspapers, she acts on screen and is seen by millions every day. How come my worthy opponent insists on her being covered?"

"Objection sustained."

"Milord, film is an illusion and here in this court, my client is in her real person. I wonder at the ignorance of the worthy defense on matters of film art. Plato, I hope my friend here is familiar with the name, says that an artist's reality is an imitation of the imitation, it is therefore, twice removed from the real world."

"By that logic Milord," said the defense, "since my friend is using quotations, his own reality should be thrice removed from the original reality."

Ripples of laughter.

"Order, order in the court."

"Milord, the prosecutor is concocting a theory of his own,

which by all standards is ludicrous," continued the defense.

"What the defense considers ludicrous is simply a matter of common sense, Milord, if we see a film or a photograph of a person, we cannot touch or feel that person. Now my worthy friend could be watching my client dancing on the screen but she may as well be praying at that time in her house. In that case, Milord, he would not be seeing the real Lilly Khanum but the celluloid image of my client. Thank you, Milord," said the prosecutor, bowing with formal dignity.

"Gentlemen, I am not here to discuss literature and art but to expend justice. Let me remind you that the case in point implies serious allegations against an honorable functionary of the Government. I therefore will not take the risk of allowing the plaintiff to appear in the court under any cover. I shall not proceed unless I see the lady by the name of Lilly Khanum with my own two eyes." The judge once again craned his neck to the dark apparition in the dock.

"Milord, it's my duty to inform the court that if my client comes out of the veil, it can cause a law-and-order situation," the prosecutor shouted at the top of his voice.

"You don't have to shout, I can hear you!" His Lordship discarded the cotton pick in anger. "Let me warn you, I will take action if you don't stop wasting my time on irrelevant issues. Miss Lilly Khanum?" his eyes drilled into the veil, "Will you take that thing off from your face or shall I order the officer to do the job?"

Hushed silence. All eyes fell on the cloaked mystery.

"Oh, I love you, Milord!" Lilly flung her burqa revealing a sleeveless top and tight jeans molded to her stout hips. "Look at me the way you want to look," she said and launched a chunky kiss at the honorable judge. The crowd went wild with excitement. The judge pounded his gavel "Order! Order!" No one listened. Like a matador, Lilly swayed her fluttering burqa against the ogling men who almost charged at their favorite star. Her guard made a reluctant move. She pinched his bottom. He squirmed in his knickers and his rifle fell off his hands. The judge became furious. "Lady, show some respect for the court."

"I am, I am, Milord!" she said, puffing her breasts out from her plunging blouse. "Here, Milord, see what you have to see." She sailed another plump kiss to the judge. The glasses he wore, fell from his eyes to his nose. Lilly turned and swung the dark rag towards Ganju, "Come, you bullhead, smell your load on it, your power-droppings." She pointed to the white splotches on the burqa that looked like bird shit.

"The court is adjourned," the red-faced judge got up from the chair and rushed to his retiring room.

The opening of the trial had sent waves of sensation around the country. Lilly, the victim of a male-dominated society had become an instant hit with the women activists. The sisters had started appearing in public and private places, dressed as Lilly Khanum. Religious parties were equally sympathetic. They were overwhelmed by her refusal to appear in court without her hijab. "She has stuck to her faith," they said.

"Order, order!"

Lilly sans burqa, swore on the Book, flashed her sleeveless arm and raised a hand covered with dazzling rings to narrate the truth of the matter. Her professionally rehearsed statement was followed by cross-questioning.

"Miss Lilly Khanum, you said in your statement that Mr Ganju called you in, what do you mean by 'in,'" proceeded the well-prepared defense.

"In his bedroom, of course, where else do you do it?" she said, looking surprised.

"What?" the judge cocked his ear, "Could you tell your client to speak clearly?" he instructed the prosecutor.

"Yes, Milord, he called me to his bedroom," Lilly repeated aloud.

"Did you say bedroom?" The judge squiggled his ear with a matchstick; he had run out of his stock of cotton picks.

"Yes, Milord."

"What time, if I may ask?"

"10:30 pm."

"And he thought you were a needy woman."

"I was, Milord."

"And what exactly was your need?"

"I had problems with the tax people. They were unnecessarily harassing me. I went to him for justice and he promised to help," she sobbed.

"And then, did he help?"

"Yes, Milord," her sighs became streaks on her face, "he did, he did, Milord."

"How?"

"Read my lips, Milord," she pouted her lips.

The judge strained his eyes behind his glasses and said, "Lady, I am afraid I am not familiar with this language. You have to speak up."

"Milord, he took my virginity," came the voice from a megaphone.

The matchstick fell from the judge's hand and the hall whined in a chorus.

"Order in the court!" shushed the judge.

"Tell us all about it, Miss Khanum," implored the judge, his eyes latched onto her cleavage.

"Your Lordship, if I may be allowed to go on with my cross-examination," intervened the defense.

"Oh, I am sorry, by all means, go ahead."

"Isn't it true that you have been a professional call girl?" the defense asked.

"What?" Lilly glared at the lawyer, "How dare you call me a call girl? Behenchod," her breasts shook with anger. "If you call me a call girl then you are the pimp who's touting a political whore, your client. If you speak to me like this, I'll chop that thing you carry in your pants and shove it up your ass." Her flying hands butchered an invisible penis.

"Mind your language, Miss Lilly," implored the judge timidly.

"Will you tell the court how you managed to get out of the house?" the defense kept up his pressure.

"How do you think you get out when all doors are locked?

Why don't you tell the court how you pulled yourself out from your mother's cunt?"

Laughter in the courtroom.

"Enough! I am warning you, Miss Lilly, watch your language or I will put you behind bars." Thrilled inside, the judge was firm.

"I escaped through the window, Milord," Lilly dropped her voice to match her helplessness. Her breathing went staccato, accentuating the bulk of her breasts.

"Is it not true that you slept with a guard who got you inside the room?"

"How dare you say this?"

"Just answer the question," said the judge, his eyes scaling the breasts under her shirt.

"Miss Lilly Khanum, isn't it true that you went to the Chief Minister in the guise of a needy woman where you bribed the guard with promises of sexual favors and then with his help broke into the defendant's bedroom? And isn't he the same guard who took you out of the house?"

"Shut up, you moron, I never mix with the lower staff, it's you who look like the hit of a sweeper, ask your mother and she'll tell you who your father was," said Lilly with authority. Everyone looked at the defense lawyer, scandalized.

"You may step down Miss Lilly Khanum," said the judge. He couldn't help a whipping glance at the sweep of hips as Lilly colted back to her seat.

"Milord, I would request the court to allow me to present my first witness," said the defense.

A corny-looking man in his twenties, oddly dressed, stumbled to the witness box. He wore an ill-fitted cap with a tight strap that hooked his chin, and flaps covered his ears.

"Will you tell your name to the court," said the defense.

"Raju," the guard proudly announced.

"Your real name."

"But they all call me Raju."

"Forget what they call you, tell us your real name."

"Mohammad Riaz, but I don't like my name, I like Raju," he insisted.

"Are you the night guard at the Chief Minister's house?"

"Yes, sir."

"Were you on duty on 14th of October?"

"Oh I am always on duty, sir," he replied and saluted like an army man.

"What happened on that night?"

"Oh that night, yes, it was a wonderful night, the night of my dreams," he proceeded to hum a film song as he ogled shamelessly at Lilly.

The judge, green in the face, warned the guard, "Mr Riaz, this is a court and not a cinema hall, I will have you arrested if you don't behave. Just answer the question."

"Forgive me, Milord. Well, after my night duty, when I was about to go to sleep in the early hours of the morning, I saw someone coming out of my sahib's house."

"Who?"

"A burqa-clad woman, I lowered my eyes, because it's not good looking at a burqa woman. You see, you can't see anything."

"Will you cut this out and tell us what happened," ordered the judge.

"I felt something touching me, very soft," said Raju coyly.

"What was it?"

"I can't say, I am shy."

"No, go on, tell us," said the defense.

"It was a tit, a real chunky one, Milord." The guard grinned with his tongue rolling.

"What did you say," asked the judge.

"Tit, Milord. Oh did I say something wrong, I mean against the law?" he looked puzzled.

"Milord, it means a female breast," elaborated the defense.

"Do they have it in the dictionary?"

"No, Milord. It's slang."

"I see, tell the witness to carry on," the judge made a note.

"Yes, Mr Riaz, tell the court what happened then."

"I looked up and found the burqa woman breathing over

me," he continued reluctantly.

"Can you see that woman present in this court?" said the defense looking around.

The guard, fixing his gaze on Lilly, shouted, "There she sits, Milord. They say when Sahibs doze off at the thighs of an insatiable whore the attendants keep the balance," he laughed, showing his crooked teeth. "*Kyoon door door rahandey o hazoor saday koloon.*" He crooned a song from her film.

"Will you restrain this joker or I'll have him removed," the judge said and struck the gavel in annoyance.

"Thank you, Milord, that's all."

"You can proceed with your cross-questioning," said the judge to the prosecutor.

"You said you saw a burqa-clad woman, was she hiding her face?" the prosecutor asked as he approached the witness.

"Yes, but she was hiding out of shame, I think it was her first time."

"How do you know it's the same woman when you never saw her face?"

"Because she whispered into my ears all those dialogues, oh, I knew it was her, the same words, the same voice, and then—"

"Yes, and what then?"

"I don't know whether I should tell you this . . . " he gave a hesitant look at the judge and the prosecutor, "you'll think I am making up a story, but it's true."

"How can you be so sure?"

"Objection, Milord, the prosecutor is turning a real situation into a figment of the imagination. He is reversing his own logic to suit his end."

"Overruled, carry on," said the judge.

"She took my hand inside. I know you don't believe me but she . . . "

"Yes, yes," the judge shifted in his chair.

"Well, she was not wearing anything underneath her burqa," he blurted out.

"What?" the judge almost jumped out of his chair. "Would you ask your witness to repeat that," he addressed the defense.

"He should not mumble, I want clarity," said the judge, his hand frenetic on the fresh matchstick in his ear.

"Repeat what you have said now, slowly and clearly in a loud voice," the defense instructed the guard.

"She...was...wearing...noth...ing...under...neath," blurted the guard like a school child repeating his lesson.

"Nothing?" said the judge in utter disbelief. "You mean no clothes, no—undergarments, nothing? Naked born?" He broke the matchstick in his ear.

"I didn't first believe it myself but Milord, she held my hand, this very hand," he said raising his hand, "and then she slipped it right under her burqa. I thought I was dreaming and this blessed hand," he again showed the hand, "was telling me a lie. To make sure, I asked her to bite my ear, and she did, but softly. I said, harder please, and she chewed at it, I couldn't help screaming, she put her hand on my mouth and bandaged my bleeding ear with her hanky," he said. "Only then I knew it was no dream."

He unstrapped his cap and uncovered the gash for exhibition. "She promised to cast me as a hero in her films. Milord, pardon me but I can sing a song on this theme . . . it goes like this," he took a squeezy start.

"Will you remove him from the stand, or I will make sure that he loses his other ear too, not to anyone but to a legal surgeon," said the judge in great annoyance.

"Milord, he is not in his right mind," said the prosecution, "and we can see that he doesn't have enough evidence to prove that it was Lilly Khanum he met on the night of the crime. In fact he had never seen this woman except in the movies. He has told the court that she was hiding under a burqa, which means there was no identification of the woman. I am sure his lordship will agree that in the absence of a proper identification, the statement of the witness cannot be taken as valid. If your Lordship couldn't proceed without the identification of my client, how can the court in this case consider the statement of this witness?"

"Objection, Milord," protested the defense.

"Overruled," said the judge and adjourned the court for noon prayers.

Once the prayers were over, the court resumed. The judge was on the dot, looking fresh after his ablutions. For him the "Lilly case" was an exciting departure from the routine cases of murder and theft. Though there were no kickbacks, the honorable judge treasured some kind of spiritual gain; the delightful presence of a film star whose company in the court brightened his dull senses and honed his blunt hearing. On that day, he had happily sacrificed his siesta, which he normally had in his retiring room.

After quickly going through the court procedures, the judge knitted his brow over a paper he had in front of him.

"Since the previous medical report submitted by the prosecutor was considered unreliable, this court had ordered a fresh medical report. The said report is still awaited. What is the delay?" the judge looked to the police officer.

"Honorable sir, I beg to submit that due to inadequate equipment, lack of female medical and legal officers and good laboratories, the report may take some time. It's not easy to detect such a breach of law, sir," said the officer.

"You'd better get it soon," the judge said and turned to the prosecutor, "You may proceed with your witnesses. The floor is yours."

Silence. No response from the prosecutor.

"Well, counsel, I am waiting."

"Milord, I have no witnesses," came the response.

"No witnesses? You amaze me. Knowing that in a case of rape or Zina, of which the defendant is accused, at least four witnesses are required and you have none. Are you here to ridicule this court?" he roared.

"Milord, I am aware of the nature of this case and I can assure you that I'll not disappoint his Lordship," said the prosecutor calmly.

"Proceed, will you?" said the impatient judge.

"Milord, I can produce not just four but four million witnesses."

Whispers buzzed in the hall.

"Don't be vague, counsel, this is a court not a magician's hall."

"Milord, I've something which undoubtedly will satisfy his Lordship."

"What's it then in your hat, out with it," said the judge sarcastically.

"Milord, the one and only exhibit . . . " the prosecutor unwrapped a packet, "I would like to present a videotape which will clearly show the accused and my client," he said putting the tape in front of the judge, "in juxtaposition."

The judge examined the tape with utmost care while Ganju sweated. He didn't have the foggiest idea that Lilly had stolen the tape. He looked at his counsel sitting next to him, the counsel looked back at Ganju quizzically, and then in a daze shouted, "Objection, Milord."

"Overruled," said the judge and slipped the tape into his bag.

"Milord, this tape can be witnessed by the jury for a fair trial," said the prosecutor.

"You mean it's all on the tape?" the judge asked to be sure.

"Yes Milord, it's all in there, in part and in the whole," quipped the prosecutor.

"The court is adjourned till next week," said the judge with a canny shiver in his voice.

"They have got the tape," Ganju panicked on the phone. "I am doomed. What future do I have if that tape is released?"

"Don't be upset, Kashif told me that she had got into the hands of the opposition. We are already looking into that. Just give me an hour, I'll come over to you and discuss the whole thing with you, alone," said Zahid and put down the phone.

It was late in the morning. Ganju was not at his official residence but in a rest house reserved by Zahid. There were no guards but police in plainclothes. He was under watch, a prisoner in his own place.

What if they found out about the pink top extension? Ganju felt the rug of power slipping underneath his feet. Oh God, what had he done? He was born with a mission to bring peace and justice to the world and here he was in the dock for raping a whore. Instead of becoming a leader he had become a joke.

How could he betray his ideals just to buy a fiction of virility? Sunk in guilt and remorse, Ganju washed himself like a maniac as he performed his ablutions. He fell on the prayer mat with a crying heart.

"I am sorry I got late," Zahid entered with a briefcase in his hand, "but I've good news for you." He took out a paper from his briefcase.

"Are these orders of my death sentence, am I to be stoned to death?" said Ganju in a bitter tone.

"Just relax, it's all over." Zahid settled himself on the sofa and swigged from his hip flask.

"No, it'll not be over, unless I expose you all, this whole godless system."

Ganju still wore his skullcap.

"Be happy, do that, there are many wannabe messiahs like you in this world, just go out and people will happily lynch you to create a martyr." Zahid looked at the prayer mat on the floor. Taking another deep swig he said, "Anyway, it's not the time to pray but to rejoice. Here," he waved the paper to him, "just read it before you make a mistake."

"What is it?" Ganju took the paper.

"These are orders from the registrar giving the judge two years' extension."

"You are getting that son of a bitch two years' extension?"

"Well, didn't you have yours, remember? He needs his, not on his willy but in years," said a smiling Zahid. "He's retiring by the end of this year, we give him two years to lean on. Come to the house in the evening, he'll be there. I'll leave the two of you alone." Zahid made a move to go.

"The burqa can hide anything. The veil has a three inch window that is manipulated to spy on the world. People usually don't register the presence of a burqa woman because she gives the signal of a God-fearing, religiously inclined female who keeps the men away. But then women often hide their paramours in their burqas," said the judge as he made himself comfortable in the basement of Zahid's house. His hand held a large whisky and a thigh-rolled cigar was stuck in his mouth. "You see the damn thing has strong cultural and social meanings. Algerian women carried hand grenades under their veils to attack the French rulers."

Ganju, his shoulders drooped and his hands still on his knees, sat spellbound, dutifully absorbing in the sociopolitical interpretation of burqa.

"You see, men want power and control, and when they can't get it up, they invent projectiles, missiles, nuclear warheads. I would say that when they can't make love they make war. I must confess, I enjoyed watching the movie, it's exciting, especially the odd angles which I guess is a modern way of making movies." The judge threw an admiring look at Ganju, "You see, I spent a lot of time winding, rewinding, using pause and replay, slow-motion, freeze-frame and zoom-in to thoroughly examine the only evidence available in this case. Now tell me something," he paused for a refill, Ganju did the honors. "I find something mysterious in this lass, I believe she is an ecstatic child. Well, sometimes you can never tell the difference between a saint and a whore." He sipped thirstily.

"Your Lordship, the food is ready," announced Zahid after the honorable judge was reasonably sloshed.

"Ah, I am having a ball tonight, this young man has promised me a special treat. I believe food is the secret of virility," cheered the judge.

Zahid led the judge to the dining table, Ganju trailed behind them, tied to some invisible leash. On the way, Zahid whispered the information to the judge about his extension. He turned back and smiled gratefully at Ganju. "Sir, I can't resist the temptation to agree that at the end of the day it's all about extensions."

Ganju returned a submissive smile.

Assured of his two years, the judge came to the point, "You see Western law is full of shortcomings, but with us it's simple, *dakhool hoa ya na hoa*, penetration or no penetration? That's the question. Well, it's the same plea the head of the superpower Mr Clinton took to get himself out of trouble. He had told the court that it was like smoking a cigar without inhaling it. Absolutely brilliant."

"Red or white?" Zahid asked the judge.

"Red I believe is good for the liver," said the judge and continued, "You see we have a very strict law and in this case, the qanoon-e-shahadat or the law of witness," the judge took a sip of wine, "ah, very smooth I must say, and yes," he continued, "I was saying that the law of witness doesn't recognize any evidence but four witnesses. One has to admit that our faith is kind to us men, it's male-friendly. Where on earth could she summon four witnesses? Sir, there is no case at all. The tape cannot be reliable evidence, nowadays such things can be manufactured and manipulated. Only four witnesses are needed by law, and that too of men because a woman's testimony is counted half. Haah, baba, just the half-truth, because she doesn't have what we men have, a solid extension," he looked at Ganju. "By the way, sir, please don't mind me asking you a personal question, I may not get a chance like this to meet you again," he said. "How was she in bed? I suppose she's virgin anytime you sleep with her, well that's a miracle. I can tell from what little I saw that she has the most robust pair of tits, pardon my slang, but I liked it and made a note when this clown used it in the court. They say tits came first when she was born. They also say she never grows old, I guess it's all a folktale, wishful thinking of our masses, but you? Only you can tell as where lies the true magic." The judge eyed Ganju with much envy.

Ganju hated the judge, who was a sweaty, obese and a dark looking slob, his face dotted by pox marks; a work of pointillism. His double neck inflated like the bellow of an accordion, pouches of weary flesh hung around his jaw, and when he spoke his thick lips overlapped like two earthworms. With saliva dripping and dentures clunking, his voice came as a slow-speed growl of a tired jackal who had spent all his life in a zoo.

"They say, at our age, one has to take the back seat as far as the sex drive is concerned, what about you, sir? You are almost fifty-eight now, I can't even find my thing when I've to piss, doctors tell me to have my prostrate operated, but I don't listen to them. Oh, that throw of the stream is no longer there, no more jet and gush but a limpy trickle. Baba, youth is youth, I believe now they have blue pills to hoist the droopy flag, na baba na, at this stage we have blood pressure, arthritis, diabetes and what not, they all come in a package. Baba, who wants to die in action? Na, baba, not me. Can you imagine sometimes I feel it's not there, then I panic, I can't even see it, this damn belly comes in the way but then as they say, seeing is believing, I put a hand mirror under my belly, just to make sure," clunked the dentures.

"Hand mirror?" Ganju was struck by a thunderbolt.

A week after that dinner, court was resumed.

"Now, before I give the judgment, I will allow a brief discussion on the medical report, which has been finally submitted to the court. Since there are no witnesses, I would like to ask a few questions to the plaintiff. Will the plaintiff take the stand?"

"Miss Lilly Khanum, are you still a virgin?" asked the judge as Lilly took the stand.

"No, Milord, not after the 14th October," purred Lilly.

"The medical report doesn't say that, I am afraid." The judge avoided looking at the plaintiff.

"Milord, my client is an evergreen virgin; she is blessed by Pir the Invisible. It may not show in the report but the fact that my client was sexually harassed and assaulted is very much evident," said the prosecutor.

"The medical report says she is a virgin and in the absence of four witnesses I don't see any point in your statement," said the judge.

"Milord, it's a miracle that she reverts to being a virgin. You may call it a freak of nature, but this is how it is. The National Geographic is already researching on this paranormal phenomenon," pleaded the prosecutor.

"I am afraid surgeons don't have any medical evidence on that, spirituality is not their forte, and let me inform you that I am here to dispense justice in the legal way, I am not here to be educated on metaphysics or the paranormal. I will only rely on medical proof," said the judge, without squiggling his ear.

"If you are still a virgin how can you say that the accused took your virginity?" the judge turned back to Lilly.

Lilly stood dumb in the dock.

"Did he enter you or not?" the judge was blunt.

No answer.

"Did he enter or not, *dakhool hoa ya na hoa*?" said the judge aloud.

There was enigmatic silence in the witness box. Ganju was impressed by the judge's display of legal precision. He was alert without his cotton pick.

The judge took a deep breath and went into a frenzy repeating his question in a see-saw rhythm; bouncing from his chair, he would say "dahool hoa" and in the same breath he would bounce back and say, "ya na hoa?" Everyone in the court was dumbfounded at the unusual performance by the judge, which went on until Lilly purred, "Hoa aur nahin hoa. No and yes Milord!"

"What?" The judge lost his rhythm, his neck deflated. He raised a cotton pick. With his hand slow on the ear, the judge spoke in a tired voice. He had spent his energy. "Are you suggesting that he couldn't perform? After watching the video I must admit that the Chief Minister is masha-allah well endowed."

The crowd gave Ganju a collective smile of appreciation.

"Milord," a smirk came over Lilly's face. It rolled into a smile and then flourished into the perennial laugh of the woman. "I don't have a hymen but an iron curtain," she said. "No one in this world can reach my secret veil. There's no man who's man enough to take my virginity. Is there anyone?" she looked around. A timid silence fell among the spectators.

"I want to be deflowered, Milord. Come unveil me! Do it, do it to me, Milord! I am dying to be a full woman." She leaped at the judge, but the prosecutor's timely intervention saved the situation and Lilly was back in the dock.

"Milord, my client is only explaining her unique biology. If your lordship will closely watch the tape, there are blood stains.

It's only that my client takes a bath and her hymen returns to its original position," said the prosecutor.

"What rubbish is this," the judge gave a furtive look to Ganju.

"Milord, it must be the Platonic illusion," added the defence.

"Yes, Milord, what you saw on the tape was an illusion," said Lilly.

"Illusion?"

"Yes Milord, just a big hoax, a bluff!"

"Bluff! You said, how can you say that?"

"Yes, Milord. The spots your Lordship has pointed are not the virginal blood."

"What is it then?"

"Hemorrhoids Milord!"

"Hemorrhoids?"

"Yes Milord, the defendant suffers from a bleeding arse," she said.

Ganju shifted in his seat as the nasty twitch in his bottom scissored through his spine.

"And what you think is the prized object of his malehood is actually an extension," continued Lilly, constantly curling her nose.

"Extension?" the judge jumped from his seat.

"Yes Milord, it's not what you think," she said in a voice vibrating with mockery.

"His thing is not as fulsome as it appears on screen," she giggled, "it's thin as a thread and big as a pea. All your lordship has seen in the tape is an extension."

The judge looked at Ganju, shocked and utterly betrayed.

"That thing is just a pinch of flesh Milord, just a pinch," she said in her Minglish.

Explosive silence.

The tiny word slipped from her lips, lobbed over the mahogany edge of the witness box, fell on the floor, bounced in the air, and touching the ceiling, it swirled back to crawl along Ganju's spine, reaching his softest parts.

Ganju died in his thighs.

Chapter 13

Hooves

After the trial, Ganju felt as if the whole world was staring at his navel, eyes spying on his genitals, as if he was being frisked at every step. At the office he would look into a file and remarks like "action taken" would throw him into a fit. At home, he would sit and brood for hours like a paranoid. He would switch on the TV and find the media discussing his private parts. Men and women in festive dresses aired chat shows, sports channels showed tennis and golf matches, announcing fault, three loves, five holes. News channels talked in codes, nuclear warfare, missiles, terrorists, global warming, ambush, retreat, surrender. Everyone conspired against him, soap operas, wrestling matches, cooking programs, weather reports, even ads for mobile phones. Music too had weird notes, cryptic and telepathic. At diplomatic dinners waiters connived; meatballs, cucumbers, sausages, chicken boties, chicken kebabs, shrimps, mutton slice.

With each new day Ganju felt an inch shorter.

A man's reputation lies in his pants and Lilly had pulled them down in public. She had exposed his power tower. Cut to size by the razor tongue of a prostitute, Ganju had fallen from his pedestal without a leg to stand on. Wobbling without an axis, he couldn't lift his head or keep his erect posture. He was the Greek hero whose penis had become his tragic flaw.

While he mourned his losses, a thin ray of evening light stole in through the curtains and sat on his eyelid like a pleasurable

fuzz. He lazily lifted his eyes and through the flurry of his eyelashes, saw a fresco emerging on the ceiling; half-men half-gods
floating around fulsome women. Goats with human faces,
men with torsos of horses, curly horns and organs of fetching
lengths, happily swinging. Young children lolling around huge
breasts of goddesses, reclining on idyllic clouds, a mandala of
limbs and flesh, a cosmic orgy sizzling with liquid embraces,
wild kisses and steaming copulation.

Struck by the vision, Ganju couldn't help shouting to a deity
higher than humans, "Oh Lord, look at these men and their
possessions. How could you bless them with such magnificent
manhoods and why from your bounty did you throw this curse
at me. What have I done to deserve this? Look at the stallions,
donkeys, porn stars, Casanovas, bulls, Tarzans, wrestlers, goril-
las, all muscled, all proud of their wistful thrusts. Is this your
holy plan of nature?"

In his desperation he knelt down, his forehead touching the
floor and his bottom facing the gods. "Oh Lord," he cried, "all my
life I've done it with the mirrors, now show me the way to avenge
my shameful defeat, give me a sign." A sharp pain zigzagged in
his rectum. It butted him out of the prayer. He lifted his head. The
ceiling was blank, only a few shadows curled around in frightening shapes. Horrified, he headed to the bathroom. Soothing his
rectum, he turned on the shower. Thin shoots of water fell on him
like splintered glass. Something happened at the time of his birth,
he thought under the shower. Doctors say, "Testosterone is the
substance that turns boys into boys. A surge in testosterone sets
in motion the formation of penis and the testes." Ganju's eyes slid
to his navel. "The testicles of a male develop in his abdomen and
descend to the pouch two months before his birth. But sometimes
the testicles are stuck in the abdomen."

"Stuck?" Ganju pressed his belly with his hands and tried to
knead down the imaginary testes he thought were still stuck in
his abdomen. Nothing moved. He dashed to the secret drawer
and took out the mirror. Once he placed the mirror at its usual
angle, the mirror dazzled back. His balls had happily rolled
down from his stomach to the pouch.

Before dinner, when Juma came to serve him drinks, Ganju didn't realize that he was sitting on the air tube the doctor had recommended for his hemorrhoids. He was still meditating the question that had stabbed him in the back; Lilly still a virgin, and he running a bleeding hole.

Ignoring Ganju's new throne, Juma lowered his eyes and poured a drink for his master.

Ganju was in no mood to confide in Juma about his ailment. It was like giving in to his own slave, offering his weakness to a blabber, becoming vulnerable to a low-class marasi, unveiling his behind to a compulsive ogler. His fear to be found out was too telling, even for a private confession, but before Juma could become unreasonably curious, Ganju took the risk.

"Juma, I haven't been well lately," he said shifting on his air seat.

"Allah may destroy our enemies, but what is it that troubles His Sarkarship?" said Juma giving a side-glance at the air tube that hugged Ganju's bottom like a swollen arm.

"Well, it's my morning stool, it's a bit tedious." Ganju moved cautiously on the seat.

"Sarkar, Bade Hakim sahib tells that morning stool is the first omen of the day, if you don't exorcise the monster, it's stinky all day," said Juma and moved to press Ganju's legs.

"I know, I know, I think I should go for an operation," Ganju said, extending one of his legs to Juma.

"Operation?" Juma abandoned the leg in horror and touched his ears. "Toba, toba," he said.

"Why, what's wrong with an operation? I believe it's a minor one," said Ganju.

"Never, Sarkar, never! Imagine a foreign hand messing up your private parts, Sarkar. They make you drowsy, strip you naked, cut, slash, mutilate and insult your body, Sarkar. Allah may forgive me, sometimes when you wake up from your dead sleep you find a limb missing, an organ misplaced and if nothing, an ugly scar, a gift for life. No, Sarkar, no, it's even forbidden in religion." He shook his head as if he was repenting.

"What should I do then, Juma?" Ganju asked.

Juma pressed Ganju's legs, as if they belonged to him; his master in his crisis had asked him for his help. Going faster on the leg-job, he announced, "Sarkar, our Bade Hakim sahib has the herbal treatment, nature to nature, not a scratch to the body. He can bring dead people back to life. To send home a reluctant stool for him is child's play. Once treated, it'll plop down like an obedient servant. It'll waltz through your passage which I tell you will be as sound as a fiddle. You could whistle from there if you want, Sarkar," he smiled.

To be naked in front of the doctor and show one's behind was no doubt a humiliating act. Doctors are scientific and scientific facts are never disputed. It was a matter of confidentiality. The Hakim, considering his position, would never open his mouth. He could be very well aware of the consequences. Ganju calculated smartly, but to be sure, he reacted negatively, "What rubbish are you talking, Juma?"

"Sarkar, Bade Hakim sahib is no ordinary man, they say his grandfather was so well endowed that when he was circumcised, it took full one week to dispose the foreskin."

"What?"

"Sarkar, he can make a woman pregnant even at this age."

"What age is he?"

"Sarkar, he looks fifty but he is hundred years old. No one knows, but his father lived for one thousand years," he said.

"How can one live for that many years, idiot?"

"Well, Sarkar, he had drunk the elixir of youth, even his son who is our Bade Hakim sahib got a few drops, therefore he's still so young."

"Juma, what has it to do with my stool," Ganju interrupted Juma with some vengeance.

"Sarkar, Bade Hakim sahib says if one part of the body is ill the other parts of the body weep in sympathy, like a single leaf of a tree, if it goes dry, the whole tree goes dry. All body parts are companions. It's not to heal just one ailing part but the whole," he said.

Ganju's mind jerked with some intuition. The philosophy was new to him but it had some logic to it. "Juma, I am talking about my piles, I am not interested in your Hakim's bullshit," he said while waiting for Juma to go on.

"Sarkar, that he can cure just like that," he snapped his fingers.

"Really?"

"Ji Sarkar."

Ganju enjoyed his own wickedness; he had discovered the cure for the weeping part of his body. In that moment, without volition, Ganju's pain took a U-turn. Ganju was surprised but without showing Juma that he had been given the sign, he leisurely extended both his legs to Juma and said, "Juma, we'll leave early morning for the village to see Bade Hakim sahib."

"As you wish, Sarkar," said Juma, keenly hugging both the legs.

It was a hot summer day when Ganju entered Noorpur village in his air-conditioned Pajero. Juma on the wheel drove faster than usual. Ganju discreetly pulled up the dark shades on his side of the window. The blinding glare hit his eyes. He could only see solarized images of buffaloes slushing in stagnant ponds and dogs with hanging-out tongues limping around in search of shade. Ganju's eyes scanned over the distant area of landlords, farmers' huts, and the slums of cobblers and ironsmiths.

"Where does he live," he asked impatiently.

"Who, Sarkar?"

"Bade Hakeem sahib, who else? Why are you speeding, we are not in a hurry, are we?"

"Sorry, Sarkar," Juma's foot relaxed on the accelerator.

"Does he live outside the village?"

"There, Sarkar, he has his baithak, it's a kind of in-house hospital," Juma said, pointing to a low cluster of mud houses beside a filthy stream that slithered like a snake alongside the slums.

"Isn't that next to the other village?"

"Ji Sarkar, it's a kind of border between our village and the Maliks."

"God damn the Maliks," Ganju made a foul face. "Where are you heading?" he asked abruptly as Juma took a sharp turn.

"To the Haveli, Sarkar."

"Haveli? What about the Hakim?" Ganju shouted.

"Sarkar, it's too early."

"Early for what?"

"To visit Bade Hakim sahib, Sarkar."

"Let me have a closer look, just drive around that area."

"As you wish, Sarkar." Juma turned the wheel. Ganju from the car window had an eyeful of kids shitting in open drains, donkeys carrying burdens, stray dogs yelping; a chaotic landscape of squalor and filth.

Juma drove back to the Haveli.

"Aren't we going to the Hakim?" Ganju asked, still looking out of the window.

"Well, Sarkar," said Juma looking at his watch, "it's four o'clock, the sun is glaring at us, people are on roads—"

"But it's only a visit," Ganju cut in, eagerly looking for the Hakim's baithak.

"Sarkar, rumours in our village spread like cholera."

"But Juma," he said shifting on his seat, "my need is urgent."

"Well Sarkar, have some patience." Juma slowed down the car. "Sarkar, forgive me but to be seen with a Hakim is like declaring oneself a leper. Imagine a chaste woman praying five times a day standing next to a pimp, what do you think people will say about her?"

Ganju was not amused by the analogy but it changed his mind.

"All right Juma, I'll suffer the pain but don't you be late after sundown," he said, dropping the shade on the window.

At the Haveli, Ganju quietly settled in the men's quarters and ordered Juma not to let anyone know about his visit.

"Do have some rest Sarkar, I'll be with you on time," Juma said after he made his bed for him and left walking backwards.

Ganju tried sleeping but images of the Hakim and the stories Juma had told kept him awake. He would open the shutters of his window and check the sun. After a few hours of torturous waiting, when the glare was doused into a dim yellow fuzz, there was a knock on the door.

"Who's it?" Ganju whispered to the door.

Juma coughed and entered carrying a bundle on his back.

"What's this?"

Juma untied the bundle. Out came balls of rags, dirty and smelly, half torn common wear. "Sarkar it's for you to disguise yourself," he said.

"Disguise? You think I am going for begging?"

"Toba, Sarkar," Juma touched his ears, "May Allah never show you bad times, but Sarkar no one should have even a whiff of your visit to the Hakim sahib. We can't stop mouths spreading dirty stories, and one thing more Sarkar, we should not go there by car."

"What?"

"We'll walk Sarkar!"

"Never! Me walking in those clothes? Take away this filth from my sight, I would rather have the operation," he fumed.

Vibes of distrust, anger and desire mingled in that silence.

Ganju stared at the clothes.

"Juma, do you know in old times kings would disguise themselves as ordinary people and find out the truth about their citizens," he paced while he talked. The thought of invisibility excited him, "I think it's good advice, I'll wear those clothes on my suit and take them off once we are there," he said.

"Good, Sarkar, I have already informed the Hakim, he's waiting for us."

Ganju quickly put on the clothes and looked at himself in the mirror. He couldn't recognize his own face. Kings in rags wandering among the humble folks, paraded in his mind's eye.

Once the sun disappeared, Ganju in a kammi dress wrapped over his suit and Juma hiding his face behind the fold of his chadder sneaked out of the Haveli. Ganju felt the ground under his feet uneven and rough. Sweating in a double wrapping, he braved his journey with the zest of a pilgrim. People carrying milk cans on bicycles, hauling buffalos, and taking fodder for their animals passed him. No one recognized, stopped or made way for him, instead some pushed him to get their way.

By the time they reached the narrow lanes, it was pitch dark. The path to the Hakim's place was checkered with ditches and puddles. Juma walked ahead with a torch showing the way to his master. Ganju followed him but once as he put his foot across a ditch he rammed into someone, and fell straight into the ditch. "Motherfucker, watch your step," Ganju heard a voice, "it's not your mother's courtyard." A drunk stood before him in the dark. Juma pointed the torch at the stranger. "Stuff it, behnchod! Are you trying to recognize your father?" The man kicked the torch, which fell into the ditch.

"Faggots," the man spat and left.

"Sarkar, it was one of the Maliks' men, good you didn't say anything," said a worried Juma groping for the torch.

In one of the darkest corners of a blind street, under a thatched roof stood a tall shadow with a garland. "Welcome, welcome," said the Hakim putting the garland around Juma, who immediately stepped back and coughed. The Hakim sensing his mistake pulled away the garland and put it around Ganju, who with a nod to the Hakim went inside the baithak. The Hakim nervously followed him. Juma stood outside, still in fear.

Inside the baithak, Ganju peeled off his dirty wrappings. The Hakim carefully dusted the only chair in the room and offered it to Ganju. Ganju in his suit sat stiffly on it. The Hakim rushed to the rickety table fan that drooped in fly shit, caught its stray neck and turned it in Ganju's direction. Breathing in the merciful breeze, Ganju looked around. Under the dim light of a tiny lamp sprawled a large divan with a slate hosting rows of small tin boxes and bottles with curious herbs. Some spooky shoots of incense burnt in a corner streaking the walls. On the floor, caked by thick soot, an old kettle was thinly balanced on a stove. It looked like a black turtle. The room bore the scent of rose water, smelling of a cemetery.

In that aromatic silence the Hakim, collecting all the humility in the world, touched Ganju's knees and said, "Sarkar, it's the luckiest day in my life. With your sarkarship, the whole universe is in my humble abode. The elephant has visited the ant's house, the Brahmin has blessed a shudra."

With the Hakim at his feet, a mortal welcoming a god, Ganju regained his composure.

"Sarkar, would you like to have some kehva, the green tea?" asked the Hakim timidly.

Ganju looked at the kettle. "No thank you, I am in a hurry," he replied curtly.

The Hakim coughed, and clearing his throat said, "Sarkar, please undress." As if reversing roles, the Hakim's voice had changed into that of some necromancer's. Ganju got upset, but the pain in his hole was too commanding to think about anything. One by one he took off his coat, his necktie, his diamond studs, his shirt, his tie pin, and then hesitantly, his pants. Standing in his shorts he looked at the Hakim, who by that time had anointed his middle finger with some unction. "You have to kneel, your face down and your posterior raised," the Hakim instructed.

Ganju did as asked. The Hakim pushed down Ganju's underwear and lifting the lamp by the other hand examined him in its light. Ganju with his clammy hands on the ground and his bottom uplifted could see the shadow of the Hakim with his finger hoisted in the dark like an arrow. "Keep still in that position," said the Hakim and in a flash darted the middle finger in Ganju's rectum. An exhilarating sensation ran through Ganju's spine. "There you are, free from the monstrous ailment," declared the Hakim. At that moment, the fan, as if with divine intent, shrugged off some fly shit, jerked its neck and with its faint breeze flipped aside the dhoti of the Hakim. Ganju was struck by the low-angle glimpse of the Hakim's knee-length penis rimed by the pale light of the lamp. He didn't wish to get up. Shrugging a bit more of fly shit, the fan spun, stealing away the vision.

"You can get up now." The Hakim put the lamp back and cleaned his finger with some solution. Ganju hurriedly dressed up.

"Well, that was quick," he said resuming his seat. The Hakim nodded and quietly washed his hands in a basin. In that gap of silence, perforated by the trickle of water, something came over Ganju. He said out without thinking, "What do you think, oh no, I mean do you think you could cure, oh no, not cure but let's say, can you with your rare knowledge, improve upon something like, well, let us say a limb of yours," he fumbled.

"Sarkar, unless the ailment is known, we don't know what to say," the Hakim replied coldly.

Ganju didn't like the impersonal tone of the Hakim. It just dawned upon him that he, the Chief Minister had displayed his bottom to a stranger in the middle of the night and had allowed him even to fiddle with it. How could he divulge his most guarded secret to an ordinary hakim? That charlatan could be well endowed only by some freak of nature. They have their tricks and props to put you in some delusion. How could anyone cure chronic hemorrhoids with the tip of one's finger, it was all a hoax. Suddenly he found himself the butt of a practical joke.

He turned to leave.

"Sarkar, do consult me for anything, I am your humble servant," the Hakim said, touching Ganju's knees.

Outside, Juma stood up for him with his torch in hand.

"Let's go," said Ganju.

"Is everything all right, Sarkar?"

"My foot," Ganju took large strides, Juma almost ran ahead with the torch. "How dare you bring me here, idiot! He's a bloody juggler, a roadside witch doctor."

"I am sorry, Sarkar," said Juma, the torch in his hand going berserk, flashing random patches of light on the uneven ground.

"I wear these silly clothes, get insulted by a drunkard, and spend my evening with a hakim who has little knowledge," fumed Ganju.

"Didn't he treat you, Sarkar?" said Juma jumping a ditch.

"How can this monkey treat me, it's all a waste of time. We'll leave for the city, soon," he said and jumped a ditch with more agility than Juma.

The next morning Ganju couldn't believe it, but when he sat on the toilet seat, he found himself a butter hole; a new man with a rectum as fresh as a coin from the mint. What a loss, how foolish of him not to trust the Hakim. We underestimate our own folk traditions, the wisdom of our elders, he thought.

Without operating on him, the wise man had nickeled his orifice. The constipated plop was no longer an ordeal but a smooth frictionless process to a decent satisfaction.

Midnight.

The Hakim in his baithak heard a knock. "I can't see anyone at this time, get off my door you lech," he cursed loudly.

"It's me, Ganju, your patient, Bade Hakim sahib," said Ganju meekly. He was dressed in kammi clothes which he had eagerly put on that night without wearing his suit underneath.

"Sarkar, Sarkar, do forgive me," the Hakim quickly opened the door and let Ganju in. "Are you all right, my Sarkar." He dusted the chair, twisted the fan towards Ganju, and sat on the floor, touching Ganju's knees.

"Oh no, please don't that," Ganju put his hands around Hakim's shoulders and gently lifted him up. "You are a noble man," he said. "Your place is not there on the floor but next to me." He smiled generously.

"No Sarkar, I can never do that," said the Hakim.

"Look I'll not be happy if you don't oblige me," said Ganju rising from his chair.

"Sarkar, please don't leave." The Hakim hesitantly sat on the divan with Ganju facing him on the chair.

"You indeed are a very gifted man, I've never felt so healthy in my life," said Ganju in a cheerful tone.

"Sarkar is very kind," said the Hakim gratefully.

"I think you deserve much more than this." He looked around the dingy baithak with a friendly frown. "You should build for yourself a new dava khana, a hospital," he said.

"No Sarkar, I am a simple man. I enjoy my anonymity," said the Hakim in a low voice.

"I admire your contentment, but do give it a thought," Ganju gave a promising nod to him.

"Would you like some kehva, Sarkar," asked the Hakim.

"Oh yes, of course," Ganju said with much warmth.

The Hakim got off his divan and started to pump the stove. After pumping hard, he lit it. Once the fire got stable, he slowly

poured water from a jug into the kettle. Ganju watched the
Hakim with guarded patience; the Hakim seemed to be performing some ritual. Now the Hakim took out two medium-size
bowls and carefully placed them near the stove. They looked like
monkey skulls. Suddenly the kettle rattled, some soot fell from
its corners. The Hakim rescued a glass jar from behind the tin
boxes and delicately coaxed out some grass. He put the grass into
the boiling water and after a few minutes poured the brew from
the kettle. He ceremonially offered one of the monkey skulls to
Ganju. Ganju held the bowl in his hands like a sacred relic. The
Hakim collected the folds of his dhoti and sat on the divan.

Ganju heard the first slurp, loud and lingering. He gratefully
smiled at the Hakim and took a sip. The hot brew suddenly lit
up his taste buds, sending an intoxicating thrill into his body.

"Sarkar, how do you find the kehva," inquired the Hakim.

"Amazing," said Ganju, taking a hearty sip.

There was something to that kehva; a few more sips and
Ganju was laughing with the Hakim like an old buddy.

"I must confess I took those stories about you with a pinch of
suspicion," said Ganju.

"Creative doubt is the beginning of all knowledge, Sarkar,"
the Hakim slurped pensively.

"I know you are a mine of wisdom, but tell me something.
Why is nature stingy to some and generous to others, I mean
why the unequal distribution of gifts?"

"Nature reveals its secrets to man through metaphors," the
Hakim stared into the cup. "There are clues for man, and not
seeing them is not nature's folly but human myopia."

"Oh but how?"

"If God is the creator, man is the co-creator, 'To shub afridi
chiragh afridam, You created night and I created the lamp, sifal
afridi ayagh afridam, You created the clay and I created the
cup,' says the poet." Prolonged lyrical slurp.

Ganju didn't understand Persian but he knew it had been the
court language of Mughal kings. "Could I have a refill?"

The Hakim poured him another cup.

"I hope you don't mind me telling you that I had a chance to peek at your malehood the other day," Ganju said.

"Sarkar, allow me to confess. I too saw yours." Bold slurp.

"Oh did you?" Short slurp.

"Yes I did." Intimidating slurp.

"Well?" Timid slurp.

"To be frank, Sarkar, great men must show solid evidence of their greatness, that's the rule, I am afraid you fall short of your stature."

"I guess you are right, but you'll appreciate that I am here to understand the metaphors of nature." A beseeching slurp.

"Only the Hakim Jalinoos had the nuskha, the secret of Tajul Kharoos, the crown rooster."

"But where is it?"

"We have no clue, we did kashf al qaboor, the ritual of opening the grave, but we never found the body of Jalinoos there." No slurp.

Eerie silence.

Ganju gulped at his drink. Before he could become alarmingly desperate, the Hakim went for another top up and taking a sly slurp said, "Sarkar, as I humbly told you, if we read nature's lips we could perform miracles."

"Teach me then, to read the lips of nature."

"Sarkar, you may find it difficult to practice."

"Oh no, I am all prepared. I'll do as you tell me, be my guide," said Ganju pressing the Hakim's hand.

"If you promise to spare my life, Sarkar, I could transfer the greatest secret of life to you," the Hakim clutched Ganju's hand.

"Please tell me, what is it?"

"Sarkar," he paused before he said, "It's an animal."

"What?"

"Sarkar, what I am talking about is eastern philosophy, something mystical. And it's not in the books. It is written on the hearts," asserted the Hakim.

"What is it, then?"

"A she-ass," the Hakim said pressing Ganju's hand.

"A she-ass?" Ganju pulled away his hand, "What about a she-ass?"

"Sarkar," the Hakim raised his eyebrows, "it's ancient wisdom. The Greeks performed on goats to produce satyrs, half human half goats. Mating with animals is the secret, it transforms their power to man."

"Unbelievable!" Ganju squirmed in his chair. "Hakim sahib, you can't be serious."

"Sarkar, nature has provided a remedy for all ailments, that's the promise." The Hakim said, resuming his seat next to Ganju, "Sarkar, a she-ass is cool in summer and hot in winter, it has good taseer, the healthy effect. Now what was the secret of the great Mughals," continued the Hakim. "How could they satisfy a harem filled with women? One bee pollinating thousands of flowers? Who do you think was behind their supernatural virility? Not a Hakim but a she-ass lounging in best climatic conditions with special food, and exotic perfumes. To practice on the unsatisfied she-ass made them aware of the satisfaction. It's only in pitch dark that we strain for light. It's like us mortals butting our heads against the unknown, knocking at the door to find out who's on the other side!"

A palpitating silence.

"Oh my God," said a mesmerized Ganju.

"You see, it's a metaphor; man lost in the unfathomable universe. The she-ass is the mother of all vulvas. *Tora na dani che raaz e kamal e sarmasti, bedil nasheeni kay alam tamaam kharmasti*," with much relish, the Hakim recited a Persian verse. Ganju looked at him, puzzled. The Hakim translated, "Oh my ignorant friend, you do not know the secret of the ultimate ecstasy. The world is nothing but the dance of a she-ass."

The cups were empty, the kettle overturned, the incense spent and the lamp dimmed in the light of the rising dawn.

Outside, alone in nature, wandering through vast fields under an open sky, Ganju jumped with joy and ran to the Haveli, singing, "*Tora na dani che raaz e kamal e sarmasti, bedil nasheeni khe alam tamaam kharmasti.*"

He was touched by the hooves.

Chapter 14

Kharmasti the Trotting Muse

Procuring a she-ass for purposes other than carrying load was not something normal. Bringing one to the house was to invite trouble; a she-ass was far from being considered a domestic pet. This species of animal was not regarded a pleasing sight even in a zoo. Noor Mohammad Ganju, the Chief Minister, asking for a creature common as an ass was like asking for the moon. Ganju, however, was not willing to give up his pursuit.

The next evening, when Juma stood before him, ready with ice bucket and bottle, "A stiff one," rippled an animated Ganju.

Expecting a dressing-down from his master for causing him displeasure the other day, Juma was surprised to find a gentle tone.

"Juma, did you know why I cancelled the trip?"

"I thought Sarkar was ... . not keeping well, not happy, I mean, with the treatment," Juma stuttered while handing over the drink to Ganju, carefully.

"No, no, let me correct you, Bade Hakim sahib didn't treat me. He healed me," Ganju said cheerfully, raising his glass to an absent Hakim.

"Oh Allah, I thank thee," Juma gasped between his teeth and took one of his master's leg to press.

"He's a true messiah," Ganju proclaimed.

"Of course, Sarkar," said Juma pacing up the pressing, "but if I dare ask, why was then Sarkar annoyed?"

"Well," Ganju started off with a feigned reluctance, "I had consulted him for something else too."

"And what was that, Sarkar?" Juma took the other leg.

"Look!" Ganju stretched out his right arm. Juma paused on the leg to focus on the arm. "Just hold this," Ganju handed his glass to Juma, and extending the other arm said, "Now look at the left one."

Juma looked up with open-mouthed curiosity.

"Can you see any difference between the two?"

"No, Sarkar, they both look fine to me," said Juma, his eyes fixed on the arms.

"Stupid!" Ganju dropped his arms. "Go and get another drink for me."

"Won't you finish this one, Sarkar?"

"No, Juma, you can finish it," came the gentle tone again.

"Me, Sarkar?"

"Yes, drink it," ordered Ganju.

"Well, Sarkar, Bade Hakim sahib tells, it's a blessing to drink the leftover from one's master." He drank it up.

"Now, Juma, if you see it from this angle," said Ganju raising up his arms again, suggesting an odd angle. "You'll find my right arm shorter than the left one."

Juma's head went back and forth to find the right angle. In utter confusion he blurted, "You are absolutely right, Sarkar."

"Good, you are seeing now," said Ganju and took the new glass. "Well, Juma, now you'll want to know what made me furious about the Hakim."

"Ji, Sarkar," mumbled a nervous Juma.

"Well, when I asked him how to enlarge my right arm, he suggested . . . " Ganju fumbled, "well, never mind, I won't mention it, but after meeting him the very next morning when sitting on the pot I found myself completely cured. And it dawned upon me that if he could be right about one thing he must be right about the other one too."

"And what was the other thing, Sarkar?"

"A she-ass!"

"What?" Juma clutched at Ganju's leg.

"Yes, the Bade Hakim sahib advised me to exercise my wrist . . . " he took a pause, "well, you know, in that thing of a she-ass," explained Ganju hesitantly.

"Oh, khoti tuppen," shouted Juma with sudden joy.

"What?"

"Sarkar, it's an exercise they do to enlarge their members."

"What nonsense are you talking about?" Ganju was shocked to find that his metaphor had not worked.

"Sarkar, you'll be surprised, Allama keeps his she-ass in the backyard, everyone thinks he carries books on it, but that's an outside tag. It's ancient practice, Sarkar, like young lads hang on to the branches of the trees to get taller, and Sarkar—"

"Idiot, it's my wrist I am talking about."

"I know, Sarkar," conceded Juma, "but it's a cover to hide one's secret. Like Allama uses it for books, they call it a metaphor, Sarkar."

"Metaphor?" Ganju said grudgingly, "Don't you talk rubbish, just come to the point, tell me where can I find this springboard?"

"What Sarkar?"

"I mean a she-ass, for my wrist."

"Oh Sarkar, that's no problem it's right there in the local mela."

"You mean the open fair?"

"Yes, Sarkar, the animal is kept secretly in a tent for men to practice on it, only for a few rupees."

"Oh, I see, but how would I go there?"

"Sarkar, like you went to the Hakim, under disguise," replied Juma, going for the other leg.

The next evening, Ganju and Juma sneaked out of the Haveli and reached the mela which by that time was drawing to a close. Many people had left and the rest were doing their last-minute shopping. Away from the main stalls, Juma pointed to a tent sagging among distant trees. A young lad came out from the tent laughing, other boys made some lewd gestures at him and they left, joking with each other. Finding the tent free from any more customers, Juma said, "Sarkar, go ahead, it's time for your exercise."

Passing by the flying dwarf and the cobra woman of the

wayside entertainments, Ganju edged his way to the tent. There it stood, the promise of his revenge on all the women in the world. Walking towards it, he could prophesize the deflowering of the stubborn virgin, Lilly Khanum, and could hear her cries in throes of multiple orgasms.

He entered the tent.

A sudden darkness attacked his senses. Havocked by the stench of manure and urine, he staggered back and watched her, wide-eyed. Tied to the ground, she stood motionless. A small rickety stool lay behind for the customers to mount her easily. Rose strings fell over her waist and a small bell swayed around her neck. Unaware of her new lover, she languidly swung her tail. Ganju's lips murmured the Persian verse, "*Tora na dani che raaz e kamal e sarmasti, bedil nasheeni khe alam tamaam kharmasti.*" Kicking off the stool, he jumped into the labyrinth of that erotic horror. Floating in a pitiless swamp, the lack of hold made him wobble into futility but then he felt as if his penis was being inflated. With each thrust the bell announced his victory, faster and faster, making music of the exotic copulation between human and beast. Somewhere in that, he heard himself braying.

A few days and the mela was over and the she-ass gone. Ganju didn't change his clothes for days. He didn't want to take off that smell from his skin.

At night when Juma visited him to press his legs, he said, "Juma, a head of state is visiting the country," his voice soaked in anxiety.

"How tall is he, Sarkar," asked a worried Juma.

"Quite tall, and that's making me nervous, and as you know, the mela is already over."

"Why, Sarkar, didn't it improve?" Juma gave a sneaky look at Ganju's wrist.

"Yes," Ganju replied, stretching out his arm, "but not enough to shake hands with the president of a superpower."

"Well, Sarkar," Juma became alert, "the Chief Minister's office with its open courts could move from village to village, following the mela, and Sarkar can have both political and personal gain; mass-contact and his arm growth."

"No, Juma, I can't have all those masses at hand while I am doing my arm lengths. And I can't deliver speeches with a short arm, can I? Oh Juma, I am a kotah dast, a short-handed man who can't reach the roof of his destiny, try to understand, I am a lonely hand," choked Ganju.

"How about doing some renovation of the great Ganju House on this occasion," Juma said, after giving the matter some thought.

"Are you out of your mind, idiot, what has it got to do with my wrist?"

"Sarkar, please try to understand, once the renovation starts there will be plenty of she-asses to carry the bricks around the house and there you can choose the one you like. Sarkar, by doing this, we can have both the blessings of people and our own she-ass. A reward in Heaven and reward on earth." Juma smiled.

"But it's looking, not touching, isn't it?" Ganju asked cautiously.

"No Sarkar, we can steal the one you like."

"No, that's not nice, stealing is immoral."

"Sarkar, we can pay the contractor for the missing one, double the price."

"Well, that makes sense. But where do we keep her?"

"Sarkar, in the basement of the Ganju House, where else? No one lives in the Ganju House except a few servants. Sarkar can easily practice there day and night. And if Sarkar wants an out-door training, we could clear the back yard and build a garden with a little hut for the animal."

"I think you are right, but we should be doing it fast." Suddenly he became a man in hurry. "This head of state is no ordinary man, he's the president of a very powerful country and I don't wish to give him any wrong ideas. The wrist has to grow to the occasion," he said.

When Ganju announced his decision to renovate the Ganju House, his intentions were hailed by the devotees. His wife found no objection against shifting him to the Ganju House for a noble cause. Ganju had already arranged for himself the upper bedroom with large balconies. It assured him a smart view of the daily ass walk.

The renovation started and in came a train of donkeys, their necks bent with weight. All day Ganju would sit by the window and gaze at the animals, sorting out females to spot a substitute for his lost beloved from the tent. Among males, some were regular flashers with their one o' clocks. They were beaten mercilessly by the contractor for obscenity. Once the contractor was out of sight, they would again be up with their tricks. Ganju noticed among them, a fierce-looking ass, rather bigger than the others. Ganju came to know through Juma that he was known as Laado. Finally one young she-ass of a stone-grey complexion and most sought after by the one o'clocks, was chosen. On the last day of the renovation, as the evening approached, Juma lured the filly with the choicest of grass and whisked her away into the basement.

"She was the best, Sarkar, the only one," said the contractor shedding buckets of tears at his loss. "And Sarkar, to tell you the truth, she was Laado's heart-throb, barely two years old. Now Laado will not work anymore, he'll either die or run away. May God punish the thieves."

Jaana, as she was lovingly named by Ganju, stood tied and bewildered in the basement of Ganju house. Within the next day, all servants except the ageing maid were either transferred or sent on vacation, and Ganju disappeared inside his hideout for a long honeymoon.

No more tents, smelly clothes, no dung and dirt but silky tail bags for her daily plops, cushioned rugs to trot upon and a large bed for her to rest. No more fighting pillows, no more groping through heaps of drapery, no more seeking out for his wife in the folds of darkness. Nature was bare and without moral pretensions. In Jaana, Ganju had found his soulmate. She quite willingly forgot the good old Laado.

Now for hours, Ganju would bathe her in rose water, spend quality time putting kajal in her large eyes, apply henna to her shoeless hooves, and comb her tail with gripping dedication. She moved in the room generously displaying her charms. With expensive cosmetics, herbal shampoos and bubble baths, she had been transformed into a glamorous puss. Ganju would talk to her and she would respond by swaying her neck or by teasing his bottom with the soft whip of her tail. He would kiss her and she would flap her ears around his over-shaved face. He would touch her sloping waist and like a ballerina, she would raise one of her hind legs to provide an eyeful of her inner delights to him.

Ganju's dream of lengthening his penis was now only a tail away. He would enter her and his thing would shoot up to the height of the one o'clocks. He would desperately wait for the weekends when he could be back in his village and metamorphose the five days' human Chief Minister into a full-length ass.

It was one of those milk and honey days when Ganju got possessed by the Muse. He saw a vision on an early summer night. Moonlight flowed through the little window in the basement and Jaana after her bath stood fresh in the mystery of the dim light. Tiny droplets of water had made a starry halo around her. Ganju felt a curious turn inside his mind. Chords of her tail riffed his soul, the scale of her ears raised his imagination, and the sweep of her waistline stirred in him a lilting cadence. To his amazement, the manure and the rhythmic hips rolled into a poem. He could no more talk to Jaana in prose. Out in the garden she would graze and he would watch the poems in her curves. Inside the basement, she would move and he would burst into a gush of hot couplets.

Soon the word went out and the discovery of Ganju's hidden talent was made public. He was promptly welcomed by the National Academy of Letters to recite at a mushaira. Overnight, he became a sought-after poet. Editors of literary magazines sat at his door like dogs waiting for a bone of verse to be thrown at them. Sycophants hoisted him on the pole of immortality. His verses touched jilted lovers, aging critics, doe-eyed rural women wandering in the Mughal Bano bazaar waiting for urban princes. Women deprived of love, bored housewives, retired bureaucrats, half-literate scholars, travelling salesmen, rickshaw drivers, dancing women and impotent men all of them found in his poetry eternal solace.

His maiden collection, *Bahana-e-Jaana*, All For the Pretext of

Love, hit the stalls and within weeks thousands of copies had flown from the shelves.

No one in his family had the gift of writing a simple letter. They say a poet is born out of a wounded heart. Only crushed souls can make the poetry of love, and yes, there is always a woman behind a great man.

"Who is the dark lady of his sonnets?" Critics and literary sleuths failed to track down the mystery woman. On the political front, the Trio was equally puzzled; it was not a favourable sign for a politician to turn into a poet. They couldn't believe a Caliban assuming the elegance of Ariel, or an ill-shaped crow strutting with the grace of a peacock. They suspected some deep-seated despair due to the Lilly trial, but Kashif, who had a nose wider than others had, was not convinced. He had smelt a rat.

At the end of the year, The National Academy of Letters announced its highest award for Ganju. He was given the title of Khuda-e-Sukhan, the god of poetry. The ceremony took place in the spacious lawns of the Academy. Ganju was seated on centre stage with the literati of the country. He was presented with a brocade turban. Amidst thundering applause and showers of petals, Ganju emerged in a godly turban and a three-piece suit. He thanked his well-wishers and started to recite his poetry to a mesmerized audience. When he reached the most popular verse, "Jaana Jaana," his voice was drowned by a rude braying. People ran for the doors in panic. A startled Ganjo saw Laado mercilessly tearing down the shamyanas and stepping on people. Fuming at the mouth, he galloped to the stage with his shockingly well-struck one o'clock. Kicking at the cushy chairs, toppling tables, and smashing flowerpots, Laado charged towards the poet. Ganju's mike flew into the air like a hand grenade, his brocade turban fell and rolled down the stage like a guillotined head. Guards jumped on the stage and baton-charged the beast, but ignoring the barrage of batons Laado attacked Ganju from behind. Finally the Chief of Police ordered his men to open fire. Laado fell like a villain in the movies. What was witnessed as an untoward incident was actually a spectacle of martyrdom.

A few weeks later the scandal had died down and Ganju was

back. He had no time for political controversies, he was much too happy enjoying his honeymoon with Jaana. But then, fate had something else in its sleeve: a divine messenger and poetic justice.

On a long weekend after two blissful nights with his Jaana, Ganju felt an unbearable urge to write. While she snorted on the bed, he took his beyaz, the book of verse, and went up to the balcony bursting with inspiration. As he dipped the nib in the ink, he saw a pigeon sitting on the balcony. He forgot to write. There were birds in the garden but he had never seen any like this one before. Blown over by its exquisite beauty, he became still, fearing that if he moved, he would scare away the heavenly visitor. The pigeon swung its wings and perched upon the middle of the blank paper. Ganju was taken aback by its boldness. It cooed softly and with a quick dropping, embossed the white paper. Ganju couldn't believe his eyes when he saw a pink envelope dangling around its little foot. Was it a vision or a dream? He untied the ribbon, opened the envelope, and removed the paper inside, which revealed a poem calligraphed by some gifted hand.

What passion? Ganju became absorbed in the letter and before he could lift his eyes from those words, the pigeon was gone.

For days, Ganju floated in the air of that scented letter. He had been receiving a huge number of fan mail, but this was a page from the romance legends. How could he reach his invisible admirer? There was no name or address on it. Every evening he would sit by the balcony and wait, but there was no sign of the postman bird. After several rounds of the vacant balcony he discarded the pigeon as a figment of his imagination.

It was weeks later at the launching ceremony of another edition of his book that, amidst the flashes of cameras while he signed his book, he heard a scream. Ganju saw the pigeon fluttering its wings nearby. Hurriedly moving aside, he wrote a love note and grabbing the bird he tied the paper to its foot and let it fly through the window.

"Even birds are his fans," remarked the dumbstruck crowd.

That day onwards, the bird followed him everywhere; it flew in from the windows, sailed down in his lawn, appeared inside his car and sometimes visited him in the privacy of his toilet. A torrent of passionate letters passed between the two lovers through this messenger.

"I am desperate to see you," would be the ending line of his letters now. The image of the invisible lover haunted him day and night. Finally, the mysterious lover wrote, "No one knows where I live except our messenger, the pigeon. It will guide you to me."

It was Thursday night. With Juma in the driving seat, Ganju was on his way to Zahid's house for a rendezvous with the spirits. He had not attended those soul sessions for some time now. The sky was unusually dark. The wind was drunk on the monsoon and the clouds were laden with rain. Roads were deserted.

"Stop, stop!" shouted Ganju as he saw a white comet flying across the sky. Juma hit the brakes. The comet came gliding down and crashed against the windshield. Ganju rushed out of the car. To his surprise, the thing flew back into the dark like a moving star. "Get out of the car," said Ganju to Juma, "get a taxi and go home." Ganju got into the car and followed the bird. Flying ahead like a guiding pilot the pigeon took him through strange routes. It went on until they reached an obscure wayside shrine built upon a mound. In a dark corner, he saw the pigeon perched on the shoulder of a woman who was shrouded in many-layered veils.

"Is that you," he stopped and whispered.

The layers shivered into a gentle nod.

"Oh, my love, so it's you!" he said. The pigeon dove from her shoulder and strutted on the ground. The woman walked behind him. A spellbound Ganju followed them. The pigeon skated down a slope to an antique door at the foot of a small hill. It knocked on the door with its beak. The door opened. The woman went inside and Ganju followed her to a cavelike room with modern settings. A giant bed lay in the center. She sat there while the pigeon perched on a statue of Venus that stood at the door.

"Do you live here?" Ganju asked.

She didn't answer.

"Can't I see you?"

No answer.

"Why don't you say something?"

Silence.

"*Zara niqaab uttaoo bara andara hey*, please lift your veil, there's too much darkness here," he recited a verse.

Layers of the veil moved. She took a piece of paper and wrote a verse on it "*Parday mein rehnay do, parda na uttaoo, parda jo utth gia to raaz khul jayai ga*. Don't lift the veil or the mystery will evaporate."

"I beseech you, show thyself to me," he pleaded.

"Are you sure you wish to see me?" Her hands fluttered on the paper.

"Yes, yes, I am dying to see you."

"Close your eyes then," she scribbled in haste.

Like a child, Ganju shut his eyes. Suddenly he felt her hand on his hand. He shuddered with excitement. The hand gently led him inside the heap of layers.

"Is that you?" Ganju jumped in horror. He lunged at her burqa and ripped it apart, unmasking a face he knew too well, Lilly Khanum.

"How dare you come here? You slut. I'll murder you," he roared.

"Don't leave me, please." She limped down and hung onto his legs. "Forgive me, please, I know I made you suffer. So much so that you had to become a poet. I can feel it in your poetry, pangs of separation, oh that yearning. It's all about a faithless lover, and that's me," she said, all in tears.

"No it's not you." He tried stepping out of the noose of her arms.

"Who else could be the center of your words but me? I am your muse!"

"Well, it's someone, not human like you," said Ganju looking away.

"What?"

"Yes, it's Jaana. A she-ass tied in my basement."

"A she-ass?"

"Yes, she's pure nature, without human follies, and of course she can never betray me," said Ganju with a heavy heart.

"Oh, but I never betrayed you."

"Liar!" He growled, dragging along the half-naked Lilly.

"Listen," she tightened her grip on his stiffened calves, "Whatever you heard in the court was not your Lilly but your opponents speaking through her," she said. "They kidnapped me and threatened to kill me. I didn't care, but when they told me about the assassination plan I couldn't resist."

"Assassination?"

"Yes, they wanted to assassinate you. I appeared in the court only on their assurance that they would spare your life. Oh, can't you see, your Lilly never wanted you to die." She moaned.

Ganju stood still, weak in the knees.

"I prayed day and night for your safety," she moved up from his calves and nuzzled against his groin, "One day while I was telling my story to the grave in a shrine, I saw a devotee of the great Pir," she said looking at the pigeon. "I saw tears in its tiny eyes. It had overheard my plight. I could feel that it was no common bird but someone else in the guise of a pigeon."

"What? You mean that's not a pigeon?" Ganju sputtered, looking at the bird.

"No, it's Pir the Invisible, no one has ever seen him, he only exists in the forms of birds and plants."

"What nonsense? Pir in a bird?" Pulling away in anger, Ganju forced himself out of her arms.

"All right, don't believe me. Don't!" Lilly sprang up in fury. "It's better I disappear from your life and from this world," she said taking out a pistol from her bag and pointing it to her now fully exposed bosom. The pigeon hovered between the bosom and the pistol anxiously.

Watching the holy bird defending Lilly, Ganju was moved. "Please don't do that, I beg of you," he said.

The pigeon cooed slyly, "Pir the Invisible sends you the blessed curse."

Ganju in his awe felt the presence of the Pir. The blessed curse? Strange were the ways of God. He shed all his doubts and embraced Lilly with a clean heart.

"Forgive me my love, I misunderstood you," he cried.

Lilly flung the rags of her veil and throwing her legs up yelled, "Come give it to me, hurry, I can't wait. Come! Come! Give it to me!" Ganju turned her over and she, on her knees, thrust her behind towards him. Ganju sniffed around her bottom and, braying ferociously mounted her.

"Oh yes, I am your she-ass, your Jaana, your muse, take me, deflower me, show me the blood," she moaned hysterically.

Shove! Shove! Ganju was transformed into a one o' clock.

"I've been raped!"

Shove!

"Molested!"

Shove!

"Assaulted!"

Shove!

"Abused!"

Shove! Shove!

"But I am still a virgin!"

A sudden halt.

"Touch your Lilly's virginal secret, the twilight veil. I've kept it only for you. Come on, give it to me," she begged.

"Yes, yes," Ganju puffed enthusiastically and fell on her still braying.

"I want to see the blood! I want to see the blood," Lilly pestered rolling over on the bed.

What? Ganju shrank in fear. There was no sign of blood. In his ecstasy he had forgotten that he no longer suffered from hemorrhoids.

Lilly pouted her lips and purred, "Darling, don't be disheartened." She caressed his deflated one o'clock which by now was diminished into a harmless zero. "I love you and only you," she slurred. "When I was in prison, men sent pictures of their malehoods for me to choose. Look at these tempting offerings." She spread a collage of photos in front of him. "Your Lilly rejected them all, because," her hand cuddled his thing, "it's small but it's mine," she said. Ganju sized up the humongous hulks with envious rage. "Bitch!" He slapped her. Lilly curled her nose. Ganju kicked off the portfolios and left the room.

Chapter 15

Naked in a Hammam

"Who killed Jaana?" The question hovered above Ganju like a rapacious kite.

The Hakim had diagnosed the sad incident as death by poison. "A vengeful assault, not by a man but by a woman," he had said. Seeking forgiveness of Allah, he had touched his ears and quoted a Persian proverb, "*Rask e zenaan, al-amaan*! No one escapes the fury of a woman."

Lilly's mocking face flashed before Ganju.

"Why?" He turned in his black robe, a symbolic coffin he had started to wear under his clothes. His grief was much too personal to be shared. Even Juma Khan, the only sympathizer at the secret burial, had not been able to fathom the extent of his feelings. He had kept measuring his right arm by stealing glances at him while he prayed for the departed soul.

"Why would she ever commit such an inhuman act, killing an innocent animal? Was it a fit of jealousy, a crime passionel?" Ganju groaned in delirious mourning.

"I'm your muse, your muse!" Night after night, the voice would choke him to suffocation. "Bitch!" How could she ever be his muse? Wasn't she the one who had defiled his reputation in a male-dominated society? Immortality, yes, that's what she could be jealous of; Jaana's immortality. People sell their souls, conspire, murder or even die for it. Tormented by wild thoughts, Ganju would bray in his dreams, run to the basement, and sniff at Jaana's hovering smell. During those hallucinated trips, his olfactory senses had become alarmingly sharp; he could even smell a pleasant or a foul thought brewing inside someone else's brain.

Ganju would have tossed forever in his black robe with his hands flailing to reach the throat of Lilly Khanum, but on a late afternoon, he received a phone call. "You have been marked absent for the past one month, naughty boy," the General boomed on the line. Ganju had not realized that it was Thursday afternoon. He pulled himself up and honed his voice from a dirge to a chirpy, "Of course, I know."

"If you don't turn up tonight, we'll take action."

Sniffing in advance a nasty thought, Ganju braved an unruffled, "sir I'll definitely be there," and calmly put the phone down.

On a cold winter evening, donned in a bright pink suit upon his mourning skin-hug, Ganju sat in the car. "Let's go to Zahid Sahib," he said to Juma.

On the door he was welcomed by the maid, who led him down to the basement. "Welcome! Welcome!" they greeted him warmly as he walked in with a firm smile and a sore heart. Shaking hands, he withstood the juxtaposition of pain and pleasure with dignity. They were all unusually pleasant to him. "A drink for you, yes? I know, whisky with water, and two cubes of ice, right?" said Zahid.

"Thanks!" said Ganju and lit a cigar.

It started as a slow evening; they listened to music, played bridge, drank the bar dry and savored their dinner. It was during the nightcaps that the General spoke.

"Gentlemen, our fate is linked with our malehood and what I mean by malehood is frankly, the hood of the male." Polite laughter in the audience. "And that hood," continued the General, addressing the three people in the basement as though addressing a battalion, "is ultimately our umbilical cord to power. We men, draw our identity and energy from this piston of pleasure called the penis."

Ganju was lost in memories of his honeymoon with Jaana.

"Allow me to declare that out there it's a war of the genitals. In this warfare the untrained soldiers suffer the anxiety of a combat. They long to blow up those intimidating retreats, but alas they fall. The helplessness provokes a rage born out of the chill of defeat. That chill runs down their spines. They collapse in surrender."

Muffled laughter.

The General stepped up to the bar and took a refill of red wine.

"Gentlemen!" he announced, "We must wake up to the disturbing reports of wives knifing their husbands in their groins. This is no small matter, we can't just sit around and do nothing. Mind you, this is the direct result of the movement called women's liberation. I must warn you that these dick-choppers are right in your bedrooms, sleeping with you. Brothers, it's a war on the male, to disarm and de-weaponize him." He paused. "Talking of feminism," he added, "you'll hopefully agree that in all fairness poetry stinks of femininity."

Ganju was kicked out of his thoughts. He nervously puffed at his cigar.

"Poetry creates an effeminate yearning by some moonstruck lunatic separated from an imaginary beloved. It's nothing but verbal masturbation." He smirked at Ganju who worked hard to keep his composure.

"Now gentlemen, imagine if a leader of our country turns into a poet, what will happen to that nation? Hats off to Plato, who banished those insane creatures from his utopia," he fumed.

Ganju tried getting up from the sofa, but a wall of eyeballs closed in on him. He crouched back.

"Wajid Ali Shah, the dancing king of India, lost his land to the white man." The General's nostrils flared. "Remember the last Mughal emperor? He attended more mushairas than his court meetings, some girly eunuch of a king. They all were pussies wrapped in the velvet of poetry, spineless ninnies who brought about the fall of an empire. Gentlemen, what they lacked was the phallic image." The General glared at Ganju. Other eyeballs bulged at him. "I hope we are not witnessing a replay of history today!" The General chuckled, maliciously. Ganju took a long puff, spreading a cloud of smoke. To avoid any hint of sorrow, he had shaved and was wearing a festive necktie. The necktie fluttered.

"I don't mean any harm to our poet laureate here," said the General casting a severe glance at Ganju, "but gentlemen, let me say that at the end of the day, poetry is a metaphorical castration of the male."

"Here, here!" Jumped the eyeballs.

Among thundering laughter and jeering faces, Ganju leapt up from his sofa and with a violent jerk tore his shirt. "Look at me," he shouted, flashing the black coffin that had become his second skin, "I am a living corpse and there you make fun of my sorrow."

Everyone fell silent.

The General coughed, discreetly breathing in the humid silence. "Of course, we all know the sad denouement to that revenge tragedy," he said in a mournful voice.

Ganju stared at the General. "Was it you—sir?" he asked timidly.

The General shook his head, "No."

"Then who?" Ganju glared at the others. They lowered their eyes.

They are all murderers, driven by greed. Political agenda doesn't have a human heart, why must it be so inhumane? Why such cruelty to animals?

"Who killed my Jaana?" Ganju howled.

"You would know better." The General buttoned up Ganju.

Ganju stood still, simmering like a volcano. "Oh God," he quaked, "the Hakim was right, it's that jealous monster! She destroyed my muse, the fountain of my poetry. Bitch! Bitch!" he ranted.

"Hold on my friend, hold on!" said the General softly. Ganju became quiet. "Now think! Why her?"

"Jealousy!" Ganju cried. "That slut couldn't bear to see my

Jaana, her gait, her beauty, her exotica." Ganju ripped the remains of his shirt and wailed in his skin hug, "Jaana, Jaana!" He hit the walls.

The General took hold of the hysterical Ganju and held him in his arms. "Calm down my friend, just calm down!" He whispered softly and made him sit on the chair next to him.

"Look," the General addressed the others, "this is what they do to us men, make tragic clowns out of us. Who can believe that the Chief Minister of this country and a man from the nobility is mourning not for any human being but for a she-ass." He paused, took a glassful of punch from the bar counter. "Frankly speaking what he needs is an antitetanus shot," he said pouring the drink into Ganju's mouth. "He suffers from bestiality!"

Half-hearted laughs.

"But was it the loss of Jaana or his separation from Lilly that turned him into a poet? The question arises as how could a she-ass make him write poetry? Do we live in an age where birds and animals talk? No. Gentlemen, it was not Jaana but his unconscious hankering for Lilly that poured out in his verse. It was a libidinous release. Jaana was merely a bahana, an excuse, an alternative, a sublimation of the repressed passions. After all what is poetry but the wish-fulfillment of a destitute mind. Once Lilly, his true love, reappeared in his life he forgot to write. I, therefore, would say that Jaana was nothing but a poetic alibi, a metaphorization of his love for Lilly."

All heads nodded in appreciative compliance.

What a blunder! Ganju suddenly woke up to the love of Lilly, her image fuzzed his brain. It was his own Lilly that he loved and not Jaana, who to be honest, was only there to grow his penis, and that too, if he had listened to his conscience, was for no one else but Lilly. Clearly he was a victim of misunderstood love. "Oh my love, how can I ever wash my sins? Forgive me, forgive your slave, Lilly, Lilly!" Ganju stumbled to the door with his eyes swamped in tears.

"Wait!" said the General pointing his finger to him. "I feel sorry for you because now you can never reach her."

Ganju stumbled back.

"Lilly Khanum has left acting," said the General.

"But where is she?" Ganju asked in desperation.

"Right after her rejection by you, she abandoned the world and became a hermit. You'll find her at the shrine of Pir the Invisible. She sits there under a veil. Her only companion is a pigeon."

"Oh, the holy bird?" Ganju almost fainted.

"My dear, why don't you sit and listen to some reason. The clue to this murder mystery is not easy," said the General and conducted Ganju back to the chair.

"Now gentlemen," the General resumed his air of high seriousness, "we have to trace the motive behind the killing of Jaana. We as rational human beings can't be satisfied with the subjective notion of our friend here. Now what could be the primary motive? Can you guess?"

They all looked at each other and then to the General.

"Well, gentlemen, Jaana, the prettiest filly among the lot, was not the prized object for our friend here but also for Laado."

"What?" Ganju sat up in his chair. His olfactory gift warned him of a queer smell.

"Yes!" said the General patting Ganju on the shoulder, "It's not that you chose a beast for a lover but so did Lilly. She had chosen a full-length mule instead of a human. Lilly, my friend, was not in love with you but with Laado," topped off the General.

Ganju's nostrils fluttered, recalling a smell he had savored while he had mounted Lilly. His stomach churned, he rushed to the bar. From the mirror in front, Laado stood in the shape of a ghost nuzzling against him.

The ghost of Laado sneered at Ganju contemptuously. Wasn't it he who tore Jaana apart from her lover? Who got her lover killed in public? Was it love or lust? Was he a hero or a villain? The mirror had gone blurry with Laado's heavy breathing on the other side.

"Gentlemen, don't forget, Lilly needed something more than a human to satisfy her," said the General with a triumphant smile. "Come, sit here," he waved to Ganju, "get rid of your black robe, you don't look good in mourning." He handed Ganju's jacket to him. Ganju reluctantly took the jacket and sat still without a word.

"It's all over, we are happy for our friend here. He is back to normal. However, the moral of the story has a solid message for all of us. We should never forget that it's the tool of power which has always been a bone of contention between lovers. Now the unyielding question remains, how to meet this challenge? The answer is straight. The stick of power, always at attention." The General clicked his heels. "Gentlemen in this case, the tail wags the dog. It's man's ascent and decline." He paraded happily. "All men in power in the past took extra care to assure their phallic integrity."

A little later, near early dawn when the world is innocent like a newborn and true spirits descend to the mortals. The General, knocking down the remains of the red wine, resumed with refreshed vigor, "After all, what's the purpose of these Thursday meetings? We can't simply go on talking to dead spirits. We have to attend to live issues, share our knowledge and work towards higher ideals. Now why feminists are making such a racket about science being a man's perspective, because with science and technology, men have gone one step further. Allow me to demonstrate an amazing specimen of scientific empiricism, a state-of-the-art technology." The General beeped his mobile, and a young captain marched in with a velvet-backed box. He saluted and offered the box to the General. The General took the box and saluted back.

"Now, gentlemen," said the General, "this is the workmanship of a Frenchman." He put the box on a side table and coaxed out of it a glass cylinder with a rubber tube dangling out if it, to which was attached a pistol. "This, actually, is not a real pistol," he explained, "but a design effect, it's in fact a pump," he pressed the trigger happily. "Now before I give a demonstration, I wish to say that to be erect is to be assured of your gender, your success over the female, and female, mind you, is the other half of the universe. Remember, it's 'they' and 'us!'"

The General unbelted himself.

They all shifted on their seats nervously.

The General took out a shriveled penis.

"You can see that a deflated penis is an apology, a curse, and it can't be erect if there is not enough blood rushing to this inflatable tube. And this machine," he said with admiration, "does the trick, so whenever you are in a good mood, you take out this magic cylinder from your personal cupboard where all your oils, ticklers, and other props are ready for you. Then you anoint your weapon with a little oil. It makes a smooth uprising." He applied some unction into the cylinder and placed the pump on that limp sausage of a penis. His hand went for the pistol. A farty sound wheezed as he paced up. The penis rose from its pathetic sloth to a live fish, then to a rattlesnake and then with each push it became larger and larger, rising from the floor to the ceiling. Once it was up, the General in a quick move removed the cylinder and muzzled his penis with a strong rubber band. "Ha ha," he laughed like a child, "the more you press the more it will rise. Now, gentlemen, it's there on its own, celebrating its autonomy." The General sauntered all over the room with his exhibit. "Well, let me confide in you that I had this kit made last summer on my fifty-eighth birthday. My wife who, mind you, is no ordinary gal, was totally beside herself, as it never bends even if I am spent. You see if it's up, you feel in control, and if it's down, the female overpowers you, so from the time I had this added mass and my round-the-clock stand-ups, she has been less inclined to go to her riding classes."

Ganju caught a sneak preview of the trumped-up penis. He forgot his own one o'clock rituals with Jaana.

"Well, now that you have my secret, I guess I qualify to ask you about your dawn-to-dusk stretches," said the General to Zahid, who coyly dropped his head and mumbled, "I am afraid, sir, I can't match the grandeur I've just witnessed."

"Come on, don't be shy. We know of your reputation."

"It's mere gossip, sir, I really don't merit a public showing."

"There is hardly any public here, it's a private affair, come on, I am asking you," the General commanded.

"Well, sir, frankly speaking surgical implants involve drastic methods which could destroy the tissues like splints inserted in the penis. What I have is something more sophisticated. It involves the insertion of a hydraulic device that causes a stiffening of the penis when a pump, permanently implanted in the scrotum, is activated. Here!" He unzipped and revealed an eye-filler.

The myth of dawn-to-dusk erections was exploded right there for Ganju. Zahid too had a fake penis.

Kashif kept sitting with his granite silence and dead eyes; he didn't seem to be moved by those two mighty apparitions.

"What about you, Kashif?" said the General.

A smile rippled his skin, lending a human character to his face. His lips flapped, "You have inspired me to divulge my small recipe," he lazily collected his balls. "I got it made by the royal physician in London in his private rejuvenating clinic. The charges of course were paid by the health ministry as I was on medical leave for my hernia operation, which was perfectly legal. It only took a few days and I walked out of that clinic fully reconditioned, with an extra leg to stand on."

"Could you unveil it now, so we may have a look at the superstar?" quipped the General.

Kashif released his balls and unzipped to reveal an astonishing length. "Wao, aren't you a dark horse?" shouted the General.

Ganju was dazzled by those towers of modern technology with their frightening shadows mounting over him. He was witnessing three revealed articles of faith, the axis of power, an epic of human progress.

"Ganju what about you?" They all said in a chorus.

"I am natural," Ganju murmured under their threatening gaze.

"Natural?" they laughed and lunged at him.

"Show us nature's work." They stripped him.

"Ha ha, ha," they laughed their heads off.

"Nature is weak," they started to chant in a circle, "it's imperfect."

"Man must make it perfect."

"Jaana was a folklore!"

"A fantasy figure."

"You chased a ghost."

"Degraded yourself as a human being."

"Curse of the male."

"Get real! Get real!"

Ganju under the spell of lofty shadows nodded his head, retreating into compliance.

They all raised their glasses and cheered, "Welcome to the club! Welcome to the phallocentric world!"

Shish . . .

The little glass moved on the table, they all looked at each other, and in confusion placed their organs on the glass instead of their fingers.

"Who are you?" they asked. The glass scuttled from C to A then to S, A, N, O, V and finally halted at A.

"Casanova!" they screamed. In respect, their organs shrank on the bottom of the upturned glass.

"Casanova sahib," said Zahid with immense humility, "your twelve-volume memoirs are bible to phallic worshipers. For generations, they have warmed the private parts of both young and old and your amorous adventures have astounded the celibate fascists. Sir, we are grateful to you for gracing this occasion with your spirited presence."

"Thank you, gentlemen," moved the glass, "I am still writing my memoirs. I didn't get enough time to complete the second series of my memoirs while I was alive," said the glass.

"Sir, they say you are the philosopher of the bedroom, please tell us your success story?" asked the General.

"Well, it's not easy to rise to the epic stature of a ladies' man, or a sex god. It's the performance that counts, stroke by stroke. My first success with the upper-class ladies came with an open contest. They had arranged a peasant and a lady of excitement, while I was asked to perform on a milkmaid. A wall clock was placed between us. This sturdy peasant was spent in a minute, but to the envy of the husbands, yours truly went on full-force," the glass slid rapidly, "the crowd cheered at my performance and ladies fainted as the clock kept announcing my marvelous duration that extended till dawn." The glass rested.

"What exactly was your secret, sir?" Kashif said, pressing the bottom of the glass with his knob which by now was reduced to a thumb.

"Well, you got to have the right equipment," spoke the glass.

"Right equipment?"

"Yes, of course, if your thing just dangles between your thighs, it's a liability. Now I, luckily, was living in the age of renaissance, the century of creative doubt and scientific inquiry. I had the fortune of meeting this Italian craftsman who had astonishing talent. You see, there's a difference between devoted craftsmanship and a mass-produced item. In these times there is an impersonal attitude towards the art of crafting human genitalia, but in my age it was pure contemplation," sparkled the glass.

"Do you mean you have—"

"Yes!" wobbled the glass.

A shriek filled the room, "You too, Casanova?"

Chapter 16

Dickery Dickery Doc — the Yogi Rat

*Men would do anything to possess things that break the circle
of karma, make them soar above mortality, shape wishes into
horses.*

Ganju was booked on the Friday flight to London, and the
Trio had decided to turn its Thursday meeting into a send-off
dinner for him. He had agreed to acquire a new penis. It was a
cloudy night with unpredictable weather. As usual, they drank
themselves silly and kept fumbling for a wandering spirit to stay
in the ouija glass. Nothing stirred. It was a spiritless night.

Disappointed, the General decided for everyone to go to the
rooftop and piss together. "Come boy, it's a sign of solidarity,"
he commanded a reluctant Ganju. Ganju's sixth sense told him
to stay back.

Left alone in the room, Ganju looked at his watch. A few
hours and he would be gone. Why on earth was he going? For
several days he had been mulling over the idea. What would his
wife say about his make-believe malehood? Could he ever live
with a built-in lie between his legs? Some cosmetic libido, a synthetic joy propelled by surgeons?

Images of the grafted genitalia flashed in his mind. He
became paranoid. Knives, scalpels, anesthesia, a foreign touch
to his private parts, some simulacrum reality, blow-ups of
male egos, macho postures, an insult to nature. There must be
another way. He looked at the lifeless glass upturned on the

Ouija board, at the marbled dervishes in idle postures, and at
Shiva and Parvati mute in their tantric asana. She had power
over him, Lilly. Under that silk lingerie and a romantic celluloid
image bristled nothing but an animal. His own poetics was born
in a homemade zoo. Under the angelic wings of the poet had
trotted a she-ass. Suddenly, Lilly's abysmal obsession for Laado
tormented him. "Revenge," he cried, "I must take revenge."
In a week he would be as tall as his partners. He stood in
haste as if to board the plane, but then the glass moved on the
table.

"Who are you?" he whispered, putting a startled finger on it.

The glass gently towed his finger to the letters, one by one:
J-A-L-I-N-O-O-S.

"What?" He shuddered in disbelief. "Are you the great
Jalinoos?" His finger trembled with excitement.

"The one and only," rebuffed the glass, flourishing a majestic
glide.

Ganju almost fainted, his finger slid down the glass. "Jalinoos
possesses the secret of Tajul Kharoos, the crown rooster," Bade
Hakim sahib's voice thundered in his mind. "It carries virginal
mercury, the mother of all elements. Its meat spurs masculinity
and lengthens our tool beyond human understanding."

The General and the others marched into the room finding
Ganju bent over the tiny glass.

"Shish!" Ganju signaled.

"Who?" asked the General under his breath.

"Jalinoos, the one who has the nuskha, the scripture of the
crown bird, Tajul Kharoos," said Ganju.

With a nod of his head the General gave the command. All
at once put their fingers on the glass, touching the very pulse of
the universe.

"Gentlemen, I am in a hurry," moved the glass.

"Oh, please don't leave us, we need you," they urged. "We
want the nuskha of Tajul Kharoos."

"I can't do that," the glass toddled.

"Oh please, we beg of you!"

"I know you all have organs of poor quality manufactured by

western nations with cheap labour from poor countries. I pity you all."

"But sir, if you don't share our own national heritage with us, we'll always be dependent on others. Make us independent."

"Independence comes with responsibility and my fear is that you will misuse it and trouble the world," said the glass.

"No, never!"

"I want a firm promise!"

"We promise!" They all raised their hands.

"Then be ready," commanded the glass.

Letter by letter the kind spirit unveiled the ancient formula. They faithfully noted down, verified, double-checked and finalized it to the last detail.

In that descent of the oracle, Ganju missed his flight.

With the recipe in hand, a revolution hit the dull lives of the Trio. No more mujras or soul-searching at Thursday night parties. They were committed to a cause.

The first step was to find a halal chicken, hatched by a blue-blooded hen with noble ancestry. Its DNA revealed its breeding behavior, plumage, and song. A swift whistler with liquid calls, Tajul Kharoos the crown bird had its lineage in the crested kingfisher, lanceolate falcon, and the imperial eagle that rooted back to Tair-e-Tooba, the paradise bird. The feathered wonder was dainty-toed, red-legged, fan-tailed, yellow-fronted, ivory-billed, and blossom-headed. Once the prominent artists of the realm had finished the sketch, a team of bird-watchers was created to spot the rare bird.

Wildlife experts reported elusive sightings of the rare visitor. The resident Himalayan species with Phoenix-like reappearances could occasionally be seen on its migratory flyways, in well-wooded parks and sometimes in garbage dumps. Day and night the team scanned the skies and finally captured the legitimate Tajul Kharoos. With its puffed up chest and a tail furled out like a spangled scythe and its stately gait it put peacocks to shame. It croaked the prayer call with full-throated ease.

Since the rooster had to be left in the open, CCTV and mobile units were set up to monitor its movements. It was not to touch or eat anything impure, therefore an army of sweepers walked ahead of the chosen bird. They would be followed by ambulances, emergency kits, and military police. After an assassination attempt, it wore a metal jacket with a hypersensitive alarm system attached to its tail.

The next step was to procure the essential ingredients of its feed. Those were the roots of rare plants scattered all over the world. The list was long and demanding. Kashif had already left for Korea to get a blue carrot. Zahid was in China arranging to smuggle some exotic stuff: saliva of a bat, a toadstool squeezed at sunrise and baked in the early mist of winter, hog blood, and an owl's morning piss. But what panicked headquarters was the shrub coded as dodai, a catalyst which could activate all other ingredients It was nowhere to be found.

The General, who was heading the project, felt challenged. He sent for gynecologists, experts in herbal magic, and dealers in charms and amulets to trace the herb. Soon his search engines identified a jungle in a remote island in the south.

For days the General and his commandos exerted themselves tirelessly and combed the entire jungle, but the celestial herb was nowhere to be found. The General was upset; he couldn't go back without the booty.

One night when it was dark and humid, without a whiff of breeze, the General, while he slept in his camp without his clothes, his cheerful snoring changed into an alarming scream. A sharp pain in his bottom had woken him up in terror. He lit his torch and brandished it around. A rat with a penis sizzling like sin stood over his back, its whiskers thicker than his. Shook by anger, the General stood to attack the horny animal, but before he could reach his revolver, the rat somersaulted like a pole vaulter and catapulted out of his sight. In panic, the General took a shot in the air. The guard instantly rushed in.

"Sir, are you alright?" Saluting, the guard glanced over at the half-naked General.

"Oh yes," said the General, covering his back quickly. "I'm fine, never mind. Did you see anything?"

"No sir, I thought I saw a mongoose."

"Mongoose? Are you sure, I mean it could be a rat or—"

"No sir!"

"But how could you tell?"

"Well sir," he grinned, "anyone could tell."

"Oh really?"

"Yes sir, it appeared to be chasing its female sir, you know what I mean. A rat can't be that lucky sir," he said with a funny smile. "Sleep well, sir!" he saluted and left.

Torch in one hand and revolver in the other, the General with an aching bottom was left defeated in a surprise attack. Should he order his commandos to shoot the culprit at sight? He paced restlessly. But what if they came to know of what it had done? He halted. The guard had said mongoose; if he had said rat, he could have been acting fishy. In the military, contradictory statements land you in crisis. Why make a mountain out of a molehill, a sword out of a needle? It was better for him to go back to sleep and forget the whole thing. He went back to sleep.

The fantasy of Tajul Kharoos relaxed him; success of the mission could bring him honors. A rude tug in his bottom kicked him out of his dream. He sat up, wide awake. What if it gets into the newspapers? He panicked. History will never forgive a General buggered by a rat. Generations will spit on his grave . . . his wife would divorce him, he'd be shaved off his moustache and spend the rest of his life in a harem to play the head eunuch.

In a fit of moral outrage the General moved to the cupboard and rescued his cylinder with the pistol pump.

"Kill! Kill!" he pulled the trigger. Honor-killing was the custom; he had a legitimate right to avenge his humiliation. "Kill! Kill!" With a pumped-up penis, the General felt in control. "Come, you son of a rat," he challenged, flaunting his penis, "see for yourself, I am no eunuch. I can bugger you and your generations to come." But he couldn't find his enemy when he was ready for him. Touching his bottom with an unsure hand he released a fart. A meek whimper blew out. He was proud of his healthy farts. The wretched creature had upset his biorhythm. His orifice lacked the authoritative baritone, a pledge that announced masculinity. His depression, nevertheless, put him into a reflective mood. He would teach the insolent animal a lesson. Torture! Slow physical affliction! It'll give him satisfaction, a creative catharsis for his embarrassing defeat. He loosened his grip on the pump. His penis deflated. The General imagined the rat hung by its tail and being castrated, slice by slice with his shaving blade. While he wallowed in that weird pleasure, as if by divine will, his finger brushed against the aching spot. No less than Newton, the General, assessing the gravity of the situation, had an intuitive opening. How come a small creature like a rat could flash a member bigger than himself? It was not natural. There must be something more to it. "Hurrah!" He had unraveled the thick mongoose-rat mystery. It was no one but the lucky rat who had tasted that rare and unreachable dodai. The rat he was cursing was actually his mentor. The holy guide who could take him to his conquest. To kill it would be a blunder, and to torture it, a sacrilege.

He fondly remembered the folktale where a rat had nibbled away the ropes of a net to liberate a lion caught by a hunter. Wasn't he re-living that fable? Could it be that it was the same rat and he the lion. The yogi rat had not opened his bottom but his mind.

The General put on his uniform ceremoniously, with flicks and medals. He was all ready to get his wishing plant.

While he recited the soldier's prayer under his breath, patriotic sentiment welled up in his breast. They are a bunch of sapped-out pumpkins, those politicians scrabbling around for selfish gains, he thought regretfully. They can't even perform a decent image let alone rule the world, selling the cream of the nation on the pavement of history. It was always a soldier who rescued this nation from failing. A good soldier never gives up his target, it was his national duty to serve the motherland. He saluted his image in the mirror.

In order to perform his duty, the General had to make a sacrifice. Touchingly, he was painfully chaste. To lose his virgin hole to the lowliest of creatures was a tall order. "But people in history had made sacrifices for their motherland," spoke his conscience. To be poked by an innocent rat was a small favor to his nation, thought the General as he opened a whisky bottle. It was just a casual dalliance with an insignificant creature. He took a deep swig. It'll never be able to claim victory over him, it doesn't have human language, it can't speak the jargon of war and terrorism. No one will ever know, no foreign correspondents, no media coverage but just a dark murmur not heard by the manic public. What had looked like a rat was in fact a dark horse galloping him to the great victory, the mystery shrub dodai.

At dawn the General wisely ordered the commandos to leave; it was solely his operation. As evening approached, he anxiously awaited his midnight caller.

Nothing.

Days went by and there was no sign of the visitor.

There must be something to attract the stranger. Why not make a juicy bait, some rat trap to snare that wonder animal; but rat traps could be frightening. Think, think, he clasped his hands. How utterly thoughtless of him, he frowned with pensive wrinkles, what could be a better rat trap than the General himself? He unclasped his hands in a fit of joy.

Next evening, the General passionately oiled his orifice, delicately rouged his bottom cheeks and carefully layered some cheese around. A special chord with an attached micro camera went right up to his rectum. With the rat on him, the camera could be hooked to the rat and go with it.

Each night he waited with his festooned posterior hung propitiously in the air, a Kamasutra position, where devotees offer themselves to their idols.

On one of those humid nights, the General felt the breeze, as if spring were round the corner. He heard a thud, the rat was on the table. The General thanked his stars and took his position. The rat sniffed at the leftovers of his dinner and tumbled his whisky glass. The General eagerly mooned to the visitor and twittered, "Dickery dickery doc, dickery dickery doc." The rat didn't budge, it kept nibbling away at the leftovers.

Disappointed, the General lit some incense, unrolled a red

carpet and scattered rose petals on it. "Dickery dickery doc, Dickery dickery doc," he cooed again from the bed, resuming his Kamasutra position.

The rat jumped on the carpet and twisting its tail around like a bow fitted its penis in it like an arrow. Some cunning Cupid in the garb of a rat? The General wondered. To attract the rat, he moved to the floor and started crawling on his fours. The penis of the rat appeared and disappeared like a piston in a sheath, teasing the General by touching and not touching. Was it playing hard to get? Torturing him with its tricks of seduction?

Near dawn when all persuasions of the General failed, the Cupid mouse shot the arrow in the air and slinked out. The General fell on the floor like a collapsible chair. Undeflowered.

He had been abandoned and rejected. In that hour of gloom he sat in front of the TV set and watched for hours the wiles of his fickle beloved; the camera had recorded all the movements of the rat. At early dawn in his despair he found among his personal belongings, the trumpet from his boy scout days. He had been a great scout and an exceptional trumpet player. They had called him the Pied Piper.

Here comes the scout
  With a barrel-like snout
  Upright folks
  Cover your butts
  The great scout blows his trum-trum-pet.
  Girls would appear in the balconies.

In that hour of rejection, the General, with tears in his eyes lifted the nostalgic relic. Under a wet moustache he breathed in. The wailing sound hit the walls and went beyond into the wilderness. The jungle resounded with the hypnotic melody.

In that spell, suddenly the door fell apart and an army of rats with their dickeries up, charged in. The trumpet fell from the hands of the General. He started to recite his soldier prayer while the rats with their brandishing tools, mercilessly buggered him. With each dig, the prayer went louder.

Gang raped, martyred, the General fell unconscious.

The next morning a hurriedly bandaged General followed the tiny monitor and reached his magic plant. There, under the infernal helmets of the forest was hidden the elixir of life, the chosen dodai. He had a cheerful glimpse of the inner parts. He snipped off the soft strands and touched the wings of that erotic mystery. A sudden flush of energy hit his body.

"Dickery dickery doc!" he shouted with joy.

"Dickery dickery doc doc oc oc oc!" echoed the jungle, far and beyond.

Chapter 17

Mr Halal

After a hurried celebration of the General's unrivaled success at finding the prime ingredient Dodia, covert operation with the code name of "Doomsday Caller" shot into action. Away from city, on vast tracts of barren land, a dome was built with a huge cauldron in the center. At midnight, the exact quantity of each ingredient was carefully put inside the reflective mirrored pot. Nothing happened. They panicked. Each wing, feather and limb of the rooster was worth millions. In a quick move, leading biochemists, ecologists, and environmentalists of the country were pulled out of their beds in the middle of the night and whisked away to the secret site.

The experts frantically thumbed the instructional manuals and repeated the process again and again until they found that the broth was to remain at a certain temperature and the climate had to be conducive for the precious mess to alchemize into an offering fit for the table. Also, the crown bird, before it was fed, had to be deprived of all nourishments until it was on its last leg.

The process commanded a complex infrastructure and tons of money. In view of the project's towering budget, a high-powered anticorruption committee was set up to crack down on wealthy families and take over their assets. Investment and lottery schemes were launched with the help of banks, fake winners, and runaway corporations. Taxes were bumped up to an alarming scale. People came out on the streets to protest, but oblivious to the trivial issues of poverty and inflation, the dream of erecto-imperialism went on, unhindered.

The only failing, however, was that the money they had collected was not enough.

The General discreetly started a mini war with the neighboring country, which had been under the control of communists. Hoping to drill a hole into the plump pockets of affluent nations, he invited them to invest in his war of liberation. To his disappointment they donated what the General termed as mere peanuts. In that crisis Kashif, the intelligence chief, suggested a two-pronged strategy to win the free world and at the same time scour around for the pounds and dollars of the expats in foreign lands.

"It would be unethical to put financial pressure on the expats, as they are citizens of the free world," read the report based on joint deliberations of the Cultural Ministry and the Intelligence Bureau. "We, however, believe that separation from their birth places burdens them with emotional baggage which could be released by bringing to them live performances of their cherished singers and dancers. Once they are drugged with the smells and colors of their native soil, we could invoke the specter of foreign debt that has long been haunting their motherland. As true sons and daughters of the soil they would contribute with vengeful generosity. A show with patriotic dressing and nostalgic cheese could bring in millions. Our declaration of self-reliance would also send a signal to the free world of our defiance and the possibility of us joining hands with the communists."

Time for psychological warfare. No one was more suitable than Noor Mohammad Ganju to head that mission. Anwara, the popular TV star, was summoned to line up a cultural troupe.

On the evening of their departure at the airport, Kashif briefed Ganju about the sensitive nature of the visit. Among other things, Ganju was given the name of a certain Lord Fazzle who lived in London but had businesses all over the world. "He's one of the richest men in Europe," he was told. "He'll contact you, and yes, for identification the password is *halal*."

Armed with a troupe of saucy women and singers and stand-up comedians, Ganju toured the free world. Though the show was hyped up by the media and had some thrilling moments, Ganju, unfortunately, couldn't raise funds even to pay off the artists.

"We are not getting the desired effect," he warned Anwara at the backstage after a show.

"I've an idea," said Anwara, mopping his sweaty face with his handkerchief.

"Like what?"

"Hold . . . an . . . auction."

"Auction? Of what?" Ganju glared at him.

"Sir, auction off our national relics."

"What?"

"Sir, imagine those historical relics on the stage, powerful images of patriotism. Sir, you know people like to boast about their rare possessions. They'll go to the highest bid just to show off their love for their native land," he said, his eyes drooping down to his lips.

"Not a bad idea, yes . . . not bad at all," reflected Ganju.

Encouraged, Anwara brushed a drop of sweat from his nose and whispered, "After all, what are the relics good for? Just laying eggs in museums."

They laughed heartily.

The first national flag ever stitched by a little schoolgirl, the fraught monocle worn by the founder of the nation, the eagle-shaped pen used by the national poet to write falcon poems, a cricket bat of a world-class player, and the disheveled and unwashed turban of the folk hero who fought against the colonialists, all were airlifted under strict security and at the end of each show thereafter were ceremoniously brought to the stage.

Anwara paraded the historical charms to the expats and touted the qualities of each item with the persistence of a street hawker. None came under the hammer.

A monocle was out of fashion, they said, nobody wanted to see the world from a half-cracked lens. The eagle pen had lost its sheen; the sharp quill drooped like the thumped nose of a catfish. All they wanted to see were the dances of their favorite starlets on whom they had showered their hard currency. Appeals for self-reliance fell on deaf ears.

"We are treated like dogs at airports," they protested, "custom officers rob us of our cameras, TV sets, deep freezers, and VCRs that we buy for our relatives. And over here they want us to bring porn videos and sex toys. Go and clean your own shit. Hold fair elections and then come to us!"

Exhausted and disappointed, Ganju was now on the last leg of his mission. Anwara had already left a day ahead. The show in London was his only hope. The English were more civilized, he thought and hoped to make up for his losses. He was also eager to see his secret host who had not contacted him so far.

At the airport there were no flags or protocol, no salutes or handshakes. He spotted a limousine with tinted glass windows and a uniformed driver holding a placard with his name on it. Who had sent him? He didn't feel comfortable to ask.

A few miles away from central London, the car moved into a posh area and entered what looked like an old castle with a mile-long driveway. He was ushered in by a Filipina maid and a British butler greeted him with a bouquet of flowers and led him through the vast corridors of the castle.

"Your Excellency, if you are not tired, I could show you around," the butler said.

"No, thank you, just show me my room," said a mesmerized Ganju.

"Feel free, sir, you are the only guest here," smiled the butler, "but just for your information, there is the pool out there," he said, pointing to an oval swimming pool. "And those stairs lead to the library. On this side is the gym and that's the main bar."

Ganju went to have a look inside the opulently furnished bar. Besides the rows of wine bottles, he noticed huge portraits of Karl Marx and Engels. The two bearded men looked like unwanted guests in a landscape of surplus affluence.

"On your right is the dining room," announced the butler. Ganju peeped in and was struck by a statue of a starving Buddha sitting oblivious to the plateful of fresh oranges on the table.

When he reached his room, he noticed the bouquet he was given had the *halal* brand on it. He was obviously the guest of his secret friend. He felt relaxed, set the roses aside and fell on the bed.

At dinner time while he waited for his host he was told that no one was expected. A series of dishes came and went. Whatever was edible carried the imprint of the word *halal* in crescent-like calligraphy: halal sauce, halal bread, halal butter, chapattis, fish, lamb, soup, jelly pudding, and even the tooth-picks. After dinner, when he went to the bathroom, he noticed that the shampoo, oils, and soap all were branded *halal*. On the toilet seat he was relieved to find the Muslim shower.

Ganju had never felt so halal in his own country.

On the eve of the show, the main hall thronged with swishy shalwars, flowing shirts, and starched sherwanis. Women with sparkling jewelry and sizzling makeup lit up the place. Men with paunches bursting out of tight national dresses and girls in dopattas, jeans, and hijabs promised a great audience. Local businessmen with shining pates sat in front while petty workers and their gaudily dressed families filled the back seats. Ganju anxiously waited for his host, but there was no sign of Mr Halal. Tense with anticipation he fidgeted in his seat. Another flop was at hand.

After the scintillating bhangra, ludi dance, epileptic prancing of pop stars, and a national fashion trot, the curtain was raised on the major event of the evening: a tableaux based on love for the motherland. Before Anwara could start with his speech of "spare some change," a sudden intermission was declared. Ganju sank in his seat. There were whispers backstage and hooting from the audience.

Quick curtain-raising in response.

Two stage hands brought a huge bowl on the stage and placed it under a spotlight. Ganju was mystified.

From the big bowl appeared a clown.

Applause.

"This is the begging bowl we were given on our Independence Day," said the clown.

"We were born in this womb of miseries. A nation of beggars." Tears fell.

"We are the wretched clowns," he sobbed.

"Shame! Shame!" A shout came from the hall.

"Are we slaves?" The tone changed dramatically from pathos to shrill rhetoric.

"No!" shouted the crowd.

"Aren't we the proud citizens of a sovereign state?"

"Yes!" thundered the hall.

"Then let us pledge from this day that we shall never beg," he boomed.

"Never! Never!" chanted the hall.

Patriotic music on dhols.

"Free the body, free the soul!

Let us break the begging bowl."

The song brought the bhangra dancers on stage. Some members of the audience ran up to the stage and joined the dancers. Lighting effects and music roused the crowd. In that hysterical moment they smashed the bowl into pieces. The audience choked with emotion. There was a sense of accomplishment.

The clown shouted from the stage, "Who is the superpower?"

"None but Allah," came the answer.

Ganju in his seat overflowed with tears of gratitude.

Accompanied by two celebrity queens in sexy ghararas, the clown now moved among the audience extending a huge chadder. Women took off their gold bangles and diamond sets while men purged their pockets of their last pennies. It was a historical loot.

Ganju could smell the chicken feed. Brewing.

After the show, Ganju rushed backstage. There he ran into the clown, who wore a plastic smile on his face. "May I offer you a halal chewing gum," the clown chirped, peeling off his mask. A human face emerged: thin patch of French beard, sparkling restless eyes, and a hedgehog haircut with calligraphy in three plain curls on the forehead, resembling the word *halal*. His diamond rings stared like cobra eyes.

"Do forgive me, but I've to take off this makeup, you never

know they mix boar skin and bone powder into these chemicals, but don't you worry, brother, I've got a halal remover," he said and disappeared into the green room. Ganju was left stupefied.

"One needs to relax after a hectic job like this," said the man, now with a new suit and a Turkish cap. "We beg by denouncing begging. Ha," he laughed. "You can call me Fazzle, though my name is Muhammad Afzal, you know how it's in Britain, they call me Fazzle the razzle-dazzle."

"Oh what a pleasure," Ganju said shaking his hand.

"Well, it was my public relations department that came up with the idea. The bowl was designed by an American sculptor. Come on, the success of the show calls for a celebration," said Fazzle, walking him outside to a waiting car.

"You were brilliant," said Ganju, sitting inside the car with obvious admiration.

"Well, I did theatre in my younger days," he said.

"I could tell," Ganju said in a flattering tone.

"Our theme was 'peasants against landlords and corrupt politicians'—you see, we were communists."

"Oh really?"

"Well, yes, we were the comrades, the Che Guevaras of our times. I would die at the end of the play and the audience would chant, 'Once more! Once more!' I would jerk out of my dead posture and the landlord would oblige me with a second bullet, giving me a chance to re-enact my last rant against the tyrants of the world. What fun!"

Ganju didn't realize but they had already come out of the car and were walking into some half-lit corridors.

"What's this place?" he asked.

"It's a private club, only celebrities come here, no photos, no cameras, total privacy. I know your position, therefore I was careful," said Fazzle as they entered the hall.

Ganju had never before seen so many topless women serving around the bar.

"I also deal with immigrants—Poles, Czechs Indians, Bingos, Pakies. They enter the country without papers, I have lawyers.

I get them work, men in restaurants and young girls in clubs. I have shares in this club. Ah there you are," he waved to a topless waitress and ordered some champagne.

In that tantalizing ambience, Ganju drank quickly just to get drunk.

"That's the maypole dance, pagan ritual in modern times." Fazzle pointed across the room where strippers danced around a pole. "It's the seduction of the gravitational center, flesh convulsing against the immobility of the pole. You know the urge to go higher and higher is as old as the pyramids. You see all those power towers? The American dream of human progress, the concrete phallus, a male thrust into the unknown, perhaps into the womb of the heavens," he said, turning to Ganju.

"You like women, sure we all like them," he said looking around. "I'll host a blonde for you tonight, take your pick."

Ganju swiveled his head and threw a glance at the strutting beauties. He ogled at bare bosoms and baffling curves as they bent and served on high heels. His eyes stumbled at a tall and well-built girl.

"Don't you have the perfect eye, she's pure breed, all English, no mix here, fresh from summer school, not a regular but very very special, perhaps you don't know Nazo, my wife, she owns a beauty parlor and runs an escort service on the side, only for multinationals and celebs, no pressure on girls, hi, join us," he waved at the girl. Ganju couldn't believe his eyes as she walked over to them in measured steps, pantomiming his fantasy.

"Hi, I am Roma," a white husky voice lathered his ears, her hand embracing his as she planted a favorable kiss on Fazzle's cheek.

"Meet my friend, Moh," said Fazzle.

"Hello Moh," she almost sang his fictional name.

"Hello," said Ganju with a tipsy tongue.

"I've to catch up with an appointment, someone from the royalty. Can't be ignored, give my friend company," Fazzle winked at Roma. "Here is the key to my private suite," he said to Ganju, giving her the key. Next minute he had disappeared through the door into the winding darkness.

"I admire your choice," said Fazzle the following morning at the breakfast table. "I can see you are keen to discover new avenues of erotica." He flicked his three calligraphic curls. They moved to the bar. "By the way I like your project. I am concerned, very much concerned." He opened a bottle of champagne.

"I keep them as souvenirs of my past," he pointed to the sepia frames of Marx and Engels. "My mother was stronger than my father but he would beat her, a low-paid police guard, fed on small change, stinking of bribe and corruption. He would tie me to a tree and thrash me with his belt, a knuckled belt. I wish I could kill him but the bastard died in my absence. I had to dig him out of his grave and hit his dead balls. After his death my mother became a monument of despair. Rosary in hand, she sat on the prayer mat and became a hunchback. She was a caricature of pathos, only sadness made her breathe. I dreaded that illness of poverty, her thick tears and her God, who was callous and without mercy. And my sisters? They stared into the mirror like frightened ghosts, plucked the white hair that slyly crept into in their heads and pinched skin balls on their faces. I had to run, and I did, stealing all that money the bastard had got in bribes. I joined the underground communist party, I wanted to wipe out poverty from the face of the earth. Cheers," he raised his glass to the portraits.

"Cheers," said Ganju, reluctantly raising his glass.

Fazzle looked at his watch.

"Oh my God, I must leave, another pressing appointment, see you around. By the way, Marx, I concluded, was averse to barbers. Too much hair means too much confusion." He laughed and left Ganju with the dialectical stares of the two communists.

Walking through the corridors Ganju fancied the gym, the center for shaping up the ultimate male. He did a few push-ups and then start lifting weights. He felt weak. The weights were too heavy for him.

"Excuse me, sir," a Filipina maid brought the phone to him, "it's for you, sir," she said and, giving him a quick bow, left.

"Haven't you reached a deal yet?" the General exploded on

the line. "We are running out of time! Get him to talk about the seed money, that damn Halal seed."

"Sir," Ganju squeaked.

"We have to enter global politics. Now don't you act dumb, you could be the prime minister after this project," said the General and put down the phone.

The next day Ganju waited for Fazzle the whole morning. Disappointed, he decided to go to the city and have a stroll. He could no longer bear the luxurious wilderness of the castle.

While taking a walk on Trafalgar Square, he was distracted by the sudden appearance of a procession. Algerians, Arabs, Turks, and Pakistanis were shouting slogans against a Hollywood actress who had flayed Muslims over goat-slaughtering. Ganju had read this in the papers but had no idea of the violent reaction. Police stood on guard, some tourists took pictures.

The crowd went wild, the police advanced. Someone nudged him, "Hi there." Ganju looked back, saw the calligraphy of three curls. "Get in," said Fazzle opening the door of his car. Seen from inside the car, the procession passed by like a silent film but then started the commentary, "That aging whore from French brothels had to make such outrageous comments about Muslims. She spends millions on her woofi dog, why? Because she fucks him, isn't that cruelty to animals? Doesn't the bitch like koshered cocks?" Fazzle the razzle-dazzle kept talking without a pause. "These white motherfuckers have no respect for anyone's religion. First they ban the hijab now they wish to ban our food. Where is their bloody secular liberalism? Now she's a vegetarian, but knows a hundred other ways of enjoying meat. Ha ha," he laughed and Ganju noticed a gold tooth.

"If she wants to protect the rights of animals, I've to protect the rights of Allah, it's my religious duty. Now this protest is the show of power, such investments pay off well. The General told me that you are the next prime minister," he said, wheeling into a deserted street. "The army is the only political party in the country, isn't it?"

Ganju smiled.

"Well then, we have a deal," said Fazzle smiling back.

"We have to discuss the future of our homeland. Perhaps you don't know that I started my career here as a bus conductor, then I worked at a grocery store till I opened a halal meat shop near the Muslim embassy. They were very particular about halal and haram but they trusted me. First I catered to Indians and Pakistanis but then I started catering to the English. I am a major donor to causes such as the perCent Club and the Prince of Wales Trust. I thank my Allah, today I have ninety-nine retail and fifty wholesale stores. The turnover is above eighty million dollars and we deal with 50,000 traders in Britain alone. I am a devout Muslim and have set up a zakat foundation to help the poor. I am also a member of the prince's education and sports aid organization for the welfare of immigrants. But let me tell you, it's my homeland that I yearn for."

Ganju was impressed. Lord Afzal had made it into British royalty by selling halal meat throughout Europe.

"I tell you it's a dog-eat-dog world around us. In the white world I was without a dwelling until I found a foothold, an anchor." He stopped in front of a building.

"It's not a butcher's plaza, it's my identity, my shrine that gives me a sense of belonging," Fazzle said as they entered the halal slaughterhouse. "Unlike those hybrid bastards, the homeless vagabonds, the so-called diaspora, I have something legitimate, something solid. Those pasty cockroaches cling to the skin of water in an English bathtub. They hate their religion, their culture, their own people. They sell their motherland, her innocence, her naivety to the West, her tales of papaji and mamaji, projecting our faith as some primitive mumbo-jumbo, they think the West is rational. Fuck all. I know my country is in need of me."

"Why don't you come back to your homeland, we can look after you," said Ganju.

"I give you forty millions pounds and you'll give me one ministry, three coal mines and Tamgha-e-Hilal, the national award for my services. That'll bring me home, I want to enter into politics, that's my passion."

"Done, you have it," hiding his excitement, Ganju spoke

with the confidence of a prime minister.

Hunks of slaughtered goats passed by them. They walked through the cold storage, wrapped in icy shadows, skinned goats dangled in polythene bags. In the fog they could hardly see each other until they entered the main slaughter hall. Hundreds of steel stands with electric choppers filled the space. Goats were huddled onto iron tracks one by one and were neatly hung upside down, their hooves tied by chains. Butchers bustled around with gloved hands.

Seeing their master, everyone greeted Fazzle. He waved at them, told them to take a break and leave the room.

"All ideologies kneel to a slaughter house," announced Fazzle. "You see, it's violence which is the primary passion of man. Battlefields are readymade arenas of human slaughter. All clashes of civilizations end up here. Man takes long to die a natural death and the tragedy with man is that there are too many of them, it's the excess, so it's ordained that they should be killed—birds, trees, animals men, women, children—as quickly as possible for man's own survival. I was a devoted slave of the revolution but where did I end up? Here! Oh, I love man's sanctified obsession with blood."

Fazzle pressed a button. Hundred choppers fell on the necks of live goats. "La-illaha, la-illaha!" came a recorded voice from a loudspeaker, full volume. Heads of goats rolled with their mouths open like shoes, eyes like fading glow worms, the room was filled with blood flowing in torrents.

"This is the darkness of love and nature. Guts, that's all. Here," he came to Ganju and took out a cheque from his pocket, "Forty million," he said.

Ganju noticed that Fazzle had a limp.

"Are you all right," asked Ganju glancing at Fazzle's legs.

"I didn't tell you the whole story."

"What story?"

"You never asked me why I left the country."

"Oh, yes, you are right," said Ganju.

"I had fallen in love."

"Really?"

"She was the daughter of a feudal politician."

"Who?"

"I don't remember and frankly I don't care. We tried to run away together. They came to kill us. I was shot in the leg but I escaped. I still have a steel rod in my leg. Usually I manage, but you are quite perceptive, I must say," he said, looking Ganju in the eye.

"And the girl?" Ganju took the cheque.

"She was perhaps killed."

Ganju felt a jolt inside him. "Who got you out of the country?" he asked.

"I was sent to London by a high official from Intelligence whom I had sold the secrets of my communist party."

Who was Lord Fazzle? wondered Ganju.

"Oh how I love the stunned eyes of the goats, still and calm, without complaint," said Afzal limping towards the severed heads. "They remain alive for a few seconds to picture their death."

There were thousands of daughters and fathers in the world, Ganju rationalized and neatly slipped the cheque into his pocket.

Chapter 18

Tragic Draw

On his return from London, when Ganju arrived at the Haveli, he was greeted by a procession of heads sunk in despair. An eerie silence surrounded Razia's room where the maids, cloaked in their chadders, stood like frozen ghosts. Juma, while he took off Ganju's shoes, broke the news; Razia had shot her child husband and, just before Ganju's arrival, had fled the Haveli under the guise of her maid Cheemo. His wife in hospital was never told the news.

Without waiting for Juma, Ganju put back his shoes and called the inspector. The case was registered as an accident; young Nadir while he played with the revolver had unintentionally shot himself. The corpse was hurriedly dumped in the family courtyard without autopsy, and under secret orders a picture of Razia was sent to all police stations and airports.

Sometime near dawn there was a call from the Immigration Desk. Razia had boarded the plane to London on an employment visa.

Ganju recalled the calligraphy of three curls. He felt a sudden heat inside his pocket, something burning. He shoved his hand inside his pocket and pulled out the cheque. Squiggles in black ink jumped at him like a hairy monster. He wanted to rip apart that cheque, go back to London and behead Mr Halal with his triple curls. He clutched at the revolver.

"Hello," he heard the General on his mobile. "Today, the

first thing on my 'things to do' was to call you, welcome back, we have a press conference in the afternoon, the whole nation is grateful to you for liberating the country from the shackles of debt. Don't be late," he clicked.

Ganju still holding the cheque looked away, the inky quigles bulged at him, forty millions pounds. "Forty millions," he recited unconsciously under his breath. His hand on his revolver slid; there was no one around to shoot.

He fell on the bed with the revolver cold against his chest. Girls are a curse, some punishment from Allah, a liability. He should have killed her on the very first day. Good, she chose to disappear from his life. Out of sight is good as dead, isn't it? Her husband, who could share his property, was no more in this world to make a claim. A blessing in disguise. He polished the revolver and carefully put it in the drawer. Going back to bed he settled the pillows; he was too tired to change his clothes. The man who had eloped with his daughter had been his host; he had lived in his house, ate, drank and womanized with him. He hid his face under the pillows. Mr Halal did say he treated his women like princesses, Ganju reminded himself. With his boots on, he closed his eyes, negotiating a dreamless insomnia.

The next day at the press conference Ganju had emerged as a saviour, one of the most popular leaders in the history of the country. It was peace time, there were hardly any news of protests or hunger strikes. People were never so happy and content with their leadership. Now they were the proud citizens of a sovereign state. There were no more questions about his trial or his masculinity. People had short memories; they had forgotten even Lilly Khanum, once she was wiped off from the billboards.

After the conference, in a confidential meeting they all reviewed the report on their project Doomsday Caller. They expressed their satisfaction on the health of the rooster and commended the progress on the project. At the end, the General made an impassioned speech, addressing as usual a battalion with three people in the room. "We need generations of good breeds. This miracle bird is a Godsend. With this bird in hand, we can produce a whole new lineage of a blue-blooded race, a crop of fine soldiers. Gentlemen, people die every day but in war they die a dozen a minute. What do you do then? Mothers grieve and are too tired to reproduce for a new battle. You see, Hitler gave it a serious thought. He unleashed soldiers on the young females of Germany, they would copulate in order to fertilize the wombs of national mothers. Gentlemen, we have to squeeze the yawning vagina of space, replace the solar system." He paused and pointed to the television in the room, "Now the satellite tube is gazing at our women, they have invaded our bedrooms, shameless oglers from the West, peeping toms, sneaking, poking and raping our civilization. This must stop! Brothers! It is our patriotic duty to counter it." He saluted the half-mast flag that sat on the table in front.

That day Ganju walked on clouds with stars in his pockets. All his bad dreams had evaporated under the sun of his rising fame. Now with Doomsday Caller at his doorstep, he was destined to take his revenge on Lilly Khanum.

Lilly, after she had renounced the world, was living at a shrine. Following her, Goga, the wrestler, had turned into a malang, an unshaven fakir with heavy locks and wearing beads and chains on his body. He was known as Talian wali Sarkar, the Locked One. He had taken a vow of celibacy. He was now an angel cleansed of the baser instincts and Lilly the queen of seduction was Mastani Mai, the ecstatic mother living as a recluse.

"Lilly Mastani, the film heroine turned mystic, gets raped." The news hauled Lilly from anonymity to the front page. Twelve masked men had abducted and raped her for full two days. Maliks were suspected. They had offered her a seat in the senate but Lilly had chosen to sit at the threshold of the shrine. Some believed that her growing popularity had turned the shrine into a cinema house and the devotees who had flocked around her were receiving more than her blessings. Therefore, other Pirs, the custodians of rival shrines who had lost their crowds in her presence had punished her out of jealousy. Lilly however had survived as a spotless virgin.

"This woman is a mystery, she has something where all our reasoning fails," said Zahid, passing the newspaper to the General.

"It's her impenetrability which is alarming!" Kashif mumbled weakly.

"Sir, her virginal autonomy is a threat to our masculinity," warned Zahid.

"Don't lose heart, gentlemen, just wait! Wait till she comes to know about our Tajul Kharoos, the Doomsday Caller," said the General, thumping his belly with the newspaper.

"Yes! Yes! How long mama will protect her Billy goat?" Zahid shouted on top of his voice, "It'll be slaughtered one day and that day isn't too far."

In a shelter home for aggrieved women, Lilly sat in her virtuous calm. Under a large chadder that she wore in toga style, she took tea from her silver thermos that reflected the light on her contours. Hanging on to her cup of green tea she took her sips languorously. The mystic star had turned into a surrealistic deity. The wardens had brought their families; they took her autographs and had photos taken with her. It was Sunday. Inside the corridors of the shrine, a flood of people jostled to get a glimpse of her. Outside, street vendors and stalkers who were deprived of her sight felt a pleasurable tremor as they keenly pissed against the walls of the building.

Among those clamouring to see Lilly the Mastani Mai, was the inspector Sher Mohammad. He was in plain clothes. He made his way to the warden, showed her his id card and told her that he had to ask Lilly some questions regarding the case. The warden told him to wait and disappeared through the door where Sher Mohammad could see flocks of people struggling to get in.

It was a sad day for Sher Mohammad. He was deeply touched by the news. The room was empty except for a table and two chairs. Sher Mohammad sat on one of the chairs and waited. Looking at the chair across the table, he imagined Lilly sitting face to face with him. He took out the box of mithai which he had hidden under his shirt and placed it on the table. He was well bathed and perfumed. He had oiled his moustaches with care. His eyes sparkled from the shiny antimony, the black surma he had applied. "Oh God, let my body turn into thousand eyes," he kept humming a folk song, "if I close one I can see my beloved with the other." In silence, he felt Mano's presence. He could hear slow whispers, as if someone were reciting a prayer. "Ah it's my Mano," he sighed and heard her saying, "Oh how nice of you to come, Inspector sahib." She hooked her nose with her eyebrow and her nostrils puffed seductively; this was Mano's nakhra, which now only Sher Mohammad remembered. He lovingly put a piece of mithai in her mouth, she bit the tips of his fingers, and a sensation sharper than lightning pierced his heart.

"Sorry, Inspector sahib, but Mai is too busy, there are guests from foreign countries," he heard the warden say. In her white uniform she stood against the empty chair, her eyes on the mithai. Sher Mohammad quickly grabbed the box and left; he didn't anyone else to taste it. He threw it in the garbage can and spent the night sobbing on the thighs of a local whore.

Far from the low-class hordes of fans and spiritual maniacs, Lilly had landed in New York City. Within days the press, NGOs for women's empowerment, and the human rights activists had got her out of the country.

At the World Trade Centre, the navel of the superpower, she was received by no less than the first lady. Hollywood stars were awed by her presence. She filled the front pages of glamour magazines.

"Stunning act of defiance," said the defence secretary at the award ceremony.

"This courageous woman from East has educated the West," declared Dr Smoocher, the noted anthropologist. Lilly the Mai Mastani mounted the stage and they gave her a standing ovation.

"Honor cannot be avenged by sitting idle with your legs apart but to come out of your shame and confront the rod-waving machoism. I am not afraid of the male gaze. Each assault on me refreshes my perpetual honor," she said.

Next to a fading book of poetry by a has-been poet called Ganju, lay the glossy best seller on shelves. "Lilly Mai Mastani, the Bandit Queen of Coital War."

Back home a warm welcome awaited her. Her fame had activated the multinational companies, the NGOs and the aggressive entrepreneurs. An international wedding company announced that Lilly had decided to marry anyone who could deflower her. The news turned boys into studs and old hermits into horny bulls. The entire male population of the world stood to the challenge. Sure males from Sudan to Arabia fought, bribed and lobbied for visas to enter the race.

"The time has come to release the pressure on my loins," declared the General, scratching his balls. "After all who found the dodai for you?" He farted casually. Kashif went into total silence, probing the depth of the matter. The uproar about the wedding lottery had whetted their appetites.

Ganju, who always imagined himself to be different from his competitors, firmly believed that the whole drama of the lottery was staged for him and him alone. Knowing about his hot affair with Jaana, Lilly was sending a message to him. The Hakim had said that women in Mughal harems were overawed by the king because he could satisfy a she-ass. To sleep with Lilly Mastani was no small matter, especially when he was the proud possessor of Tajul Kharoos, the crown bird.

While they all secretly celebrated their weddings, the National Security Chief broke the news that turned their wet dreams into soggy nightmares.

The rare bird was missing.

Sabre jets, F-16s and choppers mobbed the skies. Commandos shook the ground upside down like a piece of rug, submarines sniffed along the floors of oceans and divers outnumbered the fish.

"She has rendered us into potential eunuchs," the General raged in impotent anger, "a low-class whore is mocking our erecto-imperialism, her virginity has become a war of resistance," he said in a defeated tone.

Ganju was so depressed that he had gone into a maraqba, a meditative comma.

"How could we watch the contest go by without the primary contenders," Zahid, said in a worried tone. "I was all ready," he said, sitting still in his yogic position.

The wedding date was approaching and there was no sign of the bird. They tried to put pressure on the organizers to postpone the date, but they declined, saying that the male population of the world was charged with libidinous energy and if deflated, it could turn into a sexual tsunami that could be a threat to the whole world. The multinational companies who had bumped their products on this occasion were also not willing to suffer any losses.

"We have to find the bird," the Trio shouted in a chorus.

"Let's watch," said Kashif staring into vacant space with his stony eyes.

"Watch?" the General fumed helplessly. "Are we khusras, the castrated men who can only watch. You want us to chew meat with toothless jaws? Shame on you."

"Sir, we know for sure that anyone who deflowers Lilly could be the one who stole our bird, it's simple." Kashif gave a meaningful smile.

"But the man who could deflower Lilly doesn't exist," spoke Ganju breaking his maraqba. They all looked at him with suspicion.

With the disappearance of the bird, Ganju had felt betrayed. Someone was playing foul, maybe one of them had stolen the bird; Lilly's challenge could have provoked his betrayal. But it was he who had given them the secret of the bird. He had always seen himself at the head of the table for the last supper. He was the rightful bridegroom, the suffering hero waiting for poetic justice. In that state of mind Ganju wanted to dig in the earth, squeeze the skies to punch out the bird, but instead, he had to helplessly watch the city jeering at him.

On the day before the lottery, while he was on his way to his office, he ran into a traffic jam. He noticed hoardings proclaiming Lilly everywhere. Taxi cabs carried her portraits, shouted her name on the loud speakers. Where ever he looked, he found

Lilly Khanum Mai Mastani, her eyes lit up with mischief, lips taut with lust, inviting, yet murderous, her long neck a delicate sword rising out of a silken sheath, her breasts towers of female pride, from every nook and corner she stared at him. At his office an invitation for the lottery jumped at him from the centre of his table, and a brochure about the life of Lilly.

Ganju was almost at the verge of committing suicide when he phoned Juma, "Send the inspector to me, immediately," he ordered.

"Sher Mohammad, do you know the Chief of Police is retiring," said Ganju revolving on his chair.

"Yes sir," the inspector standing on his toes saluted him.

"Good," Ganju threw the brochure to the inspector, "burn that face," he ordered.

The inspector glanced at the picture. He felt as if his heart had stopped beating. He looked at Ganju. Ganju with the wave of his hand dismissed him.

There were medals on the well starched uniform of the inspector, but underneath that uniform, Sher Mohammad was a man of flesh and blood. It was not easy for him to burn the face he had loved all his life, but the temptation to move up into power had blinded him.

Next morning when he stood to dress up he looked at himself in the mirror without his uniform, which hung on the wall. His eyes fell on Lilly's picture lying on the bed. He froze for a moment and then burst into tears. Who was Lilly, what was she to him? Now that she had touched the ceiling of fame he had no future with her. At the shelter home she had not bothered even to see him. He had to throw the mithai in the garbage. She never touched it. The man and the uniform grappled, but the inspector gently numbed the man underneath and put on the uniform; promotion as the Chief of Police was too strong a drive to sacrifice his primary love. Images of Lilly kept fading against the glare of the brass.

He tightened his shoelaces and trampling on Lilly's face walked out the house.

On the very first day of the lottery, among thousands in the queue, the inspector entered the well-guarded wedding arena. On pretext of keeping the order, he went ahead of everyone and once he was inside the building, a modern day replica of a Mughal palace, he slipped into the bathroom. A few minutes and a handsome raja with a turban and a beard appeared out of the bathroom. In that guise of a wanton lover, the inspector queued up among the contenders.

The best way to burn the face of a woman was to throw acid on it. This was the common practice from ages. A woman must become ugly. She should never be able to look at herself in the mirror. Defacing and disfiguring a woman was the best revenge a man could take in this part of the world, it becomes a reminder to her whenever she sees herself in the mirror, and it's a walking ibrat, the moral lesson for all other women. Sher Mohammad in his bag had carried a bottle of whisky filled with the acid.

The lottery results were quick; the contenders were disposed rapidly. They would faint or puff off at the mere sight of the virgin bride. Shrunk in shame they were ejected from the bridal room like popcorn from a popper. With crumpled faces and wobbly legs they would stumble out and disappear into dark alleys. The crowd booed the losers and cheered at Mastani Mai's victory.

"Come show me your credentials," the inspector in the guise of a maharaja heard a familiar voice. There she was, his own Mano whom he had loved and hated, whom he had seen in torn clothes with hair full of lice, with the smell of vomit and filth around her. She had been transformed into an elegant lady, shrewd and smart. Overawed by her presence Sher Mohammad shook inside his guise for a moment, but then Ganju's voice ignited his brains.

He took out the bottle.

"No liquor, you have to be clean," she said.

The inspector looked at that beautiful face, at her heaving bosom covered by the fall of a dopatta accentuating a figure sculpted by the gods.

"Why must God give a heart of stone to this little angel? Must beauty be cruel and indifferent to its worshipers? Wasn't she the one who came to him begging? Wasn't he the one who saved her from the curse of poverty and wasn't she the one who had been unfaithful to him? She was an exploiter, a blood-sucking vampire who didn't even return his call, she thought he was after her money. Bitch! Finish that face, let her deeds become her features, they all are whores, they have to burn in hell, hell," the thought reverberated in the inspector's mind.

She smiled at him. He closed his eyes on that dazzling beauty. In a quick move he threw the acid, on that face. The acid lit her face into flames, she screamed. The inspector putting a cloth in her mouth gagged her, she fainted in his arms. Sher Mohammad saw those lovely features melting into a lava of blood, a mess of dangling skin. Horrified he ran out of the room.

Lilly, the icon of the century had been turned to ashes, her face a bombsite. Next day the news was in every paper, with Lilly's burnt face in close up, a haunting nightmare.

It was a day of sorrow for the whole nation. In a ceremony at police headquarters with the Chief Minister as the Chief Guest, Sher Mohammad was decorated as the Chief of Police.

During visiting hours, Inspector Sher Mohammad entered Mano's room in his shiny uniform sparkling with new stars on his shoulders. His personal guards stood outside on the door with their guns. He wanted to see her alone for which the permission was promptly granted by the hospital authorities.

Inside the room, he quietly sat next to her, eyes down; he didn't want to face the face he had burnt the other night. He coughed discreetly.

"Who is it?" she asked.

"It's me, Sher Mohammad," he said.

Lilly's eyes struggled against the coverings to see him. "Oh it's you, Inspector sahib," she said and tried to hook her nose with her eyebrow. Only a small movement ran through the layers. There was no more the nakhra of Mano; the final curtain had been drawn on the theatre of her face. The Chief of Police tried to keep her quiet but she was suddenly animated by his presence.

"When I renounced the world and sat at the shrine," she slurred in a broken voice, "I discovered the power of love. I looked back at my past and found the love of only one man." Words slid from the holes which once were her lips. "Your memories have remained with me forever, no fame or wealth could erase them from my mind. There was not a moment when I had not breathed without remembering you," she said fumbling for his hand.

Her words suddenly put a dent in his composure. He couldn't say anything.

"I wanted to live with you, iron your uniform with my own hands, bear children with you, eat and sleep with you, wake up with you in the morning and sleep next to you at night. Oh nothing stays in the end but love," she said.

The Chief of Police felt the man inside the uniform raging.

"I knew they had captured the crown rooster. They wanted my virginity, but Inspector sahib," she paused for breath, "I stole that bird for you."

"For me?" the inspector was shocked.

"Yes, yes, for you," she whispered and with great difficulty raised her head and bent towards her feet. "I wanted you to take my virginity." Slowly she pulled her shalwar down baring her thighs. Her legs parted and to his amazement, from her womb, flew a bird he had never seen before in his life. "It's for you," she wheezed. The bandages on her face went still.

The bird lovingly fluttered between her breasts.

Outside, the guards heard the shot. Nurses ran into the room, the guards rushed in.

Blood spurted against the ghastly face of Mano. Sher Mohammad's pistol, still clutched in his hands, lay a few inches away from his temples and his blasted head calmly rested on her charred hand.

The bird flew out of the window.

Chapter 19

Satjug the Age of Truth

Lilly Khanum's charred face on placards held by protesting crowds, on TV screens, and in every newspaper screamed justice. Who had killed that woman with the divine face? Beauty gone to ashes! Venus deformed by male pigs. Burn alive the culprits! Protesters said.

Ganju, leafing through the papers on his breakfast table, looked away from the dark print but a mere glance had changed the taste in his mouth. He wiped his face with his napkin, but the image of that ashen face choked him. What was between Lilly and the inspector? Did she kill him or he killed himself? Was he in love with her, was there something secret between them? Did it have to do something with the burning of her face, buzzed the questions.

In that chaos, neither the inspector's suicide nor Lilly's death was of any interest to the Trio. They were only concerned with the bird, which was sighted by one of the nurses at the scene. It had raised hopes of the troika for their plans. But the identity of the bird was unclear.

Was it the stolen bird, the bird of the Doomsday Caller, or any other bird? If it was the crown rooster, then who would abduct it? CIA, FBI, or RAW agents or the local agencies? What was it doing in a hospital?

There was only one eyewitness; a nurse who had entered the room exactly at the time the inspector had pulled the trigger. And she had seen a bird.

"I believe you saw a bird," the General said to the nurse. She was dressed in white uniform buttoned to her neck.

"Oh yes, I did," she giggled, head down.

"A real bird?"

"Yes!"

To his surprise she giggled again, helplessly.

"Are you alright?"

"Yes yesss . . . "

"Well, in a situation like that one could be in a state of shock. Are you sure you saw the bird, or could it possibly be a hallucination?"

"Well, I couldn't see it properly sir, it just dazzled before my eyes . . . "

The General noticed every time she uttered something about the bird she blushed.

"What happened then?"

"Oh, ha, oh," the nurse went into a pleasing convulsion. "A bird, oh, a bird of unbelievable beauty, white and yet oh not so white."

"Did it look like a duck, a fowl or a rooster?" asked the General, excited at the description, which nearly matched the crown bird.

"Very much a rooster sir," she said, one of her buttons breaking against her panting bosom.

"Did you touch it?" the General said, half rising from his chair.

"Touch? Oh no, no sirrr," she giggled again.

"I said did you or did you not touch it?" Something stirred inside the General.

"No sir, I didn't."

"Tell me about the shape of that bird."

"Shape?"

"Yes yes, the shape!"

"Well, it was, oh, what it was, some special shape."

"Answer me!" thundered the General. "What was the shape of that rooster?"

"Long tail, golden crown, blue crested . . . " She fidgeted.

"I asked you a question, didn't you hear me, did you see the bird you are describing, did you see a royal crown on its head, tail of a miniature peacock?" The General circled around her with one of his arms lifted. "Did you? Did you?" he crooned.

"Yes!" screamed the nurse, her buttons flying and her body going through orgasmic shuddering.

The General relaxed in his seat. He was more than sure that she had seen their bird, the very crown rooster.

At the hospital, each time the nurse narrated the story of the bird, she would go funny. Her shudders gave the patients a pleasure beyond anaesthesia. Her story went from patient to patient and from patient to visitor until it became a buzz in the entire nation. Within weeks on every nook and corner appeared barbeque shops with skinned chicken hung on display, named exotically; murgh-e-musallam, the ultimate chicken, shahi murgh, the royal chick, and Mughliyee, the descendent of the Mughals. Chicken tikka and karahi became popular. All sorts of people would come and eat chicken with a hunger they had not known before.

The Trio got alarmed. "What if our chicken is already skinned, hung, and cooked," panicked Zahid.

"Well, if someone ate that bird it would show. To eat that bird is to grow something that would pale Eiffel tower to a hunch," said the General confidently. "We have to come up with some strategy. Imagine some common hustler carrying the burden of the ultimate organ of penetration. No never, it will be blind men leading the mad. We can't let it happen."

"What about bird flu," Zahid said, serving a strong dose of vodka to the General.

"Bird flu?"

"If some dying patients in hospitals are diagnosed as victims of bird flu, the government can declare it illegal to slaughter a chicken without it being checked by the health department. We can then check out all the chickens."

"Excellent," said the General emptying his glass.

Ganju had become a victim of futility. His wife was on the operation table for God knows what surgery, his daughter had left him, and his son had stopped responding to his letters. The virgin he wanted to deflower was no more in the world. He might never taste that bird and leave the world without ever having to become the doer or the ideal male. He would die a truncated eunuch who could only hobble into the bed with a coffined wife.

That evening Ganju in his despair left the house, without informing anyone. His feet carried him to a park in the interior city. He had never been there before but he felt as if he had lived there forever. It was Sunday, and most of the people were out. In his ordinary guise no one recognized him. He walked past a row of jugglers, wayside palmists, and entertainers. A man flashing a sword came in front of him. He froze on his feet. The man laughed and swallowed the blade up to the hilt. Ganju hurriedly moved away as the man bowed to the applauding crowd. At a corner, he saw a woman's head stuck in the ground. The head smiled at him. Horrified, he turned away and saw a parrot that hopped onto a small cannon. It ignited the cannon, a big blast, children and their parents laughed and clapped. Now a pigeon pulled a cart of birds and a monkey paraded in army uniform saluting an effigy of Uncle Sam.

Ganju kept walking away until he reached the top of a hill. No one was around; he sat down looking at the sky with vacant eyes thinking about those faces he had seen, a pageantry of God's plenty. What was he but a speck of insignificance against the vastness of the universe? Lying down, he stretched himself and closed his eyes. He would have liked to die or sleep forever in that serene moment. Suddenly he felt someone was watching him. He opened his eyes and saw the image of Tajul Kharoos, the aphrodisia of paradisia, the crown bird. It watched him with the eyes of a human.

"No it can't be true." He sat up with a start.

"It's true, I am Tajul Kharoos, the first bird ever conceived," it said. "I make nests in the minds of people, flutter in their souls. I am the fantasy of mankind. I can curl into the darkness of the night and with my beak can nip into the very human race. My eyes can see beyond seeing. I am the invisible dream people dream, and I can take wings after my death, from my own ashes I am born again and again."

Ganju almost fainted at this miracle. How could a bird speak in human language?

"I've little time," the Crown Rooster lifted its long neck and said. "Ganju it's you who brought me to life. It was your desire for a longer and firmer future that moved Jalinoos out of his grave. I am given this power of speech only to tell you a secret. I belong to you and you only but your own friends want to steal me. They are after power and your calling is love. Pir the Invisible," it flapped its wings, "sends you the blessed curse!" It eased itself onto Ganju's shirt as if embossing it with some divine seal. Ganju, wonderstruck, stood up watching it disappear.

At night while Juma pressed his legs, he said, "Why Sarkar is so quiet, is something wrong, should I inform Bade Hakim sahib?"

"No."

"Is it your haemorrhoids?"

"No."

"Sarkar, to keep something within your body is to give room to a burglar. Bade Hakim sahib tells if something worries you, you must spit it out or it will poison your heart. A secret becomes an ulcer, Sarkar, a stone, and that stone can destroy you from within."

"Juma, you are my trusted servant, but I know if I tell you something even you'll not believe me," said Ganju.

"Never, Sarkar, whatever you say is sacred to me, toba toba," Juma touched his ears. "How can I ever disbelieve you, death to me if I do so."

"I saw a bird," said Ganju.

"Sarkar a bird, what kind of bird?"

"A very special bird."

Juma nodded in utter awe.

"And that bird spoke to me," said Ganju, his voice going heavy.

"The bird spoke to you, Sarkar?" Juma looked at Ganju open mouthed.

"Yes, it spoke to me in our own human language," Ganju said as if he himself didn't believe in what he was saying.

"Oh Sarkar," Juma shouted and kissed his hands and then fell at his feet. "Sarkar, it's a great sign, no wonder that bird was from Satjug and you are no less than a saint."

"Satjug?"

"Ji Sarkar, Satjug, the age of truth where even stones talk and trees have tongues, they all speak like humans. Satjug is where man and nature live together. But Sarkar, in this age birds speak only to people who are nearer to truth. They bring prophecies, like huma, the invisible bird who if it ever sits on your head, you are declared the king. Sarkar, you are selected for some higher task. You are the chosen one." Juma kissed Ganju's feet again.

"Juma, I know you believe me, but I still doubt the bird," Ganju said gathering his legs.

"No, Sarkar, toba, toba, never doubt, that will be sacrilegious, never, Sarkar. If you don't believe in things they never come back to you."

"Really?"

Ganju had always felt some invisible force surrounding him, some spirit protecting and guiding him. Maybe that spirit had visited him in the form of that bird. And now that Juma had told him about the Satjug, he should justly consider himself the favoured one. This feeling transformed Ganju into a new man, a man with lofty ideas and unbent will.

The General summoned all the bird catchers in the country. After testing them out, he picked one who among his numerous achievements, had captured a flying dinosaur for a Hollywood producer.

Knowing the instinctive behaviour of a rooster, the bird catcher told the General that in the mating season, which was about to start, hens could attract our rooster. The General could nab it in the act. The General liked the idea but feared a law-and-order situation with millions of hens on the roads. It was also ungraceful for him or for the army to run after a chicken in the open public. At night while playing his games with his wife he thought of something.

"I want only one hen, the hen that could turn on the rooster," ordered the General to the bird catcher.

The bird catcher produced an attractive well-plumed chick, an ultimate femme fatale who could twirl like a cheer leader and seductively lift her scanty tail to reveal her pleasure spot.

The General, to carry out his plan, needed a decoy female. Only the nurse could recognize the bird but keeping in mind the utmost secrecy, the nurse was an obvious risk. Why not someone near and dear to himself? Why not ask his own pretty wife to give a little sacrifice while he volunteered to be the cuckold. After all it was the question of his loyalty to his country. He had the hormones of the hen-on-heat squeezed out and doused them on his favoured cushion. He hid himself with the hormonal cushion and waited for his wife. She came in her lingerie and sat on it. She smoked a cigarette. The General had an unbearable urge to crow while she wiggled on the cushion. He restrained himself and on the pretext of being tired turned to sleep on his side. At midnight hearing his wife snore, he left the bed and went to the closet to wait for the expected visitor. Sometime past midnight the wife in her sleep thought the very moustache of the General was touching her bare flesh. She happily responded to those kinky feathers with her blinkers on.

Cluck cluck, cluck cluck.

The General heard the sound, a commotion in the bed. Maybe she was having a nightmare or a wet dream, he thought and fell asleep. At dawn he came out of the cupboard and saw the sheets on the bed rising up to the ceiling, moving fast in whirlpools of circling movements.

"Oh God, what am I seeing," the General muttered to himself. He was shocked to see thousands of roosters with their crowns up and tails stiff, jostling to enter his bedroom. In a quick move the General ordered the commandos to enter and complete the mission. They pulled off the sheets, the wife shrieked, and they captured the rooster and left quickly.

Attracting stray cocks around the country, the wife was fittingly flattered but it took the army two weeks to clean the chicken shit in and around the General's headquarters. Once caught, the crown rooster was sent for an immediate checkup. The doctors reported that it was fine.

To celebrate the successful recovery of the Crown Rooster, Zahid had arranged a mujra in his house. The sauciest dancer of the city hit the male company with her voluptuous charms.

Whirling like a tall flame, she teased their imagination, rubbed herself against their bodies, and put her arms around them. Late at night when the musicians and the female artist had left, the General as usual addressed his battalion of three people,

"Gentlemen, why is the oldest profession in the world still going on? In ancient monarchies it was never the throne or the palace but the king's sceptre that was the most intimidating prop in the theatre of power. And what were those harems but an extended womb. It's the harems with hordes of royal bastards that speak of the ever-present virility of the kings."

He paused for a drink. After a cheerful quantity of intake his neck erected and his face became red with passion, "Did you notice that woman," he referred to the dancer of the evening. "She looked at us with an eye keen to feel us in our balls. She was a challenge, a vertical question, sharp as a blade, stripping us naked. Her gaze was penetrating, her moves provocative, and yet she remained distant, inaccessible. Now who among us had the spunk to grab and give to her what she demanded so aggressively." He looked one by one at everyone and they all lowered their eyes. "Never forget that women read faces." He looked at Ganju who obediently listened. "One look and they can tell not only the size of your penis but also the weight of your balls. Can't you see, she reads the hidden contents through the open books of our faces." The General twisted his nose, drawing a bold expression on his face.

"Now, gentlemen, the good news is that operation Doomsday Caller is our gateway to the international club of he-men. Now we are self-reliant. It's the success in our pants that bounces to our faces, the self-assured smile of a king. Remember, a failed penis is a failed state. Let's march to our destiny!"

"Ignorant fools," Ganju pitied their ambition and their greed for the bird which only he knew would never be on their table. Suddenly he felt taller than them. With the height of a newly born Adam touching the skies, he lifted a triumphant glass; it was he to whom the bird had spoken. Only he was invited to the final dinner. With a smirk he gulped the drink.

Chapter 20

The Last Bath

Like a gushing stream under the earth not finding an opening, Zeenat had died like an unheard whisper.

All her life, she had been possessed by the weary ghosts of the Haveli. Its cold walls had finally closed in on her. While she lived, her only adventure was to open a window and feel the sun on her skin. Shivering in her loneliness, she would dissemble part by part and spend the whole day collecting her arms, legs, breasts, and her pelvis from different corners of the Haveli. Moving like a shadow against the chandeliers with dust murking their glassy lungs, she would pass by the sofas lying stagnant in their isolation, walk on carpets with hunting images, peacocks, roses, nightingales, castles, and deer fleeing from tigers with woolen skin and silky teeth. Suddenly the silence would be riddled with the intriguing stir of insects.

She was the muse without a poet.

Her greatest passion was her embroidery. She was happy with a needle. Her fingers would come alive at the thin glare of silver weaving in and out through the plain cloth, carving patterns on it. There was no ambition in her to conquer or liberate the world. She only fought with her needles, heroically.

It was one of those late evenings when she was watching the sun go down over the courtyard that she felt an urge to take out her embroidery. In dim light of the lamp she sat on her bed and fondly placed the frame on her knee with a neatly stretched cloth. It was a rose she had drawn, a full-bloomed rose. As she moved her hand, the needle led her to the mystery of her flesh. It slyly slipped into her skin and pricked her finger. Blood spurted, the twinge of pain tingled her body like the wind shaking a tree. She liked it, the hurt, the tiny bob of red bubble on the tip of her finger. In that blood-soaked moment, she had become real. Maids rushed to dress her wound but she kept smiling, thrilled to be one with her body.

The greatest celebration of body rites came when she was on the operating table for the first time. Under the knives, she had felt resurrected. Their keen stare had cleansed her soul and blessed her flesh with bolts of sensation and a sacred rage. Flat on the table with floodlights, the scalpel had cut and sliced, performing some ritual on her bare body. The serpentine hiss of stitches had excited her. She had loved those scars on her body; the indelible memories of congealed sensations. Since then, she would want her body to be slashed, manipulated, mauled, wrangled, molested, ripped apart, limb by limb.

"Allah, and to Allah we return."

Voices of sorrow-women reciting Quran reverberated in the emptiness of the Haveli. News of Zeenat's death had spread through the village. She was the Naik Bibi, a kind-hearted woman who on the quiet had always helped the poor and the needy. She was the silent savior of Noorpur.

"Allah, to Allah we return."

In middle of the night, the heart-rending wailings of women made Ganju tremble with fear. Just an hour ago, he had been horrified to find a dead body under his weight. He had torn himself away from her cold embrace and in panic had switched on all the lights in the room, but seeing a portion of her thigh exposed from the covers, he had instantly switched them off. Later, the local lady doctor had checked Zeenat's pulse, prodded her chest with her stethoscope and had declared her dead. Once the doctor had left, Ganju had rushed out of the room, which was now filled with the odor of death.

Sitting in the lounge, he had tried to calm himself, but knowing that Zeenat lay in the next room had made his heart sink.

Images of her lifeless body kept haunting him.

Did he ever love her? Was it duty or love? All his life he had never seen her body bare. Perhaps he didn't have the eye. They say beauty hides itself when it doesn't find a beholder. Why couldn't she unveil herself to him? Was he too selfish, busy in his own things? Ganju wept. He felt all alone in the world.

Near dawn everyone was at the funeral except his son, who was to reach the village by evening. Allama stormed in with his orphan children dressed in white caps. The shamyanas went up and Ganju sat in an enclosure receiving the guests. By evening the government officials arrived in their flagged cars, mostly wearing the starched national dress. That turned the funeral into a national ceremony. The prime minister had sent him a condolence message. All those cars, men in power and women in their silk dresses under their chadders appeared like shadows to him. They were all crawling to their graves he thought. "Allah and to Allah we return," the Quranic recitation went on forever.

His son Taimur had arrived. He had taken a flight from the US. To Ganju's surprise he had grown a beard and was dressed in the traditional Muslim attire. There was something in his look, something hypnotic and penetrating. His walk was of a follower of someone invisible. He looked like a youth educated not in California but in some local madrasa.

Inside the enclosure Taimur stared at his father as if he had killed his mother. To avoid that look, Ganju, reluctantly introduced him to the guests.

The General was exceptionally warm in greeting Taimur; he embraced him and told Ganju that he should be proud of his son who had not given up his Islamic traditions in spite of western education. Kashif glanced him over, his eyes working like a metal detector. Taimur, without responding to anyone, left and sat in a corner to read the Quran. He recited in an aggressive tone as if he were possessed.

Late in the afternoon, a servant came to Ganju and told him that the professional women who prepare the body, had asked his permission to give the deceased her last bath. Something came over him, he shook his head. "Pay them and tell them to go," he said. The thought of professional bathers touching his wife made him puke. He stood and walked to the room where Zeenat's body lay.

Just before her death, Zeenat had partially recovered from one of her operations. After taking a long bath, she had sat in the window looking into the garden. It was a lovely day. The light on the leaves had made exquisite patterns on the grass. Slowly the sun had melted in the foliage of pensive greens. A colored mosaic of glass ventilators had cut the shadows, making furrows of light in the room.

Once the sun had gone down she had walked to her dressing room. Large cupboards had greeted her with ivory handles and sylvan embroidery, but she was held by the mirror; something alive, a full length dreaming box. She had taken off the chadder. Her bare skin had fogged the air. Mesmerized, she had loosened her hair. Turning to the closets, she had rummaged among her wedding-night clothes and the jewellery lying bright in their velvet boxes. Her eyes had wafted through bottled perfumes, layers of silk rub, and the impossible shine of diamonds. Tempted she had stood among her bridal ghosts.

All those years she had been dressing up for someone who would never come. Often she would fall asleep with her clothes on, but on that day, she had kept herself awake for her husband. She had wanted him to look into her eyes, touch her, put his arm around her waist and sweep her away like an insatiable wave of the ocean. She had longed to shout, dance, and grab her husband in bed and never let him go. She had fantasies of stripping naked and climbing on top of him. She had a raging urge to see him naked. But as the light on the window sills vanished and darkness swallowed the huge Haveli, there was no sign of Ganju. Exhausted, she had curled up to her only companion, the insonomic ghost, solitude. That night was longer than her life. She was too exhausted to recollect her body.

When Ganju entered the room, he was greeted by the ice slabs and the smell of camphor. Zeenat's body lay on a marble slab covered in a white cloth. It gave him the chill. His own room looked alien to him.

He locked the door.

Alone with Zeenat, he sat next to her body.

With her eyes closed, Zeenat looked beautiful as ever. Unaware of his gaze, she had a smile on her face.

Images of young Zeenat flashed in his mind, he could see her in her bridal dress, she serving him food, talking to their daughter, giving him his vitamins, moving in the house, half revealed and half concealed. All his life he had never seen her without clothes and there she was lying in front of him waiting for him to undress her for her last bath. He looked at her. The afternoon sunlight had lit her majestic contours. Ganju, reluctantly uncovered her upper part. Her beautiful breasts emerged like twin moons. With trembling hands he poured the water from the clay jug. The water fell on her skin giving it a divine shimmer.

In a mist of fear and fascination, he slowly pulled the cover down to her feet. It took away his breath

Ganju saw his wife. Naked.

Chapter 21

Labaika Labaika, I Am Here I Am Here

Even with his eyes wide open, Ganju couldn't shake off the image of Zeenat's body lying naked on the marble slab. He tried distracting himself by drinking but it was engraved in his mind. Zeenat's flowing saris, silk blouses smelling of perfume, embroidered scarves and large chadders hung lifeless in cupboards. Her shoes lay neatly in a row awaiting her footfall, and her jewellery sought her arms like clusters of fainted fireflies. He ordered the bedroom to be locked and shifted himself to the guest room.

The forty days of mourning became a soul-searching journey for Ganju. Imagining Zeenat's body being devoured by worms gave him the shudders. He pondered on the conflict of good and evil, God and man, fate and human will, on angels, on hell and heaven, on jinns and witchcraft. What was man? What was the purpose of one's life? Was death the final end? Was there a God? Stuck in the abyss of his own introspective cinema, voices of condoling crowds and sorrowing women passed over him. During this period, the maids forgot their cackles and their courtyard games. Alcohol had lost its bite and food its taste.

Ganju, in his mournful solitude, noticed his face going awry with wrinkles, his cheeks splitting into chipped coins, his head balding, and his belly sagging. Sunk in remorse and spent with guilt, Ganju had suddenly gone old.

It was a message from his daughter that pulled him out of his stupor. A condolence message appeared in a few printed words without emotions and without address. Suddenly he wanted to ransack the world to find her. How could she miss the last look of her dead mother? Everything came back to him; the three curls, the murder of young Nadir, and her disappearance. Oh, she was the cursed one who had brought shame to the whole family. For him she was already dead. He tore up the message.

"Chhotay Sarkar has not been well," said Juma as he pressed Ganju's legs in the evening.

"Why do you say that?" asked Ganju taking a sip from his glass.

"Sarkar, something is happening to him, no one knows what's going on in his mind," said Juma.

"What's going on in his mind?" Ganju nudged him with his foot.

"Well, Sarkar, I can't tell you exactly, but Taimur sahib goes to the bazaar and," he hesitated, letting out a sigh.

"And?" Ganju asked sharply.

"Sarkar, he shouts to everyone that qayamat, the doomsday, is nearing," lisped Juma.

"What?"

"Ji, Sarkar."

"What the hell are you talking about?" Ganju exploded. He pulled back his legs and sat on the bed, leaving Juma's hands in midair.

"Sarkar, Chhotay Sahib says the world is coming to an end. We must pray to God to forgive our sins. We should not lie, cheat, fornicate or lust after worldly power. And we must be ready for the final judgement," said Juma, his hands clasped to his chest.

Ganju was silent.

"The other day," Juma continued, "Chhotay Sarkar held the scales of the local shopkeeper while he weighed. 'Do not deceive your customers!' he warned him, and 'Do not hoard, because hoarding is to store fuel for hell.' He caught hold of a landowner who wore a silk shirt and a gold chain. Chhotay Sarkar pulled his chain and said that his silk shirt will whirl into flames and gold will turn into red-hot iron." Juma touched his ears, "Toba toba," he clattered his teeth.

"What's wrong with him, has he gone mad?" said Ganju in a fury.

"Sarkar," Juma lisped once again, "the little master says we must wait."

"Wait for what?"

"For the savior of the world, Sarkar," droned Juma.

"Saviour of the world?"

Ganju hurriedly pushed off his whisky glass as if it were a fiendish object.

"Do you think qayamat is nearing?" he asked.

"Sarkar, the scholars say on doomsday the maid will give birth to the mistress, Dajjal, the monster, will appear on a donkey wearing a crown of blood. He will have only one eye on his forehead and his body will be covered by kinky hair. Sarkar, Chhotay sahib says, 'The earth will crack and the sun will fall from the sky.'"

"Enough, enough. Idiot! Playing some wayside clairvoyant," rebuked Ganju. He leaned back and took his whisky glass.

The next day Ganju called Taimur and hugged him with great warmth. He was met with a metal chest. Ganju begged him to show some sympathy for his father. How on earth did he become a preacher instead of an aeronautical engineer, Ganju wondered, as Taimur stared at the ground, panting, as if he was reciting something under his breath.

"Your mother was a good woman, she loved you," Ganju put his hand on Taimur's shoulder. "You are a grown man, you have to look after the jagir," he said, giving Taimur a whiff of power. Taimur looked up with one merciless stare.

That night Ganju switched on the TV. Every channel flashed news of wars all over the world, killings in Africa, in Iraq, Afghanistan, children bombed, people dying everywhere, earthquakes, suicide bombers, poverty, crime, rape, hunger and natural disasters. He got depressed, maybe his son was right.

But before he could see the earth cracking and sun falling from the sky, Zahid called. "You have suffered a great loss, I can understand, but now you must pull yourself up and join our Thursday meetings. There are some new happenings you'll like to mess with."

Ganju politely thanked him but then abruptly blurted, "Are you watching the TV channels?"

"Why, are there some new ones?" quipped Zahid.

"No, I saw some horrible images of war and suffering in the world," said Ganju.

"What's wrong with you, war has been there from the time of Abel and Cain. We all have to go through some kind of war, history is full of them, there are water wars, world wars, ethnic wars, star wars, and God knows what wars. What about Mahabharata, the longest war where even gods participated. War hones our life instinct, it's an incentive for us to survive, and man's evolution lies in this very secret."

"Do you think the world is coming to an end? Is there any saviour?"

"Now don't tell me you are as stupid as those half-educated lot in this country. After every war, which is no less than a qayamat, they wait for the saviour who never comes. Look, the world is going on, people are shopping, picnicking, eating, dancing, fucking, going to places, having fun and you are stuck in your cynical cocoon. Have you forgotten the story of Mr Cheerful we read in our fifth class? 'Always look at the brighter side,' would say our teacher with her half-exposed bosom. Don't ignore the ads between those gruesome war scenes, you'll have a different feel of the world. Life is overflowing with seductive women, shampoos, anti-aging creams, chocolates, funny movies, and lot of digital reality. They have already cloned a sheep, man is not too far. It's sad that you act dead when you are fully alive. Cheer up, old chap! Put on your joggers to join the race. It's the century of man's ascension."

Before Zahid could switch off the phone, Ganju reluctantly asked him about the bird.

"Oh, the bird is in perfect health. Our success is around the corner. Now don't be a killjoy, be ready to taste the Aphrodisia of the Paradisia. Unite all the cherries of the world. You have nothing to lose but your juices," came the drunken voice skidding on ice cubes.

As if woken from a bad dream, Ganju shook his body like an

old rug, opened the window of his room and aired it in the sun-shine. Taking a deep breath, he hastened to the bathroom for a quick shower.

"Welcome back to life," said the General after the last day of the mourning period. "I am already smelling the divine barbeque on our table. This last supper will make difference both in bed and in war, the two most important portfolios of us men. We just need the last push, a couple of millions for the missing feed and then we'll blow our palates. You'll be glad to know that we have already started the programme of poverty alleviation. We have engaged some left-wing social parasites obsessed with upward mobility. They are keen for cheque-licking projects like the liberalization of arts, theatre for social change, and empowerment of women. Affluent western donors are eager to support these leftovers of the left. We are also collecting a host of rich kids, to start the fashion industry. One has to show some flesh on the media, give a taste of carnal pleasures in the name of enlightenment, and yes, we must get some retarded urban pirs to form an official Sufi counsel for a moderate view of religion. But, mind you, against this liberaliza-tion, we must create a media war, unsafe borders, soldiers dying and killing, some kind of upsurge. I mean some nationalist groups have to be hoisted alongside religious groups to create a pseudo opposition. You know all those gruesome images of bombs and human limbs flying in the air, it could challenge the patriotic mania among liberals and peace-loving people. You'll agree that at the end of the day, fear is the key to good rule. Hurry up and don't waste a minute. There's this Hajj coming up, we've already arranged your meeting with the Arabian princes. It's an appropriate time for you to pay homage to the house of Allah, especially after your personal tragedy. The public will look at it as a pious gesture from your side. Try convincing the princes to dole out money, since they too need our Doomsday Caller," said the General.

With his wife in the grave, his daughter disappearing into anonymity, and his son hallucinated by visions of the qiamat, Ganju was indecisive. Once the bird had promised him his wish, why should he be going to Hajj and beg for money? But could the bird be a figment of his imagination. Ganju was pinched by his own doubting instinct. He should face facts, the bird was in the custody of the Intelligence agencies and the army was guarding it. There was no chance for its escape from such security. But birds have mysterious ways of escaping and satjug bird is no ordinary bird.

"Juma, do you think man could live more than a hundred years?" At night he couldn't help confiding in Juma.

"It's not easy to fool Izrael, the angel of death, Sarkar," said Juma pensively.

"Did I tell you about the bird?"

"Oh the satjug bird, yes, Sarkar!"

"Did I tell that the very bird spoke to me?"

"Of course, Sarkar."

"But I guess I didn't tell you what it told me."

"No, Sarkar."

"Well, the bird told me that if I would eat it, I would live for more than a hundred years," Ganju said drinking deep from his whisky glass.

"Wah, Sarkar, the bird was so right. Adam was five thousand years old, and Prophet Noah survived for three thousand years. Now people don't exercise, walk or eat pure food. Sarkar, you know the story of Khizar, who still lives on but is hiding somewhere. Maybe it's one of his birds. You are lucky, Sarkar, he has sent you a bird of life."

"Do you think I should go to Hajj, I mean proper Hajj this time?" asked Ganju, waving Juma to get him a refill.

"What else does a Muslim want in his life. Once in a lifetime every Muslim must perform the Hajj. It is one of the five pillars on which our religion rests. Your sacrifice of a goat at the house of Allah will relieve you from all worries and fears. Go to Hajj, pray to Allah, thank him for sending you the bird, and," he waited while handing over the glass to Ganju.

"And?" Ganju took the glass.

"Once you go to Hajj, your son will find in you a true father, he'll listen to you and you alone. Our whole nation will appreciate that you are doing your duty to God."

"But I've just gone through the mourning period."

"Sarkar, the dead cannot return but you are living. Sarkar, you only live once and if you live in humiliation it's not good, I can do that because I am born that way, I am humiliation incarnate, but you are born to be a king, a powerful king. Emotions make us weak, and the weak are eliminated. Once you have power, you can raise a harem. There will be thousands of nazrana women, and you can have as many wives as the Mughal kings," Juma paused, his hands running like puppies on Ganju's legs. "They built nice mausoleums for their beloved wives once they died. You must build a shrine. That's the best gift to your spouse," he said.

That night Ganju couldn't sleep. Once again, lustful desires stirred in him. After having invested so much of his life in this project and now that he could smell a future steaming with the bird stew, he should not step back. To perform Hajj was a matter of few days. He would be back after enjoying the hospitality of the princes and earning a reward in the world and the Hereafter. His wife's death was ordained, no one could stop it. Once the shrine was built, her soul would rest in peace, he rationalized. With a charged libido, he looked at himself in the mirror. His wrinkles had already disappeared.

The ritual of Hajj started with a prayer. Ganju repeated after the prayer leader:

"It's time for departure from the world
From my family and from my children
From my wealth and from my home
It's time for departure
Even from myself . . . "

He took off the blue jacket, pink necktie, grey shirt, checkered socks, black shiny shoes and his undergarments.

A white unstitched cloth wrapped his stark naked body.

"Cloth around your body is nothing but your kaffan, the burial shroud. You are alone as in your grave."

His self was shed like a wornout skin.

"Labaika, labaika," millions recited as they performed the ceremony of Arrival. Pulled by some invisible force, Ganju was driven along waves and waves of people who leapt to the Kaaba like moths circling around the flame. "Mothers will forget feeding their babies and all pregnant women would abort." Voices of the prayer leaders thundered on every step. Ganju was hit by the weird images of women dying in labour, abandoning their babies in deserted places, disowning their own flesh and blood. He moved faster in the circumambulation, chased by the screams of babies.

"Mankind would be in a drunken riot, and yet not drunk. All who are in graves shall be raised."

Divine verses fell on his heart like bolts of lightning. His body shook. He could hear the trumpet of Esrafil, the doomsday caller.

As if awakening from their mortal sleep, people ran around at a quick pace touching the covers of Mahmil the sacred cover that wrapped Kaaba like a bride.

"Those who will touch will accompany Kaaba to Paradise on the day of judgement."

Ganju reluctantly touched the hem; a gust of sensation swept him off his feet. He hung on to the cover like a fallen creature, desperate to be lifted.

Nearing the black stone his heart jumped. He felt as if something living was looking at him.

"On the day of judgement the black stone shall appear with an eye that sees and a tongue that speaks and it shall testify in favour of only those who have kissed it in truth."

His lips shivered. He leapt to the stone and kissed it hard as if to imprint his face on the stone. He wanted to be remembered on the Day of Judgement.

At the seventh circle, people moved to Multazam, the sacred wall where they thrashed their keen bodies as if they were beating and punishing themselves. Some hit it so hard that their foreheads had bumps and their chests got bruised.

The touch of the wall flared Ganju's skin; his body pulsated against the wall to embrace all the miracles of the wall. Each time he hit it, he felt lighter and calmer.

Stopping by Mizab-ar-rehma, the fountain of mercy, he

looked at the benign flow shimmering in cool purity.

"Once you are forgiven, your sins will be washed away, and you shall be fresh as a newborn."

He eagerly drank from that well. Rinsing his soul, it washed away all the dirt of his sins.

At night he couldn't help wondering about his curious transformation.

He seemed to be losing control of his position, his status, his family; he was not even remembering his own name. Was it a collective hypnosis that had disoriented him or was there some power above humans? Earlier, he had been there for Umrah, the casual visit to the Kaaba, but this time he was going through the entire ritual with millions around him. Well, another few days and he'd be back to his normal life, things would settle once he had his meeting with the princes. It'll be all over, he assured himself. Thinking all that, he didn't know when he fell asleep.

In the middle of night with one rapid eye movement his dream jumped from one image to the other; a beautiful woman in a garden appeared and disappeared. A sudden jolt of delight, her lithe skin surrounded him. With the next rapid eye movement he found a serpent winding round his body, nipping him at the navel. The sting shuddered through his groin. His bones expanded into a huge skeleton, his nose unfolded two heavy nostrils, his tongue fell out of his widening mouth, his ears flapped and his body parts swelled. He struggled hard to get out of that coarse hide but it kept growing on him. He screamed in fear.

The rapid eye movement stopped.

He woke up and discovered that he was not clean. He felt horrible, ashamed. His mind was riddled with hysterical questions:

What was man but a two-footed beast embedded in lust, defiled by bias, sullied by hatred, pocked by greed. It's the spirit that floats above furs and faeces. Lust was the unbridled stallion without a rider. What about higher things: love for mankind, helping the poor, compassion, charity, and tears for the suffering people. Humans had risen from their animal selves by raising their forelegs and now from humans they should become angels. That is the spiral flight to divinity. He must muzzle his bestial appetites. Peasants had to castrate overheated bulls and donkeys. They became gentle once the unruly libido was trimmed. Sacrificing lust was the rebirth of man as an angel. Laado, the major donkey, will be measured only by his penis but man was created in the image of God. They say Adam was so tall that he could hear the heavenly music but due to his fall had shrunk into a mortal. Ganju too was a fallen Adam, and this was his chance to become tall and touch the celestial harps. Suddenly his fear to be debased into a penis made him shudder with disgust.

He quickly washed himself.

"Time to repay your debts. Seek cure for the sickness of your heart." At Arafat the mountain of mercy they halted to meditate on events after death, to beg mercy and cry out loudly for their saviour. Running seven times between the two hills of Al Safa and Al Marwah, he moved between his good and bad deeds, between punishment and forgiveness. His memories of life were fast erasing, a void was growing inside him; nothingness resounding nothingness.

"Waswsa is the whirlpool of fear. Before you are sucked into it, thou shalt shout, I am here, I am here, labaika labaika to your creator, only then thou shalt overcome it."

He felt the tremors of doom inside him.

"Here we have imprisoned Satan."

Prophet Abraham's footprints were still fresh on the rock from where he had called aloud, "Labaika." God had given Abraham's voice such energy that the whole world could hear him; a loud universal labaika was the answer from the living and from those still unborn.

"Labaika!" shouted Ganju, his voice rising from his guts like a cry.

"Abraham tied Satan at this place by throwing stones at him."

"Labaika labaika."

Everyone was driven by the passion to attack Aqaba the devil, a crude pillar standing in a basin-like enclosure of more than one yard in height.

They ran, collided, and jostled to be the first to hit Satan.

Ganju looked up at the pillar, a projectile of lust and depravity. From nowhere, his body was filled with energy. He threw the stone in his hand with all his might, hitting Satan. The hideous pillar moved. Ganju was astonished to see the appearance of a massive moustache, brass, and medals; it had turned into the figure of the General. For a moment Ganju's hand froze in the air. It was the General who had instructed him to beg money on the pretext of performing the Hajj; a sacred duty of all God-fearing Muslims. "Labaika . . . " Ganju's voice joined a million others.

With each stone, he was released of his anger against corruption, greed, lust, and his own sins. By the last stone, he was relieved of his burden. In perfect calm his heart prayed and his lips thirsted to kiss the very dust of Mecca.

"Sacrifice is a covenant with God, it's not the flesh that reaches God but your devotion."

"Allah o Akbar!"

Thousands of animals were slaughtered, blood flowed all over for the celebration on the tenth day.

The razor flashed.

They shaved his head.

Shorn of intellect and his worldly powers, Ganju felt like an angel.

On the last day, inside Kaaba, the sweet voice of the muezzin beckoned Ganju to his creator. He performed his ablutions; water ran over his hands like splashes from heaven. He stood among millions for the prayer. All of them kneeling on the sacred ground. Loud and clear commands of God rising among the millions made him tremble with the awesome fear of God. He looked up at Heaven and cried, "Oh God, this slave of yours will only serve you and you alone. All worldly gods are false and there is only one God." After losing his wife, his daughter and his son, he was now left alone with his Allah. Allah and to Allah we return. His soul melted into tears. The next day the princes waited for him at their dinner, but he had boarded the earliest plane home.

"Labaika labaika!"

Ganju had flattened the serpent.

Chapter 22

Divine Buzz

Unlike before, when he traveled first class, Ganju returned on economy. Still wrapped in his ahram, the white kaffan, he was without any baggage except a computerized rosary which he held tightly in his hand. No one recognized him in that dress but everyone regarded him with some kind of reverence. Some shirked at his sight, pretending he was not there. When the air hostess approached him, he lowered his eyes and ordered nothing. With his eyes on the tiny thumbnail screen that displayed all his clicks in numbers, he kept rolling the digital rosary, stoically oblivious of the young girl sitting next to him. Each click boomed a warning of doomsday. It made her shudder in her seat.

After the journey prayer and a long list of safety instructions, the plane took off. Ganju, his seat belt on, cast an aerial glance over the passengers; young, old, fat, ugly, good-looking, reading papers, sipping water, sleeping, snoring, all of them forgetful of their end. What if the plane fell, he thought, looking out the window. They think the world is forever and they are here till eternity, ignorant fools. He pitied all those suited businessmen, the air hostess with her makeup, and the pilot in his uniform. He wanted to stand up and remind them of their last stroll to their graves, ask them to pray for forgiveness of their sins. He wanted to save them all. With his mind soaring above the airplane, his hands on the rosary went faster, his breathing became heavier and his recitation louder. He vowed to offer all the prayers he had missed from the time of his birth, preach the word of God and thumb that rosary until it outnumbered his sins. The young girl gave him a dirty look and muffed her ears with head phones, drowning the din of doom in some hot music.

"We are sorry the number you have dialed is off," replied the automatic voice. The General, sitting in the hideout of Zahid's basement, stared at the phone as if he would chew it off; he had been calling Ganju since early morning. He cursed, "What the fuck does he think he's doing?" He looked at Zahid and Kashif, who averted their eyes. It was the day the General had to be given the good news about Ganju's dinner with the Arab princes.

"Why doesn't he pick up the phone," growled the General. "Here we are sitting like beggars for some spare change. Now that all is set, he disappears on us?"

No one said a word.

"I've already booked a villa in the hill resort, the best one, with a massaging bed, it's no joke. What I need is a bite of that bird," he said, fondling his balls. "Aren't we all ready to enter the international club of supermen?" The other two nodded their heads in compliance. "Then how come one of our members is missing?" Silence. "Why on earth doesn't anyone give me an answer?" He stood up, furious. "Bring that failed poet to me before he turns the whole country into a failed state. Find him out, I want him right here. Now," he ordered.

"Sir," said Kashif, and buttoning up his jacket, left immediately.

Before Ganju could touch the ground, Kashif had received information about his imminent arrival. He arrived at the airport with his men and whisked Ganju away. The car with darkened windows headed to Zahid's basement where the General had drunk half of the bar waiting for Ganju.

Ganju with his shaven head, scanty beard and flowing white toga appeared on the stairs of the basement like an ancient god.

"Ah, here comes the hero of our mission, it's never too late, is it?" The General stood up in haste to greet him. Ganju, surrounded by the plainclothes police, remained stationed on the steps.

"Oh sorry about that, we were only worried about your safety," said the General, waving to the security men. They clicked their heels and left.

"Ah, my dear, you look like a pharaoh of the old times, some Egyptian model. That dress is quite sexy, I must say—what do you think?" he turned to the others. They responded with light laughter.

"Oh God, why don't you come down, it's just a catwalk. Come, show us your new fashionwear," the General approached the staircase.

"Aren't we all walking to our graves?" Ganju staring into some vacant space said in the voice of the possessed. Stepping down, he swirled his toga and implored, "Don't we all have to wear this kafan someday?"

Zahid and Kashif looked at each other, aghast. The General, however, ignoring Ganju's queer behavior, slapped him hard on his shoulder as if to bring him back from the Hajj, "What's wrong with you, boy, are you okay? I think you need a drink," he said.

"I am in perfect peace with myself," came the mellow voice.

"Oh come on, stop playing jokes with us," the General said, but Ganju remained unmoved. The General stepped back, a bit embarrassed. "Well, he may not need a drink but some shrink-wrink," he rhymed cheerfully. "What on earth did the princes do to him?" The General sat down and picked up his glass.

"Sir, that dinner never happened," whispered Kashif.

"What?" The General's face reddened with anger.

"Yes sir, this is what has been reported to us."

"Oh God, here, when we are ready to stand up with the he-men of the world, a self-styled angel stands in our way. The world is coming to an end." The General shook his head in despair.

"Sir, he needs some rest," said Zahid quietly.

"I can't rest anymore," Ganju lifted his voice. "I have a lot to do, I am already late."

"Dear Ganju, you know how eagerly we have been waiting for you?" Zahid moved closer to him.

"I saw you, I saw you all." Ganju fixed his gaze on all three of them.

"You saw us? Where?" They looked at each other in amazement.

"In the holy land."

"Really, how come?"

"Millions of people threw stones on the three pillars of Aqaba, on the devil."

"And?"

"And you were those three pillars."

Anger shook the General, his neck inflated and his eyes bulged. He thumped his feet on the ground, hit his head with his hands, kicked the table, and shouted, "We are all screwed up, the chap has gone insane. This square-headed baboon has suffered some chemical imbalance, some brain injury. We've to put him in a straitjacket. Oh God, what've we done to deserve this?"

"I have come here to save your souls, you must repent and ask for the forgiveness of your sins," said Ganju. "We all have very little time. Now I want to be excused, I have to say my afternoon prayers." He turned towards the door and left the room

"We are ditched. We can't waste our time on this punk, he's not our man, not anymore," said the General.

"Sir, we must understand, Ganju lost his wife only a few months ago, and his beloved ditched him for her lover. I think it's too much for him to take. Let him go to his village and we work on something else," said Kashif.

"What something else?" responded an irritated General.

"Sir, the new finance minister," Kashif gave a knowing smile.

"Good idea," said the General. "Call an emergency meeting and put that gelled wizard from the World Bank on the job. Why the fuck do we have him in the finance ministry? Tell him to flaunt his neckties to arrange some loan from IMF under some development plan. We are too hungry for our bird. Aren't we?"

The General looked out the window. Out in the lawn Ganju stood, leading the prayer with all the servants and guards behind him.

Back in the village, Juma was busy making preparations for his master's arrival. Ganju had asked him to arrange a huge langer, free food for the poor at the old Ganju House. It was Ganju's wish to revive the glory of his uncle and the great Pir Bade Ganju Shah. After the death of Zahoor, the Ganju House had remained empty and silent as a cemetery. Nothing was left in that house except the huge portrait of the great Ganju Shah hanging in the veranda collecting dust.

Juma was eagerly looking forward to see his master; his hands missed the touch of his legs. The night before, he had bought a nice chicken for Ganju's lunch and had safely locked it up in a cabinet. Juma now unlocked the cabinet. He was shocked to find a fistful of feathers but no chicken. He nearly fainted. How could any wild animal enter the locked cabinet? What would he feed his master? He rushed to the local poultry market but on his way a sudden storm made him run and take shelter in a forsaken corner. While he prayed for the storm to subside, he felt a breeze. He looked up and was dazzled by a light in the dark sky. A flash of thunder and his eyes were struck by the sight of a bird descending straight towards him.

"Is something wrong with you, you look worried," the bird spoke. Juma couldn't believe his ears, but finding no one around, he stuttered, "Did you . . . I mean, talk to me?"

In that pouring rain the bird was miraculously dry.

"Yes, it's I who am talking to you, tell me, what are you looking for?"

"I had to cook lunch for my master and for that I had bought the best chicken, but it has disappeared. Now I was going to get a new chicken."

"Well, it disappeared because it was not worth the palate of your master."

"Really?"

"Yes! And you'll not get any chicken in this storm."

"Oh God, don't tell me that, I'll be ruined, my master will not spare me," Juma cried. "If I don't get the chicken today, I have to kill myself."

"No, you'll not."

"But I can't face my master."

"Well, let me help you."

"How?"

"I can offer myself to be your master's lunch," said the bird hopping closer to Juma.

"What?"

"Yes, I promised to be sacrificed for him."

"Oh God! Please forgive me, but are you the Satjug bird? My master did tell me about you." Juma spoke as if he had met an old friend.

"Yes, I am the Satjug bird, the bird of truth!" The bird stretched its elegant wings, puffed its chest and lifting its elegant bill let out a song that made Juma's heart soar to heaven. The storm stopped instantly.

"The time has come," spoke the bird collecting its wings. "Here, hide me under your chadder."

Juma trembled with fear.

The bird snuggled under Juma's chadder.

Walking back home, Juma's mind buzzed with all kinds of thoughts. He had the Satjug bird warm right under his arm. Anyone eating it could live forever and who doesn't want to live forever? After all, no one was loyal to anyone else but to oneself. Humans are born selfish, aren't they? Now that his luck had smiled on him, why should he resist it? Tranced by the smell of immortality, Juma's feet caught speed.

Arriving at the Haveli, he ordered all the servants to leave. He had decided to cook the bird himself. Inside the kitchen, he locked the door and, his chest wheezing and his Adam's apple bobbing in and out, he took out the Satjug bird.

"Just take the knife and put it on my jugular. I can no longer wait," said the bird. Various knives with keen edges glittered in the kitchen cabinets. Juma looked at the sharpest one; it happily flew from the cabinet and settled in his right hand.

His mind now fogged by the wish of living forever, he put the knife on the jugular of the bird. His hands faltered. Maybe the bird was lying or testing him. But then the idea of immortality had hit him. "Allah-O-Akbar," he shoved the knife into the rooster.

"Kuk," came a sound. A sudden shiver and the bird was halaled.

Juma stood still, watching the slaughtered bird. He waited for a moment. The bird did not move. Fearing that it might speak again, Juma started to clean it slowly but there was nothing to clean.

Happily he put the Satjug bird in a pot and lit the fire. Pouring water, oil, and spices, he started to cook the ultimate chicken. Soon the heavenly aroma absorbed him.

When it turned brown, Juma was tempted to take a piece; after all, it was his right to taste it, why should anything stop him? When everyone else was dead, he would still be alive. Wao! He could inherit Ganju's lands, his havelis and his wealth. He looked around, saw no one. He stealthily took off the lid, breathed in the steam and before he could scoop a piece from the pot, the steam vanished. The bird flew from the pot and sat on Juma's head.

Juma nearly died.

"I just saved your life," said the bird, flying from Juma's head and perching on the edge of the pot. "I had forgotten to tell you that apart from your master, whosoever touches my meat will be instantly dead."

"Dead?" Juma felt betrayed.

"Yes, dead forever! Now you must repent and cook me only for your master." Saying that, the bird jumped back into the pot. A roaring echo of its last words came from the pot. Juma touched his ears with his hands and asked forgiveness from Allah.

Sometime in the late afternoon, Ganju was quietly brought to the village by the secret police and was left by himself in his Haveli. Inside the Haveli, Juma followed him to his bedroom. Without changing his clothes Ganju lay down on his bed. Juma sat beside the bed and started to press his legs.

"Don't ever do that, I am not a cripple, and you are not my slave. It's not desirable in the eyes of Allah," Ganju admonished Juma.

Juma stood up at once. "Forgive me, Sarkar, I thought you might be tired after the journey," he said.

"No I am not, I have the energy of the spirit," said Ganju in his gravel tone.

"Would you like to change, Sarkar?"

"No, I like to be in ihram, it protects me from sins."

"Should I bring lunch," Juma asked fervently.

"Not now, I have to pray first."

"Pray?" Juma said in surprise.

"I know it's not time, but I have to catch up with all the prayers I have missed so far. All my life I have been lusting after money and power, but at the house of Allah I came across my shadow. Man is nothing but dust. This world is a temporary residence, not eternal. We have to die and be resurrected on the Day of Judgment. We can't attend to ourselves without attending to God first."

Ganju stood up for the ablutions. Wondering about the change in his master, Juma left, back footed.

During the preparation of lunch for Ganju, Juma, in an unguarded moment, was again tempted to eat a portion of the divine bird, but remembering the curse of the bird, he desisted.

Well, if not he, the bird of Khizer would give his master a long life, he thought. His future generations would benefit from this. He felt proud to be able to present to his master the gift of a long life, cooked by his trusted servant.

"I've very little appetite," said Ganju as Juma spread the table.

"Sarkar, you must eat something," insisted Juma.

"What have you cooked?"

"Your favorite dish, Sarkar, it's chicken," said Juma and excitedly took off the lid from the pot.

"No, I want simple food. My appetite for worldly pleasures has faded away." Ganju took his eyes off the pot.

"Sarkar, please have a little bite, I've cooked it with my own hands," begged Juma.

"How can I eat when half of the world is starving? Remember, gluttony is one of the greatest sins. We can't stuff ourselves beyond our necks, can we?"

"Allah will give you a very long life," said Juma.

"How can you say that," Ganju said skeptically

"I know it, sir, I believe it, just eat, I am sure you'll live more than forever."

"Thank you for wishing me that. I'll take only one piece."

"Good, Sarkar, I am sure you'll like it," said Juma, watching his master take a reluctant bite.

Ganju's taste buds lit with a flavor not known to him before. Suddenly he became ferociously hungry. He couldn't stop eating.

"I've never tasted such food in my life, it's amazing!" Ganju said bolting down a big piece.

Juma was flattered, "Sarkar, God will bless you with immortality, an endless longevity," he said like a fortune-teller.

"Thank you for your prayers for me, Juma." Ganju had savaged the super bird with extraordinary relish.

In the evening when he moved to the old Ganju House, he was animated to see colorful shamianas, lights, and fluttering flags all over the place. Processions of mystical singers along with thousands of villagers, both men and women, greeted him with garlands. They jostled to kiss his feet or touch his toga.

"Pir, Ganju Shah, the holy saint, marhaba, marhaba! Welcome, welcome!"

With thunderous slogans Ganju was led by the devotees to his ancestral chair. After the welcome speech by Allama, Ganju stood and waved his hands to his people. They swayed with admiration and threw rose petals over him. Reborn to faith, Ganju was determined to lead his people to the path of righteousness.

"Listen to me, my fellow men," he spoke, "we don't own our lives, they belong to Allah the Almighty. On the Day of Judgment, He is going to take count of each breath we take in this world." The crowd went into into an ecstasy. In that silence Ganju felt an involuntary commotion inside his toga. There was a divine buzz.

"Those who fornicate shall be thrown into hell," Ganju's voice became louder. "We must control our nafas, the greedy beast in us. This is not a piece of cloth I am wearing," he said, shaking his ahram, "it's my kaffan," he roared.

In the midst of gaslights, fluttering flags and thousands of people, Ganju had not realized that a storm was brewing inside his body. Ignoring the rumbling in his limbs, he went on with his preaching, "Bestial passion must be castrated by faith and patience!" Ganju felt a jolt. He struggled for composure but as he fumed against the corruption of the flesh, his toga flung open and his penis burst out like an angry wrist.

Embarrassed, he looked at the people. To his amazement everyone stood mesmerized at the sight of his rising member.

Somewhere in the crowd he heard the familiar voice, "Pir the Invisible sends you the blessed curse."

"Curse, curse," came the rippling echo.

Hearing that, women tore their clothes and ran to him as if they had been shown a sign.

"Don't come near me," he warned them.

"Ya pir, ya pir, bachra dhe dhe, oh holy man, give us a child," they sang, circling around his penis that stood like a pillar of fertility.

"Ya pir, ya pir, bachra dhe dhe," in a mad rush they started rubbing the sacred penis on their bare bellies.

"Don't! Don't you touch it, it's a sin, you'll burn in hell!" screamed Ganju.

With each rub the penis enlarged.

Watching their women hovering around the penis, men got wild with passion. They grabbed any female around them and started copulating. The ground was filled with limbs and muscles, pulsating and writhing. In that screaming and groaning, Ganju's prophetic voice shriveled into a whine. His weight shifted from his torso to his groin. His head started shrinking and his legs and arms becoming thin and short. He was diminished into a midget. In that gravitational disaster, he couldn't hold the ground anymore. Rolling his head down, he dangled along his member like an extra growth. Penis had outsized man.

The crowd ran, amok. "It's the sign of doomsday," they shouted.

Ganju was immediately carried off the scene by his worried servants.

When Kashif was informed about this paranormal phenomenon by one of his officials, he rushed for the bird. To his horror
it was gone.

The General at that time was having dinner with his commanders. It was not wise to disturb him. Kashif sent a message requesting him to visit Zahid's house after his dinner. The
General, hoping for some good news, skipped the desert and
left in his uniform.

"What's it," the General asked as soon as he entered the
basement.

Ominous silence.

Zahid quietly handed a glass of vodka to the General.

"You look strange. Has Ganju converted you all," he said,
taking a smart sip from the glass.

"Sir, we have bad news," said Kashif, head down.

"What news?"

Kashif looked at Zahid, who lowered his eyes. Kashif cleared
his throat and blurted, "Sir the bird is missing."

"What?" roared the General. Before he could murder someone, "We have good news too, sir," Zahid interrupted.

The General was still speechless.

"Sir, the good news is that we have found the bird," assured
Zahid.

"Found it," he laughed, idiotically, "now you could have
given me the good news first. Naughty boys. Where is it?" He
sat back.

"Sir, it is there but," Kashif said and looked to Zahid.

"But?"

"Sir, but it's not there," stuttered Kashif.

"What kind of logic is this?"

"Sir, I don't know how to put it, but it's there in a way, and
it's not there."

"Are you drunk or gone insane? Stop talking through your
ass. Speak up, what is it?" the General commanded.

"Sir, it is very much there but it has taken on a different
shape."

"What do you mean?"

"Sir, now it's flying in the shape of a penis," said Zahid without wasting time.

"Penis? How can a penis fly, is it some new expression that you have picked up from hip-hop. Flying penis," he chuckled sardonically.

"Sir, Ganju ate the bird, and his penis is rising minute by minute," said Zahid, his breath stuck in his lungs.

"You must be joking," the General almost lost his balance.

"It's true, sir."

"Come on, no, no, there must be some mistake," a disoriented General mumbled deliriously.

"It's absolutely true, sir."

Deathlike silence.

The General dug his eyes into both Zahid and Kashif, who stood head down like statues in a park. He pulled off his medals, threw away his cap and stripping to his underwear sauntered like a caged animal.

"You mean that preaching monk stole the bird and ate it? How could it happen? Say you are lying to me, kidding me, say something," begged the General.

"We have no clue, sir."

"Bastard, I knew he was faking that vulgar posture of a holy man. That was his ploy to steal our bird and eat it. All! I swear in the name of God, I'll murder him, hang him by his pubic hair," he said putting back his uniform. "Cordon off that village. Declare a curfew on the pretext of religious riots. That thief should not escape," he ordered.

Inside the Ganju House, surrounded by servants, Ganju lay unconscious but his penis was awake. As if going through a rebirth, Ganju's entire body was transforming itself into his genitals.

When the General arrived, he was struck by the magnificence of Ganju's penis.

Juma, who was still pressing Ganju's tiny legs, promptly stood up and wept violently at the feet of the General, "Please save my master, please save Ganju Sarkar," he cried.

The General, his eyes glued to the penis, ordered his guards to remove Juma and everyone else from the room. He was to be left alone with Ganju.

With tears in his eyes, the General marveled at the miracle of nature. He was half pleased as he had laid the seed and was happy to see the fruit even if it was on another tree. In his empathy he had a sudden urge to rip apart Ganju's stomach and pull out the remains of the bird. He called for the doctor.

"The bird, I am afraid is fully digested sir," said the doctor.

The General dismissed the doctor. His jaws watched the gory pit of Ganju's x-ray with a crunch. Why didn't he leave some for him, greedy bastard? He cursed Ganju and hurried to the kitchen. His tongue flicked out and licked all those pots which were used for the cooking and eating, but there was nothing left for him to savor. In desperation he slipped into Ganju's bathroom. Locking the door, the General sniffed into the toilet bowl. The oval eye of transparent water stared back at him. The toilet was air freshened. Not a whiff of the chicken that could bring a freebie of extra flesh to the General. The General rushed out and stood by Ganju. He exhaled and stopped breathing. He waited for Ganju to release a fart for him to breathe in the spirit of the divine bird, but no. He pressed Ganju's belly, but there seemed to be no good news.

"Forgive me, forgive me," the General heard the screams. Juma was being interrogated in the next room by Kashif. Hung upside down he was being given the regular treatment. The General entered. "Strip him, check him," he ordered.

"Sir we have already done that, he's clean," said Kashif.

"But he is the one who served Ganju that chicken." The General glared at Juma.

"Oh God, forgive me," Juma screamed.

"You filthy bastard, how could you feed our bird to someone else?" the General hit Juma in the belly.

"This slave wanted to give his master a long life," groaned Juma.

"Long life? You call this monster a long life?" the General shouted, sticking out his wrist. "Long life, he calls it a long life, son of a bitch," shouted the General. He could see in Juma a reflection of Ganju eating the chicken and the low-class kammi watching his master eat their bird. He hit him so hard that Juma fell on the floor. Blood spurted out, his eyes went white. Half conscious, Juma pointed out to a pamphlet that lay among his belongings. The General took the pamphlet. Juma smiled and breathed his last.

"Armageddon, the end of the world," the General read from the pamphlet, "rubbish," he threw down the crumpled paper. A sudden wind swept it from the floor and it disappeared into the air.

The penis was growing, and the Trio panicked. If they let it go on unbridled, it would become public by morning. Their operation would be exposed. Religious parties, world opinion, neighboring enemies? What would the media say, why in a sea of poverty this tower of shameful obscenity? How could they keep it away from CNN and BBC? If they didn't act soon they would have a national disaster in their hands.

"Castrate the bastard," ordered the General.

In the early hour of morning, under strict security, Ganju's penis was carefully loaded in an armored tank along with Ganju.

The truck drove to the military hospital.

Twenty surgeons lined up to inspect the swollen flyer of male conceit. With that kind of extraterrestrial erection it was not wise to operate; the patient had to be deflated before giving anesthesia. To ease the erection, the hospital nurses efficiently shagged that titan of a penis. It jerked, discharging a storm of semen and collapsed like a dead cobra. The fall of Ganju's penis was a great triumph for the nurses, but as soon as they tried to administer anesthesia, to their joy, it was up again. Till morning half of the hospital nurses had swung on that free pole while there were queues outside waiting for their turn.

The surgeons reported the matter to the General. It was better to be rid of the monster than to be exposed to the world, thought the General.

"Amputate him," he said.

"It might cost him his life, sir," they warned.

"I don't care," said the General.

"Sir, we can't do that. Our job is to save lives," dared the conscientious chief surgeon.

"Idiot, here I am trying to save millions of lives and you throw a half dead man on me, who's not even a man but an appendix to a monster? Now do as you are told before you have to run for your life."

"But sir," Kashif whispered to the General, "his sudden death may cost us some political consequences."

"Let him be a martyr, the media can be told that he was our hero who died of bird flu," the General whispered back.

Next morning the national flag was at half-mast. News of Ganju's death made the headlines with his pictures all over the daily papers. It was a black day for the Trio, the corpse of their dream was going to be buried forever.

Black Mercedes came in rows with flags. Ambassadors and some of the heads of states joined the impressive funeral procession. The president and the prime minister were present in national dress and skull caps, while navy and air force commanders appeared in full regalia.

It was a murky day. It had been raining all night. A timid sun was smoldering under the clouds. The wind had the nip of winter. The General saw Ganju's son Taimur standing among the mourners. He had tied a bandana on his head. He had a well-grown beard and wore a jacket. The General tried avoiding his gaze, but Taimur's eyes chased him everywhere. At the time of putting dust on the grave, he saw him standing next to him. Exchanging a look with the General, Taimur threw a handful of dust on the grave. Some strange message was writ in those young eyes. The General patted the kid on the shoulder and prayed for the departed soul.

Twenty guns were fired. The grave was now covered by hundreds of wreaths; it looked like a small garden on a tiny hill.

After the final prayers everyone became quiet while the national anthem was played. In that stillness, the General saw something familiar rising from the grave.

Chapter 23

Proxy of a Man

The rude sight of the gaping grave had made a crack in the General's skull. He could hear his thoughts circling in his mind like a stunt motorbike in a death well. He doubted his eyes for having seen such a thing. On a muggy evening in the land of the dead, he could have been hallucinating; a slanting light or lingering shadow can play the trick on the eye. In fact no one else had shown any reaction during the silence of the prayer or at the playing of the national anthem. Even after the funeral, there was no mention of any clandestine movement in the grave. Considering all that, the General blamed it all on his own paranoia and went to sleep, but a call from Kashif widened the crack in his skull. The close-up description by Kashif was a copy of the image he had seen in the graveyard. Kashif had used his pocket binoculars at the time of the parting of the grave. The General hit the ceiling; their Frankenstein had struck back. "It's the curse of the virgin!" he shouted and ran out of his bed, wide awake.

Without losing time, the General rushed to the grave with his commandos. To his horror the monster had popped out of the ground and was now high enough and swaying next to the cypress trees. His eyes couldn't believe the sight of a corpse enjoying a flawless hard-on. He ordered the shameful spectacle to be promptly covered and asked for the health minister to consult the experts and submit a report on the consequences of this calamity within an hour.

"Gentlemen, in the next few hours the light of the morning sun will make the sight visible and clear," said the General in an emergency meeting called in the middle of the night. "Tomorrow it'll be in the press. The whole world will be chatting about us on Facebook. Before the graveyard becomes a media shrine, we have to lock this monster! Now will you read this to me," he said to Kashif, throwing a report compiled by the scientists.

Kashif, carefully took out his glasses, fixed them on his eyes and looked at the report. He took a sip from his glass of mineral water and cleared his throat.

"After a careful study of this phenomenon, we have come to the conclusion that . . . " abrupt pause, another sip of mineral water, "the penis in view is a living organism . . . triggering off an endless metabolic process." He swallowed.

"Endless process?" interrupted the General. "We've heard of the blue whale and dinosaurs with thirty feet but this thunder lizard is ever growing. Like a nail. That's the endless process, isn't it?" He shook his head and signaled Kashif to continue.

"All energies, brain, heart and liver of the deceased are now transferred to his . . . genitals. They have developed a metabolism independent, self-generating . . . " Kashif stressed the words vengefully.

"Impatient motherfucker couldn't resist the temptation," the General cut him off, swearing at Ganju. "It's all because of that virgin whore, whom he was unable to screw."

"The body of the deceased is merely a corpse, a proxy for a man," came the trembling voice of Kashif.

"Proxy for a man? That's well said, I like it, proxy for a man," the General repeated sadly.

"Such a phenomenon is yet to be seen in the history of mankind."

"True! True! Read the whole thing, don't stop," said an irritable General.

Kashif quickly fixed his eyes back on the report. "So far it had only existed in mythologies but this one is real," he read.

"Real! Real! The damn thing is real, did you hear that?" The General threw his cap on the table.

"Now the penis will move independently of any human control," read Kashif.

"We can only revel in our impotent rage," said the General. He opened the wine bottle. "We have enemies on all sides. They'll condemn us for the cheap display of hyper masculinity. The feminists will chew us alive. Nations less endowed will conspire against us and those with super balls might annihilate us. Think! Think! Do something!"

Till late the Trio mulled over the possibilities of averting an imminent disaster. Nothing but a yawing futility loomed large in the room. The General had reached a state of mind where he was left with no options but to laugh at his own helplessness. He looked at the two half asleep zombies beside him. "Are you sleepy," said the General.

"No sir."

"Well, frankly, I am not really a night bird, I do like my slumber. Do you know what is my favorite position, well not of mine but both of us, I mean me and my other half," he chuckled. "Can't you see I am trying to change the subject, just to cheer you up?" he laughed emptily. "You see, when she turns her face from me, and I, lying sideways, hug her from behind in the spooning position, yes, that's the one. Lying sideways. Sideways?" He shouted, halting midstep. "Sideways!" He jumped like a child who had just won a prize. Both Kashif and Zahid looked at the General with great curiosity.

"Lie on the table," he ordered Zahid.

"Sir?" said a confused Zahid.

"Don't waste time, just lie on the damn table," he commanded. Zahid slow-motioned to the table.

"Now, lie on your side," instructed the General.

Zahid turned his body on the side. The General put a large sheet of cloth on him. "Don't take me wrong, I am doing it all in the national interest," he whispered to Zahid, who felt the General had turned into a sex maniac after the appearance of the Doomsday Caller.

"Now, have you noticed that in the spooning position the direction of your member is not vertical, but--? Yes yes, horizontal! Now, God forbid, if you get an erection as lengthy as that of the late Ganju, it'll not be seen because you are covered by the ground. Simple, isn't it? Boys we have lot on our hands. We have to put this proxy for a man in a horizontal position," said the General putting his cap on.

Before the world could wake up rubbing its eyes with a nightmare, the Caller had gone underground. The day appeared bright and clear, without a blemish. The cities stayed calm and peaceful. There was no report or rumour about the night's event, nor was there any untoward incident.

The Trio thanked their lucky stars and said their Friday prayers in a public mosque.

Weeks later while all was quiet on all fronts, a sacred temple in the neighboring country was destroyed by unknown terrorists. Mayhem followed, a surge of religious fanaticism torched anything that came in its way. Saffron togas attacked, raped, and butchered children, burnt shops attacked the restaurants. They swarmed to the ancient mosque built by a Mughal king and razed it to the ground.

"Gentlemen, what was a tool of pleasure is now a warhead. Nothing is more aphrodisiac than the potion of power. In our Caller, we have found our hidden missile which we can maneuver and control. Of late, the neighboring country has been sending its agents to blow up our buildings and bridges, but lo and behold, we with our strategy of spooning have succeeded in creating the ever worst law-and-order situation in their own country, and mind you, without blame or responsibility. Gentlemen, with this new toy we can penetrate the impenetrable," he proudly announced to his commanders. In jubilation, they thumped the table and their feet.

Applauded and encouraged, the General planned his next move; turning the corpse towards the second neighboring country. The idea of controlling a penis gave him the pleasure of a mythological god.

During this time no one knew that Taimur, the son of the late Noor Mohammad Ganju, had been keeping vigil on the grave of his father, whose death he believed was the outcome of a conspiracy by his enemies. He had been watching the movement of the commandos from another grave he had dug himself on the night of the funeral. Huddled in that hole all night to ponder and wait for something to happen.

Studying in the US, he had gone through a psychological crisis. With the death of his father, his alienation had become more intense. He felt he was robbed of his own culture, his religion, and his identity, the essential props for a social being. He didn't have any desire to inherit the jagir, the lands of his father. All he wanted was to find the meaning of life.

One night, while he was sunk in despair, he saw a shadow hanging over his head. He looked up, startled. "Don't be afraid, here's a friend, come out, it's safe," a gravelly voice spoke to him. The shadow extended a hand to him. Taimur took that hand.

Who was he? Taimur looked at the man closely. In thin light, he could only see a sweaty forehead furrowed by wrinkles and the shadow of a rough beard. On his head a bluish turban glimmered under the crescent moon.

"I've been making room for the dead on this earth. They all come here in the end. I am the gravedigger, just follow me," he said.

They moved to a narrow path that led them to an underground groove. The gravedigger opened a thatched door hidden under a pile of grass and descended the stairs. Taimur followed.

"No one comes here, they all are afraid of the dead," he smiled. "Come, sit, and let me get you some food."

"No thank you, I am not hungry," said Taimur timidly.

"No, you must eat something. I insist, please," said the gravedigger.

Taimur nodded his head.

The gravedigger went inside and while he heated the food in the back kitchen, Taimur looked around. There was nothing much in the hut except a charpoy and a matting on the floor and in a corner an old stove with a kettle. A dim lantern hung by a bamboo pole. There were books all over. Books on religion, philosophy, and politics.

"I am sorry about your father," said the gravedigger, entering with some food. "I know how these evil men are misusing your father even after his death. Lackeys of Satan," he cursed and put the food in front of Taimur. "A young man like you should not despair. It is a sin in our religion. I can't let you bury yourself alive in that grave. Eat, this is God's blessing, one should not deny the gift of life given to us by our merciful God," he said.

Taimur took a bite, the soft bread melted in his mouth.

"I've been watching you, I know you are not happy with the world, no one is happy. More and more people are not saying their daily prayers, they are too busy making money," the gravedigger said, lighting the stove.

"Women are independent from their husbands. Young girls and boys are roaming half naked in western dresses. The new generation is shamelessly aping the white people, hopping like monkeys on devil's tunes. We are hypnotized by their satanic tricks."

Taimur raised his head, his body stiff with doubt and eyes wrought with questions. "Where are the answers?" he said.

"Answers? Yes, I understand. We all have questions and questions but do not know that the answers are around us, within us."

"Within us?"

"Yes! Within our own faith! Allah gives us all the answers, but we don't look up to our Lord. We have gone astray. Remember! We have to destroy all images of idolatry, all those false gods who deceive us with false answers, we have to seek only one God," he said while pouring the tea. The steam spiraling from the cups curled the air into grey haloes.

"Here, I've made special tea with cardamom for you." He placed the cups on the matting where Taimur had finished his food.

It was deep midnight, only the stir of insects could be heard in that silence.

"They are the hawkers of fear and annihilation," continued the gravedigger, sipping his tea. "They build high buildings from where they watch us, analyze and study our sufferings, control us. They say they have knowledge, reason, technology, but knowledge devoid of compassion is dangerous. It's vampirism. They think they are infallible, but no one is infallible, except God," he said.

Inhaling the aroma of incensed tea, Taimur could hear the flutter of an angel's wings in the voice of the gravedigger.

His eyes moist with passion, the man paused to take a sip and continued, "Can't you see, they are killing us, harassing us, torturing us, interrogating us. After the daily bloodbath, their hearts congeal into a stone that suffers nothing. Their tongues can taste nothing but blood. With full bellies they pamper themselves with gossip about us. But no one can take away our faith from us!" He took Taimur's hand. Taimur felt that the man with the blue turban was opening the secret of life to him.

"Whosoever destroys these fake idols will be greeted in heaven," he said, looking into the eyes of Taimur. Taimur grasped his hand.

The early glimmer of morning light had rendered the sky into tender blues. Taimur looked at the thatched roof above him where the light had filled the chinks in the roof. Heaven was looking at him with a thousand eyes. Taimur embraced the man. In that embrace, something invisible passed between them.

Chapter 24

The Mongoose and the Snake

"Meray aziz humwatano, my dear countrymen, today, the world witnessed the biggest disaster in human history," said the General to the TV cameras after staging a bloodless coup. The night before, he was informed by the Intelligence forces that some unknown terrorists had changed the direction of the Caller. Now that it spooned with the western hemisphere of the world, the power towers of civilization, the tall wonders of human progress known as the twin brothers springing from the thighs of the City of Gods, had collapsed.

"Brothers and sisters," said the General in his starched uniform. "We can't sit back while the rest of the world is burning. We have to be a part of the global struggle against all those unseen forces of evil which are disrupting the peace of our world. I feel my country needs me, and I need my country. To move with the world, we need a single command. Keeping that in mind, I have taken over the heavy responsibility of becoming the head of the state. God save the country."

"How could our Caller get into the hands of terrorists? Those security chaps should be sent to clean the latrines of this country," the General fumed in a private meeting with Kashif, who had been appointed Chief of Security.

"Sir. I have investigated the matter and allow me to submit that as long as it's underground, we will not be able to have full control of it," said Kashif nervously.

"Full control? Would someone tell me as how we can have this fucking full control?" said the General using his native accent.

"Keeping it a secret may cost us our lives, sir," continued Kashif. "There have been news of floods and earthquakes in different parts of the world. The Caller is havocking the world by moving in all directions. The navel of the earth is ripped and its ribs are falling apart. The DC has hit the very womb of planet earth. Sir!"

The General stood up from his chair and started his mini march. Kashif followed him with guarded steps. "If we don't stop it, any rogue state could take its control," he warned softly. "If today some unknown sources have changed its direction, tomorrow someone else can do the same. We must expose it, sir."

"Expose? Are you out of your mind?" The General quickened his march. "The world powers will not spare us! They'll not bear to see a smaller nation flaunting an organ bigger than itself."

"Please, sir, give it a thought, it's better to assert than to be apologetic about our achievement. It's a moment of historical importance. We must stand with the world powers."

The General halted near the jaded flag on the table. "Maybe you are right," he said. "It's always good to be at the front than in the trench."

"Yes sir! One in hand is better than two in the bush. Once visible, it can be watched over, protected, and can be a very powerful image to incite patriotic feelings. Sir, you can lead this war on terror and put our country on the map of the world," said Kashif, saluting the flag and the General with a firm hand.

Before anyone could discover the hidden weapon of mass erection and put his country back to the Stone Age, the General very wisely offered himself to be a junior partner in the big game.

"There is a race of phallo-hegemony in the world. All nations have overt or covert Callers," the General announced in a secret meeting with the core commanders. "We must join the club." He looked around at the uniforms and opening his thighs said with a puffed smile, "Before they smoke it out, let's declare it. Gentlemen, it's showtime."

The commanders smiled, reasonably elated.

"The Caller, my dear colleagues, is a godsent opportunity to make money and headlines." He stood up from his chair, the commanders promptly stood for him. "No, no, you don't have to stand, we are not in the cavalry ground. I just like to walk while I talk," he said waving them to sit. They all sat back in one go.

"We must not forget that we have the genuine formula, and all those eunuch states of the third world with poor libido will be ready to pay tons of money to have access to it." He assessed the dribbling faces of the commanders. "Gentlemen, we are in business," he announced.

The commanders thumped their tables in jubilation.

Within no time secret funds were distributed to journalists, political analysts and other media to create DC awareness among the masses. The new buzzwords sparked the minds of the younger generation. Full-throated poets recited qasidas, hymns for the Caller. The media invented mind-boggling theories. Sculptors erected majestic replicas of the Caller at various centers of all the big cities. Once overt, the DC stood like a pillar of power in the center of the country. The sight inspired the patriots, who walked with their heads erect with supernatural energy. Before going for their daily parade, soldiers saluted and kissed it with militant devotion. Barren women touched it with fervent hopes; fashion shows, literary festivals, music concerts, and carnivals were held around it. The whole world was chatting on social media about this new totem pole of masculinity.

At home while all was going well, a worried Kashif reported to the General, "The DC is gone on to alarming heights, sir. It's no longer possible to control it. It is feared that its autonomy could destroy the whole planet," he said.

"What rubbish are you talking?" said the General.

"Sir, with its rapid growth, the climate is changing, the seasonal cycles are losing their rhythms."

"Are you out of your mind, how can a penis change the climate? Go and get some rest, you need a break." The General offered him some mineral water.

"Sir, the environmentalists have given their warnings on world media. The thrust of DC could be a threat to the ozone. Rain forests are fast disappearing. There is global warming."

"I know the term, global warming, such terms are coined by all those merchants of fear. Some lunatics have even prophesied the end of the world," said the General with a chuckle.

"But sir, our own experts have confirmed this. As such, we don't seem to have any hold over the DC. This report by international green studies," Kashif nervously spread a file on the table, "is scary, sir!"

"This indeed is alarming," mumbled the General after he had glanced through the file.

"Sir, we have the information that the superpowers are planning to move to the ice-melting Antarctica. They are rehearsing the apocalypse, sir," said Kashif.

"You mean they'll leave the earth to us, the third world, with war, poverty, and swine flu? What can we do? We can't let it happen. We have to control the DC."

"Of course, sir, just imagine the earth like a baked lava, and we all burnt to ashes," said Kashif, gulping down his water.

The all-powerful General didn't like to be helpless against a penis. He felt as if he was a mere uniform on a hanger. That night he couldn't sleep in spite of his pills.

"Aren't you in the mood?" said the wife clad in her pink nighty to a pensive General. "Don't tell me you are bored of me?" she nudged him naughtily.

"No, no never, sweetheart, how can you say that," the General sat up, dutifully, "I want it badly, believe me," he put his arms around her ample shoulders. "It's just that I am a bit tired," he said.

"Oh then that makes me the mistress of the ceremony. I mean the active partner, doesn't it," she giggled.

"Oh that's my baby," said the General half-heartedly. She smiled and swirled to the cupboard where the General kept his sex weapons. Once she triggered the pump of the French cylinder, he was all ready.

"Just lie down my sweetie pie," the wife guided the General

to the bed. "Let me do the honors," she said straddling the General. The General lay under her commanding weight like a helpless mule, thinking of nothing but the Doomsday Caller.

Towering over the General she rode him like a racecourse jockey. "Nab me, nab me," she screamed.

The General listened to her call, but she looked distant and far beyond.

"Nab me, nab me."

Her screams excited him. In the heat of the action, he flaunted the twin ropes, his moustache. They noosed her nipples. She screamed louder. The General pulled hard. She let a hairy scream and fell helplessly on his chest like a rootless tree. In the silence that takes over after wild copulation, the General thought of the Caller. With a start, he jumped out of bed and ran naked to his home office where he put on his uniform and left long before his wife could find him.

Reaching his headquarters, the General ordered for a military helicopter. The entire state became alert in the middle of the night. The General refused to discuss anything with anyone. He wanted to go in that helicopter alone. He ordered the pilot to fly to the graveyard where stood the DC, the Doomsday Caller, in complete security.

The General ordered the pilot to circle around the DC. Envy and fear mixed in the air. The magnificent minaret of beauty stood against the thin curve of the crescent moon.

"Get near, slowly, like a moth around a flame," the General told the pilot. The DC leaned a little and the helicopter was pushed away. The General stared at the DC; it stared back with its solitary eye. The General couldn't face that mocking squint. He lifted the mighty rope, his moustache, and flaunted it at the DC. The DC smiled and swung away. The General swore at the pilot, "Get near that ruffian . . . near, I said." The pilot steered the helicopter around the DC. The General held his moustache and angling it towards the DC flung it carefully. The twin brooms flew in the air and in a flash hooked the rising DC. The General jumped with joy and laughed hysterically, "There, I got it!" The next minute he was mum. The DC had slipped out of the noose. The knotted hair hit back at the General's face with vengeful force, but the General threw his deadly snares once again. They noosed the DC in a perfect knot. The DC struggled inside the tightening grip, the General pulled and pulled. The DC scuffled within those razor sharp string of hair.

The army on ground and the half-moon calmly watched the spectacle of two flying monsters fighting in the sky-ring. The DC swiveled and tried wiggling out of the noose but the General had it in his control. In a sudden blast the DC shook with such a force that it pulled itself off the ground, tearing off half of the General's face and his moustache. The pilot lost control, the helicopter wobbled in the air, caught fire, and exploded like a firecracker. The General's cap fell like a dead duck. His flicks, his medals, his uniform, his heavily polished shoes, his shiny pips, all disappeared in a flash. Sloping down, the DC tumbled on the ground but then gathered speed and after making a few barrel rolls became airborne. In the next minute it had disappeared into the space.

Breaking News

Celestial Channel

Three seconds to go. Cue. Red light, a smile and, "On planet earth, a male organ is blown to alarming proportions," announces the ever young hoor, her figure shaped as an hourglass. "Last night it pulled itself off the ground and is annihilating whatever is coming in its way."

Blurred clip of the DC.

"This image was taken an hour ago. So far, its speed cannot be gauged, and its altitude is unknown."

Live coverage of the cities. O/L Audio commentary

"Monuments of power are cracking up like the pulp of a Lilliputian universe. Museums with rare collections, churches with divine filigree, mosques with blue arches and holy temples with golden pillars are being smashed to pieces. Blown up images of actors, sportsmen, labels of fame and glamour are crumbling down. In a sea of dead bodies, broken doors, and shattered windows, stalks the lockless monster. We'll keep updating you on this, but don't go away! We'll be back after a short break."

Fade in Title I&I Talk show

Esrafil and Izrael, in designer clothes, gelled hair and smart make up. Esrafil smiles to the camera, "Welcome to the show, I am Esrafil the angel with the trumpet and with me, is Izrael the angel of death. In view of the news about the destruction of the terrestrial world, our question today is whether man will survive or become an extinct species?" He looks at Izrael who adjusts his right wing and says, "I think man suffers from a God complex, his vertical ambition spurs him to the moon. He's the ripper of the skies who hops above the gravitational center without realizing that he has to fall back on mud!"

"Maybe he wants to find his origins. I mean the tree and the fruit!"

"Well, I think he shouldn't have tasted that horny fruit. One clown was enough for the amusement of our Master, now there are trillions multiplying trillions."

"But it was the tree of knowledge." Esrafil flaunts his left wing with much flare.

Close up of the forbidden tree with some laundry on it.

"Right, but he has turned the pleasure of knowledge into a tool of power. His brain has become his penis!"

"That's some topsy-turvy logic," Esrafil said twiddling his wings. "Well, coming back to the God complex, do you think man will eventually replace God?"

"Could do, I think he believes he can do better."

"Why because he thinks he is clever?" resumes Izrael with a suave flourish, "You know how tough it is for us on the borders. Once people die, they expect a VIPs treatment. Their documents are forged, they change their biographies, grovel, and try to grease our wings, not realizing that they are no longer in the world."

"Well, he's also the biggest sycophant, an ass licker. He has created lot of scarecrows; honor, status, religion, race, and caste."

Bell rings

Izrael presses the button. "Yes? Can you hear us?"

Caller, "Yes, I can."

"From where you are calling, sir?"

Caller, "I am not a sir, I am a lady, I've my gas mask on."

"Oh, I am sorry, it's good to take precautions, well, what's your question?"

Caller, "I ask why you don't talk about woman, who gives birth to man. Why it's always man? Just because he can dangle something between his legs?"

"We'll definitely consider that ma'am, thank you for calling."

Disconnection.

"What would you call it? Penis envy?" Esrafil swivels on his chair.

"Well, it's all about the part women don't have," says Izrael cocking out his neck.

"Good, we are free from all those attachments," Esrafil says in a chilly tone.

"Come to think of it, after all, it's a male organ blasting the whole earth, nature and the rest of humanity."

"But she's right, man is born out of a womb."

"Of course, but he denies the womb, doesn't he?"

Bell rings.

"Are there any humans left alive?" Izrael winks to Esrafil.

"Well, maybe he's the last one." *Esrafil presses the button.*

"There's some noise, please speak louder, all right, now your voice is clear. Can you hear us? Well? Tell us now sir."

Caller, "We are dying of hunger. Our village was attacked by unknown forces. I've lost two daughters and one buffalo. I am a God-fearing man, I pray all the time, but no one has ever come to our rescue. And they had said he'll come."

"Who?"

"The savior."

"Who said that to you?"

"The astrologer, the post man, the poet and the priest."

"What would you say to that?" Izrael says with a mischievous smile to Esrafil.

"I think he should wait."

"Well, we have no knowledge of it, but if he is coming then he is coming, just wait for him," says Esrafil.

Caller, "Shall we wait? Shall we wait? Wait forever?"

Disconnection.

"Who do you think is this savior?" Izrael turns to Esrafil.

"Well, he's the ultimate man spawned in fables, in dreams, in previous births of humans like the healing man, the man who could fly, the messiah, the new Adam, the proletariat, the elemental man, the ideal man, the black or white Adam, yellow or blue, the Utopian man. I think the concept of the savior is born out of man's own imperfection."

"What about hope? Is there any hope of man's survival?" Esrafil changes the topic.

"Hope, I guess never lets him die and even when he dies, it keeps seducing him."

"One last question Do you think this is the end of the world?"

"No, I don't think so. Man is born of sperm, and sperm is born of a miasmic organism. The earth planet may be destroyed but the gene of the original sin will still be there, it's the pest. It's even beyond the control of the creator. The cockroach will fly forever."

Bell rings.

"It's a local call," says Esrafil pressing the button.

Caller, "I've been living in the Hereafter for the past two millenia. I guess the very first genome in the womb of creation was depressive. Man is born out of a depressive womb. Our lord was in a sad state of mind when he created man."

"But that's what creates poetry, art, and music, I mean the sadness," quips Izrael.

Caller, "This is what it is; symptoms of a depressive womb."
Disconnection.

"What would say about our Lord's plan to abolish hell and establish the eternal Heaven sans hell, Summum Bonum?"

"Well, I think his seven days gig is irreversible," says Esrafil looking at his watch, "before we talk about this utopia, we have in our studio a surprise for our viewers."

Close up of Mano

The evergreen virgin Mano known as Lilly Khanum. Hello there. Welcome to our show.'

Mano hooks her upper lip with her eyebrow, "thanks for inviting me to your show," she says, "I must thank Triplex the makeup department of Heaven which gave my face back to me."

"Well, you have a soft face of hoori now," cheers Izrael.

"Thank you."

"Is it true that you are the impenetrable virgin," asks Esrafil.

"Yes, I've been a virgin from the time of birth to my last gasp."

"But I believe you were a prostitute," Izrael interjects.

"Yes, I was the virginal goddess. My body was a Shrine but

men visited me like a brothel. When love ends the world ends."

"Tell us how you could provoke a man to eat the bird and destroy the world?"

"Sorry, I am a simple person, I can only tell you a story if you like," she says.

"Oh yes, sure. Go on, our viewers will be very much interested."

"Well, while I was growing up, my grandma used to warn me about a snake."

"A snake?" Izrael gives a knowing look to Esrafil.

"Ah, yes, we understand," says Esrafil with an encouraging smile at Mano.

"You know she herself had seen the snake," continues Mano.

"Oh really?"

"Yes! One day when she was working in the fields she saw this snake, a real big one. She pulled her scythe and cut its head but the next minute the snake disappeared. People gathered around to find the snake, but it was nowhere to be seen. Everyone told my grandma that she must have imagined the whole thing. My grandma got worried, she started to hallucinate about the snake. She would touch anything and shout, 'snake! there is a snake!' One day the local sage told her that the snake she killed had two heads, one which she had cut and other which was on its tail. 'It will come back to you with the other head,' he had said."

"The other head?" Izrael looks at Esrafil.

Sudden cut to the title of Breaking News, thunderous music.

"A huge penis is moving fast upward into the skies. A tiny man is attached to it. We can see it clearly, it's directed towards our Heaven."

Blank screen. Red light. Cut to studio.

Izrael and Esrafil manner a smile.

"Don't go—" *The smile continues.*

"We'll be back soon." *Powdered faces melt.*

"Stay tuned." *The Wings start to burn.*

"Don't go away!" *Voices blur into a noise,* "St ttay aa y with uuussss Don't forrrrgettt there iss mo re moore to com e . . ."

End.